THE ACHING PLANE

The Aching Plane

Cody Lakin

Katalpa Press

Cover art from shutterstock.com/g/frankies
Cover design by Cody Lakin and Anjali Alam

First Printing, 2023

ISBN: 979-8-218-28461-9

EISBN: 979-8-218-28462-6

For my family, the Duncans and the Lakins. What a joy and privilege it is to be one of you.

And for Anjali. When I stepped out from it, you were still there.

Contents

"There a painless death awaits him who can no longer bear the sorrows of this life."

- from *The King in Yellow,* by Robert W. Chambers

"Throw roses into the abyss and say, 'Here is my thanks to the monster who didn't succeed in swallowing me.' "

- Friedrich Nietzsche

PART 1

River Bug (I)

1

At the party, Charlie Louise wandered without aim or pattern, bearing the vague appearance that she was looking for someone. The skin around her eyes was dark from too many long nights, and although her gaze flitted from face to face, room to room, she comprehended little of it. Drink in hand, car keys jingling around in the pocket of her overalls, she searched for something in the faces of her peers.

She could imagine finding someone here who might want to spend time with her beyond tonight, but in her mind she turned this hypothetical person into someone else—someone specific. Charlie knew she wouldn't find Marion amongst the riotous crowds that populated these tired scenes, but still she looked. And looked. And looked.

Sometimes she felt as though she were a ghost in her own life, living inside a faded impression.

After finishing her drink, she decided she was done with wandering. The living room was an eruption of noise and dancing bodies. The fluorescent-lit kitchen was a debate room for guys discussing the merits of socialism and communism. The hallway was a series of closed doors.

Sam, who had insisted she come tonight, was at the kitchen bar with a gin and tonic in hand, occasionally chiming into the debate.

Judging by the way Sam had sidled up beside another guy, laughing at the things he said and agreeing enthusiastically with his points, Charlie could tell that Sam had found his prospect for the night. She butted in just for a second to let him know she might head out soon. He waved her off. She turned, eyes down.

Charlie let herself out onto the back deck. A few people were soaking in the hot tub, but otherwise, the deck was empty. The commotion from the house was muffled through the walls; the only noise out here was from the hot tub and the quiet conversation of its occupants, set to a backdrop of soft cricket song. She looked at her phone: 1 AM. With her head still teetering—thanks to the alcohol—she considered the car keys in her pocket.

Instead, she sat on the deck's steps and looked up at the night sky. No stars, just the rumor of them behind ghostly clouds.

I want to go home, she thought—and it felt like the first time she'd thought that in… how long? Years?

Movement from somewhere ahead drew her gaze away from the clouds.

A man stood alone on the back lawn's dewy grass. Shrouded by the moonless dark, his body was too long, his arms hung too low. He lifted one of his misshapen arms and waved at her. There were too many fingers on his hand.

Charlie drew in and held her breath, careful to seal any reaction. It wasn't a *hello*, that wave. It was the gesture of somebody trying to get her attention, trying to say, *"Can you see me? Look over here."*

A young man her age stumbled out of the hot tub with his skin still steaming. His friends laughed at him and shouted halfhearted encouragements and insults as he moved toward where Charlie sat on the steps. Instead of sitting near her, which she expected, he began to descend the stairs on wobbly legs. One of his feet, still slick from the water, slipped off an edge and he dropped, sliding down the rest of the steps in the process.

Laughter erupted from the hot tub. One of the girls said, "Oh, shit! You okay, Adrian?" None of them showed any signs of trying to help.

Charlie went to him. He was on his knees now in the grass, throwing up, then retching on an empty stomach, moaning between heavy breaths.

She cast a cautious glance out at the lawn, searching for the silhouette. There was no one out there anymore.

The young man spat and wiped at his mouth.

"You okay?" she asked.

"Me? Oh… you know. Just getting some air."

"Yeah?"

He waved his arm at her, and was in the middle of insisting he felt okay when he bent forward and dry-heaved again. This time, Charlie put an arm on his bare back and rubbed. It came as second nature to her, considering the number of times she'd crouched beside her dad in the bathroom, just like this, while he stuttered through feeble apologies and empty promises.

"Some way to end a party." She ran her hand along the young man's spine. The tension in his body softened slowly as he dropped into a sitting position.

"Jesus," he said.

"Feel any better?"

"A little. I think it was the hot water. Kinda hit me all at once."

"No one warned you?"

"About what, drinking too much?"

"About hot tubs when you've been drinking or smoking at a party."

He shook his head, shivered.

"Come on," she said. "You must be freezing."

"I think I wanna sit here for a bit. It's nice actually. The fresh air." He rubbed his shoulders and kept shivering.

"Here." She left him on the grass, hurried up the stairs, and returned a few seconds later with a towel that she draped over his shoulders. "I'll get you a glass of water."

"No… thank you. In a few minutes, maybe."

"It's okay. Sit tight."

In the kitchen, pushing past the crowds—no sign of Sam anywhere—she searched the cabinets and remembered another party like this one. Someone else's house, some lost hour among so many. She had stumbled outside, into a side yard full of neglected lawn equipment, and spent the next hour dizzy and sick. A few people had been close enough to see, but no one helped her. No friendly hand on her back, no one fetching water or crackers for her.

When she returned to the back deck, the young man was seated on the steps. Color had returned to his cheeks. He looked at her as if she were his savior when she handed him a glass of water and a box of soda crackers. "My god. Where did you come from?"

She scowled playfully. "Come on. This is the bare minimum of courtesy."

"More than anyone else did. You do this often? Take care of drunk friends?"

"Something like that," she said.

"You know, before my head started spinning, I was kinda, I don't know, building up the courage to come over and talk to you."

"Is that right?"

"Just to talk. You know. I saw you come outside and you looked sorta like you were in pain or something."

"In pain?"

"Yeah, or something. How's your night? Before this, I mean."

She raised her eyebrows. People at parties, especially guys, were so much bolder than in everyday life—*presumptuous* was the word that occurred to her, yet somehow, in this moment at least, she didn't mind. Direct people were refreshing. Marion had been direct. Or *bold*, Charlie remembered thinking when she'd first met Marion.

She let herself slouch and lean back a little. "My friend Sam. He invited me tonight, and I thought it was because he wanted to hang out and catch up. Guess I should've known better."

"You like him?"

She breathed a laugh through her nose. "I think *you're* more his type. But no... he and I have been friends since we were in grade school. I had a, um..." She stopped when she realized what she was about to say, and to a stranger. But she thought about her father again. She thought about all the times in the years since her mother left that she asked him if he was okay and he simply answered, *I'm fine*. She looked at the stranger beside her, the invitation in his eyes. "I had my first depressive episode in third grade. It wasn't anything dramatic, but most of the kids in my class... let's just say they never treated me the same after that."

"Kids can be cruel," he said. "Hell, when I was that age, *I* was cruel."

She nodded. "Sam was the first person to come up to me one day, at recess. He sat down right next to me on one of the benches and said, 'You'll feel better. My dad says negative emotions are like spicy food: resisting the pain makes it worse.' Something like that, anyway." Charlie fidgeted with her hands in her lap. "I'm overreacting, I know, but when my friends and I—especially Sam—when we used to go somewhere together, it was to be together. We'd catch up on what we'd missed, even if it was just a few days. And we really livened things up. People wanted to come hang out with us."

She clenched her hands into fists. "I can be like that, though. Living in the past."

"Huh. Yeah." The guy reached into the box of crackers. "I can relate."

"Shit. I've never been this person before, if you can believe it."

"What person?"

"The one making a stranger be my therapist." She rolled her eyes.

"I haven't been this person, either—the one being taken care of by a stranger at a party."

The earnestness in his voice made her smile. "I'm Charlie, by the way."

"Charlie Louise?"

She shot him a suspicious look.

"It's nothing, just I heard someone talking about you earlier."

"Oh. Didn't realize I was talked about."

"I wouldn't worry about it. It was nothing like that. I'm Adrian."

"So what were they saying about me, Adrian?"

"Nothing, really. I don't really give a fuck about gossip, especially from Spencer and Keri and their friends." He made a dismissive gesture in the direction of the house. "You know how Keri is, anyway."

"Not really."

"Oh, it's... you know how it is. High school's never over for some people."

"Very true."

"She's the type of person who's judgmental if she doesn't under-stand someone. Her opinion's so important. All that. She's my ex, actually."

Charlie raised an eyebrow. Adrian laughed.

"I know, I know. I was pretty different then, is all. And, uh, not to bring it up again, but it's funny, that's actually one of the things someone said about you back there. I think it was Spencer. Keri was saying something about how you show up to these things a lot, and Spencer sorta chimed in and said, *She wasn't always like this.*"

Charlie lowered her eyes, said nothing.

Adrian smirked as if to show it didn't matter to him. "Reminds me of something you said just a minute ago, actually, except a little different. About the way you and your group of friends used to be, and how it's changed. It's like, we change and they change, but because we're the center of our own universes, to us it just seems like everyone else has changed."

"Interesting point." She scanned the back lawn but quickly averted her eyes.

"You sure you're okay?"

"I'm fine."

"Sorry, you just looked like— Never mind. Mind if I ask something a little personal?"

"Sure."

"Was Spencer right about what he said?"

"About what?"

"When he said you weren't always like this."

She wanted to say to Adrian, *Do you ever miss someone so much that, no matter how many years go by, their absence is the only thing you can feel?*

Instead, she asked: "Do you know the name Marion Del Rosario?" This was something she'd found herself asking more and more people lately. Somehow—though it should've been impossible —people were forgetting Marion. A name that had been in news headlines, a household name in this town. She studied Adrian's face as he thought it over.

"No," he said, " I don't think so. Does she have something to do with that? With the way you used to be?"

Charlie turned away. "Something to do with it, yeah." In her mind was the creek, the water reflecting gems of sunlight. Marion's voice reciting poetry. The sound of a fishing rod reeling in line. "I'd rather talk about something else, though. How're you feeling now?"

He grinned. "A lot better, thanks to you."

Pulling now into the driveway of her house, Charlie put the car in park, killed the engine, unbuckled her seatbelt, and rested her forehead against the steering wheel with a long release of breath. There was a ringing in her ears, a sense of imbalance from more than just the alcohol.

A moment came when Adrian asked if she wanted to join him and a few of his friends at his place.

She knew how it probably would've gone. A few people smoking, playing video games, and Adrian might've, at some point, invited her to his bedroom. And he wouldn't have been surprised, probably, when she politely turned him down.

That was one of the things Keri would've said: Charlie Louise, the girl who showed up to the parties but never went home with anyone. Charlie Louise, who was too good for guys and apparently too good for girls, too. That was what people such as Keri Gates liked to say. Adrian was right. High school was never over for some people.

But I'm like that, too. Still living in the past. She wondered what it would've been like, letting Adrian get closer to her. She wondered how long before, inevitably, she would've tried shaping him—in her mind—into someone he wasn't. Someone like Marion.

She thought, too, about what Adrian had heard someone say about her: *She wasn't always like this.* Charlie thought it of herself, in her own voice, as if realizing it for the first time: *I wasn't always like this.* If only she could leave the past behind, turn to someone like

Adrian, and say it like that, with such ease. *I wasn't always like this, you know. I never chose to be this way, and I do not choose it now.*

Her father, James Louise, had left the front porch's light on. Otherwise the house was dark. He was either asleep or awake in his bedroom. If he was awake, he might hear her come in, might come out to see if she was okay. And if he noticed she was drunk, there'd be that look on his face, one that hinted toward anger but settled on sadness. Not even disappointment, really—*sadness.*

Charlie thought she could face that, if it meant getting to fall into bed a few minutes later. The thought of getting up for work tomorrow conjured every recent memory of being reprimanded by her boss for her deteriorating performance on the job due to frequent hangovers and minimal sleep. But as she reached for the door handle to exit the car, she caught sight of the man standing on the front lawn. Here he was again, a silhouette with the front porch's light behind him. He was too tall. His body bent strangely. Posture unnatural. A hand burdened by too many fingers, waving at her, trying to catch her attention.

Chills rippled—a sharp, cold wave through Charlie's body. She turned away, brought her attention to the interior of her car. She locked the door. Pushed the seat back to give herself more room.

After her heart stopped racing, she reclined the seat as far as it would go and grabbed her sweatshirt from the backseat to use as a pillow.

It wasn't as bad as it had been. After her mom left, Charlie had spent countless nights in her car, parked in the driveway, managing maybe four hours of sleep if she was lucky. The shame of stumbling into the house drunk had been too much back then.

She thought about her job at the coffee shop downtown, how she'd probably be let go soon if she didn't leave. She thought about Adrian. Even though she'd declined his invitation to join him and his friends, he'd still given her his number. *Adrian Benedict.* He'd put his full name in the phone. She thought to herself now, as she curled up in the reclined driver's seat of her car: *Maybe I should let myself try, instead of giving up before it even starts. Maybe I don't have to just keep living in the past.*

She closed her eyes against the images in her head and the memories of the night.

I wasn't always like this, you know. I never chose to be this way, and I do not choose it now.

I do not choose it now.

2

Charlie Louise had stayed up late again, curled up in the living room with a blanket and a mug of tea and an old black-and-white Japanese film playing on the TV. She had chosen Japanese cinema for this month. Last night had been an unsettling horror film called *Onibaba.*

When she woke to the feeling of her father's hand on her shoulder—gentle, as always—she woke with the sensation of strange dreams still shadowed behind her emerging consciousness. Dreams of high grass in a night wind and a woman standing somewhere in the grass with a wide-eyed demon mask on her face.

Charlie blinked awake, already certain that the part of today she most looked forward to was eventually getting back in bed.

James Louise, her father, sat on the edge of the bed, hands folded in his lap. He wore a white button-up and beige slacks—not his best look, but nice, at least—and his hair was damp, probably from a spray-bottle. An eagerness rested on his face.

"Hey, River Bug."

He hadn't called her that in a long time—a nickname from when she was a kid. Charlie smiled, then groaned and rubbed at her eyes. "Am I making you late?"

James shook his head. "Got about a half hour."

She reached for the nightstand, knocking a paperback of pessimist philosophy to the floor, and lifted her phone just long enough to glimpse the time.

"Another late one?" he asked.

"I meant to split the film in two, but..." She shrugged.

"Why don't you stay home this time? Get some rest. I'll be okay."

Charlie shut her eyes a second, felt the invitation of the warm sheets. Her father sat patiently. She imagined him pulling into the church's parking lot by himself. Him seated at a pew alone, nodding along to the priest's sermon, saying *amen*. She imagined him making his way back to the car, a polite smile fading from his face.

She opened her eyes, forced herself to sit up, blonde hair in curls and tangles. "Nope, I'm up, I'm up. Just gotta get dressed."

James smiled, patted her on the shoulder as he got to his feet. "Tea for the ride?"

"Mmm. Please."

He nodded toward her thermos on the nightstand. "When's the last time you washed that?"

She shot him a look.

Imbued with a cheerfulness at her insistence on joining him, he grabbed the thermos and left her alone. He'd been attending church alone for a year—until two months ago. Now she came along every Sunday, even when she was tired or if it was inconvenient for her. It was kind, he often told her. Kind for her to come even though she wasn't—as far as he knew—religious.

But Charlie didn't go with him out of kindness.

While she dressed, she paused for a few seconds to glance at her desk. There were a few framed photographs staged in front of her books. They were photos of her friends, most of them from years past. One of these photos was facedown on the desk.

Two months ago, the day after the party where she'd met Adrian, Charlie had wandered into the house in the early morning hours. Twilight seeped gray through the windows, making the curtains glow. She'd sat down at her desk and looked at the picture. It was the one photograph on her desk that was a magnet for her attention. It brought a smile weighted by melancholy to her face. She had turned the photograph facedown, and it had stayed that way ever since.

Even though she was pressed for time, Charlie approached the desk. She wouldn't have been able to explain why if she'd been asked, but something was different. She felt—not lighter, exactly, but simply *different*. Like something long obscured was coming into full view. She set the picture back in its original position.

It showed two girls, both twelve, each with an arm around the other, standing knee-deep in glittering river water in the midst of summer. The girl on the left, in a green bathing suit and weathered baseball cap, was Charlie. The other girl was Marion Del Rosario, whose dark curly hair was tied up in a loose ponytail. The girls were looking at each other and laughing.

Charlie's eyes lingered on the photograph for a few seconds. No… she'd acted too soon. She took a breath, shut her eyes, set the photograph facedown again, and left the room.

As she did nearly every morning, Charlie made breakfast for her dad. When he reminded her that she didn't need to, she teased, "If I didn't, you'd be starving by the end of the service."

He showed his agreement by remaining silent and digging into the meal, all the while casting looks at her.

What James didn't know was that Charlie didn't do these things to be kind. In a worn leather journal she kept in one of her drawers was a page where she'd taped a picture of her dad. In it, he stood in front of a small waterfall. Late one night she'd penned a caption, something like a line from a poem or something spoken in a half-remembered dream:

"Not that I'd ever know how to tell you this, Dad, but you're the only person in my life who's ever given me hope."

She still thought about that sometimes, about how that one line was still true for her, while she made him breakfast, or insisted on running errands for him, or accompanied him to church. It had remained true even when she'd paid bills for him, cleaned the house without help, took phone calls for him because he couldn't form a coherent sentence, or struggled picking him up from the floor to walk him to his bed.

No. She didn't do those things to be kind.

They came to a stoplight just a couple blocks from the church.

Charlie glanced out the passenger window, and her insides felt as though they turned to stone.

There were three people on the sidewalk waiting for the light to change. Charlie's first reaction was disbelief. Did no one else notice the man—he was *huge*—or were they trying to be polite by not staring?

The first of the three people on the sidewalk was a woman with her baby in a stroller. The woman's face was red and she was trying to talk on the phone while also rocking the stroller back and forth to soothe the crying baby. Beside her, a vagrant in a dirt-caked tubular jacket which had once been blue.

The third man stood just behind these two. At first Charlie didn't believe what she was seeing, but then her mouth came agape, her breath felt as though it went cold in her chest.

A giant man stood there, his body as wide as it was bulbous, his midsection like a boulder roughly twice the size of the woman in front of him. He towered above the other two, an absurd spectacle in broad daylight. The man wore no shirt, and across his massive belly snaked blue veins and white splotches. His skin was colorless, as though no blood ran beneath it. Patches of wild hair stuck out in all directions from his head. His eyes were gray, sightless, lacking distinct pupils. Fleshy tendrils, almost like boneless arms, spilled from his purple lips. *Tentacles* was what she at first thought, as if the man were in the process of swallowing an octopus, and the creature's writhing limbs curled and flopped down the folds of the man's enormous chin where they splayed across the small hairs of his chest. They only resembled tentacles in how they squirmed; she didn't know what they were, but they were fleshy and pink and red, stained with blood.

Charlie stared wide-eyed.

"Dad," she whispered, quick and tense. "*Dad.*"

"Hmm?"

"Sh-shouldn't someone help him?" she placed a hand against the glass of the passenger window. The woman and the homeless man didn't appear to notice the giant that stood behind them—the giant with the tendrils of flesh flopping from his throat. But that wasn't possible. "Shouldn't we help him?"

"I don't have any cash on me, sweetheart. Maybe if we see him on the way back…"

"Not *him*," she said, starting to shudder. The fleshy tendrils spewed from the giant man's mouth, some of them flopping across his massive shoulders, some crawling back up toward his face.

Charlie swallowed hard, feeling her stomach lurch. "*Oh my god.*"

"Sweetie?"

She managed to tear her eyes away from the man.

"Charlie? What's the matter?"

"You don't see him?"

"Who? The guy in the blue jacket?"

"No. *Right there.* The one with the…" For a second she thought she might lose a part of her mind if she said it out loud.

When she looked again, there was no one. The woman was pushing her stroller through the crosswalk, the homeless man had meandered elsewhere, and there was no sign of the impossible giant. There was no one else at all.

But he had just been there, seconds ago, the sunlight falling flat on his gray skin.

A car horn blurted from behind. The traffic light had turned green.

James Louise got the car moving again. "I didn't see anyone, sweetie. Everything okay?"

She could see herself reflected in his concern: her skin gone pale, eyes glassy and horrified.

It's getting worse, she realized. It had never been this bad before.

The rest of the drive, she expected to see the giant on every empty stretch of sidewalk, or around the sides of downtown's shops. But she didn't see it again until the end of the service, at the pastor's closing sermon.

3

The first few services Charlie ever attended, she felt sorry for her father. He had seemed desperate, clinging to the pastor's every word, praying with a devotion so raw it bordered on embarrassing. But now, when she watched him in those passing moments, any embarrassment she felt about attending church was dispelled. She wondered what it was like to believe in something that strongly, to devote oneself with such abandon and joy. It felt good sitting beside him. Others would see them together and know she was his daughter. She had traded in her late nights, her mornings waking up in the driveway before dawn, for better things: nights in with good movies, evenings spent with her dad, more time for fishing.

For her father, where once there'd been trash bins filled with empty beer bottles—and the nights Charlie spent listening from another room to the sound of muttering and weeping and whiskey being splashed into a yawning glass—there was now Sunday mornings at church. Charlie wanted to be here with him, especially after all of that.

For his sake, she went along with every part of the service except for the communion. It seemed wrong, to her, to come here for the reasons she did and to partake of the ritual as if she were a believer like the rest.

Still, she watched him all the while. She did a lot of that through-out the service when he wouldn't notice. During some of the songs, he would close his eyes and smile a little. When the crowd was called upon to repeat the word *amen* in unison, her father did so with quiet enthusiasm.

Her mind had started to drift. Normally she snuck a book in, and to avoid being caught and therefore offending her dad, sometimes she folded the book into a copy of the Bible.

Her father probably knew this, of course. If so, he pretended not to notice.

More recently, however, Charlie had come without a book. She read from the Bible instead—by now, she must've read roughly two-thirds of it chronologically and found it to be an often disturb-ing work of mythology—but other times she simply observed the people around her, her father included.

Which was how she first noticed the woman just two pews ahead, graying black hair done up in a modest bun, skin brown and lined with more wrinkles than Charlie remembered.

Lupita Del Rosario. Mother of Charlie's childhood friend Marion. She hadn't seen Lupita in years, yet there she was, nodding along to the sermon. Charlie felt the spreading of warmth inside, as though her memories of Lupita were a fire to warm her hands around. Her nose filled with phantom scents of chicken adobo marinating in a crockpot, or pancit bihon sizzling in a pan. Marion had loved taking them (*them* being Eric, Stephen, Sam, and Charlie) to her house in the late afternoons, because Marion's mother always wanted to see them and always prepared more than enough food for everyone.

Lupita was always so animated that half of what she said was always with her body. "I cook always for too many. This is what my nay taught us kids. Cook for too many, too many will come." And she'd laugh that full-faced, full-bodied laugh, encouraging them to get seconds or thirds. "Is too bad you kids don't drink yet."

It didn't take more than a glance, now, to see how Lupita had changed. For one, she looked terribly alone. Charlie pictured her preparing one of her wonderful Filipino meals, but for an empty house. She pictured her sitting down to a meal she'd cooked for too many, at a table full of empty chairs and only herself to feed.

I should've gone to see her, thought Charlie, heavy emotion rising from her chest. *Why didn't I think of doing that? Just once a week—even once a month—I could've visited her. She would've wanted to feed me and hear how I was doing.*

God, but if years could be taken back.

Once everyone was seated again, the minister began the closing speech. This was always Charlie's favorite part of the services, in part because it signified the end, but also because it tended to be short and hopeful. Every now and then, the pastor would give an intense speech, impassioned by his faith and love of God which burned in him, making him want to spread that love like fire. At a younger age, Charlie would've felt judgmental about this, but she tended to see it differently now. That much devotion, so whole-hearted it could be called abandonment, surely felt so joyous, any-one would want to share that feeling with somebody else.

One of the pastors had even said something to that effect. "*Doesn't it just make you want to go out there, grab someone by the shoulders, and tell them it's okay? Tell them there's a love this deep, and this powerful, and this complete, and all they need to do is open their hearts to it and they'll be forgiven?*"

She couldn't judge them for that, even if it was all pointless.

But sometimes there were speeches like the one Pastor Harry had given last Sunday, about the works of man and the corrupting nature of Netflix shows.

The closing speech from the pastor normally brought the mood back around though. Back to love and joy and hope, so that the congregation could go out into their days with a sense of light.

This speech was different. This one sent a silence through the congregation like a burst of wind across a field of grass.

"I know you've seen Him out there in the world," said Pastor Joe, running a hand through his wiry brown hair. It was almost a discomforted gesture, as though the speech ahead was one that both burdened and frightened him. "I know you've seen the signs. Revelations tells us that we will see many signs in diverse places. God may grant us visions of what's to come. But if, as it says in the Book of Job, the Devil walks to and fro among the Earth, and walks up and down it, then it must be true—no, I *know* it's true—that God and His angels walk among us, too." Pastor Joe looked out at the silent congregation, his eyes wide and gleaming. "Haven't you felt it? Haven't you seen Him?"

A few people shouted *amen.*

Charlie's phone buzzed in her pocket, vibrating on and off. Somebody was trying to call her. Probably spam, she thought.

As the pastor kept speaking, however, Lupita Del Rosario stood from her pew and began shuffling past everyone. She made it to the aisle and rushed out of the church, phone gripped in one hand.

Charlie watched her, a puzzled look on her face, and then turned again to the front of the church.

"He sits among us," said Pastor Joe. "Even now, He sits among us."

Charlie's eyes fell upon a massive figure protruding from the front row of pews like a mountain in the ocean. Her breath left her lungs.

The giant she'd seen on the sidewalk was here, lumbering over the other churchgoers, its skin gray and cold. Charlie could see only its massive back, the light from the windows falling over its shoulder blades and dividing at the canyon of its spine. God, but it was gigantic.

A cold feeling gripped her body.

No one else can see him. If they could, they'd be screaming. It's in my head. It's in my head and it's getting worse.

In her pocket her phone buzzed again, indicating either a voice-mail or a text message. Maybe it wasn't a spam call. Maybe it was Adrian.

Her breathing quickened and she pulled her arms close to her body. To her left, her father listened intently to the closing sermon. He didn't see the giant man, either.

"And I tell you this now, not as a prophecy, and not as the kind of fear-mongering so many news stations and politicians would give you, not even as some churches would devolve to. I tell you this as a promise, my friends. Something about this world is changing. We may think it starts out there, out in the world with the politicians and the elite, but no. It starts inside each one of us. In our hearts, we can feel it. I know you've all felt it."

The giant began to turn around. Charlie couldn't tear her eyes away from it, though she felt a hot tension rising in her chest. If she had to see those blank, pitiless eyes again and those flopping things spewing from those purple lips, she might scream.

(*"...I've felt it in the air, I've felt it in my bones, and I know many of you have, too. We are approaching a precipice..."*)

She could see the giant's protuberant, vein-snaked belly. And the scarlet-spattered, boneless things spilling across its chest. Any second and she'd be able to see its gray eyes—the eyes of a corpse that stood upright.

("*...and if we do not receive the signs, or heed the warnings, I tell you now: we will be subjected to His wrath. This world is merely a threshold, is it not, for the greater truth that lies underneath. For sinners, a nightmare of their own making. For those chosen few, those who walk His narrow path: a kingdom...*")

Charlie, her arms wrapped around herself as if to shield from cold, couldn't believe what she was seeing. Beyond the giant who was, even now, turning around to look at her, there stood Pastor Joe. Around him reeled strange shadows. But they weren't mere shadows.

They were *people*. The shapes of people, anyway. Far taller than the pastor—taller, even, than the giant man—they were rising up from the floor, at first like shadows but their skin whitened as it took form. Melting in reverse.

("*...He is among us even now. I've felt his eyes, and I know some of you have, too...*")

It can't be real, it isn't real—

("*and it pains me to say it, but it is written that the path is narrow. That though some of us claim devotion, we haven't given all of our hearts. And He knows this. He commands His shadows to come and grant us the dreams that form the path. We must profess our whole selves, not merely in words but in actions, in our total surrender body and soul. We must lift our gazes on high to the Dusk, the Ache, and the King in Dark Katalpa...*")

Charlie felt her father's hand. He placed it over hers. She released a breath, opened her eyes.

The giant was gone. So were the rising shadows.

"Let this be a reminder," said Pastor Joe. "Go in peace. Go with our Lord."

Some people in the congregation answered, "Amen." Most, however, were silent.

4

On the drive home, James Louise was the first to break the silence.

"What'd you think about Pastor Joe's closing speech?"

Normally, Charlie was the one who asked him *his* thoughts on the service. Something was on his mind. She could hear it in his voice.

"I don't know." How to explain that she couldn't remember much of it? Not except for the words, *He sits among us,* and something about the world as a threshold, and something strange at the end. "I was kinda spacing out for most of it."

"Ah, well, you didn't miss much."

"What'd you think of it?"

He cocked his head. "It was odd. I've never heard him speak like that. Most of it wasn't even… it felt kinda—" He rubbed a hand along his jawline.

"Kinda apocalyptic?"

Her father laughed. "Hellfire and brimstone, or… some weird version of it, anyway." He sighed. "Was kinda hoping to avoid that type of thing."

"Like from when you were a kid?"

"Mm-hmm. Had enough of that to last a lifetime."

She'd heard plenty of stories about his strict Catholic upbringing. It had led him to an agnostic adulthood, at least until last year and his replacing alcohol with church.

He said, "Did you see Lupita? She looks different. I think the last decade's been especially tough on her." The sympathy in his voice was palpable. A broken marriage wasn't comparable to a vanished child, but it was still loss. He viewed Lupita as being of the same tribe, part of an understanding so few others shared.

Charlie pulled out her phone but first looked at her father. "I want to see her," she said. "If she'd want to see me, I mean. I don't think I've even seen her around town at all. Not for years."

"Oh, sweetheart, I'm sure she'd love to see you. You think you'd be ready for that?"

"Why wouldn't I?"

James sighed, shrugged his shoulders. "Just asking. You kids spent a lot of time at her house back in the day."

Charlie nodded, but she was staring at her phone. Adrian had called twice, but left no voicemail.

"I remember," her father went on, "your mother was jealous of her cooking."

"Yeah," she said. "Marion used to take us over to her house all the time." Again the ghost scents of Lupita's house all played in Charlie's nostrils.

I'll go fishing and call Adrian back, she decided. *Then I'll go see Lupita.* She looked back at her father and almost asked him why he'd called her by her childhood pet name this morning. Instead, she simply smiled to herself.

My River Bug, he used to say when she asked to be taken fishing.

5

____

It was called Catalpa Creek and she'd been fishing on its quiet banks since childhood. A ten-minute drive from her house and then a fifteen-minute walk into the woods out past the flooded quarry brought her to the creek's widest expanse. Sometimes she liked to start the walk downriver and hop along the rocks. It made for good exercise, made her feel especially agile—like a character from a video game or some wilderness adventure movie. Mostly it made her feel like a kid again. Marion, Sam, Eric, Stephen, and herself used to come out here to hop along the rocks, fasten swords out of sticks, and conjure kingdoms out of fallen trees. At places where the creek was slow, they sometimes spent hours building dams out of rocks and dirt.

She could remember they'd once built such a successful dam that for two weeks that summer they were kings and queens of their own swimming hole; no other kids had known about it.

Standing now beside the river, small tackle box at her side, Charlie thought about her childhood and wondered why it felt so impossibly far away. She'd turn twenty-two soon, but ten years ago felt like a different lifetime. The person she'd been then felt even farther away. Eons. Lifetimes. Years at the speed of light.

All circling around a drain.

Sunlight danced across the surface of the creek in shards and ripples. There was no sound out here except the chirping of birds and splashing of water.

Charlie thought of Marion and spoke aloud to her the same way some people—including her own father—spoke to God. "I wish you were here to do all these things with me."

She hadn't brought her fishing pole, but this was intentional. With casual movements from years of familiarity, Charlie stepped into the tree line, around a considerable boulder and a circle of trees, a bundle of bushes. She dropped to the dirt, slid herself beneath one of the bushes, reached her hand out. Her fingers found the cork grip of a fishing rod. This was her backup pole, one she'd been leaving out here—in this specific spot—ever since she was a kid. If ever she found herself wandering around with nothing to do and didn't want to return home just to grab her fishing gear, this pole was waiting for her. She took it back out to the water. With a sigh she sat on a flat boulder, reached for her tackle box.

The lure she selected had been part of a set gifted by her dad on her nineteenth birthday. Every couple years—ever since she was seven or eight—he'd bought her the same set to make sure she never ran out. This lure's cosmic blue rubber body ended in frills and was adorned with gold sparkles.

It was called a River Bug.

With the lure attached to her line, Charlie found a pebbly stretch of sand where the water beyond slowed and deepened. She held the bail arm back, pinning the line with her thumb. Swung the rod back, and then—swiftly, with force, but too gentle a finesse to call it a flick or a throw—she cast it forward in an arc, at the same time releasing the line. The cosmic blue River Bug flailed through the air and then plopped into the creek—about halfway across to the other side, in a spot where the water pooled before a shelf of rocks—and Charlie let it sink a little before setting the spool. She tightened the drag so she'd be able to feel any tug on the fishing line, then, content, found a rock to perch on. She sat that way, in her forest green shirt, overalls, and blue cap, her legs pulled up to her chest, hands comfortably gripping the pole. The corner of her lips tilted ever so slightly upward—a smile that appeared similarly at the corners of her eyes.

More than her own house, this was home. A creek or a river, a comfortable enough rock, a line cast out across the water. For a long time she'd stopped fishing, had filled her time with things that, now, felt meaningless in comparison. But she was back and wondered why she ever left.

With her left hand she reeled in slowly, picturing in her mind the lure and its glittering frills shimmering and twirling in the current. If something bit, it'd likely be a trout, or maybe a bass. Rainbow trout was what she normally caught.

Her first catch had been a small rainbow. Charlie was seven and her dad took a picture. The photograph hung now in the hallway: Charlie, not quite grown into her two front teeth, one tooth missing on the bottom, hair in a ponytail sticking out the back of her baseball cap; she held the fish by the mouth, its scales glinting rainbow; behind her, the gentle waters of the Sacramento River.

Catalpa Creek was no Sacramento River, but she preferred the silence here—the stillness, the echo of the woods, the inescapable sense that she was the only person for miles and therefore the only one experiencing this.

She felt something like a tug on the fishing line, but continued her steady reeling. Could've been a rock. Even though this was a deeper-than-usual spot, the creek was shallow. She'd lost plenty of bait, even a few lures, to the rocks and underwater plants.

The water was somehow both constant and ever-changing. Her mind drifted while her eyes scanned the quicksilver surface.

Hadn't the pastor said something about the creek in his closing speech, or had she imagined that? Something about dusk and Catalpa Creek? Or just catalpa. The flower, maybe. Whatever it was, it had sounded strange to her. And she'd been too consumed by the sight of the giant…

No. A cold chill trickled down Charlie's back. She pushed the thought away, brought her attention back to the taut fishing line and her own steady reeling. Soon the lure became visible, so she reeled it all the way in and then cast it out again. The motion was effortless, almost without conscious thought, so easy was its familiarity to her. In fact, the few times she'd found herself fishing in a popular spot, she'd been complimented on her casts by older gentlemen. One of those men had been a fly-fisherman, and he'd suggested she try out fly-fishing. It had made her day.

Her lure landed in the same pool of slowed water as the first cast.

No smile rested on Charlie's lips anymore, nor at the corners of her eyes. She pursed her lips tight. Her gaze was elsewhere as she did her best not to see the giant in her mind's eye. She had seen things before; it'd been happening for years. Began, in fact, not long after Marion's disappearance. But none of her hallucinations had ever been so grisly, so unthinkable.

A few times, while out for a walk—out here in the woods, even —she thought she'd seen a person far out in the trees. This alone wouldn't have been strange, except this person—a man—had been waving at her. Not just waving at something random, or at another person, she was sure. He'd been waving at *her*. Even the memory of it made her pull her legs closer to her body and suspect, for a moment, that she should check over her shoulder in case someone was watching her from the trees.

But the giant man—the corpse with the bloody tendrils spewing from its mouth—was unlike anything she'd ever seen. She'd been able to live with the hallucinations for so long, but if she saw the giant again—or anything so disturbing—she would have to tell someone. At this point, not even Adrian knew. If she told someone, they'd want to help—and she didn't want to imagine what *help* for such a thing would entail.

She remembered, suddenly, how Adrian had called earlier.

"Shit." In her eagerness to get out here, it had slipped her mind, and now she was out of cell service. "Just one more cast," she told herself as she reeled the lure back in.

She came into view of her junky forest-green car which sat in a dirt parking lot near the old quarry. Her phone buzzed.

"*Charlie?*" read Adrian's message, which he'd sent twenty minutes ago. "*Call me back. It's about your old friend Marion.*"

Charlie froze with her hand on the door handle of the car, eyes fixated on the name of her childhood friend.

The thought that fell like cold rain through her mind was this: Marion was dead. After all this time they finally found out what happened to her, but it was too late. She was dead.

In order to keep herself from falling, Charlie gripped the top of the open car door. The next thing she did was fall into a sitting position on the seat, her feet still in the dirt. She read the message again.

It's about Marion, Adrian said. No way it'd be good news. Too much time had passed for it to be good news.

On her desk at home: the framed photograph of herself and Marion at age twelve, standing knee-deep in the swimming hole they and the boys had created. The Renegade's Dam, they'd called it, because that's what they sometimes called themselves: The Renegades, or The Renegade Club. The boys had picked that one, of course. Charlie and Marion had wanted to name it something else, something about flowers and thorns.…. she couldn't remember, exactly. But it would've been better than *The Renegades*; of that much she was still certain.

But there was that picture on Charlie's desk, not of the whole group—The Renegades—but of just Marion and her, arms around one another while knee-deep in their swimming hole, looking at each other and laughing about something.

How long since I last cried about you, Marion? How long since I stopped hoping to see you again and instead started to wonder if I'd ever find out what happened to you?

Charlie looked up from her phone. Marion was standing just a few feet away, in a dark purple sundress. But it wasn't Marion as she would be now, ten years later. It was Marion at age twelve, the way Charlie remembered her—the way she imagined seeing her again.

"You took it with you," said Charlie, giving Marion her full attention. "And nothing was ever the same."

When Marion spoke, her voice seemed to emanate from the breeze. "Every summer comes to an end, Charlie."

"I know it does. But we were supposed to have more than what we got. We were so young—*you* were so young—and there was so much to look forward to. So much I…" She looked down at her hands. "There's so much you and I didn't get to do."

Marion shut her eyes. The ends of her purple dress rippled in the wind. "When's the last time you were happy, Charlie? I mean really happy, all the way down."

Tears blurred Charlie's eyes and she blinked them away. When she did, Marion was gone; the parking lot was empty.

Happiness is a fool's game, she thought. *I know that, and maybe you did too, before whatever end you met. It's like light, isn't it. Light in our universe. There are places where it can be found—places, even, where it envelopes everything. But always it's burning out, it's impermanent—and there's no point trying to hold on to it, no point fooling ourselves that it'll last. Not in this world, where darkness is how it started and how it'll end. Soon enough the light will fade. And when all lights go out, maybe none will ever come again, because despite what we tell ourselves, dark doesn't need light. And it'll become clear to us that it doesn't really matter whether or not we're happy, or for how long. The fundamental reality is something different, something so much bigger and all-encompassing than any of us are ever aware, and none of us knows how to admit that.*

But the last time I was happy, I mean truly happy, all the way down? With you, she thought, remembering that full-bodied, nerve-buzzed feeling from long ago. *That's the last time. When I was a child. When nothing could touch us and it was like nothing mattered, not the loneliness, not the emptiness,. With you—together somewhere. That's what I remember.*

She sat still for a long time, eyes closed, gazing across the aching hours of the past. With a breath she opened her phone, found Adrian's contact, and tapped *Call.*

6

Adrian answered on the second ring. There was more urgency in his voice than she'd ever heard.

"Charlie! Where were you? I've been calling and calling—"

"I know, I'm sorry. I was out of cell range."

"Where?"

"Catalpa Creek. I just got your message."

"Charlie, you aren't gonna believe it. I think—"

"Just tell me what you heard." She was sitting in her car, still in the dirt parking lot by the old quarry. Now that she was on the phone, she expected to hear the words any second now: *They found Marion's body. They found out what happened to her.*

Adrian said, "I think I should tell you this in person. We can meet, um, at the little park just outside Old Town."

Charlie inhaled sharply through her nose. "Adrian."

"What?"

"Just tell me."

"Okay, but… but I still think we should meet, okay?"

"*Adrian.*"

"Okay, listen. I heard it from my mom who heard it from the pastor of that church you go to, I think." He took a breath. "Charlie."

"What?"

"It's Marion. She's alive."

*

The second time they met, Adrian had said: "Kinda wondered if I'd ever see you again."

"Don't ruin it," Charlie had answered. They smiled at each other as he rose from his camping chair to give her a hug.

It was at a campfire with a small group of people, mostly Sam's friends from high school, and Charlie initially hadn't wanted to attend. But after a few days of thinking about it, she'd sent Adrian a text message with an invitation; she decided she'd only go if he was there.

While sitting in the glow of the campfire, with the stars beginning to burn in the dusk, Charlie told herself she wanted nothing from this new friendship but friendship, even as the conversations of everyone else at the campfire may as well have been the buzzing of mosquitoes or a backdrop of cricket song, and all of her attention was on Adrian. The ease with which he carried himself—not quite with detachment or indifference, but simply with an ease, as though nothing reached under his skin, as though nothing could bother him—this near-stoic disposition was exactly what fascinated her, made her wonder: what did he hide in his mind? What whirled beneath the surface that he didn't let show?

"I gotta say, no girl's ever made me wait two and a half weeks before reaching out to me." He said this while holding a stick out over the fire, as if roasting an imaginary marshmallow.

For the second time since meeting him, she was struck by his casual boldness. "So you give your number out often, then?"

"I wouldn't say that." He eyed her carefully. "It's just, I couldn't tell if you were interested or not."

"Interested?"

"You know. In hanging out some more." He looked into the fire, apparently content. "For the record, I was glad to hear from you."

She eyed him a second more, trying to conceal a smile, before turning also to the fire. "I'm glad you came."

"I don't usually come to these things."

"What, *these things* as in social gatherings?"

"I guess so."

"The only times we've met up have been at these things."

"True."

As the evening went on, ice chests were opened, drinks passed around. Adrian took two and offered one to Charlie. Charlie began to reach for it as though it were the most natural thing in the world, no hesitation, but stopped. It was Saturday, meaning tomorrow would be an earlier morning; she wanted to join her father for church.

"I'm good," she said. Adrian asked her if she minded if he drank, and she told him to go ahead.

"I don't think it's something talked about enough," someone was saying. It was the group of chairs beside Charlie's and Adrian's—a few guys whose philosophical conversation seemed to be overtaking the rest of the campfire crowd. "It doesn't matter what we're talking about here, whether it's death, or grief—you know, losing someone, as opposed to facing your own mortality—or whether it's literal depression, I mean like *real* depression, not like when some needy, attention-starved teenager posts 'I'm depressed' as their status on Facebook so that everyone will comment and ask what's wrong. Or some bullshit internet poet writes 'I thrive through depression, I don't suffer from it.' Not like that ignorant shit. I mean like medical depression, you know. Chronic, or whatever it's called. Or it doesn't have to be that, even. Just sadness. Negative emotions.

It doesn't matter. It's social media, it's every commercial on TV, it's the goddamn ghost of Cold War McCarthyism come back to haunt us. This obsession with happiness, or, or… or not with happiness, it's with the appearance of happiness, you know?"

"Okay, sure," another guy interjected. "I can see that with social media, obviously. We're supposed to compare our own inner lives with everyone else's outer life. But that's only if you buy into it."

"No, no," said the first guy. His name was Colin. "It doesn't even matter if you buy into it or not on the individual level. Our society is practically built on it. Generations of people raised with image at the forefront of their value systems, so what do they pass on to their kids? And what do those kids pass on to their kids?"

"What does it matter?" someone else chimed in. "We're all gonna die and be forgotten one day anyway."

Some of the people laughed, but Colin continued unfazed. "That's part of my point, actually. You say that like it's this thing you can dismiss and it means nothing matters. But that's exactly the reason why everything *does* matter."

At this point, the whole campfire was listening to the conversation. Adrian could apparently restrain his own contributions no longer. Maybe it was the two drinks in his system—two-and-a-half, considering he was partway through a third.

"I know what you mean by that," he said. Even though Adrian hadn't said anything for the first part, Colin looked at him not with disdain or dismissal, but with something near to joy. "Buddhism, or something like it," said Adrian. "No wait, more like Taoism. In the context of that being the opposite of Nihilism."

"*Oh* yes, yes, exactly. The fact that we're all gonna die and be forgotten, eventually, doesn't mean nothing matters, it means everything matters. Or, or… or if not everything, then what you choose. What you choose to make matter, that's what matters."

"Okay. What's that got to do with McCarthyism?"

More laughter around the campfire.

"Well, that's more having to do with maintaining a social image. Smiles and toxic positivity have replaced a hyper-American nuclear family image. But what I was getting at is, like, how our society primes us to not be able to basically function right, because we're conditioned to be in denial of negative emotions."

Right, thought Charlie, restraining a laugh from her mental corner. *Could've just said that.*

"When something terrible happens to us, it hits us like a meteor. I mean, it just floors people. We're emotional illiterates, most of us, when it comes to loss, or sadness, or *real* depression, you know. I mean, how many people do you think are out there—in this town or, hell, right here, around this campfire—who say they have depression, or think they know what it's like to experience something really hard, really negative and difficult, when really it's just child's play compared to the real thing? How many people have run-of-the-mill negative experiences and call themselves traumatized? When real life comes knocking, like *real* heavy stuff, there's no way to even prepare for it because, all our lives, we're living on this cloud that doesn't even skim beneath the surface. As a society we're so out of balance with the other spectrum of human emotion. What Carl Jung would've called our *shadow.*"

"Hold on," said another guy—the one who'd made the comment earlier about death. "What do you know about what anyone else has been through?"

"Well I don't mean it like that, man, but—"

"It sounded like you did," said Adrian. "I don't know about anyone else here, and none of this is anything huge, but I have my own struggles. And they're just as real as anybody else's."

"I get that, I do. But I'm talking about us as a society, not necessarily—"

Someone else from the other side of the campfire: "Isn't that what a society is? Us, our group?"

"I'm sure I'm not the only one here," said Adrian, "but ever since I was a kid, I've had pretty bad anxiety. Used to have anxiety attacks at school actually, when I was little."

Everyone else began to chime in with similar anecdotes: experiences with depression; with anxiety; with loved ones lost; with hearts broken. All the while Colin tried to stem the tide of voices with his own, trying to clarify without further dismissing or invalidating.

Charlie, however, was looking at Adrian. She tried to envision him as a child, which wasn't difficult. But imagining the anxiety underneath...

What she felt as she watched him was an unexpected warmth. A desire, almost, to scoot closer to him, as though the night were cold and he was the campfire.

Later, before she departed for home, she excused herself from the ongoing discussion—which had spiraled beyond any semblance of what it started out as—and made her way to the shore of the lake.

There was something about bodies of water in the dark. The darkness in place of reflection. The quiet of water gently splashing the shore.

When Adrian followed just a few minutes later, he found Charlie sitting atop a boulder. He paced back and forth at the water's edge, searching for rocks to skip.

"You good?" he asked.

She had pointed her gaze skyward. "I'm good."

"Not interested in the debate, huh?"

"I guess not. Not that I would've been able to get a word in, anyway."

"Yeah. Makes sense."

"I didn't know you have anxiety."

He tossed a rock, watched it splash, watched the water settle. Across the silence of the lake, the sound seemed so loud. "Ever since I was a little kid, pretty much. It's nothing, really."

"I know what that's like."

"Sometimes I wonder, actually, what would be different about my life without it. Without a lot of things, but especially that. I feel like I ruined a lot of my own childhood because I couldn't stop clenching my teeth and pulling away and just staying still."

"I'm sorry."

"No, it's not your fault."

"I know, it's just… I get it." She stood from the boulder, stepped closer to the edge of the water. "It's sort of a problem I've always had. Like I'm never done with the past. Or it's never done with me."

"Yeah, I sorta got that impression from you when we met."

"What do you mean?"

"I don't know, in a way it's like you have this weight on you all the time that most other people don't have. I don't mean that in a bad way, it's just…" He shook his head. "I guess I can relate, in some ways anyway."

She picked up her own rock, bounced it a couple times on her palm. No drinks tonight, but she felt bold—perhaps it was the crowd, or being under the stars. Perhaps it was a buzz she felt in the presence of Adrian, a pull somewhere inside to simply be honest. Maybe it'd been too long since she'd felt this safe with another person. "You know, some of the things you guys were talking about over there… it got me thinking about a lot of things."

"You should've piped in. I'm sure you wouldn't have let yourself be talked over."

She grinned. "I know. I just didn't feel like it. Sometimes it's more interesting to listen." She tossed the rock, watched it all the way to the splash. "Some of the things that Colin guy said earlier, though… you know, the parts that you started arguing with him about."

"Yeah."

"I agree with what you were saying. It just got me thinking about how much of my life has been spent around a negative space, so to speak. Whether it was feeling depressed, or how toxic my parents could be through most of my childhood with how they were always fighting. It's like… sometimes I feel like I grew up too fast. Sometimes it's more like I still haven't grown up enough."

"They're divorced, your parents?"

"They may as well be. My mom left when I was seventeen, and my dad… I mean, I think *he* still thinks she might come back one day. And I hope he eventually realizes it's better if she doesn't."

"Wow. I didn't know any of that about you."

She shrugged, suddenly self-conscious about how much she was saying—and about how she felt safe doing so with him.

"I've been in situations like that," he said. "Sort of, I mean. Just relationships, not as serious as marriage, or how it is with your dad. I just mean, the type of thing where I was holding on to something—some*one*—when I should've let go. One of those things, you know, where you're stuck on the same problem for months, so it's like you're reliving the same situation for way too long."

"With Keri, you mean?"

Adrian released a quick breath through his nose, something like a scoff or a laugh. "Keri'd like to think so, but no. It was someone else."

"Someone important."

"Yeah. And it's not like it's all over, you know, with that other person. She means a lot to me. It just… it'll never work out."

Nothing ever does, she thought, but didn't say. "How come?"

"How come what, it'll never work out? It's not like we fought or anything, or like something terrible happened. It's funny, actually." His eyes appeared to twinkle in the dark. "We just saw things differently. A little too differently, I think, because she couldn't seem to understand."

Charlie sat back down on the rock, feeling suddenly chilled. From the front pocket of her overalls she pulled a dark red beanie and slipped it on. "So it was philosophical?"

"A little more complicated than that, but basically yeah. That wouldn't be inaccurate." He stuffed his hands into his pockets, cocked his head in the direction of the campfire. "Want a drink?"

"Thanks, but I'm good. Got an early morning."

"On a Sunday? You have work?"

"Still looking for a new job."

"Ah, job-hunting. That's basically work."

"Actually, tomorrow I have church."

He looked taken aback. "*Church?*"

"I like to go with my dad."

"I didn't know you went to church."

"I just go to be with my dad."

"Oh okay, so your dad's religious, like he believes in God. What about you?"

"What about me, as in—do I believe in God?" With a sigh she turned her eyes back to the stars. "I guess I don't really know."

"Not to just ask something like that." He scratched the top of his head. "But I guess it was gonna come up eventually."

"It's okay."

"If I was gonna guess, I would've guessed no."

"No?"

"I don't mean that as a bad thing. It's just... I got that impression from you."

"In a good way or a bad way?"

He grinned as if to assure her that it wasn't in a bad way. "I don't really know either, you know, if I believe in anything. Sometimes I think, you know, you gotta believe in *something*."

Charlie shrugged again. "Not necessarily." She thought about the stars, how she used to look at them as a child and wonder how old some of them were, wonder how many of them were dead and how long before their light faded away. "But I like to think there *is* something. Not God. But *something*. And whatever it is, if there's anything, I want to think it could be fundamentally good."

Adrian watched her as she said this and his eyes filled with a reverence not unlike the way Charlie looked at the stars. "I like that. Something good."

"That's what I'd like to believe, anyway." She closed her eyes, inhaled deeply. Remained that way for almost a full minute in silence, thinking about the distance between what she wanted to believe and what she actually believed. "Sometimes I think, if there is something, it must be beyond anything we could understand."

"That's interesting."

She asked, "Do you remember Marion Del Rosario?"

Adrian opened his mouth to say something, but he stopped, his brow furrowed. "You know, that name kinda rings a bell. You asked me that before, didn't you?"

She watched him closely. How could he not remember? It was the most shocking thing that had happened in this town in decades. Marion had been a household name.

But it was as though people had forgotten Marion. Not merely in the sense of having moved on—it was worse than that. Sometimes, when she brought up Marion's name, people either needed strong reminders or didn't remember her at all.

Watching Adrian struggle to remember now, Charlie felt cold. If Adrian of all people wasn't immune, then her fears were real: people were forgetting Marion—it was as though she'd never existed.

"Wait. Yeah... I think I know that name." He reached up to touch the side of his head as if he felt a pang there. "Didn't... Wasn't she the girl who disappeared, or got kidnapped or something, a few years ago? Or am I thinking of—"

"That was her. She was my best friend." Charlie wrapped her arms around herself, acutely aware of the hole—the negative space —she'd lived the last ten years circling around. She turned her eyes skyward. "And she loved things like water, and poetry, and the stars."

*

Even though Adrian told her to wait for him, Charlie wasted no time. As soon as the phone call was over, she left the dirt parking lot and drove straight for Lupita's house.

Fifteen minutes later, Charlie parked her car across the street from the house. She felt pale, lightheaded. Now that she was here, she let herself breathe. She hadn't been back to this street in what felt like an entire lifetime. In reality, it must've been eight or nine years. After Marion disappeared, there weren't many reasons to come back here.

Except... no. That wasn't it. They could've come back to visit Lupita. They could've walked down to the end of the street, like they always did—to where the asphalt broke off into dirt, dirt into forest—and spent time out at their usual wanderings. The land-marks invented by them: familiar bushes, recognizable trees or up-turned roots, noteworthy boulders, the types of places they, with their children's imaginations, transformed into fortresses and hide-outs and battlegrounds.

After Marion's disappearance, it hadn't felt right. Nothing had. And soon enough, The Renegades were a memory.

Charlie looked down that way, to the end of the road. The old basketball hoop was still there, its rim lacking color, net torn to shreds. Stephen, the best one at most sports, had often tried to jump high enough to touch the rim whenever he walked past it.

"It doesn't look different," said Charlie, thinking out loud. "On the outside, I mean." It occurred to her that this wouldn't make sense to anyone but herself.

No, this place—Marion's street, where The Renegades had spent so many summer days—didn't look so different than it had all those years ago, not on the outside. Beneath the surface however, in that intangible, non-temporal place that made a place what it was, this street was a landscape of ghosts. A husk of memory—and memory of life.

This world is a threshold, the pastor had said. Charlie Louise understood what that meant. Beneath what could be seen, there was an invisible world, and the fabric of that world was memory, emotion, aching.

I get to see Marion again, she realized, but wasn't naive enough to hope that Marion wouldn't be like the end of the street: no different on the outside.

She exited the car. On the front porch of the house stood Lupita Del Rosario, waiting.

Charlie went to her, and Lupita met her halfway with arms wide open.

This was how it had always been. Marion brought everyone over, and Lupita would greet each person with warmth, but it was always Charlie she hugged with the most enthusiasm. "Charlie, my girl," she'd say, or just "Nenè."

And it was no different, as if no time had passed.

"Let me look at you," said Lupita, holding Charlie by the shoulders. "You've grown into such a beautiful young woman, nenè." Her eyes twinkled, and the smile that tightened her lips could just as well have been an effort to hold back tears.

Charlie felt it too. "I've wanted to come visit you," she said. "Not just once, I mean. I wish I would've—"

"You stop that. You're here now, yes?"

Charlie nodded, suddenly finding it hard to speak. "I came as soon as I found out. Is it really… I mean, is she—"

"She's inside, in bed." Lupita looked off toward the driveway where her minivan was parked. "I'm afraid Dr. Schultz will come back."

"Dr. Schultz was here? Is Marion… is she okay?"

Lupita appeared to shake her head, or to begin to. Something came into her eyes, like a cloud crossing over the sun.

"You come inside. Dr. Schultz won't return for perhaps an hour. You come inside."

Within two minutes, Lupita set out a tray of cheese and crackers and was asking if Charlie wanted anything to drink, maybe a glass of water or—oh! how about some Martinelli's?

Charlie only agreed to water. She had no appetite; in fact, she hardly felt as though she were inside her own body at all. When Lupita handed her the cold glass, Charlie examined her own hand as though it were something separate from her, a thing with its own will.

Marion was just a room away.

And just a few hours ago I was thinking about you, she thought, directed at the Marion that lived in her head. *I was missing you like I always am, and wondering what you'd look like if you were still alive.*

She tried not to remember the other thoughts she'd been having, the ones that haunted her like her own shadow, nipping at her heels: that maybe it was time to start moving on. If the past would never be done with her, maybe she could choose to be done with the past.

Lupita sat at the table, too, and looked at Charlie with something like regret.

"I think it is all right for you to see Marion," she said. "Dr. Schultz said probably no visitors yet, but if it's you…"

"Why doesn't he want anyone to see her? Is she okay?"

"Physically yes. She is healthy and awake." She looked off into the living room without seeing anything. "And you must know this, Charlie, how happy it makes me for her to be here. Not just alive, which is more than I let myself pray for all this time, but also that she is mostly healthy. It seems like a dream. Like it shouldn't be possible that she is in this house, in her own bed, alive, when all of us thought for so long that this story already is over."

"It was never over for me." Charlie's voice came low. "I've thought about her every day."

"I know you have, nenè. The two of you…" Lupita brought a hand up to cover her mouth as her voice wavered. "But there is something wrong, Charlie. I did not need Dr. Schultz to tell me this. Although my sweet girl is healthy in the body, something is very wrong here." She tapped her head. Then, carefully, put a hand to her chest, over her heart. "Here too, most of all."

Charlie crossed her arms over her chest. "She vanished almost a decade ago. I'm sure she's been through so much more than we can imagine."

"Dr. Schultz offered such terms as post-traumatic stress disorder. In some ways it is like that. When my husband returned from the war, he was not fully the man who I married. It was terrible. For him, I mean. It also made him terrible for some time. Angry all the time. Sometimes would put his food in the oven, or the microwave, and just watch it cook. When the refrigerator made sounds at night, he would jump awake. Normally he and I drive each other crazy just over breakfast, but suddenly he's sad, or staring off at nothing and looking like he's in pain."

"Flashbacks," Charlie echoed.

Lupita nodded—she had a way of nodding just once, as if to say *Exactly*. "Slowly he came back, but part of him was always still there, in *the bush*, the way it's said. He didn't talk about it with me, but I heard a friend say it that way. That the war never ends for many who come back.

"Whatever is happening with my Marion, it seems the same thing, maybe, but more than that also. Since she appeared yesterday, she has said only a little. Dr. Schultz will come back with a priest." *Pressed*, it sounded with her accent.

"A priest?"

"He thinks Marion will talk to a priest. Or he is feeling inadequate and thinks this is beyond his practice as a physician." She made a funny sound with pursed lips, indicating dismissal and disapproval all at once. "As if my daughter is possessed or ever liked going to church." She smirked at the look on Charlie's face. "Like you, a good girl. She went to church for me, like you go for your papa. Don't say it's not true." She wiped at her eyes. "But I think it's okay if you see her now. I think she will talk to you. If not today, in time."

Charlie nodded, empty of words. She felt a block of ice on her chest, both the weight of it and the cold, and the feeling only worsened as Lupita led her down the hallway to the closed door of Marion's bedroom. Charlie knew the way, had made the walk to Marion's room hundreds of times with Marion herself, but this time it was far from familiar. Charlie was making her way through the dark, with no idea what waited for her beyond the doorway.

7

"Do you remember me?" asked Marion. She was curled up on the windowsill, legs pulled to her chest, head lowered. At first, Charlie dismissed this as a silly question. Later, when she came to understand what Marion had meant, she would shudder at the memory.

The only illumination in the room was cast by thin slots of gray light between the blinds. Charlie hadn't stepped inside this room in almost ten years, but she had no problem remembering its details: the neatly made bed centered on the far wall, facing a wardrobe where she and Marion had often hid from the boys and pretended it might lead them to Narnia; the perpetually messy desk in the far corner, piled typically with books and sketchbooks.

All the furniture remained in the same place, but the details were missing. The few books on the desk were neatly organized by Lupita's hand. The walls, once featuring movie and book posters, were barren except for a few of Marion's sketches, which Lupita had left hanging.

Then there was the window. The windowsill was wide enough to sit on, and sometimes when Charlie had slept over, being the only one of The Renegades allowed to sleep in Marion's room, she had chosen to set up her bed in the windowsill. So many weekends she'd brought over her sleeping bag, and Marion provided pillows, and the windowsill was her spot. She and Marion stayed up late—

past midnight, if they lost track of time—just seated on the window-sill together, chatting, telling stories, talking about who liked who, who had done what or said what, new art projects, books they were reading, movies they needed to show each other, how small the world was next to the vastness of space, the stars and their light trapped in time...

...talking about their futures and what sorts of people they wanted to be, how they'd never end up boring like their parents, how they would never stop wanting to do fun things like build rock dams on Catalpa Creek or have sleepovers, and they'd go to the same college and Marion could punch anyone who tried to hurt Charlie; and on and on...

Kid stuff, Charlie thought.

But as she stood by the bed, looking at her long-lost friend who was curled up tightly as if trying to hide from the world's prying eyes, Charlie longed deeply for those wonderful, simple, impossible dreams she'd dreamed with her friend when they were kids—when, in the late hours after lights out, nothing was impossible. Kid stuff.

The room was the same but different. The windowsill and its loneliness. The bed and its cold sheets, the familiar quilted comforter lacking wrinkles from recent weight.

Marion was the same but different. Hair the same dark brown but longer, curlier—*wilder*, thought Charlie. She didn't look how Charlie had imagined her when, over the years, she'd played out the scenario in her head, over and over. She looked closed. Like she was a stranger inside a familiar body. The same eyes but a different mind looking out.

Charlie came to the windowsill, sat slowly by crossing her legs. It seemed impossible that the two of them had ever spent so many hours at this very spot. There was hardly any room; they sat now almost shoulder-to-shoulder on the sill's cold wood.

Do you remember me? Marion asked. Charlie didn't want to answer that question—it made her think of the people who seemed to have forgotten Marion—although the words that came to her mind were: *I could never forget.*

"I remember the first night I slept in your room," Charlie said. "And the first question you asked me, too. Remember?"

From where she hid behind her arms and raised knees and the tangles of hair that hung across her face, Marion met Charlie's eyes for the first time. She looked like a stray dog cornered, baring teeth, torn between trying to hide or attack.

Charlie restrained herself from reaching out to touch her friend, a gesture that had once come so naturally as to be called thoughtless.

Marion whispered, "I asked if you slept with a nightlight, because I was embarrassed of mine."

Charlie nodded. "And then you asked if I was scared of sleeping over at a stranger's house—"

"—and you answered, *You aren't a stranger.*" For the first time, as Marion rested her chin atop her knees, Charlie could see all of Marion's face. The shape of her jawline, the dim light glinting off her brown eyes, and the sucked-in appearance of her cheeks. Marion had grown up—of course she had—and she was as pretty as Charlie remembered. But she was thin. And, for the first time, she could make out a semblance of what Lupita had meant when she said Marion was different. When she said there was something wrong.

Marion's voice was still a tense whisper. "That's what you told me. That I wasn't a stranger."

"You weren't. There's a lot I don't remember about being a kid, but I remember how it felt talking to you." Charlie started to reach toward her, longing only to hold her hand. "It felt like we always knew each other. From the beginning. Like we'd always been friends."

These words appeared to physically sting Marion, causing her to squeeze her eyes shut and hold herself tighter.

"You're still my friend." Charlie, with hesitance, placed her hand gently on Marion's back. "My best friend."

Marion inched away from Charlie's touch. "I think you should go."

"What?"

"I said, I think you should go."

Charlie's vision swam in the low light. For a second she caught movement from the corner of her eye, what looked like a person standing in the bedroom doorway, maybe Lupita come to check on them. But when she looked, the doorway was shut, just as she'd left it.

Why was it, she wondered, that after so many years of talking to Marion in her head, she suddenly had no idea what to say?

"I have that picture of us," she said, "from the last summer. The day we built the dam on Catalpa Creek."

Marion hid her face, appearing to try harder and harder to disappear.

Charlie went on with the persistence of an ice sculptor chipping carefully away. "It's on my desk with all the other pictures of us when we were kids together." She almost said *I look at it everyday,* but that was a lie. It had been true, once, but it wasn't anymore. That same picture was facedown on her desk.

She turned around so she was facing away from the window, the opposite direction of Marion. Her eyes settled on something under the bed: a leather journal. It was old, the leather chaffed and torn. Something about it made her skin crawl, as if she were looking at a giant insect. Charlie looked down, shoving the journal from her mind. She went on. "Even after I was sure I might never see you again, you know, I never stopped imagining what it'd be like if you came back. I've imagined it so many times." Beside her, Marion had made a cocoon of herself. "Do you really want me to go?"

Marion tried to take a breath. It was only then that Charlie realized Marion wasn't just hiding; she was crying silently into her arms.

She started to reach out for her again, thought better of it, kept her hand suspended halfway to her.

"Hey. You're back. You're really here... alive. And I'm so happy about that." She made herself stand up. "And when you're ready to see me, there's s-*so* much I have to tell you."

She felt as if the solidity of her long-lost friend was inexplicably fragile, that if she stepped out of this room she might never see her again. Still, Marion didn't want her here, and it hurt too much to linger. So Charlie straightened the cap on her head and stepped away. Reached for the handle of the door, its cold silver gleaming.

From the windowsill came Marion's voice. "Wait."

Charlie turned.

"When we were kids and you slept over, I used to make a bed for you right here."

"I remember."

"But you never used it. You always slept next to me." Marion lifted her eyes and met Charlie's gaze across the dim room. "Remember what we used to say to each other before we fell asleep?"

Charlie wiped at her eyes and cheeks. "Of course I do. *Let's try to meet in our dreams.* And sometimes we'd make up a setting, a house or a castle or a forest, and... and we'd try to think about it as we fell asleep so we might dream the same dream and be able to meet there. I used to fall asleep smiling because of that."

"That's what I did," said Marion. "Every night for the past nine years. In bed, sometimes with my hands and feet tied together, I'd close my eyes and think really hard about you and me on Catalpa Creek, and I'd wish I could go there in my dreams. Sometimes thinking about you like that, while trying to fall asleep at night... it was all I really had. For so long." Marion's face darkened. "But then things changed. And it didn't matter what I thought about before I fell asleep." She took a long breath, not so much a sigh as a sound of bracing. "Can I ask you something, Charlie?"

"Always."

"Have you felt it yet? In your dreams?"

"In my *dreams*?"

"Have they started for you? First your brain goes black. And then, after awhile, they change. They become... *wonderful*."

"What does that mean?"

Marion looked away as if there were something to be seen out the window, through the thin slots created by the blinds. "You would know what I meant."

"Are those the kinds of things you dreamed about? Your brain going black?"

In response, Marion retreated into herself again, lowering her head into her arms.

"Marion..." Charlie brought her hands together at her waist. "You were... you said you were tied up at night?"

No answer.

"Someone did that to you? The someone who kidnapped you?"

"You don't remember?"

A strange feeling—a stiffness—filled Charlie's body. "I want to know what happened. When you're ready to talk about it." She opened the door. "By the way, I... I haven't had any dreams like that, but I *have* seen things. Ever since the day you left, actually."

She began to say more but choked on the next word. It would sound outlandish if she said it out loud. "Bye, Marion."

Marion lifted her head to say something, but Charlie was already shutting the door behind her.

*

Marion emerged from her bedroom on tiptoes, her destination the front door. Charlie was on her way off the front porch, probably to return to her car and then home. But Marion needed to ask her something. She needed to—

"Ah, Marion," came a man's voice from the dining room. Marion didn't stop, but caught a glimpse of a man in a black button-up shirt. "Marion?" The man called when she walked on toward the front door.

Lupita stepped out from the dining room with the man in tow. "Nenè?"

Marion didn't answer. She shoved through the screen door and onto the front porch, eyes seeking Charlie.

Seated on the curb was a young man in a brown jacket. Beside him, on the sidewalk, stood Charlie in her forest-green tank top and denim overalls that Eric had liked to tease her about. Her hair blew in a sudden wind that made the front lawn's grass twitch and the surrounding trees make a *hssshhhh* sound as their branches swayed. Marion couldn't see her face, but she could tell that Charlie was looking at something across the road, near the end of the asphalt to the left where stood the old sagging basketball hoop...

The wind seemed to fall into silence. The approaching footsteps of Lupita and the man in black faded off like echoes diminishing.

The person who stood at the end of the road was someone Marion knew. She recognized the shape of him, his long body, the confident setting of his legs, the dreadlocks spilling from beneath a wide-brimmed hat. She even recognized the way he was waving at her, as if trying to get her attention. She'd seen this gesture so many times before, from the bedroom window of the cabin, out in that impossible forest...

It was him. Impossibly, it was *him.*

Marion drew in a harsh breath, felt her heart pick up its pace. She started to turn away, equally to turn her face from the vision as if to banish it away, but she stopped.

"Charlie," Marion said, but her voice came out as a hoarse whisper. *You see him too*, she thought and wanted desperately to shout, but her voice wouldn't obey.

A hand gripped Marion's shoulder. It was her mother. "Marion? Pastor Joe is here for you."

The phantom man's attention was no longer on Marion, and he had ceased waving. He was facing Charlie, was *pointing right at her.*

Marion gasped. "Charlie," she said, her voice still low. "Charlie!" Louder this time. *"Charlie!"*

Charlie turned. Her face was pale and there was horror in her eyes. Her cheeks glistened in the afternoon light.

"I see it, too," said Marion. And then the vision was gone and the wind with it, and Marion was pulled back into the house.

8

———————————————

A gust of wind appeared to whisk the phantom man into a spiral of dust that tapered away on the asphalt like a twirling ice-skater vanishing mid spin.

Charlie had come away from the house in a daze. By the time she reached the sidewalk, hardly registering Adrian's presence, the emotions were boiling over.

She thought, *She doesn't want me anymore. All these years and she doesn't want to see me anymore. Marion I miss you so much.* Then thought, *I need to call my dad.*

Sniffling, she pulled out her phone, began to scroll her contacts, but her resolve faded.

Adrian sat on the curb. When she came and stood, crying, on the sidewalk, Adrian rose to meet her. He recognized something on her face and decided to say nothing; their shared silence was a gift between the two of them, handed to one and then handed back.

When the wind picked up, Charlie's gaze followed it to the end of the road, past the decrepit basketball hoop to where the asphalt ended in cracks and crumbles.

That was where the man stood, clear in the low sunlight, half his body and face in shadow. That shadow was somehow like liquid, restless on his body like ripples across the surface of water.

He was waving an arm back and forth, back and forth, trying to get her attention.

If anything else happened around her, Charlie wouldn't have been able to tell. Even Adrian standing beside her, ready to embrace her if she moved closer to him, seemed to fade from her awareness. Her heartbeat grew fast and heavy. Her body stiffened. Each of her senses honed in on the man at the end of the road, trying to discern the real from the hallucinated. The dark skin, the tattered coat, dreadlocks underneath a wide-brimmed hat…

The man stopped waving. He extended an arm, pointed right at her.

Then the gust of wind, the man becoming a dust-devil collapsing on the asphalt.

"I went to the Border to witness the Katalpian Dusk," said Charlie, her voice low, eyes panicked as if she were surprised at her own words. "I was sure the Second Coming was at hand. But when the time arrived, the God that emerged was a hideous spider. And his face held no mercy."

The second the words left her lungs, she threw a hand up to her own mouth.

Adrian, with fear in his eyes: "*What?*"

She shook her head, opened her mouth to speak but no sound came out.

"What'd you just say?"

Her reeling mind was trying to make sense of what had just happened when she heard Marion call her name from behind. Charlie turned.

Marion stood on the front porch, strands of curling hair tumbling out from her sweater's hood and blowing across her face, with a look of dreadful comprehension in her eyes.

"I see it too," said Marion, faintly audible from where Charlie stood. Lupita emerged from the house and led her daughter back into the house, toward the black-clad figure of the pastor.

I have to know what happened, Charlie thought, and at the same time knew—from the look Marion had given her—that, if she asked, Marion would tell.

9

"Do you remember who I am?" asked the pastor, sitting at the far end of the dining table, hands folded in front of him.

Marion stood in the foyer, brushing her hair away from her face.

"I wish I didn't."

His lips tightened with an unreadable, restrained emotion. "You can sit down if you want. Make yourself comfortable."

Marion looked toward the hallway and the ajar door of her bedroom.

"Know why I'm here?" asked the pastor. "It might not be for the reasons you think."

"If you're not here because of *him*, then… you're here to see if I'm okay. My mom was scared."

The pastor cocked his head. "You and I both know, don't we, Marion, that your mother has good reason to be scared for you."

Marion eyed the pastor the way she might an interesting animal at a zoo. After a few seconds she removed her hood and sat down across from him.

"I have a few questions for you," said the pastor. "Let's start with what happened on the shores of the Ocean of Hali."

*

The rain started after Marion was pulled back into her house, and Charlie would've stood still and let herself be drenched if not for Adrian. Adrian took her hand and led her to his car. Sat her in the passenger seat. Jogged around and sat himself on the driver's side.

With water dripping from the ends of her hair, Charlie watched the splashing of droplets across the windshield and she tried to focus on the thought that Adrian had been holding her hand, that her fingers had been intertwined with his. She trembled and thought how nice it would be if Adrian reached across the dividing cup holders to take her hand once more. But it didn't happen.

Beside her, Adrian rubbed his hands together, then started the car and clicked the heater on. "Man. Sure got cold fast." He leaned forward to peer out through the windshield at the sky. "I didn't even notice any clouds earlier, did you? And I could've sworn there was nothing like this in the weather report."

It almost struck her as funny, somehow, that he checked the weather report. It seemed like an absurdly adult thing to do: to check the weather report and to keep it in mind.

The image of the man at the end of the road lingered like an afterimage of bright light behind her eyes.

She blinked the image away, trying to remind herself of where she was and what was in front of her. The car's dusty dashboard. The vents blowing warm air. The rain-splattered windshield.

"Thanks for coming for me, Adrian."

"I would've gone in with you if you'd waited."

"I would've made you wait outside, anyway."

"Fair enough. What happened in there?"

She winced as if the memory of her conversation with Marion sparked literal pain in her body. "I don't know. I don't know how to explain it, really."

"It's all right if you're not ready to talk about it."

Charlie envisioned bidding him farewell, hurrying to her own car and waiting for the engine to heat up, then driving home in the rain without telling him anything. No. She couldn't do that.

But how to say it? How to explain to Adrian that something else was wrong? That Marion wasn't merely *off* or merely *different?*

"It's not like I expected her to be a certain way. I've played this out in my head for years, over and over, especially when I couldn't sleep. I'd imagine scenarios where she came back and we sort of just picked up where we left off. I imagined her crying on my shoulder, and me crying too, and us figuring it out." Charlie felt something unexpected rising in her chest. She shut her eyes to try and keep it at bay, to try and keep her voice steady. "But I always knew that if she ever came back, it would never be how I imagined. Even before I went to her room to see her earlier, her mom told me—she said, *Marion's different.* And it's true. But it's more than that. It's like she's at war with herself. One second she was completely closed off and telling me to leave. But then she stopped and… and then it was like her old self peeking through, just for a second, to tell me something."

"To tell you what?"

"It's like she wanted to warn me about something, or some*one.* She sounded depressed, and scared." She looked Adrian in the eye. "And then there's what happened just now, on the lawn."

"You said something strange, like really strange, and then you looked at me like you had no idea what was going on."

"I don't know how to explain it. And whatever I say, it's just gonna sound insane."

"All the more reason."

"Whatever it was I said… Okay, look. I know how this sounds. Those weren't my words."

"Something Marion said to you, then?"

Charlie shook her head. She could feel Adrian looking at her as though she were a crazy person.

"I heard a voice, but it came from far away. Like when my friends would meet me on Catalpa Creek—they'd start calling and I'd hear them and call back and we'd move toward each other's voices. Like that, but it was in my head." She felt herself shrinking into the seat. "I know how it sounds. I do. Voices in my head. Weird visions at the end of the street, which—I know you didn't see anything."

"No." Adrian looked away. "But I did hear what Marion said—that she could see it, too." He put a hand to the side of his face. "Jesus."

"I know." Suddenly there were tears stinging in her eyes.

"Did it mean anything to you? The words you spoke?"

"Adrian, what do you think?"

"I'm just asking."

"It's like gibberish, some voice in my head, and it doesn't even make any sense, so what could it possibly mean to me?"

Adrian lifted an open palm up in a gesture of surrender. "Forget it. I'm just thinking out loud. Probably half as confused about this as you are."

"I don't know what to do."

"Want me to take you home? Or you could come over to my place. The housemates mind their own business, mostly, and I can… I can sleep on the couch. Or the floor, if you don't wanna be alone."

Images of Marion flashed through her head. Marion huddled on the windowsill, trying to hide herself. Marion knee-deep in the waters of Catalpa Creek, turning to look, a smile on her face. "Thanks. Thank you." With the heel of her hand she wiped at her eyes. "I would. I mean… under different circumstances, maybe. But not tonight."

"Oh, okay."

"My dad's probably worried about me. And I need some time to myself."

Beside her, Adrian—kind and nonchalant as ever—was offering to drive her home, saying too that he could bring her back here tomorrow for her car. He was more worried for her than he was letting on. It was clear in the way he was looking at her. She saw this, but barely heard what he was saying.

The man in the house, the one dressed all in black…

Lupita had pulled Marion inside in a hurry, and the man had been standing in the front door, waiting. He had come to speak with Marion.

It was Pastor Joe, from church. What was it he'd said in his closing sermon this morning? Something about

(*dusk*)

(*a threshold*)

something about devotion to a king.

"Catalpa," whispered Charlie, forming links of a chain in her head.

Adrian started to ask her what she was saying, but he paused. "Like your creek, you mean? That's part of what you said earlier, the thing that you heard in your head. The Border and the… I think it was the—"

"The Katalpian Dusk."

"Yeah… Jesus. What do you think that means?"

She took that as a rhetorical question, and he didn't press.

"Charlie," he said. "Are you okay?"

"I don't know how to answer that."

"I know, but… you seem… you just seem—"

"I seem what? A little uneven? Like—oh, I don't know, like I just spoke with my friend who I thought was dead for the last decade of my life, and maybe instead of it being the dream come true I've always secretly hoped for, it's like realizing my life really is a nightmare—the nightmare I've always been afraid it might be—only there's no end to it in sight, no waking up from it, because the reality is even worse than the nightmare? Is that how I seem?"

Adrian said nothing in response. The emotion in his eyes wasn't shock, but a quiet resignation. Sinking disappointment, maybe.

You can't understand, she wanted to say. *There's so much I want to tell you but you wouldn't understand.*

You weren't there back then, she wanted to say. *You don't know what she and I were like. What we had and lost.*

In her head she said these things to herself as if trying them on to see how they fit, to test if she could say them out loud to Adrian. But she said nothing.

Later, after he parked at the curb in front of her house, Adrian hardly looked at her. "I'll be here in the morning," he said. "You know. To take you back to your car."

"You don't have to do that. I can ask my dad if—"

"Don't be silly. I'll see you."

She said goodbye, climbed out of the car, and stood in the rain to watch him drive away. Water splashed outward from the spinning tires. She wanted him to stop, reverse, roll down the window, and tell her it was okay. She wanted him to refuse her silence and throw his arms around her so she could be held, so she could release some of whatever was building inside her body.

*

When Charlie entered the house, her father was seated at the dining table with two dinner bowls waiting by a crockpot of stew. He hadn't eaten yet, was reading a paperback novel while he waited. This was something they both did: they waited. Whether it was putting on a movie for the evening, digging into a meal, or going out someplace where the other might want to join: Charlie and her father waited for each other.

He smiled as he raised his head, pleased to see she was back at a good hour—and in time for dinner together. But the smile faded when he saw her face.

"Charlie." He rose from the chair, not even bothering with his bookmark as he set the book on the table. "You okay? Someone dropped you off?"

She stepped onto the carpet in her wet shoes. "It was Adrian. He didn't think I should drive."

"I got a call from Lupita," he came up to her. "Charlie, sweetie. Is it true? Is she—"

Tears came. "Dad, I… I don't know what I'm supposed to do."

He didn't let her complete that thought; he put his arms around her and pulled her close. He knew, he always knew.

*

That night, Charlie learned what Marion had meant when she alluded to the black-brain dreams.

In the dream she was sitting in a camping chair in front of a crackling bonfire. The flames danced with the consistency of a buffering video on a low internet connection.

Adrian sat beside her, but he wasn't talking. He kept looking at her from the side, without turning his head. She could feel his eyes on her when she wasn't looking.

"What's your problem?" she said, certain his problem—for whatever reason—was Marion.

He said, "You used to be different. I miss the way you used to be."

"It's not my fault," she replied, or wanted to reply, but the fire was bright and its crackling was too loud. "I don't know who I am anymore."

She turned to her right. She was in a white room.

Marion was standing on a table with her arms lifted upward toward the white ceiling… or was it sky? She looked as though she hadn't slept in ten years. And she was singing, or rather whispering a song with lyrics Charlie had never heard before, her voice like moonlight glowing through drifting snowflakes.

"How much will I lose as I grow old? How many loved ones will be gone by the time I'm old?"

The room darkened. The whispering faded.

Charlie was sitting at a wooden table with her old friends The Renegades: Stephen, Eric, Sam, and Marion. Her father was there too, at the end of a long procession of candles which made a runway to the table's head.

Past all this was a sliding glass door that looked out on thick darkness. Charlie could see everyone's candlelit reflection in the glass. Something was wrong with the reflection. They all sat perfectly still and erect, eyes wide open, mouths moving rapidly and in exact unison as if all chanting the same prayer at the same time.

Charlie's heart began to quicken—pounding, pounding—and she looked at the faces of her friends. They were all smiling, sharing stories, laughing. Like old times. Like it used to be. Nothing like the reflection in the dark glass.

She missed them like this. Even after all that had happened, the rifts that had formed between them as the years went by, she still loved her old friends and missed them dearly.

"I still don't know exactly what happened between us," she was explaining to Marion. She was on the windowsill, but it wasn't like earlier. This time, Marion didn't tell her to leave, instead she turned to her and they started talking, started catching each other up on everything they'd missed. "I've never told anyone this," said Charlie, "but I think I really messed things up with Eric. And after that, Stephen could barely look at me anymore—he never said anything, not like Eric did, but I could tell."

"Because of that one night?" said Marion.

Charlie didn't question how Marion knew about that one night. Charlie was sixteen, it was her first big party, and Eric had come with her. They'd fallen asleep in a sleeping bag together, and Eric had started to touch her in the night—and she let him. For a little while, at least, before making him stop.

"It wasn't supposed to happen," Charlie explained, and it was like she was explaining it both to Marion and to Eric. "It wasn't supposed to mean anything. But, Eric, you kept bringing it up and you started getting angry at me." She closed her eyes. Pictured herself at age eleven, walking along railroad tracks with all of them. Back when things had been the way they were supposed to be. Back when Eric had sometimes put his arm around her shoulders, but he did the same thing with Marion and even Sam, because that was Eric. He was close with everyone. He liked to protect them, even though Stephen was the bigger one.

The windowsill again. Marion was looking right at her, but there was something hollow about her face. As if someone else looked out through her eyes. "*After awhile, I couldn't wait anymore. I went out into the trees and never came back. I never came back after I went into the trees.*"

"That's not true, Marion. You're here right now."

"*I pulled back the curtain and saw behind everything. Did you know, it's almost dark back there, I could hear my mom calling us back inside for dinner—almost dark, is why—but did you know there's something behind it all. Like the darkness that's always on your mind but you try not to let anyone know, you try not to talk about it with anyone else. Underneath. The nightmare.*"

"I wish you wouldn't talk like that."

"*And the dream we cover it up with. We cover it up with a dream.*"

"Marion, please stop."

Marion shook her head, but it was more of a twitch. "We used to be different. I miss the way we used to be."

Charlie was at the table again with everyone, with the strange reflections cast in the darkness of the sliding glass door. But she ignored the reflection and its strangeness. She looked around at her old friends, the people she'd once loved more than anything in this world.

She wanted to tell them this. Here they all were, together, and now was the perfect chance—maybe this was the last time they'd ever be together like this, and she could embrace them all and tell them she loved them, tell them how things didn't have to change, tell them—

At the head of the table, James Louise suddenly sagged in his seat. His head dropped down and his face slammed against the table. Something like a horrible moan, or a belch, escaped his mouth, the sound muffled against the table.

"Dad?" Charlie tried to stand up, but for some reason her body felt as though it were underwater, and her own voice was a far off echo. He was dying, and if he died she'd never get the chance to show him that page in her journal, the one where she'd taped the photograph of him at the waterfall, the one under which she'd written that he was the only person in her life who gave her hope...

Her father twitched and convulsed. No one else appeared to notice.

"DAD!"

On both sides of the table, every member of The Renegades suddenly fixed their postures into perfectly erect positions, as if they had frozen into realistic statues of themselves. But their heads, with eyes wide, turned toward Charlie.

"No," she said, still trying to rise from her seat. "No, no, this isn't happening, this isn't happening."

In her ears she could hear them still talking amongst each other, and it was a jumble of regular conversation. Some laughter, some shifts in tone and volume—conversations between people who hadn't seen each other in far too long and had much to talk about. But their mouths weren't moving, their bodies were stiff; they were sitting upright, statue-like, and staring at her, while in her ears she could hear them. She could hear them still talking amongst each other.

This isn't happening, this isn't happening...

Charlie felt her heart stop beating. Felt its last feeble pump. Her breath deflated from her lungs and slipped out of her mouth in a whisper.

The strength drained from her body, limbs like concrete; her head dropped forward, chin to chest. Her eyes stayed open, but her vision—like her thoughts—went black. Went silent.

And they were all there, watching her, and soon they'd be talking—in her ears she could hear them talking—about how much they missed her and they'd be moving her body to put it underground.

Charlie Louise woke up screaming.

PART 2

The Journal

1

The nights grew longer, shadows lengthening in late light.

In the foggy-minded mornings that followed, Charlie noticed darkening bags under her eyes when she looked in the bathroom mirror. Time seemed to drift past her before she managed to get a hold on the rhythms of the day. She stayed home, avoided her phone, thought she saw, from the corner of her eye, strange things looking at her through the windows of the house—but when she turned to look, nothing was there. Her thoughts were blurry, out of focus, and by the time night came, she'd spent so much energy focusing her mind, it was too late to do any of the things she wanted or needed to do.

This had happened to her before, and there'd been times in the recent past that it was debilitating. Her father had learned how to support her through it when it came. But this time was different. This time, the same thing was happening to him. The two of them bounced around the house like aimless pinballs in slow motion.

Charlie had slept through a mere handful of scattered hours and lay in bed for a long time as darkness became the low blue glow of predawn twilight.

She wanted to make breakfast for her dad, so even though her body felt weighted down—as though wet concrete had filled her bones—she sat up with a wince of effort. Scooted to the edge of the bed, scratched her fingers through the tangles of her hair.

At first she thought the feeling was part of everything else, the way she'd felt since Sunday. But no. Something else was wrong. She felt it in her skin first, her body reacting as if trying to recoil away from extreme heat: an unshakable suspicion that she was being watched.

2

———————————

Charlie found her father seated in the grass outside. With his arms wrapped around his knees he looked younger except for the dark skin around his eyes.

She brought him a scramble. He took it with gentle hands and a hollow-eyed smile before staring up at the sky.

"Been a little while, hasn't it, sweetheart."

She sat on the edge of the deck, facing him with concern on her face. "Since what?"

"Since we had some time together."

"We've been spending most of the week together, Dad."

"I know, but it's not the same, really, is it. We're around each other. There's a difference."

"Yeah. You're right."

"Don't get me wrong, sweetie—it's not your fault. I know you have a lot going on." He finally looked at her. He seemed wistful, distant, as though he were half awake, but she saw only lucid sobriety in his eyes. "Is that where you're headed? To see Marion?"

She nodded.

"If you don't have anything else going on later, maybe we can have dinner tonight. You can invite that boy—sorry, that *young man*—if you want. We can watch a movie or something."

"You wanna meet him?"

"If he's important to you, yes. Of course." James Louise plucked a few blades of grass from the dirt. "You care about him?"

"Depends on what you mean by that."

"Well, I guess that answers my question."

"Oh my god."

"I'll behave, don't worry. Especially if you bring him over." He took a deep breath, let his posture slacken. "But with Marion back, it must be hard for you. I'm sorry, Charlie." He met her eyes, and the effect on her was that of a freezing wind. "I won't even pretend to know what you're going through."

Charlie began to speak, even opened her mouth with the intent to say something—*Thank you, Dad,* or something small and insurmountable like that—but her voice caught in her throat. He could look at her and see right through her.

"You know," he said, "I keep having these dreams that I… that I'm with your mother. In the dreams, I can't tell if she came back or if it's the past, but it doesn't seem to matter. I'm able to talk with her about everything and—-probably because this is something I think about a lot—I get to tell her about you. About all the ways you remind me of her, and about how you've changed since she left, and about how proud of you I am." He rarely spoke this much without interruption. She could only sit and listen. "That's another thing, you know—like a conversation I keep having in my head. I think she'd be proud of you." James wiped at his eyes. "And it's the stupidest thing, I know."

"It's not stupid, Dad."

"It is though, isn't it? She left. She chose that. After all this time, I think I'd be able to come to terms with it if she was… if she at least would talk to *you.* You know what I mean? If she reached out to you, even if it was just you. It just doesn't make sense to me. These dreams I keep having, I know they're impossible. Fantasies, basically. In fact, the first night I had one, I was actually scared, for some reason. I woke up saying *This isn't happening*, or *That didn't happen*. But each night it gets a little easier, I think. And, Charlie, it's so real. It's like, if she did come back, I think that's maybe how it might be. That's how real these dreams feel."

Charlie couldn't hold back the tremors in her body. She sat as still as she could, eyes aimed at her feet.

And her father asked something she never could've imagined him asking, if only because he wasn't someone who sought other people for advice. "Do you think it's possible? That she'd come back, after all this time?"

"Dad…"

"I don't know why I'm asking you this. Maybe it's because of your friend Marion. It seemed impossible, completely out of the range of possibility, and yet, after a decade…"

"It's different. It's way different."

Her father dropped the blades of grass, closed his eyes, nodded.

Maybe she'd been wrong to assume he was lucid and fully himself, she thought.

"I still pray about it, you know. For her. For me—that I can let go of the past, stop looking back. I pray for you." He laughed, but there was irony in the sound. "You know what I pray for the most, though, for you and me? Especially on harder nights? That there's purpose to it. All the pain, and the feeling alone. You and Marion, mostly, and your depression. Everything, I guess." He sighed. "Shoot. Listen to me. I haven't even touched my breakfast." He shot her a strained smile.

When Charlie left, he was still sitting on the lawn. Rather than digging into his food, he resumed staring up at the sky. She said she'd love to introduce him to Adrian tonight.

Charlie climbed into her car with all the things she wanted to say to him burning inside of her—a furnace in her chest kindled by unsaid words that were impossible to say.

Things like, *It's not about meaning, Dad. If you could let go of your need for it to make sense, maybe then it'd be clearer—easier—for you.*

Things like, *Take it from me: Not even the good times in your memories were as good as you remember. The joy you want to feel, that fullness you keep wishing you'll feel again someday... you never will. Nothing ever comes back—and if, somehow, something does, it isn't the same, it's nothing like how you remember it. This pain and this loneliness and this aching, this is what's real, this is what most of it amounts to, anyway.*

But she said none of these things. She kept it inside and drove away crying.

3

―――――――――――――

The street was empty in a way it never had been when she was a kid, when everywhere hummed with possibility. As she pulled onto the street and parked in the shade of trees across from the Del Rosario house, she thought: *There's no possibility here—only memory.*

Lupita was seated on the front steps, arms wrapped around her legs, and she was staring up at the sky. As Charlie approached, she noticed how far away Lupita's eyes were, as if she were asleep and dreaming with her eyes wide open.

Like my dad, she thought. *I wonder what she sees in her dreams, lately.* But Charlie didn't really need to wonder.

"Lupita?"

The older woman's eyes drifted down until settling on Charlie. There was delight there, a dazed sense of warmth, but it was like an impression caught through dense fog; a far cry from the way she normally greeted Charlie with an overflow of gracious words and open arms.

"Nenè," said Lupita. "So pretty now. So grownup. Here for Marion?"

Charlie nodded. "I need to talk to her."

"For the story."

"If she's willing to talk about it, yes."

"The priest," she said, though in her accent it sounded like *depressed*. "He's in there now with her."

"The priest? You mean Pastor Joe?"

Lupita nodded, made a dismissive clicking sound between her lips.

Pastor Joe, dressed in funereal black like an imitation of a Catholic priest, sat alone at the dining table, an open bottle of beer in front of him. He was slouched with the manner of a defeated man, someone who'd just learned their wife was cheating on them, or someone trying to drown out suicidal thoughts beneath the haze of alcohol. He didn't look up when Charlie entered the room.

"Pastor," said Charlie. It felt strange being in the same space as him. His recent closing sermon cast a long shadow.

His eyes tracked Charlie's shy approach, but he remained stagnant. "You must be James Louise's girl, the one that accompanies him to our service every Sunday, rain or shine."

"I'm Charlie."

"Well it's good to meet you, Charlie Louise. Officially, I mean. I apologize that we've only met in passing before this. I've had my attention stolen by a number of… obligations, of late." He took a sip from the bottle, then he leaned in her direction. "You were here before, weren't you? Sunday, mid afternoon?"

"To see her, yes."

"Ah. Interesting that you were here—and are here again today. Some would call that providence."

Charlie took a step toward the hallway, wondering how long she would have to entertain this man before she could slip away to Marion's room.

"Tell me, if you would, please," said the pastor. "Humor me, let's say. I've noticed you stay seated during the communion part of our services. Do you feel unworthy of it, for some reason?"

"I go to church for my dad."

The pastor's eyes lifted up and to the side while something like sorrow flashed across his features. "Any man would be blessed to have a daughter like you. That's what I believe."

"You don't even know me."

"No, I don't, but I know something about your heart." He took another sip from the now half-empty bottle. "You accompany your father to church every Sunday even though you, yourself, don't believe in God. Is that accurate?"

Charlie flinched as if tasting something bitter. "Not exactly..." She thought of a similar conversation she once had with Adrian.

"Then what do you believe in, Charlie Louise?"

"I don't know."

"You have no certainty."

"There's things I... things that I'd like to believe—"

"Ah, yes." The pastor appeared to suppress a grin just a second too late. "I've seen you in church, the way you look around at everyone else, especially at your father. I notice these things. You're not like the others there." He tapped the side of his head and pointed at her with the same finger, as if recognizing her as a person similar to himself. Her stomach tightened at that. "It's as though you see the way they pray, the way they listen, and you *want* to believe. You want to believe in a God that accepts the imperfections and hurts and uncertainties of the world, and washes it all away—*bathes* it, bathes *you*, in love and forgiveness and purpose. You want to believe, maybe because then it would be easy, everything would have meaning, packaged up and prescribed, but you can't."

Charlie crossed her arms over her stomach. She felt as though she'd shrunken in size, while the pastor towered like a mountain. That magnetism again: his words like invisible hands slithering their way to her brain.

"Either way," said Pastor Joe, "you go for your father. Not for yourself. *That's* what I know about you, Charlie Louise. And that is a good thing. Any priest or pastor or true man of God would attest to that."

With some effort, she found her voice. "What about you?"

The pastor blinked a few times as if the question stung. "What do you mean?"

Charlie couldn't believe she was engaging him like this. "The things you said in your closing sermon last Sunday," she said. "Those didn't sound like the words of a man of God."

Pastor Joe nodded once in slow motion. *He* was the one shrinking now.

"If you'll excuse me, pastor, I have to see Marion. After ten years of wondering what happened to her, there's a lot that she and I—"

"Ten years?" the pastor sat erect. "Did you… did you remember her all that time?" He didn't wait for an answer, taking her silence as confirmation. "You and I have more in common than you realize, and more to talk about than I previously thought. You've had the dreams, but unlike the others—like Miss Del Rosario out there—here you are, wide awake." He gestured to one of the dining table's wooden chairs. "Have a seat."

"I'm here to see Marion."

"I'm sure a few more minutes won't make any difference." He gestured again with a stiff arm, palm wide open—as if, by the forcefulness, the desperation of the gesture, he could simply cause her to do his bidding. "Please, Charlie. I can't understate how important this is. For you. For your father."

This has nothing to do with either him or me, was what she wanted to say. But she saw something in his eyes that challenged her preconceived distrust: *fear*. Pastor Joe wasn't trying to trick her, and he wasn't doing this because he was a creep, no; it was clear in the gleam of his eyes that he was afraid. Maybe he didn't know her, but he was genuinely afraid for her sake, and whatever it was he wanted to talk about, to him it really was as important as he claimed.

"You can trust me." The pastor's lips were trembling, eyes widening. "I'll tell you what I know. I'll tell you about the Aching Plane. I can tell you about Katalpa and its dreaded King."

There were those words again, resonating off the walls of Charlie's denial. The very air seemed to shudder, to quake and then to dim, as though the weather were rapidly changing outside.

Charlie took a shaky breath. "*What?*"

"The trees fade, the skies darken, the shadows open their eyes beneath the strange hunger of Dark Katalpa." The pastor closed his eyes. Charlie half expected him to lift his hands upward in praise. "I can still recall Terry's words about it. 'Death himself trembles before the void of The Aching Plane. The veil undone. Past becomes future. Our agony is borne for us.'"

Of all the thoughts that flashed with panic through her mind, the loudest was simply: *I need to tell Adrian. He needs to hear this.*

A voice cut through the room, falling like a shadow: "That's enough, Joe."

It was Marion. She stood in the hallway, in a black nightgown, hair damp from a recent shower. She looked as though she hadn't slept at all since Charlie had last seen her.

Pastor Joe nodded a few times, blinking rapidly as if all this reality in front of him was too much to bear, and he lowered his head and took another drink. He said nothing more. Marion's words had done more than silence him; somehow he cowered beneath her, refused to look up and meet her eyes, as if she were of considerable stature and he a lowly servant caught in an act of delinquency. Charlie had never seen anything like it before.

With a nod toward her bedroom, Marion bid Charlie follow. But not before she gave Charlie an almost mischievous look, and Charlie—in response—felt an emotion sprout inside.

That's my friend, she thought, and could've thrown her arms around her. *The one who would've punched anyone on the playground who was hurting my feelings. She came back. She really came back. That's my best friend.*

But in the bedroom, as Charlie gravitated naturally to the windowsill, Marion faced her with somberness.

"I know why you're here," she said, sitting on one side of the windowsill. "And I think I'm ready."

4

Later, when reflecting on everything Marion told her and trying to reconcile that with the new question of how to carry on with these things encroaching upon her world, Charlie would think Marion's words had a similar effect as Pastor Joe's. Charlie didn't notice in the moment, hypnotized as she was by being in Marion's presence, but Marion's story—especially as it progressed—had an apparent physical effect on the very molecules of the air. Her bedroom seemed to shrink, the walls at first melting into blurred impressions of color in periphery and then shuddering inward before dissolving altogether. The air felt, on Charlie's skin, as though it trembled—as if it were a singular conscious thing, made to quiver around a fact it was too afraid to accept.

*

She sat cross-legged on one end of the windowsill, Marion sat on the other. The blinds were drawn, leaving the room gray and dark. Thin bars of light seeped through the gaps in the blinds, falling across both the girls' faces. Charlie felt the familiar urge to reach out just to touch her old friend, to feel her skin, intertwine her fingers with hers. But she restrained herself, let the warmth dissipate.

"I'm not sure where to start," said Marion.

"Start at the beginning."

Marion briefly grinned. "Like *Alice in Wonderland?* Begin at the beginning."

"Then go on until you come to the end."

"Then stop," finished Marion, and they both laughed. It was the first time they had laughed together since they were twelve years old. But as with any levity now, it was like a candle blown out. "When you were here before," said Marion, "you said you don't remember what happened."

"I remember fragments. Like calling your name as I wandered in the woods around our creek. I did that every day for weeks, starting the moment I heard you were gone."

"And you don't remember anything else? Like, anything specific about my kidnapping?"

"No. It's like a blank space in my head."

"What about Peter Doloria?"

"I feel like I… like I know that name, or I've heard it somewhere."

Marion nodded. "Then I'll start there. Peter Doloria was the man who lived next door, literally just a house down. He was sort of a hermit. You used to call him Boo Radley."

Wrinkles showed in Charlie's brow. "I can't believe I don't remember that."

"Eric and Sam even snuck up to his house one time, at night, to peer in through some of the windows. You and I thought they were crazy." Marion looked down at her hands. "Peter Doloria is the man who kidnapped me."

The blood drained from Charlie's cheeks. "Why don't I remember that? I mean… did I hear about it?"

"It was regional news. The Amber Alert. Newspapers. TV stations. Search parties. You knew, but you forgot."

"Marion…"

"That's why, when you first stepped into this room on Sunday, I asked you—"

"You asked if I remembered you."

"And I had every reason to think maybe you didn't." She turned away, searching for something to look at. "That's what happens when people go too far. They're forgotten."

"Oh god. Marion, people were forgetting you. I used to ask about you, and… and they…" She felt her voice near to breaking, felt moisture pooling atop her eyelids. "Marion, I never would've forgotten you. I wouldn't have let myself."

Outside, the wind was steadily building, now a low whistle but soon to be a howl. Charlie checked her phone, saw two missed calls and a number of text messages, all from Adrian. She returned the phone to her pocket, her attention to Marion.

Marion had her head bowed and eyes closed. The way her arms were wrapped around herself suggested a need for comfort, a battle inside.

It wouldn't have mattered, Charlie realized, a coldness sinking inside her. *It wouldn't have mattered how tightly I held on. I would've forgotten you. One day I would've looked at that photograph on my desk and maybe you'd be gone, I'd be alone in the waters of Catalpa Creek on that summer day.*

Or maybe there'd be no picture, and I would never have noticed the lack of it from my life.

When Marion next spoke, she began to tell her story.

Sam and Marion were the only two who understood the reference; the other Renegades thought Charlie had made up a funny name for the seldom-seen hermit who lived on Marion's street. None of them knew his real name. By the end of the summer they would all know. The whole town would know. And, far too late, Charlie Louise would realize that the man was no innocent, childlike Boo Radley.

It began one night when Eric and Sam decided to sneak up to the quiet house and see if they could catch a glimpse of the neighborhood recluse through the windows. This, of course, was after they had already been warned by Lupita to leave that poor man alone. *He's not like other people,* she said, which was as close as she could come to saying *he's dangerous* without scaring the kids too much, but she didn't know much about Peter Doloria; she only knew that the handful of times she had ever seen him, there'd been a look in his eyes she didn't like.

The Renegades, however, loved to live up to their self-appointed name. Between eleven and fourteen years old, their options for rebellion and adrenaline were limited, but they had their ways. Even Charlie and Stephen, the more reserved ones—the two more likely to hang back and be the lookouts while their friends did something stupid and possibly illegal—even Charlie and

Stephen secretly enjoyed the thrill. Stephen's protests, tonight, were half-hearted, while Charlie rarely went further than merely voicing her concern.

This time, Marion decided to stay back with Charlie and Stephen.

"So you're gonna be a wuss about it," said Sam to Marion.

Eric started to say something to defend her, but Marion shoved Sam's shoulder. "Tumahimik. He's my neighbor."

None of them spoke Tagalog, and what Marion knew was an inherited not-quite-fluent grasp from her mom, but each member of The Renegades had come to understand a handful of words because of Marion. Mostly swear words.

"I'm just saying," said Sam. "It was practically your idea, chica."

She got up in his face and shoved him in the shoulder again. "*Tumahimik ka*, asshole."

Sam laughed, along with the others, as he walked away with his hands up in defeat, saying *Okay, okay*. Charlie alone noticed the hint of a smirk at the corner of Marion's mouth.

So it began. Charlie, Marion, and Stephen waited in the trees on the other side of the street while Sam and Eric, crouched down like they were playing commando, crossed to the quiet house. The Boo Radley House, they'd all taken to calling it, thanks to Charlie.

Sam and Eric went around the side yard. A sedan was parked in the driveway, meaning somebody was home, but there were no lights on in the house. The windows felt like eyes and the house's unseen interior felt alive, as though the entire structure was watching, waiting to alert its master of trespassers.

Stephen, on this side of the road, crouched on one knee in case he needed to sprint for his friends.

Charlie and Marion hung back in the shadows of the trees, shoulder-to-shoulder.

When the boys thought they heard a noise, they shoved each other away from the house and came running back. Marion's hand found Charlie's hand and squeezed. It was a moment, no longer than a few seconds before they let each other go, but it was enough for electricity to sing between them, as if they were conductors for each other. The night's darkness lessened, slightly, and the Boo Radley House was, again, just a house.

But as the boys regrouped, both Eric and Sam excitedly explaining what they thought they'd heard, Marion's gaze flitted to the old sedan parked in the driveway. She saw what had to be the silhouette of a person's head above the back of the seat. Someone was sitting in there. Somebody was seated, perfectly still, in the car, and had been there the whole time.

Chills flooded Marion's body. None of the others had noticed.

Later in the night, in her room, she would tell Charlie, but she would say she *thought* she saw someone. She wasn't sure, because when she looked back at the car, there didn't appear to be anyone there. It could've been a trick, the night reflecting off the car's windows. It could've been her imagination fueled by excitement.

Still, she slept restlessly that night, unable to shake the feeling that she was being watched, even in the safety of her own bedroom.

The following day, the boys decided to see a movie in the mid-afternoon, but Charlie declined to go. The day was overcast but not cold—her perfect weather—and, besides, she thought the movie looked awful. So, when the group text went out, Charlie sent Marion a private message: *"Gonna head to the creek instead of the movie. I'd love it if you came, even if it's after the movie!"*

Marion was in her living room when her phone buzzed. She'd had a late breakfast with her mom, gotten dressed in preparation for going out—probably to the movie—and was sitting on the couch reading a book of poems from W.S. Merwin, when she saw Charlie's name on her phone. She read the text, and that warm feeling sparkled in her stomach. She typed: "*Just the two of us on Catalpa while the boys are out?*" and then she paused. The next phrase was almost too scary to consider, but it flashed vibrant purple in her mind, like a neon sign: *Sounds like a date.* Would that be too weird? Would it scare Charlie a little or a lot? They were moving at a steady pace. Were they ready to start making cute comments like that to each other? She thought of something else to say—something safe like *I'll see you there*—but then she remembered last night. Standing with Charlie in the tree-line while Sam and Eric peeked through the windows of the Boo Radley House. How, just for a moment, their hands found each other in the dark.

It wasn't the first time it happened and she knew it wouldn't be the last. Few thoughts had ever excited her more.

"*Sounds like a date,*" she added into her message, and before she could overthink, she sent it. Her phone made the little *whoosh* sound and she gritted her teeth and squealed internally.

"I'm gonna go meet Charlie on the creek!" she called down the hallway to her mom.

Lupita was in the spare-bedroom-turned-office, and called back: "Be careful, nenè! Make yourself food!"

"Love you, Mom!" Marion went out the door while still pulling her shoes on. Those were the last words she would say to her mother for nearly ten years.

*

Marion was a few minutes into the woods when she began to feel like something was wrong. It started on her skin, as if there were eyes on her, eyes in the shadows between the trees. But as she pressed on, she felt it was more than that. At intervals it felt as though someone walked beside her—a person, a man she glimpsed from the corner of her eye—but when she turned to look, there was no one. As if her own shadow had become a separate thing from her, stalking her in the rays of light through the trees.

Soon she heard the sound of the water and she could see it in her mind. That soft sloshing and crinkling of the current on its path over stones and logs and fallen branches, its quicksilver surface catching gems of afternoon sunlight. Even clearer in her mind's eye was Charlie. Charlie perched atop a boulder, probably wearing denim overalls over a forest green shirt, and a cap of some sort—occasionally a sunhat. Maybe she'd have a fishing pole in hand. Maybe she'd just be sitting there, gazing into the water the way some people do into a campfire.

With this image in her head, Marion picked up her pace.

When she reached the creek, the banks were empty. This spot, where a simple deer trail led, was a frequent meeting spot of The Renegades. Farther downriver from here, a quarter-mile at most, was where they'd built the dam. Farther *upriver*, however, was where Charlie normally did her fishing.

Since Charlie's bike hadn't been at the dirt parking lot by the quarry, Marion deduced she'd beaten Charlie here, meaning Charlie was likely to show up any minute. Marion sat on a boulder at the water's edge. The quiet of the woods filled her ears as a backdrop to the creek's running.

She sat this way for ten minutes, sustained by the excitement in her body, knowing Charlie Louise would come walking up that trail any minute now. Marion played out the possibilities in her mind. Would it be awkward at first? How long would they walk together, either up or downstream, before one felt brave enough to reach for the other's hand?

But there was more to it than that and they both knew it. Twice now, when it'd been just the two of them, they had kissed. Both times had been in Marion's room, on the windowsill. Somehow the image of kissing Charlie out here on Catalpa Creek, under the afternoon sun, was different from kissing on the windowsill at night. This would have a degree of naked realism to it. No hiding under cover of night, no pretending it was a stolen thing in the dark.

The image of it made Marion's blood rush, made her insides feel as though they sparkled and danced like sunlight atop the flowing surface of the creek. It had been hard to feel like this country was her home for quite some time, but being with Charlie made her forget about all that.

Marion looked over her shoulder, half-hoping to see Charlie coming up the trail. There was no one there, just the quiet of the trees and the sensation creeping in again that she wasn't alone.

Marion returned her gaze to the river, but she froze. Her eyes had caught sight of something in mid-turn from looking over her shoulder to looking at the river. Something by a nearby tree, some-thing gray nestled against a bush. In the span of a second, her mind reeled with answers: a rock, a tree stump, a deer, a misshapen bush. But she knew what she'd glimpsed: it had eyes. She looked again. Her entire body locked up.

In a bush fifteen feet away, a man crouched. He was watching her.

She had time to note the pallor of his skin, the raccoon eyes, the gauntness of his features. She had time to think: *I've seen him on my street. I saw him sitting in the car in his driveway, watching Sam and Eric sneak around his house.*

Marion stood up on the boulder. The man stood, too, as though he were a reflection.

And then the man shouted and ran at her.

She tried to jump backward, her body reacting as if away from a massive spider, but she slipped and tumbled backward off the boulder, landing hard on her back against dirt and rocks. The force of the landing huffed the breath from her lungs.

She rolled on her side and put her hands to the earth, trying to push, trying to rise so she could run. But the ache in her chest spread through her limbs like poison; her body felt as though it obeyed her willpower in slow time.

Marion glanced up to the riverbank and, for just a second, thought she saw someone there. A person, but a person without details. No sense of clothing, no sense of skin, no face. Except—at least in some distant way—for a second it looked like...

"Charlie?" Marion said, her voice broken and desperate. She wanted it to be Charlie, but maybe no... no, she didn't want it to be Charlie. That would mean Charlie was in danger, too.

At the same time, the indistinct shape of a person by the riverbank was no more—there was nothing there—and a thought crossed Marion's mind: What if she never saw Charlie Louise again?

The sound of boots stomping across dirt. A shadow fell across her vision. A trembling hand gripped her shoulder. She stared up at a pair of wide, frightened blue eyes inside a pale face. The man's breathing was labored, hissed between gritted teeth.

He looked at her as if searching for something on her face. "Hey... heyyyy. You in there, sweetie? You can come out. It's safe."

Marion tried to bat his arm away, but he held firmly onto her with the strength of a deep-rooted tree. She struggled, started to writhe and kick, telling him *Stop*, telling him *Get the fuck away from me*.

But the man slapped a hand over her mouth, pinning her to the ground. With her shallow breath she tried to scream into his hand, but he pressed down hard until she felt throbbing in her head.

He leaned in close. He smelled like sweat and dust.

"Don't know where you hid her, but I saw her alright. I'm sure I don't gotta remind you how much easier this'll be if you stay calm."

He cupped both her mouth and nose under his massive palm and he pressed. She tried to scream again but there was no air. In seconds her vision fluttered under purple darkness and her mind popped with twinkling numbness, all thought ceasing.

*

Something I didn't tell the police, or the doctors, or even my mom, is that I don't remember how we got to the cabin. I told everyone that I woke up in the backseat of his truck, tied up, my mouth duct taped, and that we must've been driving for a long time but I didn't really know.

But it wasn't true. When I woke up we were at the cabin already. He was untying me and dragging me to the cabin, telling me I could scream for help if I wanted and I could try and run but that it wouldn't matter. We were so far away from anything, he said, it wouldn't matter if I screamed or ran.

I didn't believe him. I thought we couldn't have been very far from Catalpa Creek, like maybe he'd just taken me up into the hills. That's what I thought at first.

And there is something else I remember. It was like having a dream, but the thing is, I remember waking up at some point after he knocked me out. And I wasn't tied up or duct taped or anything like that. I woke up but it was like waking up dead. There was a thick, thick fog—so thick it felt almost like moving underwater or like I was inside a cloud—and my breathing felt more like sobbing. Like when you're crying so hard, taking a breath is almost impossible. That's how it felt.

There was a horrible darkness above. I couldn't tell if it was the sky, or if there was a ceiling… it just didn't feel like anything was there. Like a darkness deeper than darkness. Nothingness, I almost want to say.

And… I know what this must sound like to you, Charlie. All of it. But I could hear the sound of breathing somewhere nearby. Somewhere in the fog. Heavy breathing, and it sounded like how the word "lonely" sounds, if that makes sense. Lonely or… empty. This tired breathing, so heavy with emotion—with longing, maybe—that just hearing it made my heart ache. I thought, maybe I'm dreaming and I'm hearing the sound of my own breathing. But it couldn't have been me. I knew I wasn't dreaming, even though that wasn't possible.

You know what comes to mind when I speak of it now, to you? Sylvia Plath. I think she was always your favorite of the poets I used to show you. A few lines from her poem Sheep in Fog, about far empty fields, and a starless and fatherless heaven.

And then I woke up and I was in the forest, being dragged into that cabin.

I started to think, this is how I die. It doesn't matter where he's taking me, what he'll do to me, how much longer it lasts—this is probably the end. And I thought: I hope I'm awake when it happens. I want to choose what my last words are. I want to choose what—I mean, who—I think about when I feel myself dying. Like how you and me, when we had sleepovers, we used to talk each other to sleep. We'd paint images with our words, taking turns building a scene that we'd both think about as hard as we *could so that maybe, when we fell asleep, we'd go there in our dreams. I used to fall asleep so excited at the possibility that I'd meet you inside my dreams.*

I don't remember if it ever happened. I just remember the feeling of your voice filling my mind, and the warmth at the thought of not being apart from you even in my dreams.

So when I first thought I was gonna die, when I had no hope at all that I'd ever see you again, the most I could hope for was to be aware when the time came, so that I could do my best to think of you until the end.

And then came the cabin, and the strange forest. The things I learned about Peter, my kidnapper, before he started to change. And the shapes I started to see out the windows at night—the shapes out in the forest, like people waving at me, trying to get my attention.

*

There came a point in time—weeks, maybe months—when Marion accepted two things: that she understood nothing about her kidnapping; and that she wasn't going to die the way she at first thought.

She was allowed to roam around the cabin, having proved to Peter Doloria that she had no intentions of making a break for it. This was the truth. She had spent every waking moment of the first few weeks designing an escape in her mind, running through scenarios, accounting for possibilities, discrepancies, factoring in likelihoods and trying to stay realistic about it all. But then she was allowed outside to gather firewood, and when she cast her gaze at the density of trees in all directions, the realization came in a sudden wave that she had no idea which direction to escape toward. Underneath the sound of wind through the branches, the chirping birds, the skittering of small critters over leaves and twigs and bushes, even at night, beneath the constant cricket song and occasional whooping of vigilant nightbirds—beneath all the noises of the forest there crept an incomprehensibly gigantic silence. Not a speck of human noise as backdrop: no drone of far off highways, no voices, no rumble of distant airplanes or helicopters.

One night, while stepping outside to grab firewood, she looked up at what patches of night sky were visible through the trees. Though she looked for several minutes, she couldn't find a single familiar constellation.

This, Marion realized, was so much more than some remote location, a mere drive into the woods. Out here, she was like a self-aware particle of dust swallowed up by a vast desert.

Doloria had been telling the truth. It didn't matter if she screamed or ran.

So within the first few months, Marion gave up any ideations of escape. To escape would be to abandon any vestige of shelter or familiar structure and to throw herself at the mercy of a wilderness that was either pitilessly indifferent or actively hostile. So she made herself trustworthy. Did chores, stayed quiet, kept her distance.

But even as she learned to navigate the shifting moods and wide-eyed, stifled madness of Peter Doloria, she didn't learn more about him until she turned her attention from escape to survival under his rule.

*

Marion stacked a bundle of chopped firewood against the side of the house, each piece another week gone. Peter Doloria tied her legs together with old rope that burned into her skin, and a month passed. She tried to slow her heart rate, unable to sleep in the middle of the night because she thought she heard something moving outside the cabin, she thought she heard footsteps crunching through pine needles, and a single night felt longer than an entire week. She woke up in the morning from a dream about Charlie Louise, and six months passed.

But one night, alone in the bedroom, she heard Peter Doloria across the cabin. He erupted into loud, shuddering sobs. Screams, almost.

A chill shot through Marion's body, causing her to stiffen where she sat on the bed. She had never heard a sound like that before—not from him, not from any adult human she had ever met.

When it became clear it wasn't going to stop, Marion resisted the strange feeling that it gave her and she left the room, emerging into the hallway on tiptoes. Out here, the sound was even louder—almost as if it were directly in her ears: a broken dam of sound, pure unadulterated sobbing. It sounded as though a newborn baby had been suddenly transmuted into the body of a full-grown adult. There was no audible effort to hold in the sobs, no adult rationale behind it, no shame, no self-awareness. Just wild, animal sobbing.

Marion emerged from the hallway. The kitchen was on the right and the living room to the left.

Peter Doloria stood at the living room's picture window, both hands pressed up against the glass. He was silent. The mad weeping of seconds ago had ceased, and somehow the silence was louder and so much worse. There was no fire in the fireplace, no lanterns or candles lit. Even the forest outside had gone strangely quiet, as if the critters and the trees were holding their breath.

Doloria spoke, and the way his voice cut the silence was enough to make Marion jump.

"I didn't mean to wake you." He continued to stare out at the darkness, both hands splayed upon the windowpane.

"Are you okay?"

Doloria laughed. It was a high, desperate sound. "I think I... I made a mistake."

"What mistake?"

"Oblivion. That's what she was most afraid of, not that she knew that word. *Daddy*, she used to say to me, trust in her eyes. *If there used to be no me, like before I was born, what about after? There won't be a me anymore?* I swear that's what she asked me, near the end. Only six years old and that's what her greatest fear was. Something she didn't quite have the words for: that maybe there's nothing after, and we just wink out. A star going dark in the night sky, leaving no trace, no memory." He tapped the windowpane. "Just like that."

Marion remained where the hallway ended. Was that why he'd taken her? She reminded him of his dead daughter?

He spun around to look at her, and the manner in which he did this brought the line of a poem to mind, something from Edgar Allan Poe: *Back into the chamber turning, all my soul within me burning.* Doloria's cheeks glistened with trails of tears. "Do you believe death is the end, Marion?"

"What?"

He moved away from the window. Marion flinched. She wasn't sure of how long they'd been out here in these woods, but it felt like many months. In that time, Doloria had shown no desire to molest her, but he had struck her several times. The worst had been early on. The bruises had kept her up at night.

But Doloria was in a pensive mood tonight. He moved to the empty fireplace and sat on the bricks which extended a few feet out. He gestured for her to come sit down, as if it were the most casual thing: *Let's talk, it's been too long since we caught up.*

She knew how his moods could shift, how his veneer of gentleness could peel away revealing itself as nothing more than a fleshy, smiling mask hiding the monster underneath. Marion stepped into the living room, floorboards flexing underfoot. She sat at the far end of the couch.

"Do you know what I used to do for a living, Marion? I should've told you, because you talk about the stars. I was a professor of astronomy. I taught some English and have some background in physics and chemistry, but astronomy was always it for me. It started when I was about your age. The stars were better company than other people—I learned that early on, as I'm sure you did, too. Some of the happiest nights of my life were spent stargazing, pondering the impenetrable mysteries." His gaze shifted to the picture window again, to the thick night beyond it. For a moment he appeared to search for something out there, something maybe he'd been looking at before. "I met my wife in college, of course. She died not long after our daughter was born. Car accident."

"I'm sorry."

"Do you know what was written on her gravestone? She chose the words from a poem she once framed for me on our anniversary. I thought you'd appreciate it, since you've read all the poetry that's here." He gestured vaguely toward the bookshelves on the far wall, and then quoted the famous lines from the poem *The Old Astronomer*, by Sarah Williams. "*Though my soul may set in darkness, it will rise in perfect light; I have loved the stars too fondly to be fearful of the night.*" He smiled sadly. "Despite her studies, she never lost her faith. I admired that, envied it even—the way she had answers to questions that, for me, could never be answered. I stopped believing in God long before I met her. I used to be an astronomy professor, after all. You can only learn so much about the incomprehensible vastness of the universe before realizing how much this petty world we've constructed that we call the human experience, along with all our flimsy belief systems and societal structures, it's all just layers of illusion. It feels more and more like denial to presume we have any importance at all. To say that we're insignificant is an understatement, Marion. On the cosmic scale, our lives aren't even flashes in a pan. All of human existence, all our history and evolution." He snapped his fingers. "We may as well have never even happened. On the cosmic scale, we wouldn't even be worth mentioning—our lives make no difference at all."

Unconsciously, Marion held herself. Doloria's words gave her a cold feeling. Even so, her mother's spirit was instilled in her, and despite how Doloria sometimes beat her for saying the wrong thing, she refused to hold her tongue.

"You must've been some professor," she said. "So self-important."

Doloria stared at her, baffled. Then he threw his head back and released a strange laugh. "No, no... I was different back then. This has nothing to do with me or my ego. It's simply the truth. And it's not something everyone is ready to hear."

"Then why are you telling me?"

He shook his head, looked off to the window again. "It's what my wife told me before she died. The car accident didn't kill her instantly. She was awake for another two days... or, almost two days. Forty hours, I think it was. Emergency surgery did nothing for her. So they jacked her up on pain meds so she couldn't feel anything and just let her fade away. And I didn't leave her the entire time."

Marion shifted with discomfort. A slithering in her chest. She sometimes felt like this when people spoke about injuries or painful situations: a physical empathy she had no control over.

"She of all people, who believed in God and still went to church even though she, too, was a scientist like me... with all those machines hooked up to her, and the IV, the oxygen to her nose, her skin all discolored, one eye dark with blood… she looked at me and talked and talked… and I sat there and listened and mostly couldn't say anything back to her." Doloria locked eyes with Marion. "All the work she'd done, the things she was still doing, the ideas about the world she was interested in, the questions she had and the answers she came closer to reaching… all of it just gone. And our life together, the life we were going to have. This is what I mean, Marion. Our lives are like dreams, and we could wake up any moment and forget it all, and all of it may as well have never happened. There's no destination we ever reach, no fulfillment we receive. It could all just end, and so senselessly, for no reason, sometimes instantly, sometimes painfully. My wife suffered, yes, but not as much as my daughter a couple years later, from the cancer. Seven years old, swallowed up by the nothingness she used to wonder so much about and feared so much."

The trembling wracked Marion's body with violence. "Why did you take me?"

"I made a mistake." There was no more kindness in his eyes. "I keep having these dreams, and for awhile I thought that's all they were. But then I started to see things. And you know what? Sometimes I saw dead people. Or… the afterimage of dead people, I mean. Their spirits. Most of them looked lost, or trapped inside a loop. Some of them must've had horrible things done to them before they died. One woman was pacing in a grocery aisle, bleeding from her eyes—some of it getting on her hands—and she just kept screaming and screaming: *This didn't happen.* As if she refused to believe it even in death. *It didn't happen. This didn't happen.* Not unlike the thoughts I had when I first heard of my wife's car accident." He scoffed. "I couldn't get to the frozen food section because of the dead woman, so I had to drive all the way to the next town." He lifted a hand up to the side of his face, seemingly aware—and almost embarrassed—of how he sounded. "And then, one day, I saw you walking down the street with your blonde-haired friend. You were holding her hand, precious as can be."

"You were watching us."

"I caught a glimpse of your face…" He clapped his hands together. "And I saw my daughter. Clear as I see you now, she was there. She was inside you, a brief flickering, but unmistakable."

"Do you… see her now?"

The light appeared to fade from Doloria's eyes. "No. I think I made a mistake. The things I've been seeing don't seem… human."

Marion's face felt suddenly hot. "Then let me go! Take me back, or… at least show me which way to get back."

He made a dismissive tilt of the head. "It's too late for that."

"Please. You saw me with her. You saw how happy we were. Would you have wanted someone to take your daughter away from something like that? From being that happy?"

Doloria stood and paced carefully over to the picture window again. "Sometimes I swear I see things out there… moving in the dark."

"I wouldn't tell anyone if you let me go. I swear."

"You said you were happy with that girl. I suggest you hold tightly on to that in the time to come. We've crossed into the borderlands already." He cast a sorrowful glance back at her. "She's likely starting to forget you."

"No. She wouldn't forget. She'll keep looking."

"It doesn't matter. Past the borderlands, in the Dusk, we are all forgotten by those left behind. Like entropy in fast motion. She might not notice it at first, but fresh memories begin to age, like old photographs losing color, then cracking. Her memories of you might already be vanishing. I'm sorry, Marion. But it's only a matter of time."

6

───────────

That's when I started seeing things outside the windows. Sometimes at night, sure, but not always. Sometimes I'd be outside the cabin during the day, either doing chores or reading a book. That was one of the only good things. He had a lot of books around the cabin, so when he let me, I took a book from the shelf and read in my spare time. Some of the books were fiction, mostly classics, as well as weird stuff about supernatural arts, afterlives, other worlds, like that. There was only half a shelf of poetry anthologies, and I consumed those within the first few weeks. Some of the other books were biographies or autobiographies from people I'd never heard of. I tried a few of them, but a lot of them read like journals or research papers, and some were written in sort of hard language, like older English. And honestly, most of those were just really boring.

But there were times when I'd be sitting against a tree, or out on the cabin's porch, and I looked up and saw what looked like a person out in the trees. The first time it happened, it was the middle of the night. I had a dream that someone was standing out in the trees—in a small clearing—and was waving at me, trying to get my attention. Just standing out in the dark, waving. So when I woke up, I went to the window, you know, just to be sure.

And I saw it. Someone was really out there, waving in the dark. And I couldn't believe it. I think I stood there for ten minutes, just staring. All this time I hadn't actually seen another human being in... I don't even know how long it'd been, at that point. But out there in the dark was a person, just like in my dream. It looked like a man. There'd be no way for him to know somebody was seeing him, but he was standing out there in a clearing in the middle of the night, waving an arm like he was sure somebody could see him and he could get their attention.

I woke Peter up because I thought... I was still hoping that I was imagining it, maybe my mind was still dreaming.

He went outside to make sure, which is how I found out he had a gun. He went outside and... and this is going to sound strange, I know, but I didn't want him to go. It's not like I cared about him, it wasn't that. But at that point, he wasn't the way he'd been at the beginning. As unstable as he could be, he could also be kind, and I could tell he cared about my well-being, if that makes sense. He made me do chores to help take care of the cabin because we were really living out there, and it was for my own good as well as his. When he grabbed the gun and went outside, I felt like, what would happen to me if he died? I don't know if that makes sense. Maybe it doesn't matter.

But he went out there to see if it was really a person outside.

Everything changed after that. Peter came back claiming he hadn't seen anyone else out there, but something was off about him. More than what was already off about him, is what I mean. And I started seeing shapes of people out in the trees, even in daylight. It felt like it wasn't just a forest anymore. It felt like we were trespassing in a strange country, and the things that lived there were closing in on all sides. I couldn't step outside without feeling like I was being watched. It's sort of like how I felt when my family first moved here to America. I felt like people were always looking at me and judging me for looking different or for not being as good at English as my dad.

Peter didn't answer my questions about any of it, not even when I asked him what he'd meant when he used words like the Borderlands, or the Dusk, and he never talked about the things in the trees. He just kept his eyes out the windows, and started carrying his gun everywhere. Sometimes I woke up to use the bathroom in the middle of the night and he'd be standing by the bedroom window or sometimes the picture window in the living room. One night I got up to use the restroom, I noticed the front door of the cabin was wide open and Peter was gone.

I didn't see him again for a long time. And you know how I said he was starting to change, like... he was different somehow? It was like that, times a hundred. Whatever happened to him out there, he didn't come back the same person. I could see it in his eyes. Someone else was behind them and looking out through them.

*

With no survival skills except the most basic knowledge about a few edible plants, Marion was left with what food was already in the cabin.

After two weeks, she discovered the cellar doors outside; they were embedded against the cabin's foundation. Inside, the walls and floors of the cellar were cavelike, made of thick concrete, as if the cellar were part of an entirely different building than the cabin above. Encased by cobwebs in the corners, there were shelves and shelves of canned food and groceries. Beyond this was what appeared to be the remnants of a private bedroom. Not a bed, but a stretch of tanned leather and a blanket of fur. Against the far wall, a slab of wood propped up by cinderblocks, constituting a make-shift desk atop which an oil lantern and a dusty old journal rested.

There was something about the journal. It didn't merely sit atop the desk, rather it called out—something about it felt like a *call*—to be picked up.

Marion grabbed food—a few packets of pasta, some canned goods—and brought them up to the cabin. She tried not to think about the journal sitting down there in the dark, on an old desk, beside a bed that looked like it would've fit in one of the old westerns that Charlie sometimes liked to watch.

A week later, while retrieving more food from the cellar, she took the journal up with her. On its first page, in rough but surprisingly elegant handwriting, was a name: *Terrence Forgaill.*

Marion started to read.

7

Crickets sang outside, making a long, steady wisp of sound that drifted like dust particles and reached Charlie and Marion through the screen of Marion's bedroom window. It sounded like a lament or a warning. Beneath the cricket song, folded under its pervasive cover, was a silence. The silence of soil under grass. Of a graveyard at night. Of tears choked behind smiles. Of void between stars. It carried on, undisturbed, until Charlie Louise noticed it was there and, blinking as if waking suddenly from a dream, realized Marion had stopped speaking.

Marion had scooted closer to the window, was staring out, her face illuminated by the dim orange glow through the blinds. She had cried through some of the story, but now her eyes were dry. Studying her, Charlie thought she hadn't stopped because of emotion, no; she was hesitant to continue. Afraid, maybe.

"Do you know how long it'd been, at that point?" asked Charlie. "When you found the journal?"

Marion shook her head. "I didn't keep track of the days. Sometimes I tried counting, but four months was as far as I got before I stopped. It seemed pointless." She breathed in through her nose. "It's late."

"I know."

"And your phone's been going off this whole time."

Charlie glanced at her phone. Somehow she hadn't noticed: nine missed calls, nearly a dozen texts. Most of them were from Adrian. The last one he'd sent, almost an hour ago, was in all capital letters: *PLEASE CALL ME.*

She tucked the phone back into her pocket. "You were saying? About the journal in the basement."

"Charlie," said Marion. "It's late."

"And I came to listen to your story."

Marion turned away, eyes twinkling in those orange slots of light.

"I didn't expect it to be easy to hear," said Charlie. She surprised herself by not hesitating: she reached out and put her hand on Marion's hand. "I wish I could've always been here for you. But now, being here is all I can do, so… whatever comes next, I'm right here."

Marion swiped away tears as if offended by their audacity. "It's not just that, you know. It's not just that it's hard."

"Then what is it?" She refrained from saying *You can tell me.* Whenever someone said that in a movie, it always sounded forced and artificial.

Marion held Charlie's hand as a precious thing. "I never deserved someone like you."

"Don't be an idiot."

"No. I mean it. Mahal ko. You were always a light—not just to me, but to anyone who knew you. I heard your name and it made me mad if somebody didn't say it right, like they didn't deserve having your name in their mouth. I used to think—*me and her. That was the time of my life.* And it was. It really was."

Charlie felt like standing up and taking a step back, but she rooted herself, using Marion's hand as an anchor. "Why are you talking like this? You're here now. You survived. And I know nothing is the same and it'll never be again, but... *you're here now.* That's something."

Marion shook her head. "I don't know how much time we have."

"We have all night. And more than that. I'm here for you."

"No. I wish you would go. What happened to me after that, what I learned and what I saw..." No more swiping at the tears; she let them fall freely. "Charlie, you are a light in this world, the only one I ever wanted to stand in. But I'm a black hole. That's what happened to me. I became a black hole. And it'd be better for you if you left and... and if you forgot me."

Charlie released her hand, black disbelief eclipsing her vision as she moved to the edge of the windowsill and looked down at her own feet. Slowly, with the stillness of resolve rising in her like anger, she clenched her hands into fists at her sides.

"How dare you."

Marion flinched as if she'd been slapped. "What?"

"You don't get to speak to me like that. Like I'm this beacon of light in the darkness, like I'm innocent and oblivious, a child who doesn't know what's best for her and needs to be shielded from the chaos and horror of the real world."

"That's not what I meant."

"For the last ten years, I mourned you. I may not have gone through the hell that you did, but I went through my own. We all do—that's life. A constantly growing collection of unmanageable hurts and anxieties and horrors and longings and aches and desperations that can't be carried, yet we carry them—one trembling step at a time, praying or at least hoping that it'll all mean something one day, that we'll cross some line before the end and at least some of it will make even just a little bit of sense. And... and I shouldn't even be telling you this. You already know, probably better than I do. I carried the weight of you around with me every single day, sometimes grieving, sometimes still hoping you'd come back, sometimes just remembering everything because—because after awhile, I started to look around at my life and wonder, What happened? Where'd everybody go? Wasn't there something else I meant to do, or someone I meant to become, or somewhere I meant to go—and someone I meant to do it all with? What happened? So remembering was easier, because everything seemed so simple in my memories, it seemed so perfect, the way memory does. But after awhile, even remembering got too hard, it hurt too much, because it just reminded me of how I had all of that back then, I had you, and there was so much still ahead… I mean, it was like we had everything still ahead of us. Remember? Our whole lives. I had all that, and I took it for granted."

"Charlie…"

"So don't tell me I should leave and forget about you, and then say it's for my own good or some bullshit like that. If I could forget you, Marion, don't you think I would've by now? Don't you think I ever wished I could, because maybe things would've been easier? You owe me this, at least. For me. For yourself, maybe, if you…" She restrained a sudden sob. "If you still care the way I *know* you do."

She spun around so she didn't have to see herself looked at by Marion with such dismay.

A few seconds passed. Marion came up behind her and, in the tenderest gesture since her return, wrapped her arms around her and rested her head against the back of Charlie's shoulder. Charlie felt her shaking. Or maybe it was only herself.

Charlie said, "I know all about light and the way it fades. The inevitability of it. I'm not some light in the dark, Marion."

"You are to me."

God, but if years could be taken back. She thought of all the things she wished she would've said to Marion all those years ago, when they'd been just kids. It would've been the time to do it. They were so different now, so altered. The things she wanted to say felt as far away as the kids they'd once been.

"I don't even know the whole story yet, but I'm sorry. I'm so sorry."

"It's not your fault."

Charlie turned around so she could throw her arms around her in return. "I don't wish I could've forgotten. I didn't mean that."

Just like that, as if it were the most natural thing, Marion moved her face close to Charlie's and kissed her on the lips. The tears on both their cheeks intermingled. Charlie pressed forward before Marion could pull away, kissed her in return.

In her pocket, her phone buzzed with another text message. She ignored it.

"You know," said Marion, "I've never heard you talk like that before."

"Like what?"

"Just a minute ago. Twelve-year-old you would've never said things like that."

Charlie couldn't help it—she laughed. "A lot's changed, what can I say."

"I want to hear about you, you know. What I've missed out on all this time."

"It's nothing compared to yours."

"All the more reason I want to hear it."

"What about you? Still stalling on telling me the rest."

Something settled across Marion's face, eclipsing what joy and warmth had briefly flickered there. What she said was a poem, a short one, from W.S. Merwin.

"Please one more kiss in the kitchen," she said, "before we turn the lights off."

*

It was after 3 AM when Charlie pulled into the driveway of her house. The house was dark except for the front porch light which her father had left on intentionally, the way he always did—always had, back when coming home too late every night had been routine for her.

She killed the engine, unbuckled her seatbelt, sagged into the seat. This was a feeling she was familiar with, but hadn't felt in a long time: the concrete path from the driveway to the front door seemed miles long, the journey from there to her bedroom even longer.

"Shit," she said to herself, realizing why Adrian had been so urgent to reach her. *Dinner.* She'd forgotten about dinner—about having Adrian over for the evening to meet her dad.

Her father had left a voicemail a few hours ago, explaining that he'd put leftovers in the fridge for her. "I know you've got a lot going on, sweetheart," he said, and although there was that subdued tone to his voice, he didn't sound too disappointed. He merely sounded concerned about her. "Let's plan another night, yeah? I'd love to meet your friend and, you know, make you feel awkward in front of him and everything. I'll be up for just a little longer, but probably heading to bed soon. Goodnight, sweetie."

Charlie felt her heart ache for him, wishing she'd thought to send him a message at least. She'd make it up to him in the morning, she thought. An apology. Then breakfast and tea, the way he liked it.

She read Adrian's text messages, listened to his voicemail—words formulated through restrained panic. She began typing an explanation which doubled as an apology, but she kept remembering the softness of Marion's lips, her hands clinging to her, trembling with something that resembled desperation.

No. Adrian could wait until tomorrow. She tucked the phone away, looked up at the house.

There was a man standing on the front lawn, silhouetted by the front porch's light behind him. Charlie had seen him before. As she watched from her car, frozen, the man lifted a hand up and waved at her.

Hours later, just before dawn, the front door of the house opened and James Louise stepped out into the misty blue of morning's brightening twilight. He wore a soft brown robe. His hair was still a ruffled nest; his eyes drooped from lack of caffeine. He squinted at Charlie's car in the driveway, then stuffed his hands into the robe's pockets and fast-walked over. When he peered in through the driver's side window, the concern that wrinkled his brow softened into an expression of relief. Charlie was asleep, slumped awkwardly back in the seat. As quietly as he could, he opened the door and took his daughter in his arms as though she were still the child she'd once been. Before using his knee to shut the car door, he noticed an old leather journal—one he'd never seen before—in the passenger seat. Something about it made him want to be away from it, so he left it in her car when he carried her inside.

Charlie was stirring when her father set her down on her bed. Before James could close the bedroom door on his way out, Charlie muttered, "I don't know how much time we have."

This made him pause, holding the door. He looked closely at the face of his daughter, as if trying to make sure to remember every detail, before he turned and left her there.

8

Even in the beige warmth of the coffee shop, enveloped by bustling human noise; even at the small black table, sitting across from Adrian and his concerned or frustrated stare; even with the scent of coffee wafting through the air, thick, textured, dusty in her nostrils, making her think of early mornings with her dad; even with all that, Charlie's mind orbited in the gravity of the old leather journal which sat like a time bomb in her satchel. Any other thoughts meagerly flitted across her mind, here and then gone like birds glimpsed in flight.

Adrian's voice cut in and out of focus.

"You're not even really here right now, are you," he said. "You agreed to meet here but—are you even listening?"

She blinked at him over her drink which issued curls of steam. "I'm trying to apologize."

"No, you're not. To be honest, you don't…" He ran a hand over his lips, his eyes searching off to the sides. She had never seen him so shaken, so uncertain. Not long ago, she hadn't been able to picture him in the throes of his anxiety. Normally it sat underneath, invisible. "Charlie, I'm sorry. I don't mean this negatively, but you don't seem like yourself lately."

She fingered the steaming cup, tried to look at him and comprehend. Her own emotions were signs held up inside her mind like cards for an actor to read out loud, but she didn't recognize the words. Somewhere behind the barista's counter—in the back of the coffee shop, most likely—a glass shattered. She thought, *There. That's what I feel in my chest.*

Shattered glass. Shards reflecting indistinct shapes and shadows.

Her gaze slipped to her satchel in the chair beside her, then guiltily back to Adrian.

"I'm sorry."

"Will you stop apologizing, please? And just say something? I feel like I'm losing my mind."

From the corner of her eye she could track the movement of passerby outside the shop's front windows. People walking the sidewalks, going nowhere. There seemed to be somebody standing still amongst them, and this person—glimpsed from the corner of her eye—was a wide, titanic shape, towering like a streetlight over the small people going about their normal days inside their normal lives. But Charlie refused to turn her head to catch a better look.

In the store's far corner, somebody was holding their head in both hands and moaning. One of the baristas—or someone behind the counter, at least—was facing Charlie directly, posture stiff, eyes wide, waving at her. Charlie tried to ignore this, too. Her eyes flicked to the satchel and back to Adrian. To the satchel and back to Adrian. Didn't he feel it in there? Couldn't he feel it and its whisperings? Its pull?

Adrian leaned back in his seat, not to relax but as an expression of sinking disbelief at her behavior. She was hurting him, it was obvious, but this awareness fell flat across the emptiness she felt inside, eclipsed by the awareness of the journal in her satchel. The journal, its contents, and—

Marion. Marion in the orange slots of light. Marion's soft lips, the warmth of her breath. The horror in her eyes as she told more and more of her story.

"I don't know what to do." Adrian looked away.

She panicked. What had he said before that she hadn't responded to? He wanted her to say something. And—and she wasn't acting like herself.

Instead of letting her attention be pulled to the old journal, Charlie closed her eyes and focused on inhaling through her nose, the feeling of air moving through her nostrils and inflating her lungs.

When she opened her eyes, Adrian was looking right at her. He wasn't like a lot of people she'd met before. He was still here. She had hurt him, was at this very moment unintentionally causing him pain, but Adrian was still here and he was waiting for her to give him another reason to stay.

She thought about all the times she'd spent with him at parties, at bonfires, at potlucks. The long conversations. The aching that had burned inside of her but which his presence had soothed even if incrementally.

"Adrian." She looked down at her hands. "I think it's just I... I'm afraid. It feels weird to admit it, but I'm *scared*."

He leaned in. "Afraid? Of what?"

"When you kept trying to reach me last night and I wasn't answering, it's... it's because I was with Marion. I went back because I needed to hear her story. I needed her to tell me and I knew she would."

"Jesus, Charlie. You could've just told me that. I figured it had to with her anyway—I mean, of course it does. I just didn't want to make any assumptions."

"I meant to call you back, I really did. But then it was around three in the morning and I got back in my car and started to drive, and I just started crying, and I got into my head about so many things... about everything. You and—and her. My dad. The things I keep seeing and how I know it's in my head, except there's... there's things Marion said, and things Pastor Joe from church said, and even things in the first few pages of the journal..." She lifted a hand up to her face to find how badly she was trembling.

"Wait," said Adrian. "What do you mean me and her? You were in your head about Marion and me?"

"About everything. But the reason—"

"So, what—just that you're worried about her and me? Like for our safety? Or is it something else?"

"It's hard to explain. I'm *scared*. I'm still seeing things, and it's getting worse, but I don't think it's just in my head anymore."

"Okay, okay, slow down. I think we should get out of here. This is all a lot to process."

When they were out on the sidewalk, headed for Adrian's car, Charlie stopped and put a hand around her own arm. "I think I should go."

Adrian scoffed at her. "You're leaving?"

The ferocity of his tone made her flinch.

"Charlie..." He came up to her and appeared, for a second, like he meant to reach for one of her hands. He didn't, but she wondered what she would've done if he had. "Why do I feel like, if you just leave now, I won't hear from you again?"

The trembling worsened. The satchel over her shoulder felt as though it contained a cinderblock; the strap dug into her shoulder.

But when she met Adrian's eyes, she felt a fogginess recede from the edges of her mind. In the clarity, she suddenly couldn't remember why she'd wanted to leave for home just now. Hadn't she agreed to meet here because she wanted to be around Adrian? Wanted to tell him something?

She looked down at the satchel. Without ceremony, she took hold of it and let it drop to the concrete. Before Adrian could ask, she pointed at it. "Will you do something for me?"

"What?"

"Will you put that in my car for me?"

He picked it up, though as if he expected a giant spider to hop out from it. "What's in it?"

She handed him the car key. "I'll explain at the lake."

A fifteen-minute drive later, they sat on a boulder just a few feet from the shore. The sun hung in the far end of the sky, dropping past late afternoon.

Charlie pulled her legs up and hooked her arms around her knees. For the moment she felt that she could breathe again.

Adrian fidgeted with a few small rocks. "Why here?"

"I feel better when I'm near water."

"Let me guess. All that's missing now is your fishing pole."

"You know me so well."

"Yeah, well, you're not exactly unpredictable."

"I was in love with her."

He stopped fidgeting, met her eyes for a passing second and then looked out at the water. "I guess I kinda knew that."

"It wasn't supposed to be a secret. If you and I... if..." She tried to slow herself down with a deep breath. "I would've told you at some point. I thought it'd come up eventually, on its own, if we started asking each other about past relationships."

"Yeah. We've had so many kinds of conversations, I kept meaning to ask you. You know, like, if you've ever been in love. That type of thing."

"She's the only story I have, in response to that." She shook her head as if to say, *Can you believe it?* "It's funny, in a way."

"What is?"

"It's so easy for me to just say it. That's the benefit of retrospect, I guess—the illusions it lets us have. How am I supposed to know that my memories aren't just tinted with nostalgia, a story I tell myself about it, compared to what really happened? It's no wonder it's impossible to ever really know someone, or to ever truly connect to another person. We construct our identities by the stories we tell ourselves about our own pasts."

"Is that how you really feel? That it's impossible to connect to other people?"

"It seems like it's true, doesn't it? We relate to each other on the surface, but the deeper down you go, the worse it gets. The deeper you know someone, the more you see how much of them—how much of any of us, I mean—is held up by illusions, and traumas, and flimsy belief systems that could fall apart like a house of cards in the slightest breeze."

"Jesus, Charlie."

"It happened to my parents. And, my dad, he's able to miss my mom because he idealizes the past. My dad looks back on his marriage and it's this perfect thing, the thing that casts a shadow over the rest of his life. The ache of nostalgia, the rose-tinted lens. But it's only like that because it's in the past and he tells himself a story about it, he idolizes it. When he was actually living it, it was hell. They were so toxic to each other. All I remember about them when they were together is how much they fought, and how intense those fights were, and how my mom took out all her bad moods either on him or me."

Adrian had turned on the boulder so he sat cross-legged, fully facing her. Her words had a physical effect on him, like freezing drops of water. "I didn't know about all that. You haven't talked about your parents much. Their marriage, anyway."

"I don't look back on it the way my dad does. In that way he's like most people, clinging on to the hope that any of it—all the pain, especially—will make sense one day. But life isn't like it is in stories."

"Is that how it is with Marion?"

"What, like a story?"

"No, the—well, you know, the nostalgia. Idealizing the past. Is that what you do with her?"

"I don't know. Sometimes I think, maybe I do. Back then, if you would've asked me if I loved her, I would've said— It would've been simple. I would've said I had a crush on her. Actually, I probably would've blushed and said we were just best friends… I used to keep it a secret, and so did she. But for the past ten years, every person I've gotten even sorta close to, I just end up trying to turn them into her."

"Can I ask something about that?"

"Of course."

"Did you do that with me, too? Try to turn me into her?"

"No. You're the first person where that didn't happen… and it still hasn't." Her own lack of hesitation surprised her. "Maybe I was in love with her, but I was twelve. Sometimes even now I'm not sure I really know what it means—what it really means—to love someone. So many people use that word but they mean something else, or they say it but their actions show otherwise. Sometimes I don't even know if it's possible to love someone in the way we mean to when we say *love*, anyway. And, again… I was just a kid. What did I know?"

"You know, kids might know more about love than most adults do. We complicate it in our heads, but kids, they just do it."

She gave him a look of surprise, which softened toward fondness.

He went on. "Really. If you say you loved her, then you loved her. Not that I have any place to speak about it, but I think of love as more of a verb, anyway. In movies, or with the kinds of people who really idealize love, they're always talking about how they *fell in love with someone*, or the whole love at first sight thing."

"Yeah," Charlie laughed without much humor. "It's bullshit."

"It is, I agree. But I think of love as an active thing, an active verb. It's something you do, not something you feel."

"Maybe you're right about that."

"Do you still feel that way about Marion?" he asked. "You love her?"

She could hear the unspoken questions behind his words.

"I did love her," she said. "And I wish I could tell you it's different now, because, I mean, it *is* different. I thought she was dead for most of the last decade. We're entirely different people now. And nothing's the same. So I don't know, Adrian."

"Okay." He dropped his eyes but nodded. "I understand."

Despite the resistance in her body, she reached out and put a hand to the side of his face. She felt a tear against her fingers, followed by a deep echoing pain in her heart for him. "Adrian," she said. "For whatever it means, I never thought I'd ever meet someone like you."

"I'm just me."

"No. You're the only person who's ever made me want to forget the past."

But the past is so big, she thought, *and it's only gotten bigger the more I've turned away from it.*

She let her hand drop away from his face and, just like that, the moment was done. Whatever longing to feel his skin, to stay that close to him, she needed to let it recede.

*

Before he dropped her off at her car, back at the coffee place, Adrian turned to her.

"Earlier you said there were things you were scared of, and I didn't mean to brush it off, there was just so much on my mind…"

"It's okay."

"I'm guessing it has to do with what happened that day at Marion's? And whatever's in your bag?"

"I don't understand most of it, or why Marion won't tell me the rest of what happened to her. But when she was there, in that cabin, she found a journal. And whatever's inside it…" Marion flashed in her mind. Marion saying, *It's not that I don't want to tell you, Charlie. If I tell you, if you read this, you're a part of it.*

Without much hesitation, Charlie had told her she was already part of it.

And then, after some time considering this, Marion had handed her the old journal.

"You also said you were seeing things? Did you mean like hallucinating?"

"I'll tell you, but… later. Whatever's in the journal, I think it's the key to what came next for Marion. And maybe for me, too. The key to everything that's been happening, and the things I keep seeing." She looked Adrian in the eyes and was unsurprised at the fear there.

9

From the journal of Terrence Forgaill:

Entry 1

My research, my time, my searching, has led me here, finally,
though it seems not to matter what I've learned of the place—if it
can be called a place—known as Katalpa. I still do not understand
it, nor can I be certain that there is a path forward nor a path back.
But I am here on the Borderlands, and I have brought with me
most of the old journals and books that have served as my studies,
and enough food to last the foreseeable future. I hope.

The bunker was waiting for me when I crossed over. The
journals of J. Hodgson and Sora Nakadai both mention a house, but
their respective descriptions differed enough that I believe this
very bunker did not exist for them. They spoke of many things I
still do not understand, such as the Katalpian Dusk and the spider
god. Maybe what they experienced as a house, somehow, is what I
experience as a bunker.

It resembles an old war bunker, the kind built along coastlines
to watch for enemy ships and to fire upon them and possibly re-

ceive fire in return. I've chosen one of the empty concrete rooms as my own. I would try and sleep up above, where the lookout point provides some natural light, but the forest makes me uneasy. Which is saying a lot, I suppose, because the darkness of this underground hallway is no comfort, either. But I have the lanterns, and my research, and my photograph of Alice. It is the only photograph that remains of her. All the others have either faded into blackness or simply vanished.

Alice, my beloved. This may be the answer, finally. I know in my heart that I will find you, no matter how lost you are, beyond these borderlands and in the aching, starless realm of Katalpa.

*

As she read, the words adopted a texture, and then they were no longer words on a page at all. She heard his voice, like sandpaper and running water all at once, infused with the weariness and wisdom of age, yet from a person who couldn't have been much older than her own father.

*

Entry 2

The path that led me here began, I believe, when I was just a child. But I didn't realize this until that day in December over seven years ago. I was home, sitting at my dinner table which seemed too large, and I had too many leftovers and couldn't remember why I had cooked so much for myself. It seemed a meal for two—large enough for multiple helpings—and yet it was just me.

That night I dreamt I was making love with a beautiful woman. She lay atop me, and she loved me—I could feel that in the way she moved against me, the way she held me and looked into my eyes.

I said her name and suddenly her eyes froze, the pupils vanished and then blackened and leaked blood down her cheeks and onto my face, reeking of copper. She opened her mouth and out came the buzzing screech of a cicada, that sound heard in summer heat as if the trees are screaming. Her face and then her entire body simply blackened, softening into something like swampy mud, and then it began to melt.

I woke from this dream covered in sweat, my heart like a heavy drum, my body gripped by the lingering arousal intermingled with disbelieving revulsion and something like a terrible sob issuing from my lungs. It was a strange, mournful sound to awaken to, alone in the dark; I hadn't known that a sound of such horrible, unbearable sorrow could arise from my own body. I felt a hole in me, something wide and fundamental lacking where once, I was sure, there'd been something. I was reminded of a poem, though I had no idea how I knew it, since I'd never been especially interested in poetry of any kind. This was a line from a poet called William Stafford, about losing someone you cared for so deeply that you never cared again. The world lost its color and sound, and it was suddenly easy to imagine living alone across a river, with no one to wait for you, nothing to look forward to.

Entry 3

Some people live their whole lives in the shadow of something from their past. In my years as a minister, then as a professor of Eastern religions and philosophy, then as a scholar of esoteric arts from early human history onward, I've seen how there is a trace of these shadows in nearly all people. For most, it is the innocence of childhood. No matter the degree of happiness or fulfillment they find in their later lives, when asked what the happiest time of their life was, many people will refer to when they were children. When what little they had was more than enough. When everything was still ahead.

I've seen young people shape their own lives into a rebellion against something and call that freedom, not realizing that they were still controlled—albeit in a different direction—by the thing they were rebelling against. All that just to say, much of my own life took on the shape of existential crisis: status quo; crisis; the crumbling of all foundation; and the construction of new foundations. I chose to let go of my past and shape the present free from any prisons of my own making. Until that day with the dinner, the house seeming too quiet, and that dream of a beautiful woman whose name I had spoken with love.

Suddenly my life existed in this shadow, but I couldn't make sense of it, as it seemed to have materialized from nowhere. Even the memories of my life seemed wrong, like a house built without a single right angle so that everything feels pervasively off. What had driven me to live in this lovely home, in this remote place? Why were there so many books on the shelves that I didn't recognize? What had I been doing for the past decade of my life, going where, and with whom?

My bed as big as they come. Two closets in the room, one with a few shoes and pieces of woman's clothing—but only a few. Most of the drawers and hangers were empty. There were picture frames around the house, but many of them framed empty space, or the occasional photograph of me—but taken by whom? I stood at one of these photos and just stared and stared, thinking I looked so happy in these photos. That smile, that sparkle in my eyes. Almost unrecognizable. I couldn't remember having been so happy, not since I was young. Not since I was a child.

And so I began my investigation into my own life, the findings of which provided only more questions, and each question left me desolate in the face of the seemingly unanswerable. Colleagues were confused by my questions; friends looked upon me with concern. I played with the possibility of amnesia, but it wasn't that I'd forgotten any gaps of time or anything of that sort. It was, rather, this unshakable feeling that I'd been holding on to something and, despite my vigilance, it was gone and—even more inexplicable—I couldn't remember what it was. I stumbled through any free time in a nauseous wave of disorientation, as though my life had been upended. But no one I spoke to gave any indication that my life, as seen from the outside, was any different than it'd been before. I remember the lines of another poem recurring in my head, yet again one I've never read, this time from Edgar Allan Poe:

> " *You are not wrong, who deem*
> *that my days have been a dream;*
> *yet if hope has flown away*
> *in a night, or in a day,*
> *in a vision, or in none,*
> *is it therefore the less gone?*
> *All that we see or seem*
> *is but a dream within a dream.* "

After months of unanswerable questions and the quest for answers leading only to more questions, I wondered if these might not be signs of some degenerative sickness in my brain. I had relatives who had, over the course of years, succumbed to dementia. Never mind that I was only in my forties.

It wasn't a degenerative disease, of course. A year passed. I threw myself into my work, feeling—intuiting, perhaps—that if there were answers, I could find them in the mysteries of my work.

The answer came two years after that strange day in December, when I returned to my hometown. A place called Two Pines Mill.

My parents died when I was young, and I am an only child, so I had no roots in that town. I returned there because of the photos of me in my house. If it was true I'd not been so happy since my childhood, perhaps I could find some answers within the landscapes of that childhood. I found only ghosts on those streets: the old shops now renovated; the long dirt road that went out through the fields and into the woods was now paved. I regretted my visit, feeling only more alone in the world, more isolated than ever before.

What meaning had I extracted from my own life so far? What purpose? My life appeared to be a collection of whats, without signs of a single why. The things I owned, the work I did... but what made it worthwhile? What was I working for—and why? And why couldn't I remember? Some key ingredient was missing. There were shadows of it cast across the map of my life as now I knew it. But it simply wasn't there.

I found myself, then, at the one place that still felt vividly alive in my memories: Tullapa River. Ironic, I know, that later I would travel to the remote Tullapa Islands and the isolated indigenous tribe that inhabited them. The only commonality is the name... but when you've seen what I've seen, lived the life that I've lived, you wonder if there is such a thing as coincidence.

My family, we were part of a small minority in Two Pines Mill. It was technically a sundown town, though none of the locals actively enforced those laws. My parents explained to me that it was a gentle community of folk who didn't want to cause trouble, and whose ignorance was not willful. I don't remember enough about it to confirm or deny those things. I only remember feeling always like an outsider, and, for some reason, my haven, my refuge, was Tullapa River.

It was while I sat atop a small rock, kicked off my shoes, and dipped my feet into the cold water, that the name returned to me like the details of a dream.

Alice.

The name opened something in my brain and body, and I tell you, fully honest: it was like a crack of lightning inside my head. A sharp headache pierced through my brain. Most of the headaches and migraines I'd ever had tended to come on slowly, like the ocean tide reaching farther one wave at a time. This one, though, struck me like a baseball bat to the head. I actually fell from the rock and clambered in the dirt, crying out in pain. And suddenly I felt fatigued, as if I'd been working all my muscles in a full marathon.

Alice. My memory of her leaked through the cracks and presented itself to me: my wife. My beloved partner of over ten years. Alice Hassan.

The headache faded to a more manageable level, at which point I remembered her completely, as if a dam had been constructed in my mind and, moments ago, a leak had formed, and then the entire dam collapsed.

Strangest of all, she had been here with me. Here on this river. Alice Hassan, a young girl with an indigenous mother and a foreign father. We'd been here together as children. I never had many friends, but with Alice it was different. She knew something about being an outsider, about feeling alone even when around other people. I think that's how we were drawn to each other.

It all came back to me. How she and I stayed friends even after my family moved away from Two Pines Mill. How she was the first person I thought of and wanted to talk to when I heard the news of my father's heart attack. How she and I reconnected, years later, when I showed up at one of the stops on her lecture tour, and thus began our affair which would lead to our marriage.

On the banks of Tullapa River, I collapsed and wept. Alice was renowned in the scientific community, commanding respect and admiration. Her circle of influence, of peers and friends, was far beyond anything I had ever achieved in my obscurer fields of study. I remember thinking, I will marry this woman—this woman who will change the world.

But she was gone—and, beyond anything I could comprehend, I had forgotten her. Everyone had. The traces of her existence were like distant memories themselves: a few pieces of clothing in my house; a few photographs of me that only she could have taken. She had loved poetry, had read her favorite poets to me out loud again and again.

The missing piece clicked into place. The empty expanses of my life had meaning again.

And once I recomposed myself and was on the road home, back to the world of the living, I discovered a fire burning within me. A fire fueled partly by baffled curiosity, but partly—almost entirely, I should say—fueled by inconsolable rage. The injustice of it. The senseless unfairness of it.

I would find out what happened to my beloved Alice, and why the world—why I—had forgotten her. It was as though she'd been wiped from the slate of existence, not merely from the present but also from the past. I would find out, and maybe I'd find her.

Oh, but I didn't have the slightest idea of where that path would lead me.

So that's where it began. If this journal is lost to time as I—like Alice—very well may be, then, if nothing else, I have written this out for posterity, for the need to remind myself of why I'm here. To remind myself that it began decades ago, with a little boy and a little girl on the banks of Tullapa River in a town called Two Pines Mill. That's where the path began, and it has led me all the way here to the Still Woods, near the mists of The Ocean of Hali, to the borders of what Alice, in her journals, called The Aching Plane.

Entry 4

When I trekked out into the woods the last few days, my intent was to begin acquiring at least some understanding of the landscape around my bunker. I know I cannot stay here, and all along my intentions have been to press forward, but I must tell the truth. For perhaps the first time in my life, in a true existential sense, I am terrified. These months of confusion and disorientation were one thing; this is unlike even the worst of my darkest imaginings or childhood nightmares.

It isn't merely what I am witnessing in this unnatural landscape —it is also seeping into my dreams. Whatever's happening here, whatever proximity to the lost realm of Katalpa does to you, there is no refuge from it, not even in dreams.

Throughout the woods, there are clearings. They seem like stages of a journey, landmarks on a pilgrimage. The first handful were empty clearings. But one I came across was host to something like a shrine. In the middle, beneath open sky, a statue of white stone stood upright. It was human in shape, standing on two legs, one arm extended—but the resemblance to the human form ended there.

At first I thought the statue depicted a man covered in fur, but when I came close, I saw it wasn't fur. The thing was covered in *arms.* Thousands of them. Instead of pores, this figure had tiny arms reaching out from its skin, or rather, its skin was comprised of these arms. None looked quite the same as another, and not all were of the same mind. Some of the arms appeared to be grappling with each other, or caressing each other, or at war with each other. Some had six, seven, eight fingers, others no more than two or three.

Stranger still, when I built up the nerve to inspect even closer, I saw, embedded in the palms of most of the thousands of reaching hands, were *eyes*. Thousands and thousands of lidless eyes. Not a single one showed any emotion I could decipher; each one stared straight forward with gray indifference.

The statue itself had no eyes in its head. Only more hands where eye sockets should've been. And its mouth was open, not slack but—as though it were screaming. In pain, perhaps.

I studied that statue for a long time, trying to imagine what it must've taken to construct. The details didn't strike me as merely lifelike, as the very term "lifelike" implies an imitation of life. This sculpture struck me more as something alive, more like a photograph of something alive as opposed to a recreation. The scholar and historian in me was rabid with curiosity. Was this a shrine, this creature a god? What would drive a person to construct something so hideous, so repulsive? It reminded me of the Biblical depiction of angels in all their horror and glory.

Or, much more apt, I was reminded of the Hecatoncheires of ancient Greek mythology: the giants with fifty heads and a hundred arms. Monsters, in simplest terms, so reviled and repulsive, they were deemed by their own mother too hideous to be born.

That is what the sculpture in the clearing reminded me of.

But my curiosity turned against me. Once I discovered its eyes, I stepped away, any curiosity paralyzed by the clearest feeling that the statue could see me. As I studied it, it studied me back with its thousands of eyes attached to its thousands of reaching hands.

Beyond the clearing, I glimpsed movement in the trees and I looked past the statue. But when I did, I swear the statue appeared to turn its head—just a slight tilt—and that was enough. My paralysis turned to panic and I sprinted away from the clearing, back in the direction of the bunker.

For an hour I was lost, having lost track of any markers I'd left behind me to guide my way. But I made it back, at last. I confess, even as I write this, I am uncertain that I'm alone in the darkness of the bunker. Three times since returning I've interrupted my own writing in order to wander the dark hallways with a lantern, to ensure I'm alone down here in the dark. I can't get rid of the image of that thing and its thousands of hands that burst from its pores, and the lidless eyes staring from each palm.

Entry 5

Visions of impossible things standing far off in the trees. Yesterday I thought I saw her—Alice—in what must've been a distant clearing. She was waving at me, a frantic energy in the gesture, as if she desperately needed to get my attention but was, perhaps, too scared to come any closer. I wondered, *Does she want me to go out to her?* If that was her, it means she is lost here in the Still Woods, and if the world forgot her the way I almost did, that must mean I am being forgotten, too. Slowly, perhaps, or else all at once.

I don't believe anyone will remember me. I had a few friends at most, such as my protege, Joe Correy. I had colleagues, but I do not imagine that I could live on in any of their hearts. I had students, some who said I left a considerable impact on their lives: Evangeline Dawson; Anton O'Shea; Violet Doloria and her husband Peter. But I would be lying to myself if I let myself hope that any of them would remember me. I only remembered Alice, I believe, because I had shared a childhood with her, and childhood memories are the closest our memory comes to being written in stone. Her impact on my life—my love for her—stretched beyond romantic love and was something more foundational.

It wasn't Alice waving at me from the clearing in the trees. When I stepped outside to get a closer look, there was something off about the figure, something that others would describe as *wrong*. She looked too tall, limbs too long, and no matter how I squinted, I couldn't make out a face. A trick of the light, I thought. Then she spun and sprinted into the trees.

I cannot help but think of the statue in the clearing, its thousands of small hands sprouting from its skin like fur. Could there be some connection between the waving figure I've seen in the distance, and the hands of the statue? Some correlation or symbolism I'm missing?

Despite my trepidation, I must go back out there. Eventually I'll have to leave this bunker entirely, if I'm to make it beyond these woods and to whatever awaits me.

Entry 6

I didn't want to record anything before I was certain, but now I am. Twice now I've returned to the clearing, and each time, the statue was standing in a different part—and, I believe, its pose wasn't quite the same. As insane as it sounds, my initial impression of the thing may be correct: that it is, impossibly, not merely lifelike, but actually alive. The only alternative is that somebody, or else a group of people, is replacing the statue every day with a nearly identical replica.

I would like to believe the latter, because the former suggests the statue may actually come alive and move through the woods. I imagine this must occur in the night, if it is more than mere imagining. That thing with its uncountable little arms and hands with eyes in the palms, its mouth open in what looks like a scream of pure anguish or terror, shuffling around in the dark, unseen and unheard, while I huddle down here in the bunker, confounded and afraid, forgotten by the world.

Alice. I swore I would find answers and find you, if I could. I promise I won't give up. You faced a harsher world than I, and you succeeded and thrived, were revered by many, before you were so cruelly and senselessly spirited away—not merely taken, but erased.

If I could pierce the unnatural barrier of memory that shrouded you, it stands to reason I can find you in this unthinkable place. It stands to reason we can rescue ourselves and return to the world. Doesn't it?

Entry 7

Today, on my fourth visit to the clearing with the statue, I happened to glance upward, and I realized this was the first time I'd done so while this deep into the woods. I am typically an observant person, prone to tunnel-vision only when it comes to my studies or my writing. My only excuse this time is that I was unsettled by the statue, therefore it drew my attention like lanternlight for a moth. Looking up, I thought, How have I never noticed the trees before?

They were not quite like the trees farther back, near my bunker. These trees had darker trunks, the bark having an almost scorched appearance, and they shot higher up toward the sky. The geography was changing, along with the fauna, and somehow I had scarcely noticed.

And there was something wrong with the statue. There were eyes now in its face. All down its torso, regular-sized arms were sprouting outward. I wonder… was it transforming? If this strange vision before me was but a transitional stage, soon it might come to resemble a giant insect with a human face and humanoid torso.

Entry 8

No matter how exhausted I become—my body sagging beneath the weight of it—my sleep brings me no sense of rest or rejuvenation. I see Alice in my dreams, but things happen to her that I am unable to stop. Terrible, violent sickness. Her skin melting from her body even while she still lives. Her eyes turning gray and then black, her voice transmuting into a sickly, death-pale moan before vibrating into the insectile screech of a cicada. There is no respite from the curse of this place. That is, except for the last two nights. These more recent dreams contained no horror. The opposite, in fact. One was a dream of being a child again on Tullapa River. Alice was with me. The second dream was nearly the same, except we were in a house, at a dinner table, children again and lost in conversation. I awoke from these dreams feeling warm… but unsettled by the warmth.

Is it a trick? An illusion meant to make me lower my guard?

Entry 9

I have begun packing what I need for what I assume will be a long journey, but even this statement feels meaningless when I have lost all sense of time.

On my last surveying, the statue is gone. At first I thought I had lost any sense of direction, but no; I located the clearing and found it empty. Beyond it, however, in the foliage, stood what I assumed were other statues, each one facing the clearing as if awaiting the return of their many-armed god. They were little more than shadows standing upright, humanoid in shape yet nevertheless misshapen. A number of them had tall bodies with oddly shaped heads, almost triangular I want to say, for lack of easier descriptors, and their arms were too long.

I didn't approach any of them to further inspect. The truth is, I'm not even certain they were statues. I turned and ran.

Even now, if I were to set this journal down and make my way to the top of the bunker and peer through the lookout point, I fear I would see them out there in the trees, watching me. Maybe it's all they're doing: watching, keeping tabs, getting closer night-by-night, assessing me in order to ascertain exactly what level of threat I may pose.

If I had yet gleaned any sense of intelligence in anything I've witnessed here, I would hope to begin a sort of communication so that I might gain even the vaguest understanding of… any of this. But I remain in the dark. I have gained no new knowledge.

Tomorrow I abandon this bunker, and make my way beyond the dark trees.

Entry 10

There are streams that trickle through the trees. Creeks, sometimes. I filled my water at one and can only hope it does not poison me, or contain parasites, or something unthinkable. I do not trust it, but I'm left with no choice.

Far ahead of me, sitting atop a rock by one of the streams, was an older teenager, or perhaps she was a bit older—a young adult—sitting by herself, wearing denim overalls and a hat to shade her face. She was fishing.

The closer I got, the more she faded until she was gone entirely and I was alone again in the woods.

She is perhaps the only thing I've witnessed in this bleak place that did not radiate threat or menace. It was a passing thing, but I miss the sight of her ahead of me, and find myself looking ahead or off in the distance, to the side, sometimes behind me, in search of something like a light to hold on to. You, Alice… if only I could see you ahead of me, your light guiding my way.

Entry 11

My dreams are beginning to change. Up until recently I was afraid of sleeping, for the dreams were, at times, worse than this waking nightmare. But then there was one in which Alice did not transform into something hideous and dead in front of my eyes. And now they are all different. She and I were walking by a lake surrounded by low mists, just talking as we strolled. A cottage sat nearby, nestled against the tree-line, smoke climbing from the chimney. A light in the window. Inside, my parents waited. My father, who died from a heart attack when I was fifteen. My mother, who died of cancer just two years later, leaving me alone in the world.

That was it. That was the dream. No horror to speak of. Just the deepest longings in my heart replaced with the sincerest warmth—a sense of my heart being full in its entirety, which is a feeling I can't remember ever having, not at least since I was a young child and therefore unaware of the feeling.

To awaken from that dream made me wish either for it to have never ended or for it to have never happened at all, so cruel was the emptiness I was left with. By what logic does this place give such dreams? To torment us? To tear us down from the inside?

Entry 12

I camped with a man last night, and some of the things he told me have caused me to question my perceptions of this place all the more severely.

The dark trees are everywhere now, no sign of familiar foliage anywhere. Even the bushes and berries and mushrooms no longer resemble any I've seen before, and grow scarcer. I am no mycologist, or any type of expert on plants and trees, but you'd think I would recognize the geography and plant life of Earth, wouldn't you?

The farther I've gone into the woods, the more I've observed what seems to be a thinning. Fewer trees, fewer plants. And steadily, a fog hangs in the air, creating something of a cocoon, making night and day increasingly indiscernible. Or, as if time has slowed and the daylight, through the fog, suggests constant evening.

The fog had become thick, distorting my sense of direction. And it was cold. It is still cold even as I write this. I never thought I'd miss the hospitality of a dark concrete bunker in a strange forest, but—in comparison—there is no quarter here, no respite. In the fog, somewhere ahead, I heard a desperate human noise. Somebody was weeping. It sounded as if they were trying to say something, but the sobs made speech impossible.

I stood still for a long time, wondering… Was it really a person I was hearing? Could it be something that only sounded like a person, some horrific imitation?

I thought of the statue with hands and eyes for skin, its mouth agape.

Eventually I realized I had two choices: stay or go on. I went on. And found the source of the weeping.

It was another person. A human person. His clothes were tatters, fabric reduced to rags. He wore a hood, and the face underneath was a portrait of emaciation. The man was skeletal, his skin reminded me of tent canvas stretched over the ends of knobby poles. And his eyes—I saw something in his eyes.

Imagine you are alone in a dimly lit room. There is no source of light, but you can just barely make out a gray sense of things in the dark. Hold your own hand in front of your face and it's faintly there. Now imagine it is a small room, more of a cage than a room, not even enough space for you to stretch out your legs, nothing to look at, no exit, no furniture. There is only the visible darkness and your own thoughts. Imagine this was your fate for the rest of your life, the long years ahead to be counted by the seconds and by the cramping of your ever restless limbs.

That is what I felt when first I glimpsed the madman's eyes. An insanity there, a looseness of the brain dictating what thoughts passed through—and a gnawing loneliness so great, so insipid, so total, there is almost nothing left. All other sensations are swallowed up by that loneliness.

I thought of him as a madman, and that is how I shall refer to him here. I do not use the term as an unkindness.

He was crouched at the dark trunk of a massive tree, using a stone to try and carve something into the bark. When he looked up and saw me, he burst out in wild laughter, stood, and put his arms on my shoulders.

"It's you," he said, elated. "You're here."

I shoved him away, fearing—despite rationality—that I could catch whatever madness infected him. But to my dismay, he was not an incoherent madman, no. He knew my name.

"Terry Forgaill," he said—he shouted. "That's what we called you. Forgaill. I—ha! I assumed it was an alias, you know. Is it? No, no, never mind, never mind. You—you're here. You're actually here." He kept looking all around as if worried we were being watched. "I thought I was the only one left. I thought I was alone."

When I failed to respond, the clarity went away from his eyes.

"Do you remember me? You do, don't you? My name?"

In response, I merely shook my head and muttered that I had never seen him before. For an instant I thought he was going to start weeping again, but he laughed. The laughter held no humor, rather it seemed a last stand against the incoherence of his mind's contents.

"You know," he said, "I've been having the strangest dreams. Full of warmth and comfort they are. Dreams of my family who must no longer remember me. Dreams of people I loved and who loved me back. Back then... when I knew nothing and had every-thing." The madman kept laughing, even as he wiped sorrowful tears from his eyes. "Do you know what it's like to wake up from those dreams?"

I was tempted to tell the man about my own dreams, but refrained. I told him to come with me. We walked a ways. And, in a clearing, started a fire.

I asked him how he knew my name.

"There were four of us," he said. "That's what I remember. Their names I've forgotten, which must mean they've crossed the border-lands, or even went beyond the Ocean of Hali."

"You know about the Ocean?"

"But you. I still remember you. You're the one who gathered us. Something having to do with our hearts, right, and the things we'd lost? The missing pieces, our lives like endless mazes impossible to make sense of? Oh, but you don't remember me. You don't remember any of us, do you, Terry."

I told him I was sorry.

"I wonder if it was worth it, dragging us along to be swallowed by The Aching Plane. I wonder what dreams brought you here."

His words made me consider the bunker, the dark hallway and many empty rooms, the excessive amounts of food stored there. It was perfectly possible that I did know this man, that I'd not been alone at the beginning—and that I had forgotten, the same way I'd forgotten Alice.

I told him he could come with me. I said, Whatever he was searching for, maybe he could still find it.

He merely laughed. "If you really think that you'll find your lost wife out there, why you're—you're even crazier than I am, brother. I saw it all. The rivers flowing into the Ocean of Hali. Just like the old myths that your wife wrote about. She… I mean, she wasn't right about everything, of course, but, but—but she was right about more than you'd think. The Ocean especially, and, and the people on the shores, some of them along the rivers, but some actually on the shores of the Ocean itself, completely unaware of how close they are to oblivion. One of our guys was there. Not, you know, not visiting like the others, I mean, he was *there*, dragging his feet, dreaming with eyes open, headed straight for Dark Katalpa and its insatiable hunger." Tears were streaming now from the madman's eyes, and that laughter sat manic in his throat. "I mean, I saw it. And it's not just something you see with your eyes; you feel it in your own heart and in your bones. The Ache. Like the shockwave from an explosion in the sky, pushing clouds and vibrating through the air, but without the explosion. And I felt what it meant."

The madman held up a hand in front of his own face as if he meant to reach out and grab the flames of our meager campfire. Such a haunted countenance had come over him.

"In Plato's allegory, we're supposed to be the ones watching the shadows on the wall, you know. Like our reality is just shadow-play... or that's what we mistake for reality. But what if we aren't even the watchers? What if we—what if we're the shadows. Just shadows." He lowered his hand. "You know, ever since I was a child, I walked around with the oddest feeling that I wasn't alone in my own mind. I thought I was always being watched, you know, so even as a kid I used to close the blinds on my bedroom window, and I slept on the floor beneath it so that, if someone were outside looking in through the window, they wouldn't be able to see me. As I grew up, I outgrew that, but the feeling never left, you know what I mean—like I was being watched. Like someone other than me was privy to my inner thoughts, or, or, or judging down to the smallest, most insignificant stuff. As an older teenager, I caught religion. Sorry—caught, like a disease. Ha! It made sense to me, if you know what I mean... God. Maybe that's what I felt. It was God. Later, I thought it must be a passive aspect of my own conscious-ness. The thinker behind the thoughts. The fundamental sense of self, you know... it had to be that. It's like when I look back on my own life now, I can see the, the, the shape of it. I can see how every change I made was just revolving around that sense that I wasn't really alone in some hard-to-explain, metaphysical way. It caused me so much anxiety, oh man, it did. But meditation, and, and that peaceful stuff, that started to bring things together, I guess. That's how I discovered your wife's writings, the books she published on human consciousness, the, the first ones incorporated a lot of Eastern philosophy, and that's what was helping me, that's where I was in my life. Then you and I met, and… and you don't even remember, do you. That's not your fault. That's not anyone's fault. It's mine, maybe, for how far I went."

"I remember my wife," I assured him. "And I remember most of her writings. There must be hope I can remember you, too."

The man shook his head and resumed his haunted staring into the fire. "What does it matter, anyway. Not long before your wife disappeared, I sat in a meditation session, the longest I'd ever done. I thought about something your wife had been working on, something about the primordial mythologies of civilizations mostly lost to time and obscurity. Do you remember?"

By now my entire body, not merely my mind, burned with curiosity. I knew what he spoke of, but those memories were still faint.

"In this way," said the madman, eerily calm now, "your wife either uncovered or, perhaps, translated such names as Katalpa, and the Dusk, and the Ocean of Hali. Names that once had great meaning, and which we can only guess at…. we explorers of an unreachable history and primordial reality, like small things in total darkness, wandering around with our minds which we assume are capable of great intelligence and great understanding, but which are just the smallest of candles in the total dark. When I sat and descended into deep meditation, I… I experienced an awakening unlike anything before. The sense of an awareness of my own mind, a stepping out from the immediacy of my own thoughts. And the peace that comes from conscious breathing, how the rest of the world—and not just the world, but every person—feels like an extension of yourself. Not just like you're a god or the center of everything, but that you are truly, by definition of being alive and being self-aware, you're connected to everything else. Underneath your sense of identity, there is a deeper self, a timeless self that was always there and will always be there. A self that sits behind all human consciousness, and every individual person is an expression of that fundamental self. That is what I felt deeply aware of in my meditation. Such a simple access point, you know what I mean—like a skeleton key that pulls open the door of the everyday reality of our perceptions, revealing the truth underneath."

The madman was smiling, and there was the tension of joy in his voice, but his trembling grew worse, and suddenly he looked upon the fire as though it showed him visions of unimaginable horror.

When he managed to speak again, his voice was so strained—like rubber stretched to its limit—I thought he would break into hysterical screams at any moment.

"What normally comes of these rare moments of transcendence, as in what mystics call an awakening, or ascension, or a transcendent experience, you know… what normally comes is joy. Peace, you know what I mean? It felt like that. All my life I'd been driven by a need for answers, and this felt like the answer. Finding that place inside of me that is timeless and unchanging, a serenity sitting beneath all the loneliness and chaos and hurt and… and aching, yes, aching, of life.

"But then, Terry, I felt something else. Something deeper."

The madman became hysterical then, sobs mingled with wheezing laughter. He even collapsed beside the fire and appeared to convulse, as though the victim of sudden seizures alongside the laughter and the tears. But he did keep speaking. And as I record this here now, the words ring in my memory, causing my hand to shake so that the words scrawl unevenly across the paper.

"I felt, then, that the serenity of this realization was a projection. My own projection. I was looking for an answer—and what do you know, I found one! And it was the one I wanted! Better, even, than what I could've hoped for. An awareness of a sense of cosmic order, as close to divine providence as a non-religious person can get. A feeling of the self as infinitely connected to all things. Oh… but it was my projection. It was the culmination of my hopes, my wishes, my desires, so that's what I saw and what I felt. Serenity, unity, peace. Transcendence. Connection. Why do you think we fall in love, or invent religion, or abuse mind-numbing substances, or project our flimsy, illusory perceptions onto the blank void of existence? Because, otherwise, the deeper reality would be unbearable. We need our illusions, our opiums, the narratives we plaster over the fundamental chaos of life in order to be able to go about our days with senses of purpose and importance, so that we don't lose our fragile minds and, perhaps, kill ourselves out of sheer horror or, or, or infinite boredom.

"The phenomenon, the mystery of human consciousness itself is just… it's this paltry side-effect, a hallucination created by existence driven to irreversible insanity so that it dreams a dream of reality as a way of coping with that unimaginable horror, a dream of sentient dust that at any moment could just end and there would never again be anything like it.

"You think you can find Alice here, don't you? That you can escape this place and forge the life you were supposed to have? We are nothing, Terry. We're shadows cast upon the wall at best. Not even fucking three-dimensional. When I stood before the Ocean of Hali, I'm telling you I saw it. The Ache. The heartbeat of Katalpa itself, and… and what it is ever hungry for. I saw. We like to think we're, you know, special. That we have souls, that we're individuals with agency, free will. We have, oh, *good energy*, you know, *good vibes*, and our lives mean something because maybe we'll be remembered for a couple generations of equally worthless and pathetic humans, or we thought we experienced some transcendent bullshit because we one time took a dose of LSD at a rave in some canyon on our insignificant little planet. Tell me something, humor me. You know those little insect things that ants like to farm? Aphids? Tell me, Terry-fucking-Forgaill, important human on planet Earth. How many aphids have you been impressed by? How many do you remember, you know, how many left a lasting impression on you? Read any interesting books written by any interesting aphids, Terry? Do you think any other aphids on any other planets in the entire universe ever look up at their night sky and wonder if they're alone? Do you think any specific aphids are gonna be remembered throughout history? Do you think they think they're special like we do just because they exist and are alive? Do you think aphids—or the ants, for that matter—do you think they labor under the illusion of having free will, the way we do, within their minuscule little lives and their inescapable programming? That is, if they even have thoughts. I mean, if they do… would you be interested in knowing their thoughts? Do you think there's anything to be learned from what an aphid thinks about? We're not just unimaginably small, *unimaginably small*, Terry. Jesus Christ. We're also profoundly delusional, especially when it comes to how interesting and how important we think we are. But what's the alternative, right? Lose our minds in the face of our own insignificance? Like the fabric of existence itself, dreaming reality to avoid the insanity. We do the same thing in our own passing little aphid lives.

"And, and, and we're alive, oh, we have, we have consciousness. But it's not what we think it is. I mean, we think our thoughts are our own, but ask certain neuroscientists and they'll tell you that cognitive agency, mental autonomy, is a myth. We're a collection of reactions burdened with self-awareness. Consciousness is the dream that existence is having to avoid being consumed by the primordial chaos. And it comes from there." The man gestured vaguely behind him, to some unspecific beyond. "Consciousness hurts, and it aches, all the while it's still an alleviation of some higher, supreme, fundamental nightmare. People like you and me, we feel entitled, like we deserve to live the lives we want, like something went wrong and we're living with a hole inside of us that we hope can be filled. But it's not that something went wrong. It's that to exist at all, to be conscious, *that's* what's wrong with the world. The emptiness any of us feels isn't an exception, it's the rule, when the very thing that makes us self-aware is the thing that's wrong. And we think we're so important, and so intelligent, so capable, when the truth is, our very consciousness isn't even our own. We're the illusions, we're the shadows. Meaning is a story we tell ourselves in order to avoid the constant underlying *boredom*, and the great, gaping emptiness, which is what it is to exist. Some of us are lucky that we can trick ourselves into thinking we're happy for most of our lives. Human consciousness is a dream, a paltry veil tossed over the nightmare—*and this place feeds on it.*"

For now that is all I can write. I must try to sleep, though how that'll be possible with those words echoing through my mind, I do not know.

Entry 13

The madman was nowhere to be found this morning—if it can be called morning, though it feels to me like perpetual evening—and so, as before, I will press on alone.

There was an insanity to the man, true, but to dismiss his words as the babbling and raving of insanity would be irrational. Comforting, perhaps, but irrational.

Alice, you often spoke to me, and at great lengths, about what you called the impenetrable frontier of our own consciousness. Sometimes you wouldn't shut up about it, so there were times when I hardly listened. But sometimes I did listen. I asked questions. I marveled with you.

Is there something wrong with the world, and is it us? Are our lives not dreams, but nightmares that are nothing but thin, pulsing membranes spread across the fabric of reality itself? Is there something behind it all—behind everything—and could it be darkness, not light?

Is that what all this is?

Entry 14

Through the fog and the trees, I see the shapes of things—some of them clearly people, some massive, hulking shapes—and I can hear what must be the sound of the Ocean of Hali. It sounds, to my ears, as soothing as any coastline, but rising above it is a terrible chorus of voices. Some of them are chants and prayers in frantic unison. Others are moans, the kind made by someone in such acute pain—physical or emotional—that sound escapes their lungs involuntarily. And others, still… I hear what seems to be people being strangled. It must be. Either that or violent suffocation, gasping for breath but not finding any to take in. I swear I hear the sound of gurgling and choking, what must be strangulation, beneath all the other commotion along those shores.

Moving toward that, my body resists my will to press onward; it feels as though massive weights are chained to my boots.

Entry 15

Earlier I came upon a small river, so similar in size and flow to the Tullapa River of my childhood—where I first met Alice—that I was struck with a strange sense of unreality, to find something so familiar in this unnatural place. I followed this river a long time, only to then come upon a rise, and the water flowed uphill.

At the top of the hill, I caught my first glimpse of the waters of the Ocean of Hali. A low, silvery mist clung to the waters.

It was here, where the river flowed downhill again, that I received my answer about the sounds of strangulation.

God… it troubles me even to write this down.

A man was kneeling on the banks of the river, leaning over across the water as if trying to see something below the surface. He appeared not much older than I, his hair medium-length and graying along the edges; he wore a simple flannel shirt and slacks. And he was crying.

I called out to him. He seemed entranced by the water, and something in my chest felt strongly that, despite how comfortingly familiar the river appeared, drawing too near to it was a bad idea, so I called out to the man and began to jog toward him.

He bent farther down until, literally, his face was caressing the lapping river's surface, and I think he drank from it… and then he jumped backward with such force that he must've given himself whiplash, and fell onto his elbows and tailbone. From there he continued to crawl away from the water. At first the man screamed, but then he began to choke for air.

I saw what was wrong only seconds later.

Tentacles were spilling out from his mouth. *Tentacles*, is what I at first thought. Long, boneless, bloody limbs had forced their way out from his throat. First one, flopping from his lips, and then a number of others spewing down his chin, onto his chest, some squirming up at his face.

With one hand he clawed at his own bulging throat; with the other he grabbed at the tendrils, attempting to pull and tear at them, but each one he grasped merely slithered out of his grip or else pulled back with equivalent strength.

I saw his eyes. They were wide, confused—horrified and confused. I'm ashamed to confess that I stood there, unmoving, wanting to help but paralyzed by fear of the possibility that this could happen to me. The man had scarcely touched the surface of the river, and this is what happened to him.

The wet sound of his choking and gurgling soon ceased; his eyes went blank, staring upward at the roofs of the dark trees.

And then his body began to bloat and derange from the inside, as if the tentacle-things were filling his body with some unknowable, unthinkable substance. The man's belly bulged as though he'd become severely pregnant within seconds, but the expansion forced itself outward beyond recognizable human function, and it spread to his chest, beginning with lumps and tumors, and then I heard meaty snapping and cracking. His bones were breaking from the expansion of his body; his cartilage was being stretched and then snapped and mutilated.

His arms ballooned and writhed, as did his legs, growing in size and length. Even his neck and his face: from disfigurement to exaggerated, impossible, bloated obesity.

When at last this process was finished, the man lay inert, a corpse. And then he sat up with a terrible urgency. I shouted and stumbled back; my skin had coated with sweat, my heart raced. Whereas before he had been no taller than I, the man now stood what I assumed to be over ten feet tall. His body was mountainous, his stomach alone like a riverbed boulder but snaked by purple veins across the now gray skin.

He turned to look at me—so tall, he had to look down to meet my eye. The man, I was sure, was dead, perhaps controlled by those spewing things, but he looked right at me through what were surely the gray, sightless eyes of a corpse. At least, I hope he was dead. To think he could have survived all that, kept just alive enough to be aware.

And then he turned and began trudging on titanic legs toward the Ocean.

Alice, listen.

I once believed in God. Not the gentle, optimistic-to-the-point-of-fantasy God of modern day Christians, but the old God of wrath and great power, a God who demanded love and devotion and fear in equal measure. The God capable of killing the firstborns of Egypt. When I could believe in the theologian God no longer, I turned toward the possibility of unnameable forces in this unknowably vast universe far, far greater than us. And I imagined, with some directionless hope, that this force might be, if not benevolent, then perhaps indifferent. I saw and sometimes felt the potential for beauty and joy in this small life of ours, and I thought, if there is a God, even if he has nothing to do with the world beyond its creation, then there is, perhaps, a kindness, a light that shines through the fabric of reality.

I don't think I can believe in that anymore.

Entry 16

I have stood here, beside the river, for what must be hours, not so much unable to move as, perhaps, unwilling.

I can't feel you, Alice. In my heart I carry not even a vestige of the hope that once drove me to find you, to find answers about what happened to you, and no matter how I reason with myself, the sense has overtaken me that when I address you by name here in this journal, on this page—right here, right now—I am speaking only to a memory.

In the side of a massive tree trunk, I happened to notice words carved by either a knife or sharpened stone: *Beware all comfort and warmer emotion. Oblivion waits in Katalpa.*

These must be the words of the madman, who was, when I first met him, weeping and trying to carve something into a tree. If I go any farther, will I ever come back? Does it even matter anymore? In my head, so vivid it haunts me, memories of standing between cluttered shelves in a used bookstore with Alice, watching her mouth and her eyes as she tells me excitedly about whatever paperback is in her hand and how she loved it, how it inspired her. Oh how I just wanted to kiss her then. Memories of being a child aloof to the aching of life to come, asking a girl my age—before I knew her name—what she was doing out here by the river.

When I look up from this page, I see the fishergirl crouched on a boulder, fishing-rod held idly. I've tried getting her attention, though I'm not even certain this is possible. Like I once did, she inhabits a space dangerously close to the Borderlands. I wonder what unplaceable longing calls her here.

I must press on.

Entry 17

There's something about the mists across the waters of the Ocean of Hali that makes me think there's no water at all. As if the Ocean isn't there, it's just that I perceive it as an ocean, I look and see strange waters because that is what my mind conjures to make sense of it.

As much as I feel compelled toward the shore with the others—dreamers, walking corpses, wanderers—there's a part of my mind that refuses the call. Perhaps that part of my mind is what remains of my reason, my rationale, my sanity.

Looming far off, there is Katalpa. But I cannot describe it. I don't mean that I choose not to describe it, or that its physical nature defies my abilities of description—nothing like that. I mean, it is both there and not there. My awareness approaches the edges and senses a shape, but there is nothing there. The sky ends in a blankness—not a darkness, not even a whiteness, just… void. The colors of the landscape and sky begin to melt away like an oil painting subjected to intense heat, before it all steps off into that nothingness like hills into fog.

But I see it. I see what the madman described as its heartbeat. I would not call it a shockwave the way he did, rather it's as though the very fabric of reality around it flexes and curls in a rhythmic pulse that radiates outward and becomes everything else. A heartbeat.

And when it reaches me, I can feel it. It's not merely a physical sensation of touch, it's literally a *feeling*, an emotion. This must be why, in her writings on the primordial myths, Alice came to call it The Aching Plane. The feeling of its pulsating heartbeat is an ache. It induces in me this feeling of shaken, inconsolable longing, so deep and so thorough that it casts a stony coldness over how it feels to have thoughts, to have a mind inside of a body, and to be. To be, as in to exist. I can feel everything that it is to exist, to have consciousness, to be aware and self-aware, like a flash of electricity through inert meat; dust that vibrates in cosmic heat and suddenly begins to dream; a swirling motion like water around a drain no longer needing a catalyst to continue its motion because it has its own momentum; a spark that becomes an ember and gives birth to a flame. Stagnancy, void, nothingness.

Nothingness.

And then *this*. Existence. And then existence opening its eyes and realizing it is conscious, it can see and feel and hear. It can become aware of itself.

And after the unknowable, tranquil stillness of nonexistence, do you know what it is to exist and be conscious? An aching. It aches.

Entry 18

I write this at my camp in the trees, atop the hill. I am afraid to fall asleep. Last night, caused by one of the dreams, I awoke standing up and far down the slope, as if I'd been sleepwalking toward the shore of the Ocean of Hali. Another few minutes and I would've found myself emerging from the tree-line, and then approaching the surf-tormented shore to join the other lost ones who find themselves drawn to the water, whether they're like me or are dreaming and have no idea where they are, or they're corpses—like the man I saw by the river, and the horror of what happened to him.

My dream was, again, a dream of warmth and comfort. I was following Alice as she led me along the banks of the Tullapa River. In the dream, it didn't matter if I tried to catch up to her or to reach for her hand; she remained always out of reach, perpetually ahead like a vivid mirage. But this did not trouble me in the moment. I knew she was leading me to a kinder place. It felt, somehow, as if she were taking me back to my childhood, back to my parents. Back to a time when loss was not part of the world, and life was full of small and exciting uncertainties, and each day was the entire future. And all I looked forward to was to meet a girl named Alice by the river, and then to return home at dusk because my parents were calling me home.

In fact, I could hear their voices calling me from across the quiet of summer evening. I knew, downriver where the form of Alice led me on, I would jump into my mother's arms, and we'd all sit around the dining table and talk about our days, talk about what was happening in town, the prices at the grocery store or the gas pump, the frustrations of the local elections. I knew I had so much I wanted to tell my mother and father, though I couldn't remember exactly what.

I think now, I would trade most of my adult life for those days. Except for Alice. I don't even know if it makes sense, but this dream seemed an expression of this yearning in my heart to take with me all that I love back to the simplicity I once knew as a child, and for that to be the life I live forever. It is a peculiar and errant wish, I know—a child's wish. An illusion.

But in the dream it felt so real. I could taste the dust along the banks of Tullapa River, could hear the water trickling and the low buzz of insects, and the fading warmth as the last of daylight seeped into twilight.

And then I awoke, alone, sleepwalking beside the replica Tullapa River, headed toward the misty Ocean of Hali.

I know I must resist the dreams, but, to confess with an honesty that disturbs me, I don't want to resist. I daydream about the dreams. Their respite is a shelter in the relentless horror of this place… and yet the better part of my mind wonders what cost do they extract.

Entry 19

I have begun the return journey to the bunker where I began. I'm not even sure it will be there, and I don't know what I intend to do next, but I fear this proximity to the Ocean and, even more, to the towering void that is Katalpa and its terrible heartbeat.

I keep seeing that fishergirl along the banks of the river. I keep trying to get her attention, I wave and shout and hurry toward her, and a few times she has looked up and appears to squint vaguely in my direction as though she sees me from an impossible distance. If, in the course of my journey, I am able to contact her and warn her away, maybe her trace will vanish from here. I don't know. Perhaps that is a lofty and unrealistic aspiration. When I was seeking answers about Alice, nothing could've stopped me from finding this place.

And here I am.

You know, I was once proud of my life. I felt I had accomplished—if not great, then good things; that is, I felt I had done good work, that I'd found and pursued a purpose, that maybe I had made a small difference in some people's lives. I felt, too, that I loved a good woman, and that she loved me in return. Happiness was never a goal of mine because I never truly understood it... but I suppose I was, for a time—in my own way—happy. I had forged a life I felt proud of, one I wished I could have told my parents about; I feel they would've been proud of me, too.

But my life was not even a chapter, not even a paragraph, not even a sentence or any series of words on a page in the story of the world. If ever I took up any space there, it has been erased.

And you know something—I'm not sure it makes any difference.

Entry 20

I'm leaving the journal here, in the bunker. If some poor soul finds it—if that happens to be you, reading this—take this as the gravest and sincerest of warnings.

As for me, I don't know where it would take me were I to tread onward, away from the Ocean and Dark Katalpa. But I'd be willing to find out, if not for the fishergirl. You see, I keep seeing her. She is not physically here, but she seems perched on the Borderlands, drawn inexorably here by something deep in her heart of which I know nothing. True she is one of an uncountable number of others whose hearts inadvertently find this place—enveloped by the essence of The Aching Plane—but maybe I was reminded of Alice when first I laid eyes on her.

Can I reach her? Would it make any difference?

Entry 21

It has been what I assume to be five nights here in the bunker. Today I set out again. My intention is to return to the Ocean of Hali, and then into the heart of Katalpa. I would not blame anyone for thinking I must be possessed by some rogue, insidious insanity. I am lucky enough to have reached the bunker alive, and with some semblance of my mind intact.

But I feel this ineffable, wild gnawing at the black matter of my brain and equally in my stomach and chest, like the emptiness of hunger, or the itch of desire, and it feeds on my sleep, it consumes my waking thoughts, as impossible to ignore as a beam of light aimed directly into one's eyes. I feel that malignant churning within me, and it's a curiousness, yes, but it's more than that. I'm not certain how else to describe it. But my proximity to The Aching Plane—Katalpa itself, the void of it both visible and unseeable—I believe the pulse, the heartbeat, is what did this to me.

That, and when I envision myself returning to the life I once had—the house, my books, the classrooms and lecture halls, highway traffic and coffee shops—I find my body filled with some unnameable resistance or revulsion comparable to actual terror. The boredom, the emptiness that I'd be returning to. It is literally sickening to envision.

If I somehow found my way back and resumed my life, I know it deeply: I would come to despair's yawning precipice, and I would step over. Despite what I've thought, in the past, about my own willpower and the miracle of existence, I don't think I could bear it. I would find a way to end my own life.

I cannot help it, nor do I want to. I must return to the shores of the Ocean of Hali. I must go further into that aching void, no matter the cost. I do this knowing full well, and of right mind, that I surely walk toward my extinction. But death, oblivion, is better than this itching, all-encompassing ache which flattens all else within me. My attempts at being rational, at telling myself that I could live again the life I once did—even if it must be without Alice—are like sandcastles built at the tide. Nothing more.

The dreams are my last respite. But as long as they are only dreams, they will never be enough.

10

Charlie emerged from her bedroom at five in the morning, dressed in the same clothes she'd worn the day before, her eyelids heavy, gaze far away, arms wrapped tightly around herself so that she clutched at her own shoulders. An urge sat in her body, roiling and thrashing like a caged animal with claws and teeth, and she needed something. Something, but nothing sounded right. A drink, maybe: a glass full of hard liquor that would burn its way down to her belly. A joint to smoke, the THC able to numb the reeling thoughts and flashing images in her head, or else relax her body and maybe let her sleep. Some part of her wanted to go to someone—Marion, or maybe Adrian—and give herself to them, and not have to think about anything else or feel anything else but them.

Her father's office door was ajar, soft yellow lamplight spilling out into the hallway. Charlie stood awkwardly in the light, looking in, wondering if she might be able to talk to her dad about all this.

James Louise was slumped forward in his office chair, asleep. On the desk in front of him were two items: a bottle of whiskey and an empty glass. The sight of that normally would've caused Charlie's heart to drop. Normally she would've felt sad and then probably angry, and would've needed to accuse him or at least interrogate him about it. But she felt only flatness. Her eyes fixed on the bottle.

On tiptoes she crossed the small office-space, past the bookshelves and the framed pictures of herself, and stood beside her sleeping father. She wrapped her fingers around the neck of the whiskey bottle.

It was full. The bottle wasn't even open. She pictured her dad sitting here with a glass and a bottle full of fire. She pictured him staring down into that glass, into its emptiness—which was all it had ever given him and all it ever would. She wondered how long he had sat here, at war with himself, before falling asleep.

Her grip on the bottleneck loosened and she turned to look at her dad. How hard he fought every day, how often he succeeded, only to realize it didn't get easier.

No respite, she thought, the words echoing from the journal. *Not even in dreams.*

Charlie let go of the bottle and put a hand on her dad's shoulder.

His breath caught up from the long restful rhythm of sleep. He blinked up at her, such piercing sadness in his eyes. It was true about the dreams. In the couple days it had taken Charlie to finish reading the journal, her father's condition had worsened. Sometimes he spent entire days with that faraway look in his eyes, as if dreaming while awake.

He put his hand on hers, looked to the bottle and then back to her. "I didn't," he said, his voice a faint whisper. "I wanted to, but I didn't."

She felt a pang, a tightening of emotion in her throat. "I know, Dad. Let's get you to bed."

He leaned on her through the hallway. "I was dreaming about your mother. You took us both out to Catalpa to your... to your favorite fishing spot. We spent the day out there in the sun."

She knew he meant the river, but still that word—Catalpa—made her feel in her stomach as though she'd stepped out over open air.

"It was like your tenth birthday, River Bug. Remember? Just the three of us out on the river together."

She helped him into bed and within seconds he was asleep again.

Minutes later, she sat down on the edge of the backyard deck, the whiskey bottle in her hands. A slight breeze wafted, unusually cold. Crickets sang. Charlie looked up at the stars and tried to conjure an image of nothing. She wondered what it would be like to look up and for there to be void, not even stars. As if nothing could be seen. The sky and the earth melting away into... would it be darkness? Gray? Or blinding light?

The images from the journal shuddered across her mind's eye and she felt herself shake. She hunched her shoulders and tried to make herself small. Her mind repeated a haunted feedback loop: *It's okay, I'm okay, it's okay, I'm okay, it's okay, I'm okay.*

Another part of her mind clung to the rationale that the journal could be nothing more than the scribbling of a person suffering from hallucinations and delusions, someone lost in an ocean of insanity. Or else a work of fiction. An elaborate and disturbing work of fiction.

The rest of her mind, however, could do nothing to stem the tide of nightmare images. She had seen some of those things—like the giant—with her own eyes.

She sat on the back deck beneath the stars, but really she was in a corner, hugging her knees to her chest, eyes clamped shut, rocking back and forth.

Charlie unscrewed the cap from the bottle of whiskey, raised the glass to her lips, and let the liquid burn down her throat. A few gulps in and she choked and sputtered onto the lawn. Then she raised it to her lips again and let it flow, flow, flow. The excess dripped down her chin and onto her clothes.

With a now desperately shaking hand she pulled the bottle away from her mouth, felt something hot and restless flare up, and she smashed the bottle against the edge of the deck. The bottle was sturdy; it didn't break, rather it slipped onto the grass. Whiskey glugged from the narrow bottleneck. She picked it up and held nothing back: this time, the bottle shattered with a thick crash, leaving her with a circular piece of sharp glass in her hand and blood from a cut across her palm.

Charlie collapsed onto the deck and cried. The tears fell in a strange silence. She felt emptied out of emotion, not full of it, and yet the fear and anxiety made her feel sick and alone and *empty*.

She sat, then, utterly still and staring forward with a blank expression on her face, occasionally sniffling and shuddering as if from cold.

In her mind, the last entry of the journal, this one from Marion.

Dear Charlie,

It feels wrong, in a way, to be adding an entry of my own inside this old journal, especially since Terrence Forgaill's story reads as unfinished. But think of this more as an afterword. This is just something I want to write to you, because leaving you alone to sit with all of this didn't sit right with me. Not that anything I say can really help with anything... oh well.

I wanted to say I'm sorry about our last talk. I did want to tell you the rest of the story, but I didn't know how, or I didn't feel ready... but then again, when you come back and want to hear the rest of it, I still won't know how, and I still won't be ready.

I know you mentioned that you reached out to Sam and Eric and Stephen just to let them know the news about me, and they've all sent messages, and Stephen handwrote a letter, and they want to come see me as soon as possible. And I know you wanting to hear the rest of my story isn't just about being curious. But I have to tell you something.

I don't think I'm supposed to be here, Charlie. I said to you a few nights ago that I've become a black hole, and I meant it. You read about what happened to Terrence Forgaill when he tried to return from that place, how it became the only thing left to him that was real. I look at myself in the mirror lately, or I catch a glimpse of my reflection when I walk around the house, and I feel as though I'm just my own ghost, haunting the landscape of a past that was the only life I ever really had. Things would've been easier, better maybe, if I had died out there in the woods years ago. You wouldn't have been trapped inside the endless grief of not knowing, and maybe you would've been able to let go. Not to say there wouldn't have been grief, but Charlie... I saw you in my dreams, though sometimes I'm not sure it was a dream, maybe it was a vision from that place.

The first dream, you were lost. You were wandering in dark hills where the ground looked scorched and the sky was dark red. You just kept wandering, calling my name over and over. I remember waking up from this dream the first time, wondering... is that what happened to you, after I vanished? Were you trapped inside your grief for me, wandering in a dark place, always looking?

But then the dreams changed. And I had different dreams of you.

I saw you free from the past in a way you never have been, and Charlie, it was so beautiful. You had a glow, like I remember how it felt to be around you when we were kids. You had mourned for me for a long time, and I knew you still thought about me and sometimes would still cry, but it was different. The past didn't haunt you, it didn't ache in your chest with so much power and hurt, and when you smiled it wasn't a struggle through the shadows of the past. You were free, and healed, and happy, and it was beautiful.

I can't stop thinking about it. How I wish it could be different.

That place has a hold on my heart that I can't shake. What I saw, what I experienced, what I lived through there, it's outside anything in my own worst dreams, and it isn't something that can be run away from.

I didn't start this letter meaning to say these things to you when there's nothing either of us can do. I think it's just, with you, I've never been able to be anything but honest.

I want to tell you, but words are so, so small... I'm sorry. I'm sorry for sharing this with you, my story, my pain, and this journal. I'm so sorry. When I tell you the rest of it, that has to be the end of it for you. The alternative is unthinkable. The alternative is something I would never forgive myself for.

Love,
Marion

PART 3

The Church

1

I know the way, said the man, or he seemed to say, even from this distance. *I know the way out of the aching. Come to me and I'll show you.*

Marion walked in his direction, alongside the river. Something looked wrong about how he waved at her.

She came closer to him, close enough she could almost make out the details of his face, could almost see his eyes. The sky grew dim, evening coming on, the sun sinking below the horizon as if in a hurry to hide from the dark.

A distant voice called. It was her mother's voice calling her name. *"Marion! Time to come home, Marion!"*

"Mom?" She opened her eyes in the dark. The river faded along with the image of the waving man. Marion tried to remember her mother's voice. She tried to remember her mother's arms. Blinking the dream away, she rolled on her side, facing the bed across from hers.

Peter Doloria was sitting straight up on the bed, staring at her. He wore no shirt, only a pair of silk shorts, and his hair was a shaggy mess.

She remembered where she was. This was the cabin. This was the nightmare. It'd been, what—more than months, more than possibly a year since she'd been to Catalpa Creek, since she'd seen Charlie Louise, since she'd heard her mother's voice? Could it have been years?

Marion sat up in bed, eyeing Doloria as though he were a poisonous snake. His eyes followed her with the unrelenting persistence of a painting. He'd been watching her sleep.

"What?" She held the sheets close to her body. "What is it?"

A hunger gleamed in Doloria's eyes. She looked at him with disbelief. He wasn't the same person anymore. He looked the same, seemed to have the same memories, but every day there was less and less of the man he'd once been.

Doloria nodded toward the bedroom window. "Have you noticed it outside?"

"What?"

"Outside. Have you noticed it?"

"Peter. I don't know what you're—"

"You don't know what I'm talking about?" He leaned slightly forward, teasing, tormenting. "You know, I guess I don't blame you. I was in denial for a long time, too. But Professor Forgaill was right—and I would've kept on denying it just fine, before it stared me right in the face and…" He rubbed his hands together, eyes growing shifty. "I think you do know what I'm talking about, girl."

She felt too stricken with fear to react to him calling her *girl*.

"Marion." His tone suggested he was scolding himself. "Marion." He lifted a hand to the side of his head.

Marion. Her mother's voice still fresh in her ears, a kitchen warm with the scent of vegetables and noodles and sauce simmering in canola oil…

"Marion," he said. "Marion. Marion. Marion." Veins stuck out from his forehead, from his neck. He slapped a palm to his temple once, twice. "Marion. Marion."

"Stop." She crawled backward on her bed, clutching at the sheets as if they could be a shield. "Stop it."

And he did. "Marion. It… It's out there." He pointed at the window. A second ago there'd been something devious about him, but now there was terror on his face. "The wandering ones, the survivors, they… they hid from it. They moved during the day, then at night they hunkered down and prayed it wouldn't find them."

"Peter, what are you saying? I don't understand."

Doloria leapt across the space between them, reached his arms out, gripped her by the shoulders. "Listen to me. It feeds on the dreams. It's drawn to them."

From outside the cabin there was the sound of the trees and bushes rustling.

"It's here," said Doloria, looking to the darkness of the window. "Marion, it's *here*."

She squirmed until he released her from his grip.

He shook his head. He was fading again, the more vulnerable and human side of him sinking underneath. He looked at her and it was like he peered at her from over a cliff edge only seconds before letting go. "Whatever I say to you, don't listen to me. You need to r-rr-rrr—"

He froze like an image captured by the flash of a photograph, his mouth stuck open. Sounds came from outside the window. Footsteps on dirt.

Something outside knocked against the side of the cabin, making the bedroom walls shake. Marion scrambled and collided with the headboard, the bed's sheets a crumpled ball she had gathered up to her shoulders.

Doloria lifted himself off his bed—slowly, slowly—appearing as though it required no effort at all. His mouth opened, closed, opened again, and the sound that croaked from his throat made it seem as though he'd forgotten how to speak and was trying to remember.

Marion watched him rise, and then she looked down at his legs. Doloria's feet weren't touching the ground, his legs no longer touched the bed; he was rising into the air as if pulled by invisible strings. His body began to shudder. It wasn't a muscular spasm, not a shiver or tremble; he *vibrated*. His body became a blur in the dark.

The sound from his mouth became a moan, and then a gurgle, a choke around words spoken through pain.

"I—I—I c-cc-cuh—couldn't f-ff-fff-face K-Kuuh—Katalpa, so th-th-the D-Duh—-Dream Eater f-ff-found me—"

Hard banging on the wall outside the cabin. The bedroom window rattled.

Doloria gurgled out a scream that sounded like the word *RUN*.

For just a breath, Marion looked up at him and meant to try and help him. But her eyes caught movement near the bedroom window, so she looked—

—and saw a hand appear through the wall. It didn't break through with force, no wood splintered away. The hand, extending from a sickly pale arm, slipped through the wall the way it would through the surface of a lake, as if the cabin were a hologram. The arm was covered in strange, spindly fur.

A shoulder emerged, the dip of a collarbone—

The room filled with the sound of skin *ripping*—thick canvas tearing apart. Marion looked up at Doloria. *Arms* were sprouting from his skin, slick and moist with pus and blood.

Marion tasted acid at the back of her throat as her stomach lurched.

Beneath the bedroom window emerged a face that was like a human's but stretched too long, mouth hanging slack, eyes wide but empty...

The sick feeling reached boiling point in Marion's throat, rising up her esophagus as her mind tried to comprehend the realness, the solidity of what her eyes were seeing.

She leapt from the bed. Before she turned to run, she cast another look up at Peter Doloria. He vibrated, a violent moan choking from his throat as his body became savagely deformed.

She looked down at the human-like, fur-covered thing coming through the wall. Trying to catch her breath, she lifted her hands up to her neck.

That's not fur. The thought was a crack of thunder in her mind. She remembered the words of Terrence Forgaill's journal like from a half-remembered dream.

Marion began to hyperventilate. She rubbed her hands across her wrists, up her arms to her shoulders, feeling as though her skin crawled and burned. If that thing touched her, would she feel its thousands of tiny hands all gripping at her skin? Some caressing, some grabbing, some scratching?

The creature pulled itself farther into the room—a diver breaking through water's surface in painstaking slow motion. Its slack, expressionless face stared, eyes bobbing across the room.

A second full-sized arm pressed through the wall. It moved with a sense of calculated certainty.

A third arm materialized, reaching through the panels of the bedroom wall.

A fourth arm.

A fifth.

A sixth.

Not legs, but *arms.*

Marion screamed, then turned and ran. There was no time to consider anything. All was deafened by the mental noise of her red panic as she sprinted out of the room, down the hall, across the living space. She shoved herself through the cabin's front door and plunged herself into the night. Sticks and twigs and rocks chewed at her bare feet with each step but she ran, eyes forward.

Her vision blotted with shining purple darkness, and she tripped into a thicket of brambles, felt scrapes and stabs in her arms and across her cheeks.

After pulling away from the brambles, she sat and took deep breaths until the faint feeling had left her head and she could see clearly again. She turned around to survey how far she was from the cabin, to make sure she hadn't been followed.

There was no cabin.

"What?"

She hugged herself and looked all around. It should've been *right there*, in this clearing, not even a hundred feet away, its front door still open from when she'd slammed her way outside. The living room lamps should've been aglow through the windows. Smoke should've been quietly drifting up from the chimney.

But there was nothing.

Marion stayed planted in one spot, arms wrapped around herself, lips trembling, a steady whimper rising from her lungs. Every second, she expected to hear movement, footsteps across the grassy floor coming her direction; she expected to see something like a human-sized spider crawling toward her, its many strangely-bent arms pulling a stretched and misshapen body forward—a body with an empty, elongated human face.

There was no sign of the thing. It had vanished along with the cabin and with Peter Doloria, but that meant it could be anywhere.

Marion turned away from the now empty clearing where the cabin had been. She looked out across the dark woods. To walk out there felt too much like being exposed out in the open, even though she was just as vulnerable here, where she now stood. It was cold. She had only her sweatpants and an old t-shirt, not even socks or shoes or a coat of any kind. And she felt as if she could barely move, so paralyzing was the fear.

She sat down. Time seemed to pass through her. She laid down and rested her head atop her arm, curled her body into the fetal position. She was still thinking how it would be impossible to fall asleep when at last she did.

She dreamt of Catalpa Creek. She dreamt of sitting on a rock there, in the sun, reading poetry, while Charlie Louise fished from the riverbank. From somewhere, she could hear her mother's voice calling her home, but it was a faraway sound, shrinking into the distance, nearly drowned out by the sound of the river.

If I could have this even just one more time, she thought, swollen with the warmth of it, *I would never leave. Not ever again.*

When she woke, it was morning twilight, and the trees of the forest were decorated with low mists. Something was standing near her, not even twenty feet away.

It bore a grotesque resemblance to some type of giant spider. Its extra arms stretched far too long and bent down like a spider's legs, but at the ends were human hands, not feet. Its body was a human's but bent and misshapen, its face too long, jaw slack, mouth open as if mid-scream. It was frozen, a statue of white stone, even though it appeared to be crawling right for her.

Marion jumped away from it, pulled from any residual drowsiness by the vividness of the thing's horror made so visible right in front of her.

She took no time to inspect it further. She began her journey into the forest, away from the many-armed spider thing. At every moment she was aware of it, casting constant glances over her shoulder throughout the days to come.

2

Looking out at the crowd of others in their groups—some tail-gating, some gathered by the ice chests, others pulling camping chairs around the bonfire—Charlie wondered how it was possible to carry on the way they did.

She could picture herself mingling with them the way she used to, taking part in the social games and sexual tensions and late-night conversations, but that had been months ago; it felt almost like a film she'd been watching about a different person.

I wonder if they'd act differently if they knew the chasm we're all balanced above. If they could just manage even the slightest grasp of how small this all is, how insignificant we all are. The senseless chattering and spinning through every day, all of us just doing what we can to try and stave off that deep, insatiable gnawing that sits in all of our hearts whether we can acknowledge it or not, the unshakable but subconscious awareness that there's something fundamentally wrong either with us or with the world.

In what felt, inside, like an emptiness that ached, Charlie didn't even notice the looks of concern Adrian often cast her direction. It didn't matter what they were doing, what the conversation around them was about, how many drinks passed between them; when Adrian looked at her, there was the usual warmth, but it darkened with worry. It was as if he didn't quite recognize her anymore and was searching her face for some familiarity.

Across her eyes, passing over like a reel of film: the mental images placed in her mind by what she'd read in Terrence Forgaill's journal.

Desolate souls wandering in dreams along strange rivers which led eventually to a mist-blanketed ocean.

A sky that grew dim through trees with black trunks.

The mutterings of a madman about dust losing its mind and dreaming a dream of walking consciousness scattered across billions of individual eyes, each pair deluded into belief of having a self.

She looked at Adrian and wondered what he might look like choking on bloody tendrils that passed through his esophagus and spewed from his mouth, his eyes turning gray as stone.

She looked at the people around the bonfire with their drinks and their words, and she wondered how they might look if their skin sprouted small hands or if extra arms extended out from their bodies so that they resembled hideously deformed spiders.

Marion had seen those things. Marion had walked through those places. Unlike the others, she had come back. Now Marion wanted to die, and Charlie realized she didn't blame her.

She thought of her childhood. How things had been back then with Marion, with the rest of The Renegades, those long summer days. Had it all been a trick? The fullness of it all? The simplicity? Would nothing like that ever come again?

Some of the people at the bonfire had started a conversation about children. One of the couples had a kid back home that was being babysat for the night.

"…and actually, I was the one," said the woman of the couple, "I was the one who wasn't sure about wanting kids. We talked about it pretty early on."

A lone girl, younger than Charlie, sat near them. She asked, "Why didn't you want kids?"

"Well really it scared me, you know, the idea of bringing a child into this world. Things are pretty fucked up out there, so it didn't make sense to me."

"And then I came along and ruined everything," said the woman's partner.

"Yep. And then he came along and I was like…" She gritted her teeth, laughed. "Sometimes you meet the right person and it just clicks."

"I mean yeah," said the husband, "just think about childhood."

"He talks about this all the time."

"Well it's important. My childhood, at least, was probably the happiest time of my life. Watching little Evie and seeing the way she looks at the world, it sorta reminds you how it's possible to look at things, I guess."

A young man in a dark hoodie who, up to this point, had been an active listener without engaging, tossed his opinion into the mix. "So what happened is, basically your evolutionary programming overcame your philosophical willpower. Sounds about right."

"Oh god. Can you not, Travis."

"It's true, right? Most people think they don't want kids, but usually it's just a knee-jerk type of thing. It's a different thing entirely than genuine antinatalism."

The lone girl cast a glance at Adrian and Charlie, rolling her eyes. "Such a downer, dude."

The woman with her partner, however, shook her head and leaned in. "No, Tiff, it's okay." Then, to Travis: "What's antinatalism?"

"Essentially it's the philosophy against having children."

The lone girl: "Are you an antinatalist or whatever?"

"So for someone who believes in that or thinks that way, they don't believe people should reproduce?"

"More like, it's morally wrong to reproduce."

"Jesus." The lone girl stood. "I need another drink." She walked away.

The young man, Travis, went on about his own version of antinatalism. By the time Charlie rose from her seat and walked away from the fire, followed seconds later by Adrian who, with concern on his face, had noticed Charlie growing pale, Travis had managed to turn the conversation toward preserving what was left of Earth's ecosystem and how humans were the most vile species, how choosing to stop procreating was a potential redemption for humanity.

Charlie meant to step away for a breath of fresh air, to put some space between the bonfire and herself, but she felt a painful churning in her belly. She put a hand over her stomach and moved to a tree, close to the water. With one hand against the trunk she keeled forward and threw up at the tree's base. When she was done, she gasped for breath between coughs, stumbled dizzily back, and then sat on the rocky ground.

Adrian was at her side in an instant, crouching beside her with a hand on her back, saying, "Whoa, whoa, you okay?"

She kept her body stiff, expecting the nausea to swell back at any second. To her own surprise, she felt tears on her cheeks.

"Sorry. I'm… I'm okay."

Adrian rubbed her back. "Scared me for a second there." He tried to smile. "Allergic to Travis's bullshit?"

"I couldn't listen to that anymore."

"I don't blame you. God. Travis is the sort of guy who uses his nihilism to justify being a dick."

"Yeah. For someone who claims nothing matters, he sure shows up to a lot of these things hoping to impress any woman who'll listen."

"Doesn't that make him more of a hedonist?"

"Probably. Or just a creep."

"You know, I wouldn't be surprised if he keeps a journal with serial killer quotes inside."

Charlie laughed. "That's… oddly specific."

"Oh, well it's not like I have experience with that or anything."

"No? Patrick Bateman isn't your sigma male role model, then?"

They met eyes amidst their laughter, eyes reflecting the firelight even from this distance, and they held onto that while they could. But even through his smile, a weight dragged from beneath Adrian's facial expressions. Charlie could almost hear what he wanted to say:

That he missed her, even though she was in front of him. That he missed this, this version of both of them. That being able to share this moment was akin to holding an old photograph of a happy moment in time—little more than a reminder of what had once been, what traces lingered of something long faded away.

She knew because she missed this, too. She missed herself, and not even a happy version of herself, but herself before all of this ineffable darkness.

While walking back to the fire, Charlie looked at him and felt a desire to simply tell him everything. To give him the journal and ask him to read it, ask him to share this burden with her. The slouch of impossibility. Chaos beneath the fabric of reality.

Do you know there's something behind it all, she wanted to say while looking up at the stars like toward a heaven she wished she could believe in. *Do you know it's been there since it all began, and it aches, it aches, it aches?*

Did you know this might all be a dream, a dream we're all having of being ourselves?

"Hey, you two," said Travis as they picked up their things, preparing to go. "How about this? It's what we started talking about. What if life is a simulation? Some scientists say there's evidence of that, like—"

"Like the Matrix," said the guy with his arm around his partner. He rolled his eyes. "It's not like a new idea or anything."

"Yeah, but what if it's true?"

Charlie sighed. "What does it matter? Whether it is or isn't wouldn't really make much of a difference, would it."

"What makes you say that?"

"You have to live it either way. Knowing whether it's a simulation or not doesn't make you any better or worse off than the next person."

Travis looked as if he wanted to provide a counterargument, but he stumbled over his words and scowled at himself.

"That," said the other guy, "is actually a good point."

Adrian and Charlie started to leave, headed for Adrian's car, but Travis—getting drunker by the sip, and strangely cheerier—needed one more thing.

"Hey, I'm sorry if you guys were offended by what I said earlier. About how having kids could be considered immoral."

"It's fine," said Adrian. "Interesting conversation, actually. She just isn't feeling well."

"Why do you think it's immoral?" Charlie asked. "I'm curious."

"Well I'm an antinatalist, is why."

"I figured. But I'm curious what *your* reason is. Why you personally feel that way."

"It's pretty complex, actually, but, like, think about what we're doing to the Earth, right? Personally, I just don't buy into the argument that individual people can make the world a better place, not when even just existing, you know… like paying rent, using resources, buying goods and services… just existing in this world is buying into a system that is too big to stop or slow down or change. We need to recognize that we're killing the Earth. We're the most dangerous animal, and if we stopped existing, the world would be better off. Wouldn't you agree?"

Charlie felt the eyes of a few people on her, especially Adrian's. She decided she would speak her mind regardless.

"And it's fine," said Travis, "if you do disagree. I'm not saying I'm right and everyone's wrong."

"I don't really see the point either way," she said, all self-righteousness gone from her tone. She spoke with her eyes dropping, realizing that she believed these things even as she spoke them. "Even if humanity stopped reproducing, it'd be for—for what? To save a small planet that's hardly a speck of dust on the cosmic scale? To call ourselves honorable? By what standard? The phenomenon of people—of us… Your argument presumes anything about this world has some inherent importance, but what makes any of us think we're capable of assigning importance to anything?"

Adrian shifted beside her. "Jesus, Charlie."

She noticed how her words had deafened the space around her, the silence broken only by the crackling bonfire. But whether it was the drinks or the nausea that made her feel numb to the eyes on her, she didn't know. In a lowered voice, she went on. "There are things in the world, which are just as real as any of this," she gestured to the fire, "that make our world seem so delicate and so, so small, and our lives so silly and insignificant, we may as well not even exist. Like maybe it'd even be… be better if we never evolved to be self-aware, so we wouldn't have to face the monstrous reality of existence."

"Dude," said the man of the nearby couple.

Adrian took hold of Charlie's arm and she gave no resistance, letting herself be guided toward the car.

Travis looked at her from his chair. Unlike the bewilderment and disgust of the others, what shined in his eyes was awe.

"What have you seen?" he questioned, rising to his feet, beginning to follow. "What do you know?"

Someone else at the bonfire circle's periphery: "No wonder she barely has friends. Good god."

And the lone girl who had dismissed herself to grab a drink: "Why would someone choose to think that way? It's so pessimistic."

Before Charlie climbed into the passenger seat, Travis approached the car. "You aren't just talking about stars and the size of the universe, are you. You've seen it, right? Or felt it? Katalpa?"

The look on his face as he said it was that of an addict pressing for a means to their fix. Charlie sat, frozen, holding his haunted gaze until the car pulled away and she could see him no more.

Adrian drove without music, his face in a resting glare, eyes watchful and reflecting the illuminated residential roads.

"Why'd you pull me away?" she asked.

"You're asking why?"

"I was answering Travis's question and you just grabbed my arm and pulled me away."

"I'm surprised you have to ask."

"What's that supposed to mean?"

He lifted a hand briefly off the wheel. "It wasn't obvious? The way everyone was looking at you?"

"What, so you were embarrassed for me?"

"Not like... It wasn't like that."

"You're welcome to explain."

"A few minutes before all that, you literally said you couldn't listen to him anymore. And you were sick and seemed… I don't know. I just thought you were…" He shook his head.

"You thought what?"

"I thought maybe you felt the way I did about all that stuff. I honestly thought it was ridiculous. But then you started talking." The coldness in his voice was enough to chill any heated resistance she felt. "I mean, do you really feel that way? All that shit you said back there?"

"I'm not sure what you're asking."

"I'm asking if you meant it. I knew you were pessimistic, but I've never heard anything like that before. It sounded…"

"Sounded what? Crazy?"

He made that open-hand gesture again, shaking his head. "You know, my aunt goes to your church—you've probably seen her, and she goes every Sunday, so she'll be there tomorrow—and a few days ago I heard her talking about the pastor, the one who was there at Marion's house. And she said the pastor's been saying some weird things lately. My aunt is weird enough as it is, but… what you said at the bonfire back there, it sorta brought that to mind. And I'm worried." He slowed himself down with a breath. "You're hard to be around, lately. Which isn't how it usually is, okay? At all. Anyway I'm worried about you. I know you're pessimistic, but it seems like you're actually getting worse."

They were pulling up to Charlie's house. Adrian parked against the curb.

She wanted to say what had been on her mind since the beginning of the night, when the conversations around the bonfire had turned toward the philosophical. She wanted to say, *We all like to think there's something special about the way we, as humans, perceive things. If you had read the journal, you'd understand.* But she couldn't blame the journal. Those things she'd said, she never wanted to believe in that. She wanted, maybe, to go to church tomorrow with her dad and to discover something like light, something warm, deep in her own heart, buried beneath all the years of pain and sadness and self-inflicted, self-perpetuated damage. She wanted a reason to smile when she closed her eyes when she was alone. It didn't have to be God, or philosophy, or anything grand, it just needed to be real. Something to hold on to.

That's what I wanted, but this is what I got instead. This shadow. This weight. Me, as I am—as unbearable and corrosive as I know I am, Adrian. You should go, and you should never look back, because I think I'm beginning to understand what Marion meant when she called herself a black hole. But you... I meant it when I said you were the first person in a long time who made me want to leave the past behind. You deserve better than to be dragged down because of me.

That was what she wanted to say.

"I'm sorry," she said. "I'm sorry, Adrian."

"Don't just be sorry. I'm honestly sick of hearing you say that. Just tell me what's really going on. I mean, you still haven't told me about that journal. Or why..." He made a sound almost like a growl. Locked eyes with her, an open, expectant look on his face. "This isn't gonna work if you don't let me in. It's okay to be vulnerable. It's *stronger* to be vulnerable, actually. To not just kill yourself slowly by bottling everything up."

"It's not like that."

"Isn't it? If you're just thinking you're sparing me something, you're not. You're really not."

"I know."

Adrian looked forward, shaking his head, and Charlie could hear the unspoken words.

When she watched him drive away from the sidewalk, she made herself imagine how it would feel if this was the last time she ever saw him. Once his taillights vanished around a corner, she turned for the house. A strange, sour stench wafted over her, a smell like skin and sweat...

Charlie screamed and fell backward, scrambling away from what stood on the front lawn.

It was a gigantic man, all clothes torn away, his body enormous, towering over her. Tendrils the color of pale flesh wriggled and flopped from the man's moist purple lips, and his suffocated gray eyes had no pupils. The hair atop his head was a familiar, shaggy light brown.

Charlie's breath came in hitches and she wanted to scream again, but when she recognized something about the man, the words rose up from her lungs. "*Dad?*"

No no no no no

"*DAD!*"

But it couldn't be him. He was inside, probably asleep...

On sea-legs she rose, gaped desperately up at those pitiless staring eyes, and ran toward the giant—then around it, giving the body a wide birth so she could reach the house's front porch.

The giant reached out for her with a titanic arm, its hand purple and flaccid at the end of its wrist. It turned its body as if to follow her. She felt cold skin touch her shoulder but she bolted away from it, whimpering and crying out as she ran for the porch.

For a moment—no longer than a stride or two—she saw trees ahead of her. Trees with gigantic black trunks and low mists between them. Then she slammed against the front door of the house and jammed a key into the knob. It was her car key. She cursed and rotated to the next one, which was either for the back door or—

"*HHHHNnnnnnnnnhhh—*" The giant moaned and gurgled behind her, laboring for air. Its feet shifted in the grass, squeezing the soil beneath as it shifted, glacier-like, toward her.

The key grated into the lock. The knob turned. The door opened.

Charlie all but fell inside, locked the deadbolt behind her, and darted for her father's room.

He wasn't there.

He was in his study, seated on the floor, slumped against his desk, asleep. On the carpet beside him, an unopened bottle of bourbon which almost looked black in the low light.

Charlie dropped first to her knees in front of him, then collapsed so she was sitting, but more so sprawled across the ground. She wept. With fear, with the draining adrenaline, with relief.

Her father, dreaming, made a face showing pain, maybe anguish, but then he smiled. It lasted less than a second but it was there. Maybe he was having one of those dreams again, of Charlie and her mother on Catalpa Creek in the summer. One of those summer days he wished had never needed to end.

The ache, thought Charlie, wiping tears, closing her eyes. *I've felt it all this time.*

The ache.

The ache.

3

Somewhere in the trudge of her wandering, Marion encountered a man.

She had lost what remained of any sense of time—minutes, hours, days, weeks—and so could not have estimated for how long she wandered. What she came to know was less a knowledge, more an awareness of daylight passing into darkness and eventually into night again, and this cycle repeating. She didn't record the number of times it happened, she knew only that it happened, and then it happened again, and then again. And she knew that in daylight it was time to move, to rest at varying intervals; but at night it was time to keep watch and to resist sleep. If she slept at night, she would dream.

The dreams were what drew the many-armed creature toward her. The Dream-Eater, as Peter Doloria had called it.

That was what Marion knew. Keep watch at night. Light a fire if she could. Don't sleep. Hold out until daylight. And in the daylight, move.

Only once did she attempt to move at night, but there were sounds in the dark, the sense of things moving just beyond her sight—things that were aware of her. So she kept to staying in one place when night fell. During those fortunate nights when she was able to light a fire, she crouched in the warm glow, stared at the flames, and recited as many poems as she could from memory. Most of those she knew all the way through were by Mary Oliver, W. S. Merwin, William Stafford, and Edgar Allan Poe. Even Poe's *The Raven*, for all its eeriness, was a comfort in the glow of the fire.

In comparison to the memories of what had happened in the cabin, the image of the ghastly, grim, and ancient raven perched above the poet's chamber door was a fire to warm her hands around.

I could be perched on the windowsill at home, she thought, *reading poems by flashlight or by the orange light of the streetlamp.*

And in this mental image, she imagined Charlie on the windowsill with her. Maybe Marion would read aloud to her. Maybe Charlie was absorbed in a book of her own: a novel or a poetry collection Marion recommended.

These were the memories, the sensations, that populated her dreams. Even in the cold that had become her life, she clung to the warmer feelings, the kinder thoughts. She told herself this would all make sense eventually. Maybe she'd make it to a safe place. Maybe she'd find something or someone that would give her answers.

But the snap of a nearby stick, or the rustling of a bush, or even the swaying of tree branches in wind, caused these mental landscapes to dissolve, leaving Marion alone in a strange, endless forest.

Soon, the forest began to change. What small comforts she'd been able to find in it, like the crickets singing to the night, or the sounds of birds singing to the day, even those things changed.

The trees were unlike any she'd ever known. They towered above all things, their bark strong and obsidian black. She heard no birds during the day, and the nights were empty of cricket song. What poems she recited that might reference these natural staples of the forest ceased to grant her any solace.

The forest no longer seemed natural. It didn't feel like a forest, it felt like a city. A city of empty streets and sickly quiet, the black trees like the skeletal corpses of abandoned skyscrapers.

I've read about this, she thought, pressing onward. Sometimes, from the corner of her eye, some of the massive trees didn't look like trees at all, no, they looked like *people.* Towering, brooding figures with eyes in shadow, observing her movements.

For a time, her feet were like open wounds unable to heal. She tried not to let the pain slow her down, but she limped through the forest. Eventually the skin hardened, grew tough and calloused. Her clothes clung to her thin, bony figure, the colors of the shirt and sweats faded, the edges reduced to scraps.

Charlie. If you could see me now, what would you think? Would you recognize me? The girl whose hand you held, whose lips you kissed?

Her bookshelves full of novels and poetry; her mother humming around the house; her phone buzzing with messages from The Renegades; her past life: inconceivable to her now.

Something occurred to her as she wandered like an ant through a corn maze; a thought that had haunted her, but which, until now, she'd been unwilling to face head-on:

She probably would never find her way back from this place. Never get to taste her mother's cooking again, or be wrapped in her mother's arms. She would never see The Renegades again. Never spend another night talking until morning with Charlie Louise.

Her walking slowed and she hugged herself as if chilled. But she pressed on.

*

After so long, Marion noticed how time no longer appeared to work as it had before. She was unable to locate the sun or any source of the unmoving daylight, and no matter how long she waited, it stayed the same. The light was low, as if approaching sunset. An evening that did not seem to progress.

The Dusk, she thought, and felt the dread creep in again. There was nothing to be done except keep walking.

*

Marion saw him from a great distance and approached with trembling caution, circling around to get a clearer look. A man knelt at the trunk of one of the massive black trees, trying to carve something into its bark using a sharp stone. His clothes were gray strips and loops scarcely covering his dusty, dirt-caked nakedness. Distance was funny in this place. Though he at first appeared not far—one or two tree-trunks away—it took several minutes before she came near to him.

His eyes were glassy and wide, and the skin around them was wrinkled, sagging, darkly discolored. His busy hair was thick and dark.

"Hello?" She held onto herself, stepping toward him. Maybe he knew more about this place than she did. Maybe he had answers.

The man hardly glanced at her. He continued his carving as though Marion had always been there, a mere distraction from his task.

"Are you okay?" It was an absurd question—he appeared as though he hadn't slept in weeks, if not longer—but she could think of nothing else to say.

"He's out there," he said. "The King. What Terrence Forgaill calls unity is only oblivion." He knocked his stone against the trunk, unable to penetrate or leave a mark. "This is only one of the layers."

She took a step back, but what began as fear on her face changed to recognition. "*You*... I think I know who you are."

The man kept trying to carve into the bark. He gritted his teeth, and a vein bulged from his forehead. "So you've felt it too, child? Me, I... I've always felt it. All my... all my life. I used to have one of those, you know. I used to, but, uh..." He tapped the side of his head with the rock. "Can't remember it. It doesn't remember me, either."

She pretended he hadn't said anything, which was easier than trying to make sense of it. "You spoke to him, didn't you? To Terrence Forgaill? I read about—"

The man's eyes widened and he shook his head with rigor. "They're arrogant, mindless *fucks*, the whole lot. As if the Dream c-can, can be—*interfered* with. As if we're anything more than afterthoughts, minuscule, tangential pieces of frayed carpet fabric— or, or, or blades of grass, deluding ourselves into thinking we might have a say over which direction the fucking wind blows. You know what I mean."

There was something in the gleam of the madman's eyes that made a siren alarm ring in her head.

The man cackled without humor. He leaned in, lowering his voice, growing somehow more serious than before. "Listen, child. Listen to me. I know you didn't know me before all this, so you don't have any reason to think there's anything but... *this*, you know what I mean? But believe me when I say, I can at least see *them* clearly—Terry and Alice and, and, and even the ones that came before them. The ones that *sought* this place. They caught a whiff of it from, from old writings, but I mean *old* writings. You know... ancient. Some of them not even on paper. All the way back when language wasn't an abstraction, when a word wasn't separate from the thing it described. They understood things about reality back then that have long, long been forgotten." The madman shook his head. "People like, like the searchers, the ones who were stupid enough to come looking for Katalpa—like the Tullapa people, sure, and myself, too—none of them ever stopped to ask *why.* As in, why is there a nightmarish, aching plane of existence tucked inside our own consciousness. Not part of us, no, no, it's the other way around. We're a part of *it. It* is as old as consciousness itself. *Way* older than humanity. As long as there's been anything at all that was alive in the universe, with anything that resembled awareness, or consciousness, there was Katalpa folded somewhere beneath the dream of that consciousness, vibrating through it— aching. You see?"

"No, I... I don't understand. Are you telling me... Are you trying to explain what's happening here?"

"Think about this, child. You should know about this. Some things we feel are *infinite.* Maybe you're too young. Maybe. I don't know. But there is a grief that can take such a hold over somebody that they never escape it. Maybe you've seen how a person can be so steeped inside their grief, it's like they're in another place, separate from the rest of humanity, and nothing you ever say and nothing you ever do can reach them. Sometimes they pull them- selves out of it, you know... sometimes they don't. Or they hang suspended in some limbo-state forever, between their present life and their memories." The madman clapped his hands. "It can be grief. It can be longing. It can be fear. It can be pain. It's there. And you're *here.*

"But don't let them fool you. The others, I mean. Just on the, on the periphery, the chaotic horrors crowd around the edges of the

Dream, *literally* impossible for us to visualize or, or, or comprehend."

Marion was backing away, shaking her head. Some of the things the man said simply bounced against her unwillingness to truly hear them; the rest of the things made it through and seemed to clasp onto her mind with claws. "I don't know what you're talking about. I don't want to hear this."

The madman's glassy eyes fixed on her, all the while he kept driving the sharp end of the stone into the tree's unyielding black bark. "Think about it. Think about why anything exists at all. Think about why we exist, you know, why we live lives, why consciousness cycles itself over and over, life and death and life and death and fucking life and fucking death. Why anything. Why this! Why, if not a last line of defense against what unthinkable, unimaginable, formless things exist outside of consciousness, outside the borders of what can be seen and felt and lived in." He let the stone drop to the dirt, lifted his hands up to his eyes. He pinched his bottom eyelids between his fingers, staring wide-eyed at her. "They want to pierce the fabric of the Dream. You know, like a pencil through paper, or a blade through skin. I can't imagine why they'd want to do that. Maybe… I don't know, maybe order insults them. Chaos desiring only chaos."

"I should go. I need to keep moving."

"There's a reason our minds are too small for it. We're barely even capable of fully understanding our*selves* as it is." Tears dripped down his cheeks, but he seemed on the edge of hysterical laughter as much on the edge of sobs. And he refused to let go of his own eyelids.

"I'm leaving. I'm sorry for disturbing you."

"If Katalpa and the ache is just that outer chaos, or darkness, or whatever it is, leaking into the dream of consciousness… what's in that darkness outside space and time? Why would we need the dream of consciousness to keep it at bay?" He laughed high and wild and—

—and then he yanked down on his own eyelids, exposing the fleshy pink and red beneath, and the bulging shape of his own bloodshot, veiny eyeballs. *"Do you think there're monsters, primordial things that dream of universes? Is time just the breath of their slumber? Could they swallow our memories without even a second thought—if they have thoughts at all?"*

The madman yanked down again, and at the spurt of blood and the sound of wetly peeling flesh, Marion screamed and ran. Her vision dimmed as her mind caught up with what her eyes had just seen, but she ran—and heard him continue speaking as if nothing out of the ordinary had happened. As if he hadn't mutilated himself in front of her. "Beware your warmer, kinder thoughts, child! Oblivion waits in Katalpa!"

*

She ran until her lungs were burning and her legs—carrying her up a sudden, steep hill—would obey her no longer. The hill began to level out but she didn't reach the top; she put her hands on her thighs, arms supporting her weight, and sucked for air.

As she regained her breath and the burning in her lungs receded, she heard voices. There were people at the top of this hill. *People.* Their voices weren't inhuman, nor lilted with madness. They sounded simply like people.

Marion crept up to the top of the hill, having to use her hands. The voices had died down, leaving just one voice. It was familiar to her, somehow, in a vague and distant way.

A man was preaching, coming to the end of a speech or a sermon.

"And then I was lying down in thick mist, on solid ground, and I could hear a sound like someone sobbing. But it was... I'm not sure how to describe it really. It was like someone so assaulted for so long by some unbearable, unending grief, completely powerless against the reckoning of their own emotions. I remember thinking: That is the sound that Job's heart must've made when he sifted through the wreckage and dust of his home and his family—his wife, his children. I remember thinking that I knew at least a semblance of that unbearable pain in my own heart. I felt it all over again every time I awoke from another dream of Darya and... and that golden time in my life. To think that all it takes is one random, senseless act of stupidity or distraction from some worthless idiot, and the life somebody else could've lived can be completely destroyed, just like that." The preacher snapped his fingers. "Gone. And the person whose fault it wasn't, the innocent party, their life takes a sharp turn down a completely different—and most likely darker—route. Like Job, holding the dust of all he'd loved in the world, all he'd made. All because of a childish, petulant God making bets with Lucifer to prove a point from all the way up there in his Heaven. And then I was here. In this place. And eventually, we all found each other."

When the speech ended, the voices picked up again. There were many people, all of them enthusiastic, all erupting into their own praises and stories in wake of what they'd just heard. If anyone might have answers for her, if anyone could make sense of everything she'd been through... wouldn't it make sense if it were a preacher? Somebody who could speak with such confidence and eloquence?

Marion began to peek her head up to catch a glimpse of the level ground and the people there, but somebody was approaching.

First she heard the footsteps, and then a man came into view above her.

"Child," he said, dropping to one knee and extending a hand. She knew his voice from what felt like a long time ago. It was unmistakable now.

"Pastor?" she gasped, all her fear draining away. "Pastor Joe?"

Joe Correy gave her a curious look. "You know who I am?"

She took his hand, nodding, wiping tears away. To come across other people here, in this unthinkable landscape… and for one of them, at least, to be familiar: the pastor from her mother's church. It was all she could do to keep from crying.

"You'll have to explain… I'm sorry I don't quite remember you." He helped her to her feet, held her by the shoulders. "Come meet the others. You've arrived at the perfect time, it's almost uncanny. *Providence*, I'd say, if I were still a praying man."

4

───────────

In the dream, Charlie had been on a couch with Marion, cuddled close together in a house darkened by a power outage. Heavy rain pelted outside, tapping on the living room window, pattering the roof's shingles. Her father had brought them mugs of hot chocolate while, in the other room, The Renegades were setting up some sort of game for everyone to play. But it was just Charlie and Marion for now, sharing a blanket on a couch with the heavy rain outside. They laughed about something. Laughed and held eye-contact that way, sparkling with light.

To awaken from the weightless sensation of that closeness, that candle-warm contentment, into the frigid isolation of her bedroom with the weight of her reality pelting down like rain, to awaken into this was a cold cruelty.

She sat for a long time at the edge of the bed, not noticing as the dim light through the window brightened from gray to gentle blue, to the first splashes of sunrise.

It was Sunday. The time on her phone showed an hour and a half until church. She pulled herself to her feet, intent on preparing breakfast for her father, even though every step felt like an uphill trudge.

After setting down a plate of eggs, sausage, and hash browns for him, Charlie went to check on her father. He was normally up by now, but considering the desolate emotional state he'd been in last night, she wasn't surprised he would sleep in. She even thought, *Maybe I should let him sleep this time, with everything going on.*

But her mind returned to a week before. The feeling of his hand on her shoulder gently pulling her from sleep. How he assured her he'd be fine going on his own to the service if she wanted to stay and get more rest. His caring, patient stare, his humility, after everything he'd been through.

And he hasn't started drinking again, she reminded herself. *He puts it in reach but he's resisted it so far. Despite the dreams. Despite everything.*

Which was better than she had done.

The truth was, she wanted to attend church today. Needed to, maybe. Even if it was a hopeless thing, she wanted to sit next to her father and watch him in the throes of willful devotion. The songs sung in unison, the scripture recited and expounded on, the silent moments of prayer, it all seemed sacred not for the reasons it was done, but for what it meant to do it.

If not God, thought Charlie, then the worship of God. The surrender.

At some point in her weekly attendance to the church, the services had become comforting, had formed a cathedral composed of sensation and familiarity around her.

So, she thought, even if her father didn't want to come, even if he needed to rest, she would go. Like he had for awhile: alone.

Charlie knocked twice, lightly, on the door of her father's bedroom. No response, so she cracked it open and peered in.

James Louise sat on the edge of the bed, dressed only in a t-shirt and boxer briefs. His cheeks, jawline, and upper lip showed thickening facial hair.

With concern on her face, Charlie went to him.

"Dad?"

His head tracked up to her but his eyes were slow to follow. "Hmm?"

"Are you okay?"

"Am I... am I what?"

"Okay? You look tired, Dad."

"Mmm." He nodded sluggishly, already trailing off.

"Have you slept?"

James squinted, lines appeared in his forehead. "Slept?"

"Yes. Have you?"

"I... I don't know. Don't really remember." He lifted a hand up to examine it, curled and uncurled his fingers. "I think I was... I was dreaming, but I wasn't asleep." There was fear in his eyes. Fear and bewilderment. Those eyes said, *I don't know what's happening to me, sweetheart.* Those eyes asked, *Do you?*

"I made breakfast for you. It's on the table."

"Oh..." He put a hand on her arm. "Thank you, sweetie. You didn't have to."

"I wanted to. I'm... um... I'm gonna go to church this morning. You can stay, if you're feeling—"

"No, no, don't—don't be silly. I'll come with you." He started to rise, reaching halfway out as if for her support. "Gosh, is it Sunday already, I—" One of his feet slipped along the carpet and he dropped to a sitting position on the floor, grunting from the impact, his body rattled. Charlie tried to catch him but merely dropped with him.

James Louise broke into tears. "God, Charlie, I'm sorry."

"No, Dad, it's fine. Are you okay? Let me help you up. I can start the shower if you want."

He nodded, seeming, for the moment, like a toddler. When he cried it was normally a restrained display, but he couldn't hold any of it back this time. His breaths were hiccups and the tears flowed freely. "That'd be… that'd be nice of you, Charlie. I'm sorry."

"Don't apologize. It's okay." She went to the bathroom, got the shower steaming warm, and returned to her father. The tears still fell but he'd gotten his breathing under control. His balance, too. She supported him to his feet and he had no trouble walking with her.

A memory flashed in her mind of years ago, when she'd done this very thing under different circumstances. He'd been drunk, unable to walk, weeping uncontrollably and cursing every thought in his own mind. She had started the shower for him, but that one had been cold to sober him up—something for which he'd cursed her, too.

This time, as she was leaving him alone to shower, he looked at her with sorrow still glassed over his eyes, enough to give her pause, and he said, "I don't know why I keep going back to the past. It's like I left some part of me back there, a part of me that was waiting for… for an ending, maybe, a resolution. Or just *something, anything*… a sign that I could pick up and move on. And that unfinished feeling, I don't know why I can't let go of it. I don't want to dream about her anymore. I just… I want to be here with you."

She didn't know what to say, and the emotions that rose up in her throat made it difficult to speak. She said, "I know, Dad. Me too."

Before they left, Charlie returned to her room for her phone, but she'd forgotten to plug it in last night and it was dead. She left it on the nightstand to charge. If there were any messages from Adrian, they could wait until she came back.

On her way out of the room, she stopped and looked at her desk. The one photograph was still facedown.

Wait. There was a reason I did that.

She lifted a hand to set the photograph up again, but froze halfway to it. A week ago she had almost set the frame upright, but faced it down at the last minute; she hadn't felt ready yet to face the reality it reminded her of. What was the reason? She pressed her mind, trying to conjure the photograph and her memory of why it was facedown, but there was nothing. Her thoughts came up to a cliff's edge, and then void. Not a barrier, but a stepping off, a blankness.

It's just a picture of me on the river. Eric or Stephen took it, and I was laughing about something... the water was cold, or I was making fun of them for not wanting to come in with me. Right? It's just a picture of me when I was twelve, on Catalpa Creek. So why did I put it facedown?

"Charlie!" Her dad called from down the hallway.

"Yeah?"

"If you're driving, let's take my car. Save you some gas."

"I don't mind, Dad."

He came down the hallway, smirked at her from her bedroom doorway, and tossed her a set of car keys. "My car. Ready to go?"

"Ready." She followed him out, the photograph already going faint in her mind.

5

When Marion entered the camp, led by Pastor Joe Correy, the inhabitants all lifted their heads to look. They carried themselves as if undead. There were tattered canvas tents, awnings constructed of leaning sticks and logs, and the beds were simple mats or nests, most of them out in the open. This wasn't a permanent camp; they probably moved—if not every day, then every two or three days—and Marion didn't need to guess why.

The people who lumbered vaguely, roused from whatever they'd been doing by the sight of a stranger accompanying Pastor Joe, they bore the drooping raccoon eyes of sleep deprivation and the wandering stares of daydreamers.

Marion was the youngest. No one in the camp appeared younger than thirty, made to look even older by the weight of prolonged existence in this merciless landscape.

"Everyone." Pastor Joe stopped in the center of the camp. He spread his arms out in a holy welcoming gesture. "Fellow seekers. I want you to welcome someone new into our company. Her name is Marion Del Rosario, and she isn't exactly a stranger. Although I don't remember her clearly anymore, she was once a member of my congregation, in my life before."

A few murmurs of affirmation. One of the men, an especially scruffy and raggedy one, actually clapped his hands before raising a fist and shouting, "Woo! Yeah!" Some of the others chuckled.

Pastor Joe pretended not to notice. "You've joined us at a pivotal moment, Marion. After dinner, we'll be setting off to meet with the Ascendant One."

"Praise his name," said a woman.

"We offer our silence."

"Behold the Dream, brothers and sisters."

"Yeah!" cheered the raggedy man. "Woo!"

The pastor rubbed his hands together. "You really have come at a perfect time. It must mean something."

"So there's someone waiting for you, where you're going?"

"Where *we're* going, yes. Some of them call him The Sacred One, or the Dark King. The madman of the woods called him friend and leader. Some of us here call him the Ascendant One."

"Who... who is he?"

Pastor Joe held out his hands, and all the others offered their answers.

"The First and Last."

"The Walker in Darkness."

"Heir to the Aching Throne."

"One who would pierce through the Dream."

"He is all of us," said Pastor Joe. "He's the one who'll show us the way."

"Salvation," said someone.

"Deliverance," said another.

"Yeah!" shouted the raggedy man, cupping his hands around his mouth. "Woo!"

Marion didn't know what to say; she felt as if she had no place. The people around her rocked with fervor and something like ecstasy. Her wariness remained, a tightness in her throat and at the top of her chest, but she saw something in all their eyes that she'd forgotten the look of: Hope. Something like hope, anyway.

Pastor Joe smiled at her. "If you have questions in your heart, Marion, he is the one to ask. Come. Let's break bread and prepare."

The people of the camp packed up what little they had. Within an hour they were on their way, leaving minimal trace that they'd stayed atop the hill at all.

Marion expected some of the others to ask questions about her, but none of them did, not even Pastor Joe. The group tread in silence except for the sounds of breathing and bare feet dragging and crunching along the forest floor.

When Marion realized the sky was darkening, she was unable to walk in peace, instead casting her gaze all directions. There was nothing to be seen, nothing alive that she could discern among the looming black trees, but it was too easy to imagine the spider-like creature and its many arms crawling its way down from one of the massive tree trunks, or emerging into view around the side of a thicket of bushes. A group of languid wanderers afflicted by the dreams would be like a beacon to that monster.

None of them, however, seemed to care that, with every step, time trudged forward alongside them. The sky grew darker, the air colder.

After awhile, Marion managed the nerve to ask the pastor how much farther.

"See that hill up ahead? He waits for us just beyond its slope."

She rubbed her heavy eyes, carried on with strains of effort up the hill. Seconds would pass in which her head seemed to reel. With every blink, her exhaustion reached out and clawed at her. When she looked around her, the others of the camp all wore stretched expressions that reflected how she felt, and somewhere in the murkiness of her mind where her consciousness dangled just above waking micro-dreams, there glowed the faintest warmth in knowing this was a shared experience. For the first time in too long, she wasn't alone.

That warmth lasted to the crest of the hill. When she reached the top, a few steps behind Pastor Joe, she looked down at the path that remained, at where the downward slope led, and Marion forgot all about the solace of shared experience. She felt the way she had all those uncountable nights ago when she'd turned around in the dark and saw there was no cabin behind her.

The pale gray light of dusk dimly glowed in the sky—light that was almost silver—and the likeness of a vast ocean presented itself through the far-off trees. She felt alone, but also as if eyes were fixed on her from somewhere she couldn't see. So many watching eyes.

She rubbed at her arms and shoulders as if to brush the feeling off her skin. There was a stream nearby, flowing down the hill. Headed toward—

The Ocean of Hali, she thought, the words sharp as icicles.

Pastor Joe pointed down the slope. "We're not far now."

"Wait." Marion pleaded. "We'll be... we'll be so close to the beach."

"Yes."

"And the Ocean."

An indecipherable smile touched the corners of his mouth. "There's nothing to be afraid of, Marion. We're safe together."

She shook her head, hugged herself tight. She felt lied to. If the look on his face was any indication, Pastor Joe had made this trek before. This was not new to him. She looked at him accusingly, wanted to resist going on, but Pastor Joe put his hand on her back and began to guide her down the slope.

The sounds of the ocean were dwarfed by the slapping splashes of a waterfall as Marion and the rest of the group reached their destination. Being this close to the Ocean, however, the feeling was more than just a thickening moisture in the air; Marion felt it in her bones: not merely dread, but a physical weight. *Depression,* she thought, having seen Charlie in its grip before. Like gravity had increased but only inside her own body.

Near the end of the trees, two small rivers came together and swirled into a glimmering pool, which spilled into a waterfall.

The group traversed the rocky slope, down toward the bottom of the waterfall. Marion kept her eyes down the whole time, focusing on her calloused feet, focusing too on staying awake. Her eyes were sticky, dry, and every blink was an embrace from the dark. Her thoughts were slippery and meandered down strange trails without sense or reason. She wanted this to be over so she could abandon these people. Maybe they were all experiencing the same fear and confusion and exhaustion as she, but she felt afraid. Maybe wandering alone, somehow, was better, was safer.

When the pastor stopped pushing her along, she stood with the others around the edges of the creek. She looked up to watch the waterfall feeding it.

We're too close. Her eyes following the splashes.

She let her gaze rise to the rocks from which the water dropped.

A person sat atop the rocks. Hardly more than a shadow in the low twilight, he watched the group from above, as motionless as the stones and the trees. He wore a wide-brimmed hat, beneath which spilled long, tangled dreadlocks. His eyes gleamed like two stars in the night sky: watchful jewels under the shadow of his hat. The rest of him was shrouded in darkness. Marion felt as though his eyes were fixed on her. Of all the others gathered here, he was looking at her.

Lines from Edgar Allan Poe echoed through her head.

"And the Raven, never flitting, still is sitting, still is sitting
On the pallid bust of Pallas just above my chamber door;
And his eyes have all the seeming of a demon's that is dreaming..."

She shuddered.

Pastor Joe lifted his hands, palms up, and the other wanderers did the same.

"We have travelled far to reach the Dusk," said Pastor Joe, speaking to Marion, "each one of us drawn by what sharp things pierced from in our hearts." He turned to look at the faces of the small, weary congregation. "Behold, Marion. We are in the presence of the only human in all of history to return from the heart of Katalpa. This is the man they call Terrence Forgaill."

6

In the church, the silence went on longer than it should have as everyone turned their waiting attention on Pastor Joe Correy. He had made his way to the front, beside the podium. As usual, he wore all black, but rather than a collared shirt it was something like a poncho made of cloth. He appeared more spiritual than religious —out of place, a single evergreen in an autumnal forest. The sunlight through the windows glinted off the perspiration of his forehead, and he rubbed his hands in front of him as if to warm them. An awkward smile appeared on his lips, vanished, appeared again.

He was nervous about something. He had never shown stage fright before; this was something else.

Charlie looked to her father, expecting they'd meet eyes and maybe smirk with some shared confusion, but James Louise didn't even seem to notice his daughter beside him. He was staring at the pastor, his expression that of blankly waiting, a cloudy absence of thought in his eyes.

She glanced around at the others in the pews, the familiar faces from around town. All of them sat erect, staring directly at the pastor, waiting in perfect silence. But this wasn't the silence of an enrapt congregation. There was something unnatural about it— inhuman, almost. Not one person appeared to fidget or shift around, no one's attention wandered, no one whispered to anybody in the back rows. It was as though somebody had pressed pause on the entire church all at once.

Is this real? Charlie took careful breaths as her heart rate picked up. *Is this really happening?*

She wished Adrian were here. He'd notice it and have something to say. Or Marion. Marion would have some idea, maybe, of what was happening.

Marion.

Charlie lifted a hand up to her face. *Marion. Oh my god.*

Marion was why the photograph was facedown on her desk. The picture wasn't just of Charlie, it was of the two of them, knee-deep in the waters of Catalpa Creek.

A sick feeling filled her stomach. She needed to get out of here. She needed to reach Marion and make sure she was okay, make sure she still—

The word that darkened her mind was *exists*—as in, *to make sure Marion still exists*—but no, she couldn't let herself think that way.

"Dad," she whispered, prodding at his shoulder. "Dad."

At that moment, however, Pastor Joe's nerve-wracked voice filled the church.

"Today," he said, "I want to begin by talking about faith. You, uh, you're all sure to find out that today's service is gonna be a touch unconventional, I guess is the right word, so I ask you to bear with me. Some of you have come to me over the past three or four weeks, voicing, um, understandable concerns and… and I don't want to say *complaints*, but doubts, maybe. And the last thing I want to do, as your pastor, is make any of you feel unwelcome here." He began to pace, each careful step producing a soft echo across the church's cavernous silence. "Faith. It's a word we use often, but sometimes I think we've, um, lost sight, if you will, of the word's true meaning. We say, *I have faith,* or *I practice my faith,* or sometimes *I have lost my faith.* I've even noticed, in everyday life, that the word faith is usually interchangeable with religious faith. It's an abstraction, practically meaningless—as meaningless as blind obedience or belief without evidence. That's how the modern world would categorize it: those who have faith are brainwashed idiots, clinging to superstition without the need for evidence. How many of you have had to defend your faith before someone who cites evidence, who takes a, um... a, uh, an *empirical* point of view, which reduces you to standing on nothing, no foundation except that one practically meaningless affirmation: *I have faith.* I. Have. Faith. But what does that mean? I don't mean a dictionary definition or the usual description. What does it really mean? To us? To us broken, battered wanderers in search of meaning and purpose and respite in this fast, merciless, unrelenting world that's so full of misery and loneliness and loss and sorrow?"

The church's silence broke with muttering and whispers.

The pastor went on. "You know, ever since I was young, my favorite Bible verse was the iconic one from Psalms. *Yea, though I walk through the Valley of the Shadow of Death, I will fear no evil, for thou art with me. Thy rod and thy staff, they comfort me.* That in itself seems, to me, a fundamental expression of faith. True faith." He paced over to the podium, rested a hand on either end of it, and bowed his head. "There's a man I want to talk to you all about today. A man of great importance, not only to all of us—in more ways than anyone may realize—but also important to me personally, because I knew him. I knew him both before and after his, um... *transformation.*"

"Amen," said someone in the crowd, and a few others echoed the word in solidarity.

"He said to me, once, that faith is a fire we create from hope. Faith is a wish, an act of defiance against what he called the Outer

Darkness. That was, of course, before any of us had ever heard the name of Katalpa, or of the great Aching Plane."

Charlie's whole body stiffened.

Pastor Joe spoke now without any awkwardness, and the congregation listened as if their attention were suspended on a high-tension wire. "I ask you all: Who among you hasn't longed for the past? Who among you hasn't longed for the return of simpler times, when life didn't seem so heavy, when, maybe, you had everything you ever could've wanted but you didn't realize it? I ask you all, today.

"Maybe what you miss is the angst and freedom and stupidity of adolescence, when you felt invincible, and your friendships were all you needed, and loud music. And the future never entered your mind. Maybe it's college, before you had a real taste of the daily grind of adulthood, and there was that bubble around everything and you could still be optimistic about things. Maybe it's a person, one person… the one that got away. Someone you yearn for, with whom it didn't work out even though you know it could've, maybe, if the timing was right, or if you had another chance. Maybe you've had profound loss in your life, and you long for the days when those people were still alive—your parents, your closest friends, your extended family members, the people you never imagined you'd one day have to live without. Or maybe it's simply the way the world used to be, maybe that's what you long for. Simpler times. When the world was slower, friendlier, familiar, and you knew where you fit into it."

To Charlie, it seemed the pastor's eyes gravitated to her. Even when his gaze swept across the attentive listeners in the pews, it always found her again.

"Whether you're willing to admit it or not, I believe this is something all of us can relate to. The longing to return to another place, another time, and to the people there. Or the yearning to go back, to make the choices we were too afraid to make." His voice broke across those last few words, and he aimed his gaze downward and cleared his throat. "In John, it is said that we should not be of this world. To belong in the world is to deny that God made us for His kingdom. This is why a true Christian often lives a life against the grain, persecuted and ridiculed and hated by the world as we walk the narrow path. I want to suggest to you all today—*that* is the role of faith. True faith, not faith as a meaningless platitude or point of rhetoric. Faith not as a path to walk, but faith as a way of walking the path. In Corinthians, a favorite verse of many is that we must walk by faith, not by sight. That's because to have faith in your heart is to trust your heart to the invisible. If you could see it, it wouldn't require your faith." He paused for laughter that didn't come. "The man I want to tell you about was a man of true faith. Terrence Forgaill was a man beyond his own time, and he, like the best of us, did not belong in this world.

"But before him, perhaps even more important than him, there was a woman named Alice Hassan. If Terrence Forgaill had faith, if he walked his path by faith, it is only because Alice Hassan showed him the way."

A few mutterings broke the congregation's silence. A woman just a row behind Charlie whispered to her husband, "What does any of this have to do with anything?" And her husband, emphatically agreeing, "How is this relevant?"

"Alice Hassan was orphaned in early childhood—her mother died in their home country not long after Alice was born, and her father died when Alice was just three years old, while living in a small town much like Matheson. She was adopted by a less-than-perfect family. The details of all that aren't something I should go into here, but it's important to remember that Alice, for all her life, felt as though she wasn't living the life she was meant to. Since youth, she was haunted by dreams—in her writings she called them glimpses—of a different life. In these dreams, her parents never died. They raised her, gave her something like a normal, happier life compared to the one she got, the one where she was neglected and sometimes abused, where she ran away to make her own living as a teenager, where terrible things happened to her and she had to overcome not just the cruelty of this world, but her own traumas and inner darknesses. And she did overcome them… on the outside, at least. She received scholarships to prestigious schools. Excelled in her fields of study with the help of considerable grants and fellowships. She made a name for herself. You see, Alice Hassan had faith. It didn't matter what the world did to her. Inside she was unshakable. She followed the guiding light of her faith, and it did not lead her astray."

As the pastor spoke, two men in dark robes quietly walked to the back of the church and locked the doors that led out to the lobby. Two women in dark dresses began to hand out plastic cups of either red wine or grape juice, starting at the front of the congregation. Charlie watched them carefully. She felt it first in her stomach: a surge of anxiety.

"How it was that Alice first stumbled upon mention of the entity she called The Aching Plane, and the primordial mythologies on Lost Katalpa and its eternal Dusk, none of us knows for certain. But they became an obsession to which she would lose herself. She wrote three texts on the subjects over the course of years, but even then, drew only inches closer to any tangible understanding of what those things meant, how they worked, why they existed. For all the digs and old texts and translations and interviews, the true nature of The Aching Plane remained a dense and elusive mystery, as it is to us all. But Alice's faith remained. Even as her colleagues grew concerned, and her funds dried up, and her reputation began to slip into whispers of obsession and even insanity, Alice stayed true to herself and to her devotion.

"And then she vanished, and all traces of her ever having existed vanished with her. And none of you, not even those of you who may once have heard of her or read about her or even knew her and read her books, none of you have any idea what I'm talking about. When she vanished, so did all memory of her.

"That is, of course, with the singular exception of the man called Terrence Forgaill. He and Alice loved each other, and had loved each other since they were children, and somehow—impossibly—the memory of her went dormant, hidden in his heart against all odds, even against the void into which she fell when she vanished into Katalpa. He remembered her. And he made a promise that he would find her, no matter what it took."

7

"This," said Pastor Joe to his weary, nearly-sleepwalking listeners, "is the man they call Terrence Forgaill."

The helium-high dread that hummed through Marion's body rose toward a scream when she heard the name.

Terrence Forgaill. The name inscribed in the old leather journal. The man that had vanished from the world, drawn inexplicably to the heart of this other world. The man who, having found his way back from the Ocean of Hali, had turned away from the possibility of finding life again. Had set his gaze in the direction of The Aching Plane once more.

He sat, a silhouette with bright eyes, at the edge of the jutting rock above the waterfall, and Marion still couldn't escape the sensation that he was looking directly at her. She felt as if she knew him, but there was nothing familiar about his gaze; it felt on her skin like the casting of a literal shadow.

Pastor Joe spoke all the while, seeming to preach to his followers while beseeching the silent, motionless figure of Terrence Forgaill.

"We have found each other," said the pastor, "and that is no accident. No. Even amidst our fear, our longings, our brokenness, we found each other and have helped each other survive. We've held on to something, if not to each other than to what little we could. Hope. The hope that somewhere we might find respite from the horrors and the nightmares. We have resisted, with what remains of our spirit, the visions given to us by this place, the Devil's own temptations. We've found safety from the horrors that wander these strange lands." He stepped forward, closer to the river and the splashing of the waterfall. Terrence Forgaill didn't even appear to notice.

No mistaking it now. He was looking at her.

"And, Terry," said the pastor, his role as preacher fading from his voice, "it's not just them. It's me. Joseph Correy. I officiated for you and Alice. Remember? I know you remember me. You have to remember me. I… I followed you. I had faith in you. You and… and…" He strained, his voice lowering to a growl. "There was another. Someone. I know it. But I can't remember. I had faith in you, and I still do. This place swallows everything and everyone, it doesn't matter… but you came back. You're still here. And we've come here many times now, begging you to speak to us. To give us *something*. Here I am, and here we all are, and we…" He wiped at his eyes. "And we're ready for you to show us the way."

"Yeah!" shouted the raggedy man. "Show us the way!"

"Show us!" another cried.

"Home," said someone. "I can't even remember what that's like anymore."

"Just let it end. Show us how it can end."

"Give us answers."

"Woo!" The raggedy man pounded at his chest. "Yeah!"

"Please," said Pastor Joe. "Have faith in us, as we have had faith in you. Guide us from our ignorance, from these horrible unknowns. Give us answers. Give us *something*."

Inexorable as the moonrise, Terrence Forgaill stood up.

Everyone went silent except for a wild-haired woman, who raised two clasped hands as if in prayer.

Terrence Forgaill stepped up to the very edge of the rock. He wore leather boots which boasted spots of severe wear, even a few holes, one peeling upward from the toes.

Marion shook her head. If he stepped off, he'd drop into the water below. It was in his journal that she'd read what happened when someone drank from the water too close to the Ocean of Hali. He had to know what would happen.

She threw her hands up over her mouth, ready to cover her eyes. Forgaill stepped out over open air and dropped, his dark coat flowing upward behind him.

He landed in the flowing water, splashing with a *thunk* beside the slapping of the waterfall. It wasn't deep—the water reached almost to his knees—and although the landing almost caused him to fall, he straightened up slowly, almost mechanically. His eyes, gleaming in the dark, again found Marion.

Nothing happened. No convulsions, no choking. He stood in the water, a dark figure in the twilight, silently watching.

Hadn't she seen him before? A distant shape, waving at her through the trees as if trying to get her attention?

With weighted emphasis in every step, he emerged from the river, the water dripping from his legs.

"Behold!" cried the raggedy man. "Lo and behold, mother-fuckers!"

Terrence Forgaill halted before them. Marion could make out the silver in his beard, the wrinkles around his eyes, the stains and holes in his clothes.

Pastor Joe dropped to his knees. "Terry, I never meant to doubt, but after so long—"

Forgaill folded his hands in front of him and gestured with a finger, prompting Pastor Joe to rise. Marion thought she saw a light flash across Forgaill's eyes.

"Tell me," said Forgaill, and his voice was like the voice of a lion, "of what do you dream?"

The pastor fumbled through uneven breaths, tears on his cheeks. "I dream of the streets of foreign cities—the cobblestones of Paris, the small hotel rooms of London, of York. I dream of the beautiful ruins of Rome made mundane, almost pedestrian in broad daylight, and streets with the music of amateur performers under street lamps, where I once walked with her. Her name was Darya. All my life, I wanted only to be closer to God, to give my life to Him entirely as if that might fill whatever hole I was born with. But all those years—the studies, the programs, the missions— all I ever felt of that intimacy I sought was silence. Waiting for a reply that would never come.

"And then I met her, and it all clicked into place. It made sense to me how someone could lay out their whole life in the service of another, or in surrender, or devotion, with or without reply. It made sense. And, as it turned out, I was her answer, too. That—I mean, her, and that life, that time in my life—is all I ever wanted in this world. In my dreams, that's where I am, that's the life I'm living. In my dreams, she is still alive and it's so much more real to me than... than any of this."

Terrence Forgaill nodded, then stepped aside to a woman with brown skin and tangled dark hair that fell all the way to her knees. "Tell me," he said to her. "Of what do you dream?"

"Me? I dream of a... of a different life, one where my family never turned me away for loving someone they did not choose for me. I keep dreaming about sitting at the table with them, and my mother asking him questions, and my father giving me small smiles to show he approves, and me not needing to tell them how I miss them, we are just together and happy in a way we have never been in reality." The woman bowed her head. The look on her face was one of shock and confusion, as if she were surprised at her own openness. "And… and in this dream, he never left me because of all the pressure, no, he is still with me and he understands. And I never had to leave my hometown, and I never tried to take too many sleeping pills. None of that. Just me and him and my family, content."

Terrence Forgaill nodded, moved to the next person: the raggedy man who liked to shout and cheer. With the dark figure of Forgaill in front of him, all cheerful pretense vanished.

"Tell me, of what do you dream?"

"I don't have dreams you, you creepy s-son of… of… ffffhhhh—" The man's eyes clamped shut. He moaned. When he next spoke, his voice was brisk and monotonous. The words spilled from his mouth like liquid out of a bottle. "I d-dream of my s-s-son. My little boy. He's a kid in the dreams, and I've stopped drinking, and I don't hit his mother, and I don't leave them with nothing so that, when I try to see him again years later, he doesn't hate me. I dream we're in that shitty trailer in that shitty fucking lot, and I've poured all the gin and every last can of Coors down the drain, and I'm letting him pick a movie to watch and I don't even care what it is, it's just me and him, and we've still got plenty of fucking time, and all he wants… just like all he ever really wanted back then, I guess, when he was just a goddamn kid… all he wants is to spend time with his Pops." The raggedy man began to sob.

Forgaill didn't move on to the next person the way he had before.

Marion began to shift on her feet, aware that she was next in line and could be staring into those gleaming eyes at any second.

Terrence Forgaill reached out and seized the raggedy man by the neck, and lifted him off his feet as if he weighed nothing. A surprised grunt squeezed from the man's mouth as he kicked his feet and swung his arms, but it made no difference as he was carried over to the waterfall.

Marion's heart pounded, pounded, and sweat wrung from her forehead.

Forgaill shifted and held the raggedy man directly in the flow of water so that his strangled choking became desperate sputtering as the water slapped his red face and leaked into his mouth and down his throat.

"My god," said Pastor Joe, but more with awe than fear. Everyone else appeared to have the same reaction, as if they had expected this. As if they were witnessing a sacred ritual.

With disturbing casualness, Forgaill tossed the man back toward the others. The raggedy man skinned his knees across the rocks, rolled over his shoulder, then began to crawl away, coughing and wiping at his face. He looked searchingly at the pastor, then at the woman, then at Marion, and the expression on his face reminded Marion of school. The man looked like a boy who'd been humiliated on the playground, a kid realizing even his friends were laughing at him.

A squelching noise came from his stomach. Seconds later he burped. "Oh... Joe, Joe please..." His hand flew over his stomach as he attempted to stand. "I, I, I think something's wrong. Inside. *Ach*... I... I don't feel so good." The low, wet grumbling noise from his intestines sounded like a sewer building pressure: churning, bubbling.

Marion couldn't stop looking at him, remembering what she'd read in the journal. Would this man mutate into some kind of deformed giant? His stomach rumbled horribly and he shook like a dog trying to dry itself. If he kept moaning like that, Marion didn't know how much more she could take. She lifted a hand to her own stomach, tried not to imagine what the man was feeling.

"Pastor," he whined. "I think there's something moving in… in my… *Oh*, fuck, ow…" He sucked air through gritted teeth. Veins popped from his forehead.

Pastor Joe cast him an uncomfortable glance before returning his attention to Terrence Forgaill, who took his time returning from the waterfall, rubbing his hands together.

"He's not the only newcomer, Terry," said Pastor Joe.

Terrence Forgaill's eyes were set on Marion once more. She would've backed away or possibly even turned and ran, but the pastor placed a firm hand on her shoulder.

"Tell me." Terrence Forgaill came to loom over her with the mien of a cloud moving across the sun. "Of what do you dream?"

She tightened her lips, pulled away slightly, but the pastor's grip tightened on her shoulder.

"There's something else," Pastor Joe said. "It's about Peter."

"Let me speak to the girl."

"She's not like us, Terry. Peter kidnapped her. He *took* her here."

Forgaill crouched and studied her as he would an animal he'd never seen before.

This close for the first time, Marion was able to take him in, to look back into his eyes. Up close, she could see the black holes of his pupils and she understood something that filled her with a feeling like cold concrete settling around her, making movement impossible even in her own mounting panic.

The man that crouched before her—looking into her, his own features shaded beneath the brim of a hat, dreadlocks and facial hair showing the fade of age—this man had a body, a voice, thoughts and maybe even memories, but he was not human. Whatever consciousness looked out from behind those eyes, it was warped and reduced beyond any resemblance to what had once been the man called Terrence Forgaill. It wore his body, it looked out through his eyes and spoke in his voice, but it was not him; it wasn't anything that could be named or articulated. In her head, Marion told herself to breathe slow and stay calm, but on the outside she began to struggle as if intending to run, and tears dripped from her eyes as she did all she could to keep from screaming.

"Shall we leave her to the water?" asked Pastor Joe.

The shape of Terrence Forgaill did not answer, showed no indication of having heard.

And then she felt him in her mind, and it was unlike any sensation she had ever known. If he had been prodding around her head with piping hot needles and blades, in search of an entry point to begin a dissection, that might have come close. She felt it as a physical sensation, but it was only his stare that caused it. Whatever inhuman thing sat behind those eyes, it reached out and crawled around the edges of Marion's thoughts. She felt its spidery steps scuttling across her mind, shadowing the images in her head, whispering beneath her own inner voice. It made her feel as if he had torn her clothes off so she could be displayed to the others, and he was touching her body all over.

When her voice came, it was not of her own will. The words were puppeteered through her. "I dream of my mom's voice calling me from the living room. And her asking me to read a poem or two while we eat breakfast together in the morning."

The Thing that was Terrence Forgaill brought its face closer to hers. It smelled of metal and moisture, stone and dust. *Go on*, its gleaming eyes said. *Go on.*

"I dream of the river, and... and Charlie sitting on the rock, and she's holding her fishing pole, and dressed in those overalls that

Eric used to make fun of her for, and her cap—her b-buh-baseball cap…"

The Thing's eyes widened with more than mere interest. When it lifted a finger up to its nose, Marion stopped speaking—rather, the flow of words stopped. She tried to say something but nothing came out, it was only a thought in her head:

What's happening? Why are you doing this?

And in her own thoughts, she heard its voice answer, its voice that of a beast, but its words made little sense.

RECOGNITION OF THE SOURCE. FOLLOW THE LINE.

"The fishergirl," said the Thing that was Terrence Forgaill. A grin peeled across its lips, and something glistened in its eyes— something human, an unmistakable flash of human emotion. A remnant, perhaps, of the man it once had been. It had started as recognition, then deepened into… longing? Sorrow? Something powerful enough, anyway, to glimmer through the inhuman essence that looked out from those eyes.

On the ground a few feet away, the raggedy man released a forceful belch, and he cried out when his stomach made a high, churning rumble. "Please. I feel like my insides are all fucked up." He groaned, rolling around on the rocks, holding his stomach, crying. His skin had gone from crimson to suffocated purple, as if he were rotting in fast motion.

"You," said the Thing that was Terrence Forgaill, speaking to Marion. "The fishergirl is what you dream of. She resides in the fabric of your being, an unshakable imprint outside of time." He straightened, something like satisfaction settling on his face. "I, too, have seen her. Her heart wanders the banks of Katalpa's waters. Perhaps she searches for you. You have not yet been forgotten by the world."

Marion felt as though a cold hand plunged into her chest.

"Do you wish you could go back to her? Open your eyes and find yourself as a child again, sitting on the river, waiting for her?"

She didn't know what to say.

The raggedy man began to convulse and flop on the ground. He seemed to be trying to call for help, announcing over and over that he didn't feel well, something felt wrong inside, he felt sick, but his voice began to muffle beneath a thick liquid foaming from his mouth. He grabbed at the skin of his own stomach, stripped away what remained of his own clothes. His bare belly showed movement beneath the skin, lumps forming which slid outward from his intestines, multiplying like bubbles in a boiling pot. His eyes, leaking blood, stared out in a plea for help, comprehending only a sense of pain and an awareness of irreversible doom.

"Diyós ko." Marion gaped at the Thing that was Terrence Forgaill. "What's happening to him? Can't you make it stop?"

"He is small," it said, as if that were an answer.

Hyperventilating, Marion pulled away; the pastor released her without resistance. "Diyós ko. Wha— Why is this happening to me?" All her fear, her disbelief, her horror, her awe of the last several years spent in this impossible landscape, it became a simmering fission-fire, its lid ready to burst from the inexplicable pressure. "*Why am I here? Why is this happening to me?*"

She backed away, backed away, while the Thing that was Terrence Forgaill stepped toward her, patient as the night sky, meaning to follow if she ran.

It spoke. "You want to know why? Because you felt it, Marion. Because, as with every person, it is part of you. And you felt it."

Enough clear-headed rationality remained amid her panic for her to comprehend that as an answer she could not accept. Her life had been stolen, her childhood ripped away, and maybe she had let herself hope—even in the senseless despair of all she'd trudged through and somehow survived—maybe she had let herself hope there would be some kind of end to it, and at that end, something like an answer. A reason, at least. If anyone were capable of providing that answer, wouldn't it have been him? Terrence Forgaill himself?

She shook her head to refuse its answer, to deny it. But there was the presence in her mind, the voice of the Thing that was Terrence Forgaill telling her there was nothing more to any of this.

"No." It was all she could say.

She ran, despite knowing there was nowhere to go.

8

A woman near the front pews stood from her seat, her face crimson and eyes boggled wide. "Joe," she said. "What is this nonsense you're spouting to us!"

Pastor Joe lifted a hand, palm out. "Hold on, Miss. This will all make sense in a few moments."

"This... *story*, this *fairytale*... I'm sure I'm not the only one here who's wondering what any of this has to do with the teachings of our church—"

"You see," Pastor Joe projected his voice, trying to slip back into his sermon. "Like Alice before him, Terrence Forgaill was well aware of the invisible forces that dictate our world: those intangible things we feel and give names to, names that are ultimately too small to do those things justice. Nostalgia, grief, longing... faith. Just as we Christians must hold fast to our belief despite a lack of such visible, obvious things as evidence and what can be seen and touched and empirically known, Terrence had faith in the unknowable nature of Katalpa. He felt the ache deep in the fabric of his soul, a longing too fundamental to be erased, since it stretched all the way back to his childhood, to those nostalgic days of his youth. He felt it. Just as, I believe, we have all felt it, one way or another."

The dark-robed women with the trays of plastic cups were coming around, and the people in the pews were distributing the sacrament down the line.

Something's not right, thought Charlie.

A plastic cup of wine was handed to her from the right. Her father already held his own.

And that was when she saw it, just as she had a week before, in the same place:

The giant.

It stood among the congregation, its bare skin gray and splotchy, sunlight from the windows glinting where the flesh of its back bent inward at the fissure of its spine. Its head fused with a bulbous neck, and what hair remained was patchy and wild, sticking out in all directions. It stood only a couple pews ahead, facing forward as if it, too, were enrapt by the sermon.

"I'm telling you all this," said Pastor Joe, "because it's personal to me, but also because I... I don't really have a choice. In a moment I'm going to ask you to take a leap of faith with me, as we drink of Christ's blood and pray."

Movement around the altar and on the walls of the church. Shadows, Charlie saw. Shadows encroached upon the place where Pastor Joe stood with his hands wrung anxiously at his stomach.

"Terrence Forgaill was my friend. He followed a path into darkness—not, in the end, for love, no. Love is what brought him there in the first place. But it isn't what kept him there, nor what led him into the heart of it."

No mistake now. He was speaking to Charlie. The rest of the congregation didn't matter. They were extras. They were collateral.

The giant lumbered forward, approaching Forgaill. Its footsteps smacked wetly on the ground, and each step made the church shake. There were shrieks from the congregation. Charlie wasn't the only one who could see it. Somewhere, a child broke out in panicked cries.

"All of you here today, you've had the dreams, haven't you? I can see it in your eyes, that unmistakable stare. The lives we live are not true reality. Our lives are small and so effortlessly tossed away. Even in the Bible it's… it's unmistakable. How else could God deem it fair to gamble on the life of one mere mortal, to destroy Job's home, to murder his family, to take everything he loved away from him, all for a wager with Lucifer? Our lives are uphill climbs through the cold and the rain, full of suffering and sorrow, loss and grief and… and pain… so much pain." He wrung his hands, his breath sounding like a carefully controlled wheeze. "A tale told by an idiot, full of sound and fury, signifying nothing. You all know this to be true, whether it's comfortable to hear or not. Why else would we cast our eyes back upon the past with such longing? Why else would you all be familiar with the ache?"

A woman yelled, "You are a nonbeliever, Joe Correy!" as she made her way to the back of the church. Several others rose—some with crying children—to join her. But they only joined the desperation of those trying to break through locked doors.

The giant took its place beside the pastor. It turned to face everyone in the church, looking out with corpse's eyes inside a hideously deformed face. The flesh-colored tendrils spewed, slick with blood, from its purple lips.

The pastor went on, unfazed, his voice barely rising above the escalating commotion. "The dreams make us see things how they could've been. And in a kinder world, that's how things would be. The things that the dreams show us would have no power over us if not for the truth of this misery, this suffering, this inescapable feeling that we aren't living the lives that we could be or even should be. This is the fundamental state. This is what it means to exist. In order to cope with it, we fabricate meaning, we tell ourselves fairytales, we... we kill ourselves, slowly, in so many different ways, just passing time until the end."

Charlie wanted to look away but she couldn't. Her gaze was locked with the pastor's even as the shadows flickered strangely around him. She knew she should be grabbing her father and joining the ones who were trying to flee, but she felt something—something with its own gravity—pulling her attention to the pastor's words.

"You're—I, I mean *we're*—Christians, so we know better than most that there is more than meets the eye with this world. Our world, our entire lives, the fact that we exist in physical space... it's a threshold, a veil, and the veil is thin. Terrence Forgaill said to me there is an edge to it, and that if we could reach that edge, we could peer over or, or pierce through it if we were strong enough. If many of us stood together. If we had faith." Tears fell from Pastor Joe's eyes. "And I had faith in him, and I would have followed him. But I was misled, along with... with all of us who followed him. Even he fell, eventually."

The strangely moving shadows converged around him. From some vague distance, there came high, shrill sounds. It was as if those shadows were slits in the very air, and the screams of Hell— or worse—could be heard echoing through them.

Charlie grabbed her father's shoulder and shook. "Dad. *Dad.*"

The screaming grew louder, bouncing off the church's corners. "Dad, we need to go. *Now.*"

He scowled. "We... we need to go already?"

"Dad, come *on.*"

"But, River Bug, we just set up. You haven't even dropped a line out yet."

"I… what?" She got a look at his face and saw a total uncomprehending blankness in his eyes. He was dreaming. Dreaming with his eyes open. It dawned on her: this was the same with almost everyone else in the church. The silence, the lack of bewilderment at the sermon except for the few strays who were now pounding on the locked doors. Her father, she thought, must be dreaming of a summer day on Catalpa Creek. Longing for those distant times.

"We may have been misled, back then, but all of us here… we can do this together," said Pastor Joe. "Strengthen ourselves by unifying our dreaming. I have faith. I ask you all to have faith with me. We can pierce the fabric of the Dream. And maybe find answers, find a catharsis, maybe find an end to this aching, find… find God in the outer darkness."

The shrill, disembodied screams reached a feverish pitch, a hellish chorus watching death rush toward them.

"Everyone! Lift the cup to your lips and drink of the sacrament! And hold the aching in your heart, don't be afraid of it—the pinpoint of your longing, the source of your sorrows—for it will show you the way. What you have lost, it is not gone. It can be yours again, forever."

All those who weren't caught up in the daydream rose from their pews—including most of the people in Charlie's and James's pew—and they fled, throwing out insults and exclamations of disgust and fear. Some flung their bodies upon the locked doors, causing them to rattle against their hinges.

Everyone else who stayed seated—more than half the congregation—lifted their cups to their mouths.

James Louise's eyes were gray and distant as he raised his cup.

Charlie grabbed his wrist to hold his arm down. "Dad—wake up!"

He looked at her—as did every other person who was seated in the pews. They all turned their heads to stare at her with their dreaming eyes.

"*Fishergirl*," said her father—and the dozens of others in perfect unison, creating a single amplified voice in the church, as if they were praying. "*Come with me beyond the Borderlands.*"

Casual and calm—as if it were the most natural act—James Louise reached out with his free hand, seized Charlie by the hair on the back of her head, and *pulled.*

"That hurts, that *hurts*, Dad, what are you—*oww*—"

The voices in unison: "*It's okay, Fishergirl.*" He yanked her down as if trying to hold her against his stomach in an embrace. He lifted the cup of red wine toward her mouth. "*I've been looking for you.*"

"You're—you're hurting me!" She grabbed at his hand, at his arm, too occupied with the pain in the back of her head to even try shoving the cup away.

If James Louise was there beneath the dreaming eyes, she couldn't tell. Couldn't get a clear look at his face. His grip tightened as he pulled her closer, closer. She felt strands of hair snap from her scalp where they met his death grip. The pointed sharpness of the pain caused her to grit her teeth in a seething gasp. Her father had hurt her before, during his drinking years, but it was emotional pain from the things he said or simply from her witnessing what he did to himself. He had never laid a hand on her with force or violence, not even at his worst. But now he held her, hurting her, with unthinking calmness. No, it wasn't him, that much was clear, but it *looked* like him, it felt like him, and it never entered Charlie's mind to attack him so she could escape. This was her father. He wouldn't do this. She knew: he would rather die than hurt her.

The pain in the back of her head became a ripping, piercing burn. She shut her eyes against it, crying out in spite of herself.

The next thing she felt was the cup's plastic rim pressing against her chin, and a splash of lukewarm liquid spilling into her mouth. She sputtered and coughed it out. Reached out wildly and felt her father's face, his chest, his arms. Any willpower she retained to close her mouth or fight back, to keep him from pouring the rest of the wine down her throat, was eclipsed by the blinding pain from his stranglehold on her hair.

"No," he whispered. His voice did not match the intensity of his grip. He was hurting her, but his voice sounded like his own. It sounded like her father.

Suddenly the rim of the plastic cup parted from her chin. Her father's hand—still clasping her hair—moved her away with authority. "*No*," he said again, harder this time, a tremble of disbelief in his tone. "*That's... my... daughter.*"

Still coughing, red wine dribbling down her chin, Charlie opened her eyes in spite of the pain.

Her father was holding her away from the plastic cup. The hand that held the cup shuddered, making the wine splash.

Before she could make sense of what was happening, her father threw her. With all his strength he shoved her away, and with the momentum she slid down the pew and tumbled to the floor.

Her father, his eyes clear for the first time since this morning, seized the cup now with both hands and lifted it slowly, shaking, to his own lips. The movement was in slow motion, as if he were lifting with one arm and resisting with the other: two halves of his body at war.

The resistant side wasn't strong enough, and Charlie was too stunned from the pain in her head to get up in time to help him.

He pressed the cup to his mouth, tilted it back, and drank what wine remained. There was no emotion on his face, but there were tears on his cheeks.

The last thing he said sketched itself across her mind. Some part of him rising up against whatever dark thing sat behind his eyes.

That's my daughter.

Coming back into focus: the sound made by the shadows at the front of the church. A sound like boiling kettles. The people pounding on the church's locked doors, their confusion reddened into panic.

Everyone else in the pews had drunk the wine and were watching the pastor.

Pastor Joe extended his arms outward, palms wide, as if to mimic the giant wooden crucifix on the wall behind him. He had no face anymore, not that could be seen. The shadows were sucking into his body, pulled to him as if by magnetism, latching onto his skin and *burning*. As they dissolved, they ceased to be shadows. Activated, perhaps, by human touch—like blood activated by water—their indistinct darkness whitened, thickened like sour milk. Melted layers of flesh stretched across the pastor's body, melding with his face, his hands, and smoldering through his clothes to find the skin underneath. His body twitched as the shadows congealed.

Others in the church saw this and cried out, and the cry became a roar of noise.

The sunlight through the windows darkened.

The sitting congregation all began to change.

James Louise cast his daughter a look of fear through bloodshot eyes, a look that said he felt it coming—whatever it was. And then it started to happen.

He bent forward suddenly, one hand going over his stomach, a strange sound of pain and distress slipping from his mouth.

"Charlie, Charlie, you, you—" He lurched, gagging on his words, and gripped the edge of the pew in front of him. "Oh, f-fff-fuck. Go, Charlie. *Now.*"

"Dad, I… I'm not leaving—"

"No. You—you can't s-see this. I don't want you to see this." He tried to take deep breaths. When she reached out to him, he swiped her hand away. "I know what he wants. I saw it. You have to go. Now." He pointed over her shoulder. "Break that window. Take the car. Anything. Just—" He groaned. "Fuck. *Go.*"

Charlie meant to protest, to tell him she wouldn't go without him, no way would she leave him, but she glimpsed beyond him the horror of what was happening to the others. She heard the sounds—skin ripping, bodies flailing, joints cracking, bones snapping, voices becoming screams, screams being torn to shreds. Her father was right. She had to go and she had to go *now*. She had to leave him.

Reaching past his protests, she put a hand on his hand and squeezed. Met his eyes.

It was just a moment, a series of seconds—there and gone. But in those seconds, the fear cleared away from James Louise's eyes, along with any awareness of the agony pulsing under his skin. Everything else cleared away, and he was looking at his daughter.

She was in her cradle with the little handle and he was walking her around the house for the first time. She fussed a little, but he brought her out on the back deck and swung her gently back and forth. He spoke to her in a low voice. "I think you'll like it here better than the hospital, sweetheart. Once you get used to it." And at the sound of his voice she smiled and made a small coo of excitement, one of the first smiles he'd ever seen from her. James laughed and then started to cry. He cried harder than he ever had, standing out there on the deck and lightly swinging his newborn daughter back and forth, back and forth, speaking soft assurances to her so she could come to know his voice as a place of comfort.

He looked at her. She held her small plastic fishing rod and was reeling in—the rod he'd bought her for her sixth birthday. The fish on the line, a small trout, flashed briefly into view along the surface of the water. Young Charlie squealed and looked over at James with the biggest smile on her face—a smile lacking a few teeth—with light shining off her eyes.

Or a different day, when she reeled nothing in and sat, arms crossed with exaggerated emphasis, and complained that the fish could be so inconsiderate, because—because didn't they know her dad had driven her all the way out here to go fishing? His laughter at that comment had only made her more frustrated, though he glimpsed the faintest hint of a self-aware smile at the corner of her mouth.

She was five, getting up off the asphalt where she had fallen off her bike—even with the training wheels on. He asked if she was hurt. She brushed gravel off her clothes, cried slightly, then bit her lips inward and said she was okay.

She was seventeen, on the couch beside him, laughing at a movie with him.

She was four, in the crook of his arm, trying to help him brush his teeth but only making it impossible, and he laughed the whole time.

She was seated at the piano trying to copy her mother's hand movements on the keys.

She was helping him off his bedroom floor because he had fallen asleep there, drunk again.

She was stirring in the driver's seat of her car where he found her asleep in the early hours of the morning. He took her in his arms and carried her to bed, telling her it was okay, telling her to go back to sleep.

She was rising exhaustedly from her bed, hair disheveled, insisting that she come to church with him because she didn't want him to be alone.

She was pretending to read the Bible during service, when really she'd snuck a paperback in and folded it into her Bible.

She was just a kid, running at him in the grocery store, crying because she had lost sight of him for a minute or two. He expected her to be mad—she could be so willful—but instead she threw her arms around him and sobbed.

"It's okay, sweetie, I'm here—I'm right here. It's okay."

"You almost forgot me."

"No I didn't, Charlie. Hey. *Hey.* I didn't forget you. I would never forget you."

She pulled away to wipe at her eyes, the sobs receding to sniffles. "I thought I lost you, Daddy. I was scared and I didn't know what to do."

He lifted her chin, smiled and she smiled back. "C'mon, River Bug. Let's get home, huh?"

In the church now, through the sounds of horror, she looked at him the same way, with fear, with disbelief, with trust. He looked back at her. "Go," he said.

James Louise managed the strength to lift his arm one more time and point her in the right direction—to the window, away from him for the last time.

It's okay. Go, sweetheart. Go.

Charlie Louise placed her hands on his cheeks, kissed his forehead. Her voice barely came through. "I love you," she told him, and then turned and did as he said. Away from the reeling shadows, the horrors, the screams. And away from him.

He raised his eyes one more time, after the window shattered, to watch her leave.

She was five years old, blowing him a kiss before she crossed the sidewalk to the front doors of her school for the first time. She adjusted the straps of her small backpack, told James she loved him, and then ran to greet her friends—the group that would one day call themselves The Renegades—who waited just inside the school's doors. It was a short distance from James's car to the doors, but she ran as fast as she could.

You go, baby girl. James Louise closed his eyes. Prayed she would make it, that she would be safe. He let the pain and the darkness roll over him—and it tore him apart.

9

She pulled over on the side of the road to throw up. A series of
police cars with blazing sirens wailed past on their way to the
church.

Charlie watched them round a corner. She could imagine their
faces as they jumped out of their cars and heard that terrible racket.
Screams of adults and children. Bodies breaking and bursting. Cries
for help. Cries of agony. Guttural *rumbles*, like growls or muffled
roars from the Changed Ones.

Would their shapes be visible through the windows, from out
in the church's parking lot? The shapes of towering giants, bodies
like tumorous boulders mutating and changing?

Would the police start shooting? Would they try to approach—
and would they be attacked? Would some of them see what was
happening—surely it was still happening, for some of the changes
were slower than others, and there had still been innocent people
inside, children even, when Charlie had fled—would some of the
officers see what was happening and simply snap? Would they lose
their sanity, unable to wrap their minds around the reality in front
of their eyes?

Full of tears, Charlie drove and felt something pressing from
inside her own mind—something pressing and sharp. It felt as if

her mind were a thin, fragile thing, and she could physically feel it close to breaking.

She had looked back just once, after shattering the window and climbing through. She had looked back. Her father appeared to be in the grip of a violent seizure, his eyes rolling up in his head, his mouth slacking open and dripping saliva and blood. He slumped forward and his face smashed against the backrest of the pew in front of him.

It was like the dream, when the dreams had first started: how she saw her father at a dinner table with all her friends; she had watched him drop suddenly, his face hitting the surface of the table —dead weight—his body gripped by convulsions.

This image played across her eyes with the unavoidability of a double-exposed image, one layer of reality hanging over the other, until she pulled the car into the driveway of her house and stepped out.

The house was quiet. Charlie hugged her arms to her body, let herself inside.

An empty mug of tea still sat on the dining table, along with the napkin he'd used while having the breakfast she'd made for him. She passed her father's study, then his bedroom. She even cast her eye in through the ajar door as she passed to see if he was there, to check on what he was doing. This had been a habit back when he'd been drinking, just to check.

In her bedroom she collapsed on the floor.

"Dad," she said to the emptiness of the house, thinking of the dozens of things she would never get to say to him. *This can't be it,* she tried to say. *There should be more.*

Behind her thoughts there was a voice—a whispering voice she recognized from somewhere, but it was a stranger's voice, not her own.

Your father is in the water, it said.

She rested her arms atop her knees and buried her face. When she closed her eyes she could *hear* the water, the quiet rushing of Catalpa Creek, its surface glittering beneath the sun. She raised her head, looked around the room. From here on the floor, she couldn't see the top of her desk, so she didn't notice that the facedown photograph was no longer there. She didn't notice her phone filled with urgent messages and a voicemail from Adrian.

Charlie sniffled, closed her eyes, buried her face again—and there, shadowing her own thoughts, not merely in her mind but vivid enough she swore she could hear it in her ears: the trickling of the creek.

She tried to will it away but it grew louder. She pictured her father stepping into the room to ask if she was okay, and the sound of the water drowned everything else out.

With her next breath she sobbed. When she lifted her head, she was no longer in her own bedroom. The rug hadn't been pulled out from under her, it had been replaced.

Charlie Louise sat not on the carpet of her room; she was perched on the banks of a river. It looked like Catalpa Creek, even *sounded* like it, as if one river's flowing could be distinguished from another's, but the light reflected on its surface, through the towering black trees, was dim. Past sunset. Somewhere in the near distance, the sound of an ocean. Just beneath the ocean's tide, there were whispering voices.

Something Marion said to her in a dream echoed in her mind: *I pulled back the curtain and saw behind everything. Did you know, it's almost dark back there, I could hear my mom calling us back inside for dinner—almost dark, is why—but did you know there's something behind it all.*

Almost dark, like it was now.

Charlie stood away from the river. The dirt was stiff beneath her feet. Through the titanic black tree trunks which stood with the steadiness of skyscrapers, a strange wind howled. She'd heard wind make a high sound before when whipping around the corners of the house, but this was different. The sound was shrill. A howl. It sent chills through her as she moved away from the river, eyes scanning the trees in search of the source.

She didn't need to wonder where she was. She had read the journal, had envisioned this place with every word. Still, there was that prodding sensation inside her mind, her own sanity apparently stabbing at her brain's fragile matter. She couldn't believe any of this was real, though she felt the air's cold bite on her skin, could see the giant trees and the dimness of the sky beyond.

Most of all, there was an emotion blooming in her chest, pulsing and widening through her body. It seemed to originate outside of her, as if her cells were drinking it from the very air, but it didn't feel alien, no; she knew it well.

Charlie followed the river with her eyes. It flowed down the end of a gentle slope where the giant trees came to a clear end. Farther beyond was the ocean and its whispering.

Her father was there. He was walking beyond the trees, into the misty dusk, toward the sound of the ocean. His shape was unmistakable; she knew it better than she knew her own.

Charlie called out for him, moved in that direction, tears already flowing from her eyes.

Her father turned around to face her, but he kept walking backwards. And he waved at her.

I'm right here, he seemed to say with the waving of his hand. *Come on, River Bug. Follow me.*

She followed.

Somewhere far off, the sound of knocking. Knuckles rapping against wood. A flurry of knocks. Somebody trying to get her attention. Somebody calling her name.

She looked ahead at her father, who walked backwards and waved at her, beckoning her to follow. But there was that knocking, that hard rapping—

"Charlie?" said Marion.

Charlie looked to her left where the slope flattened out against slate-gray sand. Marion stood there on the sand, not far from the water. In one hand she held a framed photograph.

"Marion." Her friend's name was like a memory already fading.

"Charlie… what—what are you doing here?" she asked; then demanded. "*What are you doing here?*"

Charlie opened her mouth to say she didn't know. Her own voice fell away at the sound of the urgent knocking again, but the knocking was followed by a *smash.*

All it took was a blink, an exhalation, and it was all gone. No more trees, no more strange wind or ocean of whispers. Charlie was curled up on her bedroom floor, tears marking her cheeks.

"Marion?" she said, her eyes darting all around. She heard, then, the sound of Adrian shouting her name. He was slamming himself against the front door and calling for her.

When Charlie made it to him, Adrian had given up trying to break the door down. He paced back and forth on the porch, phone to his ear, but when he saw her, he dropped the phone—never mind if its screen cracked—and went to embrace her.

"Charlie, my god, I've been—"

She swatted his arms away and put a hand on the center of his chest, keeping him from moving any closer. He gave her a look of hurt, not offense.

"I need to go," she said.

"Charlie… what happened? I've been hearing all sorts of things about the… about the church. Stuff I don't even know if I believe, you know? But you…" He furrowed his brow at her. "You were there. You and your dad, right?"

She cursed her own tears and tried to push past him. He was the one to deny her this time as he gripped her shoulders.

"What happened? Are you okay? Is your dad here?" He looked past her, then back at her leaking face. "Charlie. Please."

"Adrian, I need to *go*." She put her hand to his chest again, tried to push him away, but her strength gave out in a fit of shaking. Her knees buckled and she collapsed—but Adrian caught her. He pulled her up, straining, into an embrace.

She didn't let it happen, but couldn't fight it either. She sobbed against him.

"Your dad isn't here." His voice sank beneath the weight of realization. "God, Charlie, I… I don't know what to say."

She wrested herself away, moved from the house and toward her car, wiping furiously at her face. "I need to go. I need to find Marion."

"Who?"

"Marion. She—" Charlie stopped. The expression on Adrian's face was genuine bewilderment, on top of the shock and sorrow he shared with her. "My friend," she said. "Marion."

"I don't know her… but Charlie, let me… let me make you something, or, or I don't know. Tell me what I can do. I can just sit with you, and if you want to tell me what happened, or if you just need to sit, or to think about something else—"

For a fleeting moment she loved him. Never mind a label on their relationship to each other, never mind everything else swirling around her, she loved him for that. For the look on his face, for his uncertainty and his willingness. But there was no time.

"I need to find my friend. It's an emergency."

In the distance, sirens wailed.

"Okay, well then I'm taking you."

"Adrian, I—"

"No. I'm not letting you drive. I don't know what's happening, okay, but I know I'm not letting you drive yourself, and I'm not letting you go alone. Come on."

And for that. Despite herself, despite the brief flare of annoyance at his insistence, she loved him for that, too. It reminded her of her father, just this morning. He had tossed her his car keys despite her saying she'd be fine driving her car. When it came to things like that, there had been no arguing with him.

"Okay," she said.

PART 4

The Grieving

There were two police cars in the middle of the street, just outside the Del Rosario house. Their driver-side doors were flung open and the red and blue lights on their roofs spun soundlessly.

Adrian had driven here with little mind for stop signs or traffic laws, mirroring Charlie's urgency. He pulled the car to the side of the road, tires halfway in the dirt. "What the hell happened here?"

Charlie got out before Adrian could kill the engine. Wary of the haunted look in her tear-stained eyes, he hopped out beside her, ready to grab her arm if she went forward without any thought of self-preservation. They stepped together between the haphazardly parked police cars. Adrian gasped.

Four bodies were sprawled across the asphalt. Three of them had been police officers, recognizable only by the shines of their badges among the splattered gore of what remained of their bodies. Two of them had been torn apart upon the ground, their blood smeared in grisly trails as if they'd been smashed into the asphalt and then dragged—more so *ground* like cheese against a grater.

One of them was on his stomach, his head bent nearly backward on his neck. No face remained, only a red, concave pulp. Bloated eyeballs leaked out from meaty sockets.

The other two officers appeared to have had their bodies snapped. A few arms and legs twisted or folded at unnatural angles, with the fleshy white of bone piercing through bloodstained skin. One didn't so much have a back as a collapsed place where the middle of his spine had once been. The third's face held the likeness of a final scream—mouth hanging open—but there were no eyes, and his jaw was crooked.

Adrian threw up in the gutter in front of the Del Rosario house. Charlie moved past the bodies on the shaky foundations of her legs, showing only a sense of curiosity and near indifference at the bodies of the officers. Her attention was fixed on the fourth body, this one a few feet down the road.

Adrian gripped his stomach, tried to return to Charlie's side, but collapsed and retched again. "Jesus Christ."

"He came *here*," Charlie said, coming to a stop above the fourth body. "Why would he come here?"

"Who... who is it? Not another cop?"

Her hands clenched into fists. "It's the pastor. He was at the church but he came *here*."

Pastor Joe was on his back, arms spread out in the same way they'd been when she'd last seen him at the church's altar: spread eagle, like the image of Christ, as if he expected to rise from the earth and be swallowed by the sky. There were too many holes in his body to count, each one leaking blood.

The pastor's eyes stared blankly, the pupils holding no light. His mouth was slack, as if he'd been trying to say something when he died.

Sirens wailed far off, warbling steadily nearer.

"This is bad," said Adrian from the sidewalk. "This is really bad. We need to go."

Charlie ignored him. She moved away from the street, headed for the house.

"Charlie, this is a crime scene. I don't think we should be here when the cops— Wait, what are you doing?"

She stepped up onto the porch. The front door stood ajar. There was no sound from the house, no sense of movement.

"Charlie? Oh, fuck—Charlie! *Charlie!*"

She reached out, pushed the door open, her heartbeat intensifying. Adrian's cries dropped beyond her awareness. She didn't know what she expected inside the house, and tried not to let her mind show her the possibilities she feared.

Puddles of blood.

Blankly staring eyes.

Silence.

Lupita Del Rosario was curled up in the far corner of the dining room, in direct view of the front door. She had her head down beneath her arms, hidden behind raised legs. When the door creaked open, Lupita looked up, eyes widened, and she lifted a hand to point—not at Charlie, but past her.

"Nenè! Behind you!"

Adrian's screams reached Charlie's ears then. Her whole body tensed as she spun to see what Lupita pointed at.

Pastor Joe Correy had risen from the asphalt despite the bullet holes peppered across his body. He came toward her, but his feet barely touched the ground. He appeared to hang as if suspended in the air. Even his head lolled forward, his arms loose, shoes only brushing the porch's wood. As if an invisible hand held him up. As if he were a toy doll.

When he raised his head, what Charlie felt wasn't fear. Despite what she'd seen at the church, something sparked in her like sharp fire.

"You," said the pastor, and under his voice was a bloody gurgle, like phlegm at the back of his throat. "You got out. You must understand, by now, the gravity of Katalpa's call—"

Charlie slammed her fist into the side of the pastor's face.

His head whipped from the force of her strike, but his body remained inert. He coughed, sputtering.

She punched him again, this time straight on, and felt his nose flatten and snap beneath her knuckles. Having never hit someone like that before, she was surprised by the pain that flared in her fingers. Somehow it felt good. It fed the fire.

The pastor's eyes rolled and he spat blood, but he didn't even raise an arm to wipe it away from his face. It appeared, almost, that he might not have much control over his own body. Maybe the gunshots had left his arms useless, deadweight hanging from his shoulders.

"I escaped because my father saved me." She could hardly finish the sentence with her voice intact. "He saved me. And you killed him. You killed all those people. There were children crying…" She lifted a hand to her face, wiped at her cheeks, covered her mouth to contain sobs. "*Children.* And my *father.*"

The pastor nodded slowly. To Charlie's bewilderment, there was sorrow in his eyes. Sorrow, maybe even regret.

The wailing sirens drew closer. A minute or two more and cruisers would be roaring down this street.

"You know," said the pastor, "I once believed in a god of fear and mercy. A god I would've begged forgiveness from, for what I've done."

Charlie tightened her fists, ready to swing at him again. *I would believe in a Hell of eternal damnation,* she thought, *if it meant you would burn there forever.*

A tear slipped from Pastor Joe's eye. "And you know something else, Charlie Louise. I would not deserve the forgiveness of that god. I know that. Just as I know I don't even deserve to beg your forgiveness."

"No," she said. "You don't."

"Listen to me, before it's too late. Your friend, M-Marion, she would know what I mean. I think I… I think I knew it was wrong, I think I've known that for a long time. But it was too late. The darkness of that place has had its hold on me, its fingers too deep, for a long time now, thanks to *him*. Terry and his promises. I believed in him, I believed he knew something about the world— and about Katalpa—that I didn't." The pastor shook his head with an ironic smile. Blood stained his teeth. "I was wrong. We are motes of dust. The Bible's right about that." With a strain he lifted his hands up in front of his face. And Charlie saw despair in those eyes. "I want you to understand, Charlie Louise."

The sirens erupted. Three police cars rubbered down the street, lights flashing.

Pastor Joe, with tears on his cheeks, turned to face them. He pulled something from a pocket on the side of his coat and handed it to Charlie. "Here. Now get inside."

Adrian sprinted past him and joined Charlie. They flew into the house, locked the front door behind them, and went to crouch at the living room window. Lupita yelled at them to get away, to duck down and hide.

Pastor Joe hovered—his feet dragging across the grass, then the sidewalk, then the asphalt.

The three police cruisers came to skidding stops. The officers emerged with pistols drawn. They barked commands in shaking voices, terror on their pale faces. It was clear they had witnessed strange, unthinkable things today.

"From dust I came," said Pastor Joe. "To dust I return."

He advanced on them, floating, his pose that of a scarecrow. Whether he did this voluntarily was impossible to tell, but after just one more warning from the officers, gunshots detonated. Bullets tore into the pastor's body. He floated forward, forward. Blood spattered onto the asphalt in streaks and dots, spraying from the holes in his body.

CRACK!

CRACK! CRACK!

CRACK!

Lupita screamed from her corner. Adrian covered his ears.

Charlie only watched. The fire in her body had dampened, replaced by a coldness that made her feel as though she were shivering on the inside. There were no tears, not for Pastor Joe, but she felt something for him as he collapsed.

The gunshots didn't stop. His body twitched, his head snapped backward. Then he didn't move at all, not even as the bullets pierced through him.

And then silence.

2

Despite her wide-eyed, hand-shaking horror, Lupita took charge when two police officers approached the house. All the while brushing away her tears and patting down her clothes for dust, Lupita pulled Charlie and Adrian from the window, told them to hide for awhile in Marion's room—with the promise she would bring them something to drink or eat in a little while—and insisted that she be the one to talk with the police. Adrian tried to interject and say he had no problem answering questions, but she shushed him.

"Who will look after Charlie?" she said, and shoved him gently along. A series of knocks came at the door, and Lupita groaned. "Ay, caramba." She ran a hand through her hair, making herself as presentable as possible.

Marion's room was a chamber, its silence funereal. The wooden blinds were shut, letting only thin bars of gray light into the room.

Adrian shut the door quietly beneath the sound of Lupita greeting the police officers. He released a harsh breath.

"Can you believe what just happened? Any of it?" He released the door handle as if uncertain of the action. Examined his own hand. "He was… he was barely even touching the ground. Did you see—I mean, of course you did, you were right there." He turned around, eyes not seeing anything in front of him. "I've shot guns on a range before with my dad, but actually seeing that, seeing someone get shot... and the way he was *floating*..." He looked up for the first time since entering the room.

Charlie had curled up on the windowsill, faced away from him, and was crying silently into her arms. If not for Adrian, this could've been a scene from a decade ago, except Marion would've been there with her.

The space beside her now, on the windowsill, felt emptier than empty. It felt, she thought, not merely like a blank space, but like a black hole.

Adrian hovered in his uncertainty before amassing the awkward courage to go to her. He sat on the edge of the windowsill, touched her gently. Could feel her spine, the way her body flexed and shook with each breath.

"My dad is dead." In the brokenness of her world, this was a statement of fact, a reminder to herself of the truth she now lived in. Not a nightmare she imagined, not something she could wake from, not a scenario played out in her head as a way of expelling its possibility from her mind, no. Her father was dead. She would never see him again.

When Lupita came into the room, Adrian told her what little he knew. Charlie had stopped crying by then, but when Lupita opened her arms to her, the tears returned instantly.

"He loved you," said Lupita, cradling Charlie's head against her chest. "And he loves you still, nenè."

The voice in Charlie's head, the one that was always there, begged to differ.

No, she thought, *but that's kind of you to say. I know nothing returns from the darkness we all eventually disappear into. I know our lives, our awareness, our consciousness, it's all just a flash in that dark-*

ness, here and then gone. I just didn't know it could hurt so much. I thought knowing all this would help, maybe, knowing the cold truth of things, having at least some grasp of what lies beneath it all, but, Dad... I don't think I could ever be ready to let you go. Why won't you get to grow old?

It wasn't just that he had died, either—something she could hardly grasp, much less accept. It was that he had died so terribly, in pain, in horror.

It didn't matter what you believed, Charlie realized. It didn't matter if you held love, light, truth, and faith in your heart. Her father had fought against his demons, resisted the seductive pull of the past, even when the ill angels of that past haunted him in the form of the Katalpian dreams. He had risen to the occasion of his own life, set down the bottle, gone to church.

And had died in that church, with screams in his ears, without an answer for why any of it was happening. Without any mercy, any love, any help, any sign at all, from the god he had tried so hard to believe in.

These thoughts boiled in her mind, steaming hot to the touch, but she held them down. Buried herself against the motherly warmth of Lupita, who had been—for all of Charlie's childhood—so much warmer than her own mom, so much more than just a friend. And she tried to hear Lupita's words instead of the voice inside her own head. She wanted to believe light carried on after death, like the light of stars long dead still shining in the night sky. She wanted to believe her father would always be with her. She wished this were not her life, but a nightmare she could wake from.

Lupita explained to Charlie what she already knew: that Marion was gone. She couldn't remember where she'd left to, or why, she knew only that her daughter was gone again.

Charlie kept her vision to herself—how she had seen Marion, for a fleeting moment, in the strange place with the misted ocean and perpetual dusk. Marion, with a framed photograph in her hand and a troubled look on her face, demanding, *What are you doing here?*

When Lupita let them be—insisting, all the while, that they stay the night—Charlie sat on the windowsill again. She looked down at the small black object in her hand, the thing Pastor Joe had handed to her before turning to meet his fate.

A voice recorder. When she turned it on and navigated its small digital screen, it showed five files in its memory. Charlie held it up so Adrian could see. After a few seconds, he sat down beside her. She clicked *play* on the first file. The first two, it turned out, were errors.

On the third file, the voice of Pastor Joe wisped through the small speakers, weary and subdued; the voice of a man who had seen too much.

3

═══════════════════

FILE 1

Ah… there. Silly thing should be working now.

Charlie Louise. This, um, recording—is for you. It feels strange to be addressing someone who isn't here and who I'm not even certain will ever hear this message. Well… I'll try to be certain you will.

In case you don't know who this is, my name is Joe Correy. We've met a handful of times before, me and you. At church and, more recently, at Marion Del Rosario's house. Our conversation was cut short then, but maybe that was for the best. You may not have been ready to hear some of the things I had hoped to tell you… maybe no one could ever be ready to hear. God knows I wish I had never heard of Terrence Forgaill, nor become friends with him, nor came to follow him with my faith and my devotion… but I digress.

If it's strange that I can talk to you now as if I know you, it's because, in a sense, I do. You just don't remember. You know me as relatively new to this town and the church. It's been almost a year, but small towns take their time adjusting to newcomers, or newcomers never quite fit in. I'm still viewed as the new pastor, but that's because nobody remembers me. I was, in fact, born in this town. I was raised here, and although I spent many years abroad in my later teens and early adulthood, I came back. I've been at this church for just over a decade, and although you and your father didn't go to church back then, I remember meeting you when you were a child… but you wouldn't remember that. Nor would your father. Nor would Pastor Harry. No one would. I am a stranger. All the memories I've made in this town and in the church, they are my memories alone, unshared by anyone else. Do you know how lonely a thing that is, to hold memories alone? To remember, but to not be remembered?

But, of course, this is a feeling I knew long before this. After Darya's death. That happens to be how I was ever led to The Aching Plane of Katalpa. A hole inside me, a grave of what died within me…

There I go again. None of that is the point of this. The reason I'm doing this is because… because there is no prayer I can say to make up for what I am here to do. I am locked in, my path is laid out before me and it is… it's a narrow path, a hallway without any branching paths. That's what I'm trying to say. But it all centers around you, Charlie Louise. I'm sure you don't know that yet… or maybe, by the time you're hearing this, you have some inkling of an idea of how this, all of this, has to do with you. So I'm recording this to try and warn you, to try and, I don't know, make some things clear for you.

Or maybe I'm just doing this for myself, after all. For my own conscience, you know… I guess it doesn't matter.

I won't waste much of your time, Charlie. I'll tell you what I know, what I tried to tell you at Marion's house. And then… well, I don't know what then.

4

Where to begin?

I first heard of Terrence Forgaill here, in Matheson. Nothing special about it. I was in line at a coffee shop, the one on the corner where the new cobblestone square was set up a few years ago. It was early morning, I was on my way somewhere else… probably back home, or off to run some errands… and I happened to notice a flyer on the coffee shop's billboard. Among the dozens of other flyers, a few "missing dog" or "missing cat" posters, ads for local theater productions or fundraisers for the school, I saw it, and I'm sure it was no accident. It was an ad for a lecture series from a former professor of some renown. I don't remember it word-for-word, I just remember the brief autobiography on the back. It described Professor Forgaill as a lauded figure of many talents, accomplishments, and curiosities. I took a picture of the flyer, thought about it for the rest of the day, and decided to do some research when I returned home.

I learned of the many ways that Terrence Forgaill was viewed by the world. A scientist, an anthropologist, an archaeologist, a mythologist, a phenomenologist, a kook, a spiritualist, a false prophet, a charlatan, a mystic. There were articles meant to criticize and defame him written by a range of people—from internet influencers to scholars, historians, politicians, fellow anthropologists. But there were just as many who came to Terrence's defense. Those who knew him regarded him as a man of uncommon originality and intelligence. I read an entire magazine article from someone who had worked with Terrence for several years, and the entire purpose of the article was simply to shed some light on what it was like to know the man, to observe him in his natural environments, to see him at work and on the road as both an explorer and a lecturer.

Then I began to read more about why he was so controversial. I began to read about his actual work, and the claims he made, the things he wrote about as a result of his multifaceted career.

In the years leading up to my encountering him for the first time, Terry had honed his focus to the study of a modern-day tribe of indigenous people on a small island in the Pacific Ocean. This tribe is similar to the Sentinelese in the Indian Ocean, in that they're cut off from the modern world entirely, in a cycle of their own traditions and evolution. Terry, with his usual dramatic flair, called them Katalpians, and sometimes he referred to them as People of the Dusk. Officially, they've come to be known as the Tullapan People, or the Tullapa Tribe, because the island they inhabit is part of the Tullapa Islands.

Unlike the Sentinelese, the Tullapans aren't outright hostile to outsiders. Cautious, of course, and all records of them suggest they are highly sophisticated and potentially dangerous… which, maybe, is why they can afford not to show immediate hostility to newcomers. Terrence visited them four, maybe five times in the span of roughly two-and-a-half years. He published a book about them, having conducted numerous studies.

It's actually a very fascinating subject. Apparently the tribe is large, over a hundred people. A small group of them could build a house—a dwelling, at least—in less than a day, as well as functioning boats to move between the islands. The structures they built—ladders through trees, dwellings out of tree trunks, mud, stone, or sometimes simply built into the earth. Their hunting mechanisms, their, their… They were deeply in tune with their environment. But I digress.

I attended a few of Terry's lectures. He spoke mainly about the people of the Tullapa Islands, using his experiences with them as a gateway to speaking about… other things. The things that were at the heart of his own studies, you could say. When I finally met him, we got along like it was nothing. Like we had always been friends. My own interests sort of transcended the church, any church, even though I was fairly committed to being a minister. I think Terry saw something in me. He opened up to me further about his time on the Tullapa Islands.

What intrigued Terry so deeply—obsessed him, more like—was the religion of the Tullapans. His other name for them probably cued you in. But it's best described with one of their rituals. In his book, Terrence called it The Grieving. I can still hear his voice, how passionate he became whenever he spoke about it, whether in lectures or even just to me, over a drink.

You see, it might sound like a, uh… a superficial, very western-thinking thing to say, but most indigenous tribes are intertwined with the natural world. Nature is often their religion, so to speak. If not literally, then in practice. This goes way back in all human history, probably where the concept of burials came from in the first place. The idea that we came from the Earth—one of the first religions, Mother Earth, Father Sun—and so, when we die, we should be given back to the Earth. It'd be fair to say, then, that to people who lived this way and believed these things, death was viewed with a sense of peace. We miss the person, but we understand they have been returned to the natural cycle—one with the Earth and its changing, again.

The Tullapan people, according to Terry, did not seem to see it this way. If they did, Terry had no grasp of it. What he witnessed, more like what he interpreted from what he witnessed—and what he could manage to learn from them, which was always limited by the severe language barrier, among other things—was some kind of... I don't know, some kind of disconnect from the natural order in their Grieving ritual. Their grief, he said, was expressed with "uncommon severity." I remember he said it like that. Uncommon severity.

On one of his prolonged visits to the islands, he witnessed a Grieving. A man went out, presumably for fish, or perhaps to trade supplies with one of the nearby islands. A storm came which lasted... I think Terry said it lasted two days. And the man did not return. His woman, then, had to accept his fate. And she became inconsolable.

I wish you could read what Terrence wrote on the subject, Charlie. His way with words was far beyond mine.

The woman thereafter, he said, seemed to exist in another world, sometimes wailing with all of her voice, sometimes quiet for hours. Others would sit with her, offering only their presence, never words or offerings. And then, after six days, they took the woman to one of the far beaches of the island. This area was curiously left alone. Terrence had never been there, as apparently he had no cause, since none of the tribe ever went there. He believed it was treated as sacred, perhaps exclusively for the Grieving ritual.

An elder member of the tribe lit a torch, then took a small bowl made of hardened clay, walked to the tide, and scooped the bowl full of seawater. He returned to the woman and held both the torch and the bowl of water out to her. He was offering her a choice between the torch or the bowl. Fire or water. The woman looked at the elder—the shaman, is what Terry called him—and she took the torch.

The other members of the tribe who'd accompanied them then set about piling branches and sticks and kindling on the beach. A bonfire. When it was ready, they dispersed in a loose circle around the kindling, keeping a wide distance, while the woman took her torch and set the bonfire alight. It was like a funeral pyre without a body. Actually, that's what Terry thought it was, at first. A funeral pyre. In place of a body, they had this ritual.

It turns out—and as you may have guessed—Terry was wrong. The Grieving is not a replacement funeral. It's its own thing entirely.

The other tribe members, the elder shaman included, appeared to assume meditative positions—somewhere between meditation and prayer, anyway. The woman, meanwhile, crouched in front of the fire.

Terry told me how he felt while watching this. He said he was overcome by a sudden fear, almost panic, that he was about to witness this woman throw herself into the flames. I know I wouldn't have been able to bear it… but the ritual was clearly sacred. There was nothing he could do without risking the wrath of the tribespeople. So he watched, ready to shield his eyes.

The woman was consumed by her grief, giving into her emotions fully, wailing and sobbing without any restraint. Terrence called it the most mournful sound he had ever heard. A sound that only a shattered heart could make from the deepest night of its despair.

But the woman quieted as she stared into the fire. She seemed to look deeply into the flames, entranced by them.

I ask you this, Charlie Louise. Though I don't know you very well, I'm sure this is something we share, just as I'm sure all people share it, to some degree. For some, it's fire. You sit at a campfire, you stare into it, and it does something to your brain, as though it is singing a soothing melody only you can hear, written just for the strings of your heart and soul. You stare into it and are transported, calmed, mesmerized. From the earliest humans to us, now, in our modern times. The fire can do this.

For some of us, it's the water. To sit by a stream, the sound of it running in our ears. Or sitting on the sand, looking out at the ocean, its rhythm in our ears as much as in our heart.

For others, it's the trees. Or the wind, the dirt, the grass…

Not that it's only one of these things. Maybe you feel that way about all of them. Maybe about only one or two of them. The point is, you probably know what I mean, as you're listening to me say this.

It is this simple, primordial thing that The Grieving is all about. The woman, even amid her impossible grief, stared into the fire and it took hold of her. And right there, in front of Terry's very eyes, the woman vanished. Disappeared as if into thin air.

You can probably imagine Terry's reaction. His confusion, I mean. He searched, but found nothing. And the other tribespeople there, they remained as they were, in a wide, wide circle on the beach. They sat there as if nothing had happened, and they waited.

What Terrence had thought was going to be at most a journey of a day or two, on the sacred beach, became an ordeal that lasted nearly an entire month.

The Tullapans constructed small dwellings at the edge of the beach, and life resumed as usual. A spontaneous sub-village, in a way, on this otherwise-uninhabited section of the island. Some of them came and went with supplies to the heart of the island, others set out on their usual journeys by making boats and making their ways to the other surrounding islands. But they always returned to the beach and the ashes of the bonfire, and they sat on the sand and waited.

I'll spare you the details. In Terry's book, this section takes up a decent chunk of pages. In short, he had to adjust to the new setting, the new foundation of life on the island being waiting. And he didn't even know what they waited for, although he could certainly guess. They were waiting, he wrote, for the woman to return. Did they know when she would return? Did they even know if she'd return at all? They offered no answers to this question, maybe because they themselves didn't know.

Eventually, they took down the dwellings they had set up, and returned to their usual section of the island. By then, there was no trace of their stay. Even the ashes had long been washed away into the ocean. For Terry, this seemed like a philosophical contradiction. The Tullapan people were so in touch with impermanence in their lifestyle, and yet when it came to loss, they were severe and inconsolable.

The woman never returned.

Now, there were two members of the tribe who had begun to pick up some English from Terry as well as from past visitors to the island. He learned a few words from them, even a few phrases —though he told me they appeared amused by his attempts, no matter how good he thought he was doing. When he returned with the main group, he was able to speak with these people. He tried to ask them questions like what had happened to the woman, all the questions you'd expect him to have.

He learned very little, even from the two men who were picking up some English. However, one of them did communicate something fundamental.

Terry asked, "Why didn't the woman return?"

And the tribesman's answer, roughly translated and interpreted, was something like this: "Her roots are not grabbing at life's earth strong enough." Their language was intertwined with the natural world, so the more anglicized translation may have been: "She is wanting for life not enough."

Terry listed a few possible meanings. It could've meant, "She didn't return because she didn't want to." It could've been, "She wanted to, but her grief was too great." Or it could've been more literal. "She didn't want life enough, so she couldn't return."

Couldn't, or didn't... the distinction is so small, yet potentially so important. And we may never know.

I spoke with Terry some time later, a couple years after the publication of his book on the Tullapa Tribe, and after he'd been back to their islands again. Things were... different with him, by then. He was changing. Drawing nearer, so to speak, to Katalpa. And he told me that something had been troubling him about his own book, that being mainly his own interpretation of what the man said about the vanished woman.

He said "wanting" was the wrong word. A fault of his own misunderstanding the nuances of their language. A closer translation would've been: "Her longing for her own life was insufficient."

The Tullapan people had different words for life. One meant past life, one meant future life—as in, the life that you want to have or wish you had—and the third meant present life. In the case of the woman's longing or lack thereof for her own life, the word was for present life. Not a longing for the past, not for an imagined future, but for the present. Her longing for own present life was insufficient.

Terry suggested to me that this was an answer of immeasurable importance. The reason being that he believed, after all his time with these people, that their religion centered around Katalpa itself.

The Grieving, he said, was a direct pathway to The Aching Plane. Whatever the nature of how the Tullapans viewed death, grief was an all-consuming experience for them. They opened themselves to the loss so viscerally, felt it so sharply. Even to those of us more in touch with life and death, grief is one of the human emotions that theoretically knows no end. It is drawn from a bottomless well. I have felt this in my own life... maybe you have, too. Certainly Marion Del Rosario has, and Terrence. I only made it back to my life because I had the guidance of Terry, and by that I mean the man he used to be before he became trapped in that place.

I think the Tullapan people knew this about grief to a degree that few of us allow ourselves to. And their ritual, The Grieving, honors this. It honors how grief is a separate place from the world we know. An agonizing, miserable, aching place. You feel it deep within you first, and then—sometimes—you fall into it. Some emotions are infinite. They know no end. And if you aren't careful, they can consume you. Those who fall into their grief entirely are beyond the reach of anything and anyone. The Grieving ritual turns this into a window, or a doorway, directly to aching Katalpa. Those who do not go deeply enough into their longing for their own life, they don't come back.

5

FILE 3

I think there's really just one more thing I need to tell you.

The Terrence Forgaill that I once knew... he was a good man. Not without his rough and harder edges, not without his flaws or his difficulties; but where it mattered most, he was good. When I remember him, I remember a man possessed of an unbearable curiosity. He saw things through to their conclusion. He was the guy jotting down notes and making obscure connections as he walked through life. To me he was a mentor, yes, but also a friend.

You probably know his story, or at least... at least the most crucial part of it, if you've read the journal. And I assume you have read it. You and Marion are best friends, and I have reason to believe she must've shared the journal with you by now. What that journal wouldn't be able to tell you is how Terry wasn't always like that. By the time he gathered his group of four—myself among them—and stepped through the door into Katalpa, he was already changing. When Alice disappeared, she really disappeared. I mean... I mean it was different from the way it happened on the Tullapa Islands. Alice disappeared and was swallowed up by Katalpa, all trace of her, all memory of her, gone. Just like that. But somehow, Terry remembered her. He never went into it with me, but I think it's because he knew her as a child. He had always loved her, almost his entire life, and that love only deepened as they found each other in adulthood. Their love also grew more complicated, darker in some respects, but always it was there, it was strong, it was a fundamental aspect of both their identities. They'd been children together. That part especially. There's something different, something purer I guess, about a child's love. For that to have been the foundation of their relationship says a lot, I think, about how Terry was able to break some invisible barrier in his mind and remember Alice, even after she was swallowed by Katalpa.

But it's even worse than you may think. I don't know how else to say this without telling you everything—about Terry, about our time on that other plane, that nightmare of a… just… just that nightmare—but I promised I'd be brief, and I'm short on time as it is. If I don't finish this recording now, and if I don't find a way to get it to you and make sure you listen to it, it'll be too late and I'll… I'll change my mind. You see, there's some part of me that knows I've made an irreversible mistake. It weighs heavy on me. I can hardly sleep anymore, not just because of the dreams but because of what I've done, what I plan to do, and what I know has been set in motion, in part because of my own actions.

Something happened to Terrence Forgaill in the realm of Katalpa. He was already changing, as a person, when we mounted the… the expedition, I guess, for lack of a better word. And the thing is, I can't say what happened. I don't know. We were, all of us, separated almost immediately after our arrival in that other place. There was me, and Peter Doloria, and Terrence Forgaill, and another… someone whose name I still can't recall. The fact that I don't remember him tells me that he never came back. Whoever he was. I've said so many prayers for his sake, and I can't even remember his name.

Whatever happened to Terry, he is not the man I knew. He may not even be human anymore. The last time I saw him, I remember looking into his eyes and I recognized nothing there. It was as if something else—something, not someone—was looking out through his eyes, puppeteering his body. And the things he said… I can't repeat them, but they were not the words of the curious, intelligent, passionate man I used to know. Maybe you have some semblance of what I mean. It wasn't just what he said; it was what his words did to me, even just by hearing them. When he spoke, it was as if he had hijacked the voice in my head—like his voice became the voice of my thoughts—and… and that gave him power over me, of a sort.

Maybe some part of me needs you to hear this because I understand Terry better now than I ever have. He couldn't return to his life. And neither could I. I made it back, but… but I left some part of me there, and nothing has felt the same since. Sometimes it's like all I can feel is the ache anymore, and nothing else is real compared to it. So I understand why Terry turned back, even though I'm not sure I'll ever fully understand what he eventually became.

But there is one thing, just one, that remains of the human in him. And it is not a good thing. If you've read his journal, then you have some inkling of it, though perhaps you haven't made the connection yourself.

Terry described to me, a few times, the days of his childhood. He was certainly one to wax nostalgic. When he spoke of his childhood, his eyes unfocused and it was like he went somewhere else, to another place. Katalpa in his mind, you could say. He always talked about Alice, the little girl he met by the river. Tullapa River, actually. Strange coincidence. The name, I mean. He'd go on about that particular scene. An icon of his life, his memories. The care-free days of boyhood spent with a girl he loved, beside a river.

What I know about you, Charlie Louise, isn't much. But I happen to know that one of the loves of your life is fishing, and that your spot happens to be Catalpa Creek. Another strange coincidence. And during Terrence's long, lost years on The Aching Plane, he saw visions of you. He called you *the fishergirl.* There were others, of course… people sitting by streams, people sitting by bonfires or campfires… you get the idea. But he took note of you on multiple occasions.

You see, while the human parts of Terry faded—and were eventually replaced by something else—what little remained became hideously amplified. His original reason for seeking Katalpa in the first place was for Alice. He wanted to—he wanted maybe to find her, yes, but I think he understood that he might never find her. He wanted answers, more than anything.

But the more he sought answers, the less sense any of it made—until, I think, he began to think more about you. He'd see you, but I think what he saw was Alice. A girl by a river. Something he could cling to, hold on to, even as the nightmare of Katalpa tore him apart from the inside out.

I don't know much else beyond that. But I know—as you surely do too, by now—that he is looking for you. What that means, and why… I wish I could tell you more. But I'm in the dark. I've told you everything I can, and although I can't pray anymore, I can hope it's enough.

Be careful, Charlie Louise. Whatever comes, for my part in it… it means nothing to apologize, but… with what's left of my heart, and the man I used to be, I am sorry.

6

The silence in the room clung like fog to hills.

Adrian rose from the windowsill and paced. After a few minutes of this, he stopped and regarded Charlie with something like frustration.

"We gonna talk about this? I mean… any of it?"

Charlie looked at him, searching for words that wouldn't come.

"Jesus, Charlie… what… what's going on? I need *something*, at least. None of this makes any *fucking* sense. I want to help, but…" He lifted his hands to his face, eyes going wide. His cheeks burned red when he noticed the way Charlie was looking at him. "I'm sorry. Jesus. I'm not even really frustrated, you know? That whole thing out there just… it scared me. And I don't know what the fuck most of that recording was supposed to mean, but he… he was insane, right? Like delusional? But it doesn't make sense if he was, because… well because of everything that's been happening with you lately, and what just happened on the street, Jesus *Christ*. And it's not like someone could just make all of that shit up." He sat down hard on the edge of the bed, grasping clumps of his own hair. *Am I losing my mind?* his posture seemed to ask.

Charlie wanted to rise from the windowsill and go to him, and she probably would have under any other circumstances. But she thought of the journal.

If I give you one answer, she thought, wishing Adrian could hear her thoughts, *if I start to tell you what's really happening and what's going on behind all of this, then you'll be a part of it, too. And you're too good, Adrian. You don't deserve that. I can't lose anyone else.*

Adrian huffed. "When we first pulled up to this house, something about it seemed familiar, almost like I've been here before, but... but in a dream, maybe. Does that make sense? I feel like I'm missing something. I feel like I should know who Marion is and what she has to do with any of this. It's like I'm circling around a hole, and everything around it makes sense and it's leading toward something, but then there's just... the hole."

Charlie closed her eyes.

"Charlie, I know it isn't right of me to ask right now, after everything, but... I need *something*, at least. I feel like I'm losing my fucking mind over here."

She breathed deeply. "I can't."

"Yes, you can. I'm right here. Just tell me."

"Adrian."

"You think you're sparing me something—I know that's what you think—but you're not. I want to be here for you, but what the fuck. I feel like I shouldn't even believe what I've seen today."

"It's not that I don't want to tell you." The sense of finality in her voice was enough to silence him. He listened, stunned, as she spoke. "I know things now that I can't stop knowing, even if I wanted to. I've seen glimpses of what the world can be like, what's underneath everything that I thought I knew—about the world, about reality, about other people and even myself. The curtain got pulled back, I don't know why or how... but ten years ago it swallowed Marion up like it was *nothing*, like she wasn't a kid with her whole life ahead of her and people who loved her. Now it's happened again. The curtain pulled back, and I've barely even glimpsed across the chasm. I've felt it, I've seen it. The other side of things. And now I can't forget."

"You could show me that journal. I could read it."

"No. The next time I pick that thing up, it'll be to burn it."

"Charlie, you don't have to shoulder all of this alone. I'm asking you to do this. It's not like you're inducting me into something against my will. I can… I mean, if I can't help you, I can at least share some of the burden—"

"No, Adrian, you don't get it." She uncurled herself from the windowsill. "This isn't like anything else. It's not something where you can be there for me or help me."

"Why? Can you at least tell me that?"

Charlie shook her head.

Adrian reached out and took her hand. "I'm not scared of what might happen to me. I'm scared for *you*. Who's gonna watch your back, or at least… at least be there for you? What happened to your dad… it's not gonna happen to me."

Charlie pulled her hand back. "Don't."

"I don't mean that like—"

"I don't care. You think my dad thought any of this was gonna happen? You think Marion did? Or the pastor? Or me?"

"Charlie, I'm sorry…"

She shook her head again, eyes moving to the windowsill, the empty desk, the bed. The absence of Marion was the void around which she felt herself spinning—how familiar a feeling it was, that circling, ever since that summer day ten years ago—but the emptiness of the room had a way of muffling all sensation of a world beyond it. Lupita moving around the house. Sirens somewhere in the distance.

If I do nothing, she realized, *Marion will vanish. And the world outside will keep to its busyness, covering its emptiness in layers of illusion. The way it always does and always has.*

She said to herself, scarcely above a whisper: "And the birds will keep singing. The river will keep flowing. The fish will continue knowing nothing about any of us."

"What— Charlie, what does that mean? Are you even—"

"This started a long time ago," she said. "With Marion and me. Even with the rest of us—we called ourselves The Renegades—"

"You told me about them."

"I thought so."

"So, this friend… Marion… she was part of that group?"

"Yes."

"How come you never mentioned her before?"

"I have. We've talked about her a lot, actually. You just don't remember."

"How is that possible?"

"I don't know."

"Jesus. Okay."

"Even with the rest of The Renegades, it was really just me and her. Marion and me. Even after it seemed like everyone forgot her, I remembered. I couldn't forget, no matter how much it hurt."

"I understand that."

"I had that picture of her, which I…" She wrinkled her brow, the next words dying on her tongue. "That… picture…"

"Charlie?"

In her mind, the images from the Dusk, the beach, outside the black trees. Marion standing on the sand, a framed photograph clutched in one hand.

She took it. It's not an accident she's there.

Charlie sat on the windowsill again, her gaze far away. She knew, then, what she needed to do.

Adrian asked, "What is it?"

"I'm not sure. I was just realizing something." She looked down. "Lupita said we could stay the night here, right?"

"I think so. Do you want to?"

The thought of returning to her house tonight, of sleeping in its emptiness, was nearly enough to bring the tears swelling again. "If I stayed here, would you… would you stay with me?"

"As if you could get rid of me."

"Okay. Thank you."

Lupita was delighted to hear they would be staying. She asked no more questions and went immediately to the kitchen to begin preparing dinner. It would take a couple hours, she said, but they could eat whenever they were hungry.

Lupita moved around the kitchen, and whenever she found herself paused she would set about with busywork, scrubbing the counters or hand-washing spare dishes, even rearranging coffee mugs in one of the cupboards. Charlie tried to help her but Lupita made her sit down with a blanket and a cup of tea; she made Adrian sit with her, too.

When the pots began to sizzle on the stove, the house filled with that familiar smell: noodles and vegetables simmering in oil. Charlie closed her eyes, breathed it in, let it take her to the distant past she so brokenly longed for.

They slept beside each other on Marion's bed, at first on opposite ends, then closer together. Charlie watched him watching her in the dimness.

"I'm sorry," she said. "I don't know how to tell you how grateful I am for you."

He said nothing. Slowly, hesitantly, he reached an arm out and put it on her shoulder. Scooted closer so he could run his hand down her back. Gently. With tenderness.

He made no movement closer, made nothing of it. She tensed at first, then relaxed. Shut her eyes and focused on the sensation of his fingers caressing up and down her spine.

She kept her eyes closed until Adrian's hand ceased its movements. After a few more minutes, he turned over onto his other side and his breathing slowed and deepened.

Charlie slipped away from the bed. Changed out of the soft pajamas she'd borrowed from Marion's dresser and back into her shirt and overalls.

Before she left the room, Charlie paused and looked at Adrian.

If I never come back, she thought, mouthing the words, *I'll remember you and think of you only with love, Adrian. You'll forget me, I know... but I'll remember for both of us. I promise.*

7

———————

In the neglected shed which sat in Lupita's side yard, Charlie found the old bicycle. It sat coated in dust and cobwebs, its frame white and elegantly arched down the center. Between the handlebars sat a chrome headlamp, and beneath the lamp was the flowery basket where Marion had often stored sandwiches and a water bottle for the long bike rides around town.

Stars still glittered in the sky, and dawn was a distant rumor when Charlie, as quietly as she could, finished brushing away the cobwebs from the frame and handlebars of the bike. She patted the seat, wiped any residual dust away. The tires weren't flat, nor were they full. It would have to do.

At the end of the driveway, she sat on the bike, set a foot on the pedal, but paused a moment to look at the house. Marion's house. Frequent hangout and sleepover spot of The Renegades, more than ten years ago. They returned from their adventures in the forest or through town, hands dirty, skin baked under the sun, sometimes with marks on their knees or elbows.

We could've done anything. We could've become anything. It must've been as beautiful as I remember—that's no illusion. How we loved each other, and the small freedoms of every day, and every minute we spent together.

The way I loved you, Marion, was the way I loved being alive, back then. We lost track of time so often, just sitting together and talking through the night. Sometimes you'd reach out and take my hand and we'd just keep talking, acting like it didn't matter even though we glowed for each other on the inside. Remember?

"You," she said to the house and the memories within, and as much to Lupita. "I had two homes when I was a kid, thanks to you."

Before she started crying, she put her weight on the pedal, lifting the bicycle into motion. The air was brisk on her face. She let it fill her up as she pedaled and picked up speed.

8

Charlie left the bicycle in the dirt parking lot that overlooked the old flooded quarry. From here, all that remained was the brief trek along the forest trail.

She looked out across the quarry, beneath the still-dark sky from which the stars were sleepily fading. A man stood out there, from this distance no more than an ant-sized shape only faintly distinct against the hazy morning twilight. He was waving at her.

Charlie felt something like a scratching in her mind, as if a hand had plunged into the waters of her thoughts. She began jogging down the dirt trail, into the woods. The stars dissolved into the dim blue of dawn.

To Charlie's dismay, when she thought of Marion, there was no mental image in her mind. She couldn't picture her friend's face. What she saw instead, in place of the memory of Marion in her mind, was fog. An impossibly thick bank of dark fog, and a man— an obscured silhouette—standing, waiting for her, in the fog.

Marion, she thought, but her mind's eye conjured only that image. And it was getting clearer. The fog was pulling back. She could see his face.

Charlie wiped tears from her cheeks, careful not to glance to the sides. She could see him in her peripheral vision. He was standing in the trees, appearing not to move and yet following her like the moon. A shadowed figure that stood too tall. A thing that had once been human.

I'm coming, Marion, she told herself, but it wasn't Marion's face she saw in her mind's eye. It was the face of the Thing that was Terrence Forgaill. A black, scruffy beard caked with dirt and decay. A looseness to its skin, as though the skin wasn't compatible with the tissue and muscle underneath. It had no eyes.

Even without its eyes, it could *see* her. There was no doubt. She tried to picture Marion—Marion on the windowsill, Marion on Catalpa Creek, Marion on the sand of that other place—but her mind conjured the Thing's face instead. Unthinkably, that face wasn't just an image in her head, no. *It was looking back at her,* and its lips peeled back into a hungry grin.

Charlie, panicking, picked up her pace. Any minute now and she'd be able to hear the crinkling waters of the creek.

9

The light of fresh dawn bloomed, reflecting on the silvery flowing waters of Catalpa Creek.

At first, Charlie paced back and forth along the banks. Her heart raced too intensely, her breaths came too rapidly. Every time she thought about Marion, every time she tried to conjure a calming memory, she saw the Thing that was Terrence Forgaill staring at her with those bleeding holes for eyes and that strange, loose-skinned smile.

When she tried to focus on the noise of the water—the splashing, the puddling, the rushing—all she could think about was how urgent it sounded, how hurried.

Had Adrian woken up yet and noticed she was gone? Would he try calling her, looking around for her, and then tell Lupita? How long until they went looking for her? How long until one of them —probably Lupita—suggested they come here, where The Renegades had often spent summer afternoons?

It occurred to Charlie as she paced that she had no idea what to do. Before, the visions of Katalpa had simply happened. She hadn't wanted them to happen, and they'd been paralyzing enough that she couldn't actually imagine *wanting* them to happen again.

Except… that was why she'd come here. This seemed the place for it to happen. In the audio file about the Tullapa Tribe, Pastor

Joe had spoken about the elements: fire, wind, earth, water. The grieving woman had been offered a torch and a bowl of water: a choice between two elements.

And this place, this creek, was where Charlie felt at home. This was where she came when the noise of the world became too much, when the waters of her heart were roiled and restless and she needed to come back to herself.

A line from a poem by Mary Oliver echoed, as if from a great distance, in Charlie's memory. Something Marion had read to her, once. Charlie had been fishing on this creek, somewhere upstream from here. But no, not quite… she remembered that she hadn't been fishing yet; she'd been struggling to untangle some fishing line, and was retying a knot around a lure.

She'd been sitting on the rock, the pole gripped between her legs, a bit of fishing-line in her teeth, both hands occupied with line and lure, when Marion came wandering up to her. The boys would be along soon, announcing their presence from the trail, no doubt, but Marion arrived first and was delighted to discover Charlie already here. She asked if she needed help with the fishing-line, to which Charlie laughed and simply shook her head.

So Marion took out a book of poetry—*Red Bird*, by Mary Oliver—and found her own rock beside Charlie's. After a few minutes, she read out loud.

The lines that came back to Charlie were from a poem called *Summer Morning*. They were brief, but they were enough.

"Heart,
I implore you,
it's time to come back
from the dark."

She could remember those lines, nothing else, because for the rest of the poem, she'd been too focused on the reality in front of her: that the girl she loved sat beside her in the early afternoon of this summer day, beside gentle waters, reading poetry out loud.

Charlie ceased her pacing while swept up in this memory. No disturbing image took its place, no darkness crept underneath. It was just a memory. In that memory, her father was still alive—back at the house—and they'd had breakfast together a few hours earlier, the way they usually did. Charlie had loved to wake up early to make him breakfast, to prepare tea for the two of them. Sometimes they sat outside on the back porch, sometimes at the dining table by the kitchen, or—if it was a rainy day and neither of them had any obligations—they'd put something on TV. It must've been one of those mornings. She would've hugged him goodbye and he would've wished her luck on her fishing, with a line like "Bring back dinner!" in parting. Along with, of course, "Say hello to Marion." Always that. Never to any of the boys, but to Marion.

He probably always knew about them. That thought made her love him—and miss him—only more.

And either she would've taken her tackle box and fishing gear on her bike, or come with only a few extra lures, knowing she had the fishing pole in its hiding place in the woods.

It was a memory, a now two-dimensional image only in her mind, but it was all she ever wanted in her life. In the memory, her heart was full and she didn't even know it.

Moving now with the patience of the water on its steady journey, she came to the edge of the creek. The water soaked through her converse shoes but she hardly noticed, too sumptuous was its cold. She crouched. Reached a hand out and, gentle as a lover, submerged it. Brought it back up and touched her own face to feel it on her skin, to feel closer to it.

I know why they call it The Aching Plane.

She closed her eyes and pictured that summer day again. The sound of Marion's voice drowning out even the sound of the crinkling water. The words reaching Charlie as if they'd been written just for her, just for this day, for the two of them together. How sunlight had glittered in gems on the water's surface, and something in her chest had felt exactly like that.

In her mind she reached out for her friend. She reached out for her father, the way she had reached out for him in the church before he told her to go.

Something inside her felt like a wound releasing all the torrid aching it contained.

She opened her eyes, looked at where the water had been.

It was no longer the water of Catalpa Creek. The light of early morning was gone, replaced by the hazy, dim gray of dusk.

Charlie opened her eyes on The Aching Plane.

10

Charlie found herself seated on the charcoal-black sand of a cold shoreline, beside a dribbling creek that cut a small trench on its way to the tide. The light of dusk appeared to be in a perpetual state of dissipation, seeping toward the edge of night—but Charlie knew it would grow no darker here. She could sit at this very spot for hours, listening to the crashing waves, and time would seem to stand still.

She lifted herself up, brushing sand from her legs. Her body felt heavy on the inside, as if her bones had taken on mass.

Like my bones are filled with concrete, she thought, and the feeling was familiar. *This is the way things really are*, she used to think when in the grip of depression, while all her interest in the things she normally loved burned away to static indifference. The simplest things—even just walking from her bedroom to the bathroom across the hallway—became impossible tasks.

The feeling in her bones now, the weight—it was like that. Her depression had come with palpable weight, as did her grief. It was what she felt now, amplified beyond anything she'd ever known. A density clogging her tissue. The muscles in her legs tightening, hurting.

Charlie focused on her breathing as she stood straight. Her vision seemed dark around the edges. She felt unable to take a full breath.

In her ears, the sound of the tide—which she'd always found soothing—was shadowed by something else. A wisp, faintly audible…

Whispers. The water was *whispering.* Just beneath the sound of the crashing waves, the ocean was speaking in thousands and thousands of low voices. Charlie couldn't make out any words; all she heard was the urgent discordant whispering. The volume of their chaos seemed to rise and tumble with every breaking wave, and then falter back toward silence when the water receded.

An ocean made of voices. She began to scan the mist-blanketed water and the distant horizon.

Far off, a dark mass—sheer cliffs—rose above the whispering ocean. The mists swirled and billowed wildly around the cliffs. With her eyes, Charlie followed the dark form up, up, impossibly high—higher than any building or any mountain she could imagine. It had no end that she could see, rather it shot up into the dimness of the sky and seemed to meld with it.

Something wasn't right. Her stomach seemed to drop into weightlessness. She felt as though the ground had disappeared beneath her. It wasn't a mountain, as she'd first thought.

"Oh my god." She clapped a hand over her mouth, stumbling back.

Whatever it was, it was looking at her. Upon the towering expanse of it, conjured maybe by the way shadows fell across it, was a face. Two cavernous darknesses where, Charlie was sure, gigantic eyes watched her. A gaping hole suggested a mouth wider than a cruise ship.

Charlie couldn't tear her eyes away from it, but her brain swelled with a painful, blunt sensation, causing her to take deeper, quicker breaths. She stepped away on buckling knees, hand still slapped over her mouth.

Its eyes, if it had eyes, if she wasn't tricking herself into seeing a face there, were aimed right at her.

As she began to hyperventilate, she *felt* its gaze and sensed what could only be described as an intelligence in its stare. A wisdom she backed away from, panicked at the awareness of, and wanted nothing to do with. She could barely stand to look at it.

From somewhere behind her, where she had not yet dared to look, something like a shockwave rippled through the air. It passed through her, making her feel as though she'd been grabbed and shaken on the inside, and she watched it—an invisible force bending the fabric of the world in a visible field of distortion—as it crossed the waters and passed into the mountainous thing with its staring shadows, its maybe-eyes and maybe-face.

The whispers from the ocean grew louder, louder, a crowd of millions—hundreds of thousands of packed stadiums—suddenly screaming at the tops of their lungs with the manic urgency of an air-raid siren, but the sound wasn't in her ears. She heard it in her mind.

One second she stood on the shore, gasping up at the staring mountain; the next second she was on her knees in the sand, hands around her head, eyes clamped shut, crying out.

Millions of voices inside the locked room of her own mind, each one of them shrieking.

God, and there was *so much pain* in those screams.

Her head throbbed. Her heart beat wildly. Charlie pulled herself up, opened her eyes.

Another pulse through the air, appearing to distort or refract reality itself as it passed. Charlie felt it in her bones and knew, not merely because she'd read about it but because she felt it:

It was the *ache*.

Everything in her view, then, was engulfed by a rolling fog bank.

Charlie had never seen anything like it. The almost untraceable speed with which it moved.

The fog was a wall that swallowed not only the mountain, but the ocean and the sky. It was a hungry thing, and it swept across the waters as if savagely uncreating them, the arm of an angry god swiping clean the slate of creation. In mere seconds, the encompassing fog crossed the entirety of the ocean.

Charlie gasped and threw her hands out in front of her, a futile instinct. The world went from darkening dusk to dense, swirling gray.

The voices in her head continued to wail and shriek—albeit from what seemed a farther distance—and after seconds or minutes, the fog *whooshed* past. Charlie spun to see it follow the path of the land before it was pulled into a radiant darkness.

Except it wasn't darkness Charlie was looking at. It was *nothing*. The landscape crept upward as if on its way to forming a mountain before it simply stepped off into void. It simmered the way a mirage would simmer and distort, then appeared to melt and blend into the grayness of the dusk, as if the land inexplicably became cosmic, and then—

—*nothing*. Not darkness, not brightness, but an emptiness where something, anything, was supposed to be.

And the void—the edges of it—radiated a strange light. Charlie watched, stunned, trying to make sense of what she was seeing. It was as though, behind the distorting, bendable fabric of reality itself, something waited, emitting an unknowable energy, a light that glowed for an instant, nothing more, and then shuddered outward in a heartbeat-like pulse.

The ache.

It traveled outward from the edges of the radiant void, making reality appear two-dimensional as it moved in a refracting wave. When it passed through Charlie, she recoiled. On the inside she felt hollow. A throbbing hollowness.

She realized she wanted to go to it. Not a conscious thought, not something she decided; it was simply there in her body: the desire to traverse the dark landscape, the shadowy hills of scorched ground, and to walk into the void and its strange, otherworldly glow. Let it swallow her, let the aching be alleviated. It hurt, everything hurt. Underneath her awareness, there remained not even a trace of warmth, no memory of pleasure, or kindness, or happiness. But the looming void, her body told her, was a way out of the hurting.

In response, she tried to turn her mind away, to direct her thoughts elsewhere. She tried to think about the river again, to conjure the memory of Marion reading poetry to her, and of her father's warmth—but those images dropped away from her mind as though their edges were slick and ungraspable. It all fell away, flattened by the immensity of the emotional aching that filled her bones. She thought of something she'd told Adrian just last night—about how the curtain had been pulled back and she'd seen the way the world could really be underneath.

I thought I knew. I thought I had even the slightest idea.

She cast her own gaze in all directions—the great black trees; the sweeping coastline that stretched farther to where dusk descended into darkness; the slope of the land gradually upward through dark hills and toward the pulsing void—and realized she had no idea where to go or what to do. Any idea of why she'd come here, what she'd hoped to accomplish, was gone. Did she think she could find Marion in this place? Where could she even start? If, somehow, she did find her—then what? Bring her home? How? And what then?

Charlie wrapped her arms around herself. Her mind had no space for imagination, for rationality. What could she do? Not even her thoughts felt like her own anymore. There was her awareness of an agony, a pain that had always been with her beneath the surface now given full reign over her.

Charlie backed away from the ocean, not wanting to move toward the aching void, but every other direction seemed rife with sentient shadows that encroached upon her position. She had never felt so small, so naked, so alone, in all her life.

When she looked in the direction of the scorched and shadowy hills, she saw something she hadn't noticed before.

Embedded before the hills—where the land began its steady incline, toward the void—was a gothic cathedral. Its spire sharpened to a point; its rose window had long ago been shattered into jagged remnants; it appeared not made of wood or stone, but of something porous and stretched and rancid. It looked almost alive, as if the cathedral were made of—

No. It didn't matter. Charlie moved toward it, perceiving it first and foremost as shelter. Shelter from the dark oceanic eyes of the mountainous thing on the horizon. Shelter, maybe, from Katalpa's dreadful heartbeat which came in steady, flattening waves.

The fabric of the world was a stagnant ocean, and Katalpa was the stone dropped in its midst—which sent ripples outward across the water. Those ripples became waves, became tsunamis, became the ocean itself.

A storm that revealed itself to be truth, the calm to be the illusion.

Charlie came closer to the cathedral. It had a thick, stinging, eye-watering aroma of decay. The stench was a dry, sick green. This close, she could see its walls more clearly. Her stomach lurched and she dropped onto her knees and retched, tasted bile in her throat.

The cathedral was made of flesh. *Human* flesh. Patches of blackening green, maggoty, porous skin stretched taut across its surface.

Charlie wiped her chin and backed away, holding the collar of her shirt over her mouth and nose, hoping this was far enough away from the smell, and she sat on the cold, hard ground. She might've cried, but her senses were on high alert even with the weight of melancholy and memory sitting like stones in her body.

Where are you, Marion? If you can feel me here, give me a sign. Anything.

She sat this way, shivering, on the edge of hysterics, eyes puddled with tears that wouldn't fall. Despite what she knew about this place, she kept expecting the dusk to fade into night, but it didn't. For how long she sat, paralyzed with fear and disbelief, it was impossible to tell. Time had no meaning here.

After a long while, she heard human noise from the cathedral.

Someone was inside. Someone was laughing from inside the cathedral.

11

It was a hoarse, high-pitched laugh, that of a man genuinely tickled with amusement.

Charlie leaned forward but would not move an inch closer to the cathedral. With the bottom part of her face covered, she went from sitting to crouching, and leaned forward to try and get a clearer look.

A man stood in the doorway of the horrid structure. His clothes were dirt-thickened tatters hanging from his emaciated limbs. His hair, matted from neglect, hung nearly to his knees. His back was to Charlie; he faced the empty church with a collapsed roof, and raised his arms out in a gesture that said *Behold.*

He stopped laughing.

Charlie held her breath. All she could hear was the whispering voices of the ocean and the pounding of her own heartbeat.

She blinked and the man was gone; the doorway of the cathedral was empty.

A voice spoke over her shoulder: "*Listen.*"

Charlie yelled and leapt forward—though it was more a fall than a leap—and she spun onto her elbows to look up at the man.

There was no skin beneath his eyes. The muscles and flesh of his cheeks were exposed down nearly to the corners of his mouth in sharp open wounds, as if in mockery of tears. With his eyeballs exposed, his expression stayed perpetually wide-eyed, bloodshot, gleaming with a hungry madness.

When he saw the expression on Charlie's face, he grinned.

"Child," he said, his voice calm and steadfast. "I can see the condition of your mind. Just there, in the glint of your eyes. If it were…" His whole body froze—along with every feature of his face, including the visible muscles of his cheeks—as he searched for the word. "Fabric. If it were a fabric—no… a piece of clothing composed of fabric—you would need only to pull upon a single thread, and the entire piece would come undone."

Charlie stood up. The cathedral and its sickening smell rotted behind her, while the madman blocked her way back to the beach.

"What do you want?"

The madman pointed toward the dark hills, which to Charlie were silhouettes in the dusk—an ocean of shadows. But in the hills were other shapes: the rising steeples of other churches and cathedrals. "I'm curious what has brought you here, child. And which direction you intend on going."

"I don't know what you mean."

He inched closer, his bulbous eyes burning. "Others like myself who have wandered in between, they—we—have built these temples so that the lost ones may pray for deliverance from our sordid, trudging ache through the languid blood of time."

Charlie scowled at that last phrase.

The madman's eyebrows raised. "Oh, so you've heard these words before, yes? You must be f-familiar with the others from Terry's expedition. I was there, you know. I was one of them. Not that any of them—those that are still alive, anyway—not that any of them would remember anything about me, or, or that I even existed. You see, child, those were the words of Terry himself. One of his notorious speeches. He had quite a way with words, wouldn't you say? And his mind, oh… it certainly grabbed *my* attention."

"You," said Charlie, trying to avert her gaze from the exposed muscles of the man's cheeks. "You were part of Terrence Forgaill's group. The ones who went looking for this place."

The madman nodded. He sat carefully, as if he didn't want to startle her. After a few seconds, Charlie took a knee. She wanted to be ready to run.

"I honestly don't remember much of my life anymore," he said, his tone growing pensive. "But I do remember looking deeply within myself, making a *conquest* of my own interiority, as if I could shine a light into each one of my darkest corners and emerge, eventually, with a sense of the shape of my own soul. But, but all I found beneath every fabricated layer of identity and consciousness and awareness and personality, all I discovered was a great blankness inside of me. A hole straight through the center where I thought the soul was supposed to be. I'd ask you to imagine what that's like, but if you're here, in the Dusk, then I imagine you know perfectly well what it's like to discover emptiness, to discover nothing, where you thought there were foundations. You can deny it, if you wish, but why waste time. You're here, after all. You know the truth. If death is incomprehensible, that is, if, if it's truly impossible to imagine the world without us because even our imagining of it is still from within our point of view, then try comprehending the lack of the self. The lack of *any* self. The mask comes off and *poof*, empty clothes fall to the floor, along with the mask. That is the truth of all human identity. Imagine that." He laughed. The sound was like dead leaves scraping across pavement. "Even if you find your way back to your life, Charlie, you will find yourself no less disoriented and empty of hope than any other shell of a person. Did you think your philosophies separated you from your own heart? Every person that ever made it back, no matter how strong they were or what they believed, they eventually returned, drawn here again by the emptiness within them. The aching."

"No," she said, but the word was like paper tossed against the wind. Terrence Forgaill had nearly made it back to his life, but he had eventually turned back toward Katalpa. So had the pastor. And Marion. Of all people—for whatever reasons—Marion had returned here. She had taken the facedown photograph on Charlie's desk, the one of Charlie and her on Catalpa Creek, and had come back to this place, as if wanting to be forgotten.

From this vantage, Charlie's memory of her own life betrayed her. She couldn't picture it or remember what she liked to do with her days. Had there been pleasure, or merely distractions? Were there things she'd liked to do that brought her fulfillment, made her feel okay? It all seemed thin and artificial, a cardboard cutout.

She knew too well—echoing the madman's words—what it was like to navigate around an abyss inside herself. A vacuum which sometimes reared its hideous head into her life and drained everything of color, infecting her thoughts, sapping away any desires or aversions.

"I once believed knowledge would protect me, *shield* me," said the madman, "from the inevitable sorrows and agonies. Terrence Forgaill was the same. As is anyone who pursues what some call *enlightenment*, or salvation, or even simply distraction, in whatever paltry form. Like you, child. Very much like you."

"I'm not like you. I'm not like you or him."

"Don't make me laugh, child."

From the direction of the ocean, the movement of something gigantic demanded her attention. She looked and saw an impossibly high wall of fog, like the one from before, rushing with unthinkable speed from across the waters of the Ocean of Hali. The dim whiteness swallowed everything equally until she couldn't even make out the form of the madman a couple feet from her. But she could hear his laughter—high, maniacal, unhinged—and could still smell the rancid, decaying cathedral.

Charlie got to her feet. She didn't want to hear any more.

"Despite what you may insist with the philosophies and the ideas you hide behind," he said, "you want life to have meaning. I know, because I was the same as you. And, just like you, I went looking for answers and I found them. Some would've called it enlightenment, but those are the ones who do everything they can to keep their eyes on the light while ignoring the chasm beneath their so-called harmony. They don't see that the doorway to their enlightenment is the same one that opens into madness.

"When you go through your days and look out at other people, or at the trees, or the rivers, the streets, the shopping aisles and the parking lots, the quiet driveways at night, you harbor deep inside you a hope you wouldn't admit to anyone, maybe not even to yourself. A hope that it all means something, that there's more. Right?" He laughed. "I'm right, aren't I."

"You don't know anything about me." Even though she couldn't see him—couldn't see anything but the swirling fog—she tried to circumnavigate the spot where he'd been sitting before. If she could slip off, back toward the beach...

But then what? Where could she go?

"No, I don't know you," said the madman. "But I know you're here. I know you're like me. You want answers."

Charlie stepped forward through the fog, desperate to put distance between herself and the madman.

"If you're trying to tell me life has no meaning beyond what we give it," she replied, "you're wasting your breath."

"All you want now," he said, his voice not seeming to grow distant, "is to find your friend and then to get back. Isn't that what you want? You might fool yourself into thinking that anywhere at all, any*thing* at all, is better than this. A couch and a blanket. The counter of a coffee shop. Maybe the sand of a regular ocean, or the banks of a regular river. What's home for you, child? You think that's what you want, to get away from this place and to get back there? What's really waiting for you in those places? I can tell you what awaits you there, but maybe I don't need to tell you. You know. And you know it isn't something you can simply run away from and then call it *escape*."

Charlie shuddered at the feeling of his words like prurient fingers digging at the interior of her mind. If the voices of the ocean were still there, she couldn't hear them above the sound of the madman's words.

All around her, faces took shape in the fog. Some of them too long, stretched like clay. Others distorted, the eyes misplaced, the mouths open and bent at odd angles.

"Stop it," she said, stumbling, trying to move past the faces only to find they were everywhere. Some of them looked familiar despite the elongations and disfigurements. Some of them looked like people she knew, people she'd spoken to—in coffee shops, on sidewalks, at bonfires, in the hallways of the schools she'd attended, or in the houses of strangers.

Yes. She did know what awaited her in the landscapes of her life. The mind-numbing familiarities. People carrying their own chains and burdens. Empty spaces once inhabited by the people she loved.

Did any of it matter? Everything she'd done, all the pain she'd endured: the long nights in her parked car; church with her father; days spent trying to get to know herself better rather than seeking easy escapes outside herself; what was the point, when it had all led to this? If she found her way back to the world she knew, to what remained of her life, what could she hold on to that could keep the aching at bay?

"We'd lose our sanity," the madman said, "if we perceived things as they truly are. Some of us can feel the turnings of whatever nightmares crowd around the edges of our world. We don't know the source of that feeling, that distant awareness, but it's there, for some of us more than for others. An unconscious awareness of the unnameable things in the darkness that make our worst night-mares look like paradise. Bad enough that we're the only species on our planet that knows we're going to die. That we possess con-sciousness is the cancer of our own existence. Imagine trying to live your life now, child."

Charlie lifted her hands up over her ears but it was useless. She could hear the whispers of the ocean again, yet they had all become echoes of the madman's voice, repeating his words over and over and over and over.

It occurred to her, somewhere beneath the noise in her head, that maybe there was no madman after all. The person she'd been talking to wasn't a person.

"But it doesn't have to continue on this way for you, Charlie Louise. There's no reason for you to carry on with the weight of these terrible burdens. You had the dreams."

The voice was changing, growing deeper, more monotonous—not robotic, exactly, but losing its humanity. She had to be far from the cathedral of flesh now, closer to the waters of the ocean, but she had no way of knowing which direction she'd gone or how far she'd walked. There was only the whispering, the echoes, the voice in her head, and the melting faces in the fog.

"You saw what used to be," said the voice, *"and what could be. There is a way out of the nightmare."*

"No. There isn't."

"Follow the dreams into the void. Join the dreamers outside of the nightmare."

She remembered her father and the dreams he'd told her about. Dreams laced with his nostalgia for the past.

Her own dreams had been soft, always with Marion, with her father nearby, with the other members of The Renegades, too. On the creek, or in the comfort of her house, or sometimes Marion's bedroom. The dreams had been wonderful.

"The dreams," said the madman, *"are what brings them here. All of them, in time."*

She stopped walking. It was useless. There was nowhere to go.

"Some emotions are infinite," she whispered, remembering the words of Pastor Joe Correy. "They can consume you."

Words from Terrence Forgaill's journal returned to her, too— something about human consciousness and the aching at the center of it.

This place feeds on it. That was what the madman had told Terrence Forgaill.

Charlie placed a hand over her chest. She started to walk again, but her knees threatened to give way with each step.

When a blurry shape materialized in the fog ahead, she stopped again, gasping.

The shape in the fog was massive both in girth and height, and it swayed to and fro as it moved. A giant that had once been a person.

Emerging from the fog, the Changed Ones moved in the direction of the Ocean of Hali, their eyes gray and sightless, flesh-colored tendrils spewing from their bloodless purple lips.

Beyond them—hardly more than silhouettes—even larger, more deformed shapes dragged themselves across the cold ground, their bodies hideously mutated with new limbs sprouting from their heads, their torsos, their backs and fronts. They were like gargantuan dead trees with aimless branches clawing outward at the sky.

Monsters, Charlie thought. She couldn't imagine seeing one without the cover of the swirling fog. Clutching at her own body for comfort, she backed away.

"Marion!" cried Charlie in horror. "Where are you?"

She turned away from the Changed Ones, forcing herself to run. The fog thinned enough to reveal other things in the near distance. Other shapes.

The panicked thoughts in her mind suddenly stopped. Her father stood just ahead, dressed as if ready for church. He was waving at her.

"Dad." She took one step toward him—only one. He smiled, but the smile sat strangely on his face. Her father didn't smile like that. He was too shy, too self-aware. If he wanted her attention, he would've called out, and the smile on his face would've been gentle and self-conscious.

Chills descended her back. It wasn't her father there, waving to her in the fog. No imitation could replace him.

When she checked over her shoulder and then looked again, her father's face was caked with blood, and the smile no longer appeared joyful; it was strained, desperate, a call for help.

She turned, prepared to run in another direction.

Marion was there. She was trudging away from Charlie, shoulders slumped. In one hand she clasped the photograph of the two of them on Catalpa Creek.

Charlie hesitated only a moment before going to her.

12

Marion's eyes were gray, the pupils mostly drained of their usual soft brown. Trails of not-quite-dried tears marked her cheeks as she dragged herself through the fog.

"*I'm sorry, Mom,*" she whispered. "*I'm sorry, Charlie. I'm sorry.*"

"Marion." Charlie reached out for her friend's arm, already knowing how her skin would feel. "I found you. I was starting to think I might never—"

Her hand passed through Marion's arm as if through the texture of the fog.

"*I'm sorry, Charlie. I'm sorry, Mom.*"

"What?" She reached out again, and again her hand passed through. "Marion?"

"*Mom, Charlie, I'm sorry. I never should've come back. I never should've come back.*"

"Marion, listen to me."

"*I'm sorry. I always thought if I could see you one more time, see you smile one more time, and kiss you one more time, if I could just...*" Marion wiped at her face.

Charlie moved as if to embrace her, all her hope thrown into the gesture, ready to feel her body and to halt it in its mindless trudge.

But she passed right through her. Marion continued on, heavy with each step, repeating her apology to the fog.

Charlie followed her friend's footsteps. "Marion? Can you hear me?"

I can't touch her, she thought, *but I can hear her. So maybe some part of her can hear me, too.*

She caught up and kept pace beside Marion. Marion who was hunched slightly, frail and weary, stuck in a loop of regret and apologies.

"I'm so sorry, Charlie. But it's better this way. This is how it always should've been. This is what I want. It'll be like that dream I had of you, when you were free from me... free from the past."

Looking at her, unable to reach her, something occurred to Charlie that she'd never realized before. Marion had never truly made it back from this place, not on her own. Just as she'd been taken, she must've been *sent* back, either by Pastor Joe or, worse, Terrence Forgaill himself. Charlie felt a deep, heavy ache in her heart.

"Marion. If you can hear me, then I want you to know I understand. I understand why you think this is what you have to do. I understand why you took the photograph."

"I'm sorry, Mom. I'm sorry, Charlie."

"I understand, believe me... you know me," said Charlie. "I get it. But I'm not giving up. You hear me? I won't give up on you. And I refuse to believe that you're giving up. I..." She stuttered as Marion continued on. "But... but even if I can't find you and bring you back... you know I love you, right? You know I always have." Charlie put herself in front of Marion, facing her. "You were just a kid. You never even had a chance because you... you were just a kid." Marion continued on, one slow, heavy step at a time. "I'm sorry I let this happen. I'm sorry if I didn't make it so you knew how much I loved you and wanted you in my life. If there's any part of you that can hear me, and if there's any part of you that's still… still conscious enough… I don't want you to go, I'll never want you to go. I need you to know that. If you can fight, then please fight. Please… I know you don't know how to, but if you could give life just one more chance, I'd be right here with you. Just one more chance. You were only a kid.

"But if you can't…" She stopped walking. Let her friend pass through her once more. "If you go, go knowing how much you were loved, Marion. And how much I'll miss you."

The image of Marion walked onward through the fog, incessantly repeating her apologies, toward whatever darkness awaited her.

13

The fog vanished, sweeping its way up through the shadowy hills and toward the aching void. Marion vanished with it. Charlie stood alone.

In the distance, closer to the water, the Changed Ones wandered. The giants. Like sleepwalkers they stepped into the Ocean of Hali, in the direction of the mountainous thing which towered without a visible peak in the dusk. Charlie felt its stare, but she couldn't bring herself to look back. Looking at it affected her mind in ways she couldn't understand.

Her attention was drawn across the other side of the twilit sky to the void. The hole in reality where the land and the sky stepped off into an unseeable abyss.

It was bright somehow, despite there being no visible source of light. She couldn't seem to focus her eyes on any portion of its expanse; when she tried, she grimaced at what felt like a hammer clanging in her head. Beneath the throbbing—the incomprehensible pain—however, it was soothing. Strange thoughts entered her mind. She knew that if she went to it, to the void, it would swallow everything that had brought her here: the desperate longing to save Marion; the impossible agony of what had happened to her father; her loneliness; her guilt. Those things would be wiped away, replaced by the wonderful images of her dreams. The sunlight on

Catalpa Creek. Her father waiting at home. Marion somewhere nearby, reading poetry by the river.

If Marion was anywhere, lost in her wandering—slipping into a dreaming state—Charlie thought, *It must be there.* Along the edges of the void.

Without even an ember of hope in what she was doing, Charlie clenched her hands into fists and walked in that direction.

14

Far off to her right was the cathedral of flesh. Standing in its doorway was the form of the madman, who appeared to be praying with his arms dramatically lifted above his head. Charlie shook off the cold feeling the cathedral and its single attendant gave her, and she continued into the shadowy hills. The ground beneath her was hard and unforgiving, blackening as if it had been swept by fire.

The last remnants of light grew pale, burning a sickly orange and red. Scattered through the hills were the silhouettes of other cathedrals.

Charlie stopped to sit and catch her breath. The incline was not steep, but her body felt impossibly larger—denser—than it should have. Her mind, unable to reconcile any of what she'd seen and all of what she'd felt, had dropped into a fog of its own. All she could do was carry herself forward, stop when the strain of motion became too much, and then pick herself up to continue on.

The ache pulsed outward from the edges of the void. Breathing the air made her feel as though she'd been trying to run a marathon. The sickly dimness of the world around her darkened red, as if she were seeing everything through a sheen of blood.

Every part of her brain shouted in protest to what she was doing, but she stepped forward in defiance of reason. If she left the shores of the Ocean of Hali and somehow found a way to return to the world, to her life, to Adrian and Lupita and the emptiness of her own home, she wouldn't be able to live knowing she hadn't tried as hard as she could to find Marion and bring her back.

This was the only thing she could do.

There were other people walking in the shadowy hills. When Charlie approached a crowd of them, she saw their eyes were gray and sightless, aimed vaguely forward. They dragged their feet across the dark ground and muttered words of regret. She searched their faces in hopes of finding Marion as she continued toward the void.

A voice spoke from somewhere behind her—a voice like mist clinging to a mountainside.

"Fishergirl."

She froze for only a second before breaking into a full sprint, not even bothering to turn and see.

It was as if she were running in a dream. As if she were underwater and her feet were embedded in slabs of concrete. Her momentum was sluggish, but she pushed.

"Fiiissshhhheerrrrgiirrrrrl."

The ground leveled out into a gravel plateau beneath the dim red dusk.

Ahead: processions of dreaming wanderers headed straight into nullity. It hurt her mind to look at it.

Charlie didn't understand what she was seeing—it hurt her eyes, made her chest sink with a thrumming weight—but she ran for it anyway. It was a mirage, the way the ground grew blurry, fading away as it stretched on. The sky distorted, bending above into a terrible shimmering. There was a sense of movement beyond the edges of the void, a vague sense that something lived within it and swirled and churned there.

It occurred to Charlie that the void was not a *thing*, not a physical space; it was a *feeling*.

On the path ahead, the shapes of more people. She ran through them, each one slumped over, each one clutching an object in their arms—an old book, a photograph, dead flowers, a clay urn, a jewelry box. Some of the people wept. She glimpsed their dead-eyed faces as she passed, hoping one might be Marion's.

Sweat shining on her forehead as she huffed for breath, Charlie skidded to a stop. Her eyes went wide when she saw what was happening to the people farther ahead as they drew near to the shimmering.

A woman turned her pale face away from the void and met Charlie's gaze. The woman looked confused as she opened her mouth, maybe to call for help, to ask what was happening. She was blonde, there were wrinkles along the edges of her eyes and at the corners of her mouth, but she couldn't have been much older than Charlie's father. Charlie could even imagine how her voice would sound. But when the woman opened her mouth to speak or to call for help, her mouth kept dropping down. The skin on her face loosened like putty.

It was as if the woman were made of wax and standing beside a raging fire. Her face dripped downward, the bags beneath her eyes becoming fleshy sacks, her mouth drooping into a hideous, gaping frown as her teeth rained from her gums and clacked onto the gravel. Her wide eyes peeked out beneath the melted skin. The woman reached out. Her arm flopped and stretched bonelessly. She tried to speak, but all that came out was a choked warble—a dying cry for help.

When the woman collapsed, it was not a physical body striking ground, but a puddle of liquified skin and meat and muscle slapping wetly against the gravel.

All Charlie could do was stare, hyperventilating. She felt dizzy.

NO, NO, NO, NO THIS ISN'T REAL, THIS ISN'T HAPPENING—

Charlie felt her stomach rise and she keeled over and retched violently, but there was only acid and bile in her stomach. It stung at her throat.

"Fiiissshhherrrrgiirrrrl."

Charlie couldn't avoid it any longer. She got to her feet and, swaying, turned to see.

The creature that loomed behind her hardly resembled a human anymore. There weren't even legs. It floated, the tatters of its long coat dragging across the gravel.

There were arms, but they were too long, hanging low along with the tatters of the coat. Its wide-brimmed hat was sliced into various pieces that stuck jaggedly up and resembled a crown.

Charlie covered her mouth, her body coated with chills.

The Thing wore Terrence Forgaill's withered, leathery face like a mask. The eyes, sunken within the sockets, glittered like dark stones, but there was something horrifically artificial about them. Beneath the ruin of the Thing's decay-darkened skin, its eyes were like painted objects: not dead, not alive, with nothing—no emotion, no intelligence, no substance—behind their doll-like stare.

Its lips were peeled away from an emotionless, skeletal grin of rotted teeth.

"Dream with me," it said. Its sticky, rancid breath reached Charlie like a low breeze, so horrible it made her grip her stomach.

It floated at her, one of its long, spindly arms raising up and reaching for her with too many fingers. Its skin was dark and restless, as if made of unsettled shadows.

She could hear it in her head. Its voice was hundreds of tiny spiders skittering across the surface of her brain, searching for an entrance point to nest. The sensation made her squirm.

dance/
come/
ride/
walk/
dream/
with me, Fishergirl…
forgetting is the
gift/
opium/
privilege/
given to us by this place, this place that we both have sought for so long/
time out of mind/
come dream with me again
remember the way it used to be/
can always be
again
from now on/
forever…

"No," she said, hands up as if she could stop him. "I'm not who you think I am."

A strange, high-pitched sound emitted through its breath, while its voice skittered across her mind. The sensation, she realized, was not wholly unpleasant.

sometimes I

when I am drifting

falling

dreaming, maybe

as if asleep

almost remember us by

the river in summer

the words you said

promises you/

we/

made

remember?

"Listen," she said, backing up through the lines of people who walked toward the void. "Terrence. I know you think my name is Alice. I know you saw me by the river, and you remembered her. That was her name, wasn't it? Your wife?"

"Alice." Its head tilted in surprise and recognition. "*Alice.*"

"I'm not Alice. I know you can't remember very much anymore about… about who you used to be, and what your life used to be. But there's some part of you still in there, and you remember her. Even if she's the only thing you remember."

"*Alice… fishergirl…*"

"I'm sorry you lost her, Terrence. You've been looking for her for… for I don't even know how long. I know. I know what that's like."

The Thing hovered closer, but she kept backing up.

"I've been looking for someone, too. A girl. Someone I loved when I was young. Just like you, actually—the way you loved Alice. She was my Alice and I lost her, too."

The Thing's spidery fingers became a fist.

"Taking me won't fix it. I'm not her. I think maybe she's gone. And I think you know that."

The Thing that was Terrence Forgaill swooped forward, swift as a gust of wind, and seized Charlie by the shoulders. It lifted her off the ground, its hands like icicles against her skin, its face inches from hers and stinking of viscous rot and coppery blood. The screech from its throat filled Charlie's ears, growing louder with every heartbeat. Its eyes stayed the same, indifferent as death.

Stricken with fear, Charlie looked into those eyes. In her mind she saw Marion on Catalpa Creek, laughing, and she wondered if—somewhere in the remnants of its memory—Terrence Forgaill could see Alice on Tullapa River, in the glittering sun. Laughing, maybe, like Marion.

Charlie said, "It never makes sense and it isn't fair, and there's no reason for it, there's no answers, no bigger purpose. It's just the way things are. We let go."

Alice.

The voice in her head, laced now with desperation.

Alice

no

fishergirl

why?

"I don't know." Charlie felt her tears returning. "I just know it doesn't make any sense why we love anything when it's all over in such a short time... and we lose everything anyway, and we die, and that's it. Eventually no one will remember us, either, or the people we loved. I just know we do it anyway, and—"

Alice
the Dream
come with me
dream with me
no goodbye
no letting go

The Thing set her on the ground again, released its long, cold fingers from her shoulders, and spoke out loud. "*In the Dream, it lasts forever. Come dream with me, Fishergirl.*"

Charlie looked over her shoulder at the figures, the people, all of them gravitating toward the aching void. There was no sign of Marion.

She faced the Thing that was Terrence Forgaill, stared into its inexplicable eyes.

"On Earth, we might be the only species that knows we're going to die. I used to think that was a curse, but I'm not so sure anymore. Maybe… maybe I'd do it differently, if I'd known how little time I had with her. But that's just the way things are. I know you understand that. I know you do."

The Thing's eyes shifted from Charlie and looked beyond her into the shimmering, transfixed. It floated past her, drawn toward the void. Then it turned to look at her again.

"*Come dream with me. Forget the pain.*" It lifted its arms toward her again, long fingers brushing up her body. Maybe it was immune to reason. Maybe it didn't care.

Charlie heard something from behind her. She turned her head and saw movement from down the gravel path, past the sleepwalkers.

Her mind jumped at the possibility that it could be others—more wanderers, their eyes gray, their minds hypnotized—and maybe, just maybe, one of them might be Marion.

Charlie had read about the thing she saw come up onto this ridge where the gravel earth leveled out, but no corner of her imagination could have envisioned it in all its vivid, disgusting reality.

The thing that emerged onto the level path looked like a human-sized spider. Jagged hairy legs jutted out from its bulging abdomen, each leg bent sharply and ending in *hands*. Not the points of a spider's legs, but *human hands*. Its body resembled a human torso, stomach and chest and shoulders—from which more spider's legs jutted and bent—and a wide-eyed, slack-jawed human face.

Its flesh was coated in uncountable tiny arms with reaching hands. And upon the palm of every splayed hand, an eyeball stared.

The spider stepped up onto level ground. Another followed behind it. And another behind that one. And another.

There were maybe a dozen of them, a horde of things that looked as though they'd once been humans.

The first one lifted itself up, and the eyes of the human face fixated on Charlie. The slack mouth opened wider and *roared*, its eyes going wide as it did, and it was a human sound made insectile: a perfect mixture of human scream and monstrous cicada's buzzing.

The horde of spiders swarmed down the gravel path, their many arms kicking up dust and rocks.

A few of the wandering dreamers fell beneath the scuttling hands of the spider-creatures, and the hands didn't merely step over them, they ripped into the bodies, snapping necks and pulling heads from shoulders in fountains of blood. The human faces of the creatures dipped down to bite at the flesh of the beheaded victims, and came up smeared with chunky red matter.

For the first time in her life, Charlie froze. Panic seized her in an electric grip, her mind told her to run—it didn't matter which way, just *run*—but the *things* were upon her already and they were too fast. She tasted dust, felt the ground tremble beneath her.

She was shoved violently to the ground, tossed with such force that she skidded on her left leg at a forceful angle—felt bright pain shoot through it—and then she rolled and felt the gravel rip at her skin.

Hands, too many hands, grabbed at her, their owners screaming with voices half-human, half-insect, half-something else entirely. Those hands found her injured leg, pulled. Charlie screamed when she felt teeth pierce through the skin of her heel, then other sharp things—maybe teeth, maybe fingers—digging into the meat of her thigh. *Fingers*, she thought in a flash of horrified absurdity. Fingers plunging into the skin and flesh of her leg. The blood was warm dripping down, soaking through the denim of her overalls.

She screamed. And then it all stopped.

15

The sound of carnage.

They were tearing into her body, she thought. Her mind had broken from the pain and this had to be the final numbness, the slipping away. She would open her eyes to see her own body torn into pieces, blood everywhere. Her thoughts flew first to her father. What would he think of what became of her? How deeply would it have horrified him and broken his heart?

But she thought, too, of Adrian. She remembered the feeling of his hand on her back, tracing the contours of her spine.

Suddenly the grabbing and slashing halted. She opened her eyes and wasn't sure, at first, what she was seeing.

A dark shape rose above the ground. The shape, at its center, was a man's body, but splaying outward from it were dozens of— tendrils? cables? Arms of some kind reached out from the dark shape. The arms pulled the dozen spider-creatures in. The creatures thrashed and bit and swiped at the shape, inflicting bloodless damage to it, but the shape's arms held on, squeezing the life from the spiders, and the spiders squealed and screeched into the void.

Charlie tried to rise to her feet, but bright pain shot through her leg and she cried out through gritted teeth before falling onto her hands. The gravel bit into her palms.

Charlie dragged herself down the gravel path, hobbling, grunting with each step. When she reached the place where the ground dropped down into hills again, she turned around. Just once, she needed to see.

The Thing that was Terrence Forgaill was the shape floating in the air. It had sprouted dozens of arms, grabbed each of the deformed spiders, and pulled them to its own body. Tatters of clothing and rotted flesh flew outward from the seething mass of struggling bodies.

Charlie turned from the scene, fighting through the throbbing and burning in her thigh and her heel—and, for the moment, trying to ignore the blood soaking through her left pant leg—and she began the trek down into the shadowy hills.

16

Other people wandered from the cathedrals in the hills, each one of them like Marion: the way they hunched and walked on heavy feet; the grayness of their eyes, the words they repeated over and over as they made their way toward the gravel path and the shimmering void.

Charlie tore a long branch from a tree that appeared to have fallen an impossibly long time ago. The wood was stiff and hard, strong enough for her to lean her weight upon with every other step. Whenever she saw a group of wanderers in the dusk, she moved toward them, inspecting every face, searching for Marion. It was as if their bodies were no longer their own and their minds were already gone. They seemed unaware of Charlie's presence, even as she tried to stop them.

The burning sensation in Charlie's left leg flared up when she came down on the leg with too much weight. The sensation in her heel was a dull knob of pain. She cried out and fell.

Having to use her teeth and pieces of the dead tree branch to get a tear started through the denim, she ripped the pant leg at the knee.

Blood leaked from the puncture wounds at the tendon of her heel and from the flesh of her thigh, trickling down her shin. She wrapped the denim tight around her thigh, and did her best to wipe away the blood. As for her heel: every time she rotated her foot, or lifted or lowered it, the knob of pain grew sharp, making her pull breath through gritted teeth.

On the move again, she hovered toward every crowd of dreaming wanderers, just in case one of them turned out to be Marion. Her limping worsened, her mouth dried up, but she kept looking.

She found a young woman with dark curly hair, and Charlie's heart lifted as she went to embrace her. But when she drew nearer, the woman was just another stranger. So Charlie kept looking. A familiar silhouette. The distinct appearance of the back of her head. The curls of her hair. The roundness of her cheekbones and slant of her eyes. Charlie found all of these things in the scattered lines of lost wanderers. Marion had to be in the next group, or the next one, or the next one, or over the crest of that far hill, or around the corner of that cathedral. Marion seemed ever closer, just one more step away, one more stretch of ground, over one more hill.

Charlie kept on, grew tired, stopped to rest. She winced every time she got back to her feet. She wandered through the hills without aim or pattern beyond the vague appearance that she was looking for someone, like a refugee searching for loved ones in the aftermath of a disaster.

She glanced over her shoulder just once, drawn by the temptation of the shimmering darkness beyond—and by the fear that she may have been followed by Terrence Forgaill or one of the surviving spider-creatures—and was stopped in her tracks. A blonde-haired woman stood on the scorched ground at the crest of a nearby hill. The woman was waving at her.

Charlie squinted, even took a few steps in the direction of the woman, before stumbling away in revulsion, her skin rippling with chills.

It was herself up on that hill, waving. *Herself.* For a moment, though it could've been an illusion, Charlie thought she saw the woman's face. She was too far away, but somehow Charlie saw the lines of her face; she saw wrinkles, laugh-lines, the marks of age. It was herself, but grown old.

When she managed the strength to look away, Charlie realized how far she was from the ocean. A heaviness sunk through her. If she kept searching for Marion in the face of every lost soul in the hills...

I could lose myself here. The image that materialized in her head was chilling:

Days passing, weeks, months even, as she limped through the darkness, caught in the black hole of her own desperate search, never knowing when to give up, never knowing when to let go. How long had it been already? The fatigue, the sweat on her skin, indicated it could've been hours. Not a whole day, she told herself, but wasn't sure. It was impossible for her to keep track of time here.

With tears forming, she aimed herself in the direction of the Ocean of Hali. She cut a clear path toward it, trying all the while to not look back in case the vision of her aged self still stood there waving; she tried not to notice the lost wanderers in the hills, to not hope she might come across Marion after all and be able to throw her arms around her.

Something Marion had said haunted her as she walked:

I'm a black hole. That's what happened to me. I became a black hole. And it'd be better for you if you left and... and if you forgot me.

Sniffling, limping, Charlie shook her head. It was as if Marion walked beside her.

"No," she told her friend. "You were a light. For me, you were a light, Marion. And I'd rather die than forget you."

The fog returned.

The cathedral of flesh stood silent, and the madman sat cross-legged in its decrepit doorway. He said nothing, made no sound, only grinned strangely and watched Charlie as she passed.

She hastened for the black trees. If the fog cleared, she'd be able to see the mountainous thing looming in the ocean—she'd be able to feel its pitiless, indistinct gaze on her—so she hurried. There were shapes in the fog, lumbering things, but she gave them wide berths. The wounds in her left leg felt stiff, and tears leaked from her eyes because of the pain.

The fog thinned as she hobbled through the forest. Dusk lightened, if only slightly. The trees held an unnatural stillness, as if time wasn't the only thing that stood still in this place.

It was impossible to tell how much time passed before Charlie let herself collapse. She had navigated a considerable hill and found herself in a vast clearing beside a gently flowing creek. If not for the gargantuan size of the trees around her, the petrified coldness of the ground, and the sky's unmoving light, this could've been a normal place, she thought. The sound of the running water lacked only reflected sunlight on its surface and the ambient songs of birds.

Charlie tended to her moaning wounds. She wanted to keep going, to put as much distance between herself and the Ocean of Hali as she could, but her body ached, her leg was stiff, her bones felt heavy, and her thoughts trailed off into gray. She drew her knees up to her chest, wrapped her arms around them, lowered her head. A few minutes later she laid on the cold ground, beside the running water, and shut her eyes.

She dreamt of things with too many legs, arachnid bodies, and human faces. She looked down at her own arms and the skin was melting away, drooping toward the ground. Voices crowded around the empty spaces of her mind, and somewhere Marion was crying for help.

When she awoke in a sweat, she counted it a good thing that she hadn't dreamt of wonderful days under the summer sun.

She decided she'd travelled far enough from the Ocean of Hali, and risked drinking from the creek. The taste made her grimace—metallic, coppery, almost like blood—but it quenched her thirst. She washed her face with it, then her wounds. And she sat and stared at its surface and thought about home.

Without her father, without Marion, she didn't know what home was supposed to be anymore. There was Lupita, whose love was unconditional—but Charlie could not burden her with the wreckage of her life. There was Adrian, whose kindness she had done so little to deserve, who would surely be there for her even after the way she had treated him, the way she had shut him out. But no matter his caring, no matter how he listened, he would not understand. No one would.

Her father, she knew, would have welcomed her with open arms. He wouldn't have needed to understand; he simply would have been there for her.

And you, Marion. You understood. You understood even better than I do.

Charlie felt tears in her eyes and she let them come.

Maybe there was no home for her anywhere in the world. But as she sat by the river, she wished the flowing waters belonged to her creek, and she wished there were a fishing pole nearby, and a tackle box, and her phone with a message from Adrian to respond to.

She wished she could settle into this new, fresh grief, without it pulsing like electricity through her every nerve.

She kept to the river, let it show her the way. Her progress was incremental, one painful limp at a time, but she kept moving.

Eventually the trees lost the blackness in their trunks, appeared to shrink toward a normal size. The dusk lightened enough that it was almost sunset in reverse. Charlie came to another clearing.

She drank from the river. Sat with her feet submerged for awhile, even entertained the viability of trying to fasten a shoddy fishing pole from tree branches. It was a pleasant enough thought without considering what she might use for line or bait. As long as she sat, she didn't see a single fish.

When she slept, this time she dreamt of the walkers in the shadowy hills. In the dream, she could see Marion reaching the place where the ground leveled out, where the gravel path opened up toward the pulsing hole in the sky. Charlie ran for her, calling out her name, but couldn't seem to gain any momentum no matter how hard she pushed herself. Her body was too heavy, the air too thick. Marion disappeared behind the crest of the hill. Charlie could imagine Marion's face melting, her body dripping like melted wax to the ground.

She startled awake, flying upright, and cast her gaze to the other side of the small river.

A human-sized spider watched her from the riverbank. At first it looked like a statue, but then Charlie noticed how the human face twitched every now and then, and as she stood up to face it, its eyes tracked her movement. Not merely the eyes in its face, either, but the hundreds of small eyes in its skin.

The creature stood perfectly still, its many legs perched as though it were ready to leap at her, its many hands splayed upon the dirt. But it did not move. It only stood, watching. The human face—a man's, with a balding head—wore a slack-jawed, unreadable expression. She almost expected the face to speak in a normal human voice, the way it looked at her with the face of someone completely normal, but she remembered the way the creatures had roared on the gravel path, their voices grotesque and inhuman.

Charlie thought to run, but the creature only stared at her with its uncanny human face.

All I have now are nightmares, she realized. It seemed, so far, that there were no more dreams of better times for her. No more visions of warmth, of longing, of nostalgia. Only nightmares which, somehow, were solace compared to the wonderful dreams from Katalpa.

After some time, the spider crept away silently, its human hands making only the softest sounds on the dirt.

Charlie let herself exhale. She sat on the riverbank and looked into the water. Longed, again, for her river, beneath her sky. Part of her—a voice in her mind—shouted that she should first go back to the shadowy hills and the cathedrals of flesh to keep searching for Marion. Maybe it wasn't too late, said the voices in her head. Maybe it wasn't too late.

Charlie curled up beside the river. Those voices became tears at the corners of her eyes. She could go back, she could wander and wander, searching...

But she thought of her father in the church. The way he had looked at her one last time, urging her to go. Telling her to live.

She thought of Adrian laughing with her as they sat by the lake.

She thought of Lupita, the way she clicked her tongue or smacked her lips; the way she moved through the kitchen, expressing love with every word, every gesture, every meal.

I'll tell you what I'll do, Marion. I'll place a picture frame on my desk, but I'll keep it empty. You took the one from my desk, you took it with you, so I'll put an empty one there and never face it down. Every time I look at it, I'll think of you. Even if my memory of you starts to fade, that empty frame will trigger something deep down, even if it's a distant thing or little more than a vague impression. It'll be my way of remembering you. I'll bring books of poetry with me to the river and I'll read those poems aloud as if you were there with me. Maybe I'll dream of you sometimes, and I'll wake up alone but with warmth somewhere inside, even if I don't remember what the dream was about.

I'll carry you with me, Marion, like I'll carry my dad. I won't let it destroy me, the way it destroyed Terrence Forgaill and the people who followed him.

I'll carry you with me for the rest of my life. That's what I'll do. That's how I'll remember you.

Charlie closed her eyes and the sound of the river filled her ears.

That poem—the one Marion had read to her one summer day—seemed to echo off the riverbanks of her mind.

"I implore you," she said to her heart, "it's time to come back from the dark."

A weight seemed to leave her body. The ground lost its coldness. The sound of the river changed, became familiar.

When Charlie opened her eyes, she was looking up at a dark sky. Dark, but filled with stars.

AFTER

1

———————————

When Charlie reached the dirt parking lot by the flooded quarry, her bike wasn't where she'd left it. Instead of carelessly dropped in the dirt, it was leaned up against the wooden fence.

Adrian, she thought. There was no way of knowing for sure, but she had a feeling Adrian had been here, had found the bike and propped it up for her in case she returned.

The next feeling she had was a pressing sense of urgency. She had no way of knowing how long she'd been gone. A day? A week? Longer? Time had been inexplicable there.

She struggled to sit atop the bike, wincing and groaning not merely from pain, but from exhaustion. Once she was moving, she rested her left foot on the body of the bike and pedaled awkwardly with her right leg.

It crossed her mind that her dad would be so worried about her and so glad to see her… but she corrected this thought. The house would be empty. The thought of limping into the darkness of her house to be met with its cheerless silence was unbearable.

The distance—which was normally a fifteen-to-twenty-minute ride—took Charlie nearly an hour.

She stumbled up to the dark house. There was no way for her to know if it was late or early as she knocked on the door, first gently, then louder. From inside the house she heard movement, steps approaching the door.

Charlie knocked again. "It's me," she called out. "It's Charlie." In the context of being here at Marion's house after everything, her own voice sounded strange to her ears.

The porch light buzzed on. The door opened.

Lupita gasped, throwing her hands up to her mouth, her eyes instantly welling with tears.

"Diyós ko! Nenè? You... you are living?"

Dozens of things rose to Charlie's lips. None of them made it before she burst into sobs.

"You poor, poor thing." Lupita held Charlie's face, kissed her forehead.

In the bathroom, Lupita examined Charlie's leg, smacking her lips and clicking her tongue with every observation. As she got the water running, then dipped into the first aid kit and got to work, she sometimes muttered to herself in Tagalog, sometimes conveyed entire sentences with only those clicks and smacks. She asked no questions, only worked without complaint.

Charlie pulled breath through clenched teeth at the application of rubbing alcohol and bandages. Lupita made her take pills for the pain, staunchly insisting when Charlie said she was okay.

When she was finished, Lupita sat on the stool she'd dragged into the bathroom and looked at Charlie, just looked at her, a great sorrow glinting in her eyes.

Charlie started to cry again. "I tried, but I couldn't find her. I went... I went as far as I could."

"It's okay, nenè."

"I didn't know what else to do. She could still be out there somewhere. Lost. Waiting f-for me."

"Ssshhh." Lupita leaned forward and held her again. They both wept under the bathroom light with the fan rattling away.

2

Charlie had no sleep by the time morning light glowed from outside. She sat in front of the living room's picture window, the same window through which she and Adrian had watched Pastor Joe meet his violent end. This time, alone—with a blanket wrapped around her shoulders—she watched the dawn brighten. She couldn't remember if she had ever done this before: just sat to watch the sunrise. Certainly there'd been countless nights that she'd been awake through the dawn, usually drunk either in the company of others or parked in the driveway of her house, but this —quietly and intentionally watching the sunrise—was new.

Even now, however, she didn't see it fully. The images in her mind's eye were impossible to ignore. The images paired with the words of the madman in her memory.

The sunrise was pretty. So what? Even if this was the first one she had ever watched, she felt nothing inside, not even when the dusty rays of light filtered through the trees, and the sun breaking the horizon bathed the world in gold. Was it beautiful on its own? Or was it only beautiful because she was here to attach some idea or emotion to its process, and to assign to it—according to her own standards—such words as *ugly* or *beautiful,* as if it meant something either way?

She heard Lupita's movements through the house. At some point, the sound of Lupita crying in a bedroom, possibly Marion's bedroom. It sounded, to Charlie, like a requiem of her own failure.

I could've turned back, she thought. *I had every chance to turn back and to keep looking, but I didn't. I gave up. I ran. I saved myself.*

Somewhere beneath the storm of conflicted emotions, there was a stirring, a desire maybe to cry, but she looked out the window, expressionless.

Why did I come back? Why did I do that?

After awhile, Lupita emerged. She insisted on warming up left-over food even though Charlie said she had no appetite. Lupita served her something anyway, a scramble from a tupperware. Charlie forced herself to take a few bites, but then set the container down. Closed her eyes, bowed her head.

"How long was I gone?" she asked Lupita. "How long since the night Adrian and I stayed here?"

Lupita looked at her solemnly from the couch. "Almost a whole month, nenè."

"A month." She showed no surprise on the outside. It didn't seem possible. If she'd made a guess, she might've said two or three days. A week would've been a stretch. But a month? A whole month in that place? How could she have lost time like that? "It didn't feel that long," she said. "Not at all."

"I'll call Adrian. He checks in every day, asking if you returned."

Charlie barely heard her. "Marion was there for ten years."

"Did you see her, nenè? In the place where you went?"

She shook her head. "I looked. I didn't know where to go, but I looked."

"I know. It's okay. You think... you think she is in pain?"

Tears came suddenly. "I don't know."

"Okay. It's okay, Charlie. You don't need to speak about it anymore."

Lupita called Adrian on her landline, told him to come as soon as he could. After, she went back to her daughter's bedroom and prayed.

3

Charlie met him in the front yard. Adrian stepped out of his car and stood, stunned, before rushing over and throwing his arms around her. He pulled away, hands on her shoulders, just to look at her. He tried to say something, but no words would come and all he could do was give her a smile that rested on the line between sadness and relief.

They sat on the front porch, shoulder-to-shoulder. Birds sang to greet the morning in the silence between them.

"You know," said Adrian, after a time. "I was starting to think I was never gonna see you again."

She nodded, having no idea what to say.

"Did you think, at any point this month, that you could've contacted one of us? Just so we'd know you were okay? I mean… it's been a *month*. You didn't even say goodbye. No note or even a text. Nothing."

"It wasn't like that."

"Wasn't like what?"

"If I could've contacted you, I would have."

"Why couldn't you?"

"It's not a simple or easy answer."

"Okay, then where were you? You just disappeared in the middle of the night and it was like… it was almost like you didn't exist anymore. No way of contacting you, no way of knowing where you might've gone. When Lupita mentioned Catalpa Creek, I went out there. I spent a whole week going out there every day, calling your name and… I don't know. No one in town knew anything. I even contacted that Travis kid."

"Travis kid?"

"Yeah, from that bonfire at the lake. The guy who was obsessed with you or something, he kept talking about why he didn't think people should reproduce."

"Oh… him. Why'd you talk to him?"

"He seemed intrigued by you, and that night you gave him this look that I… I couldn't get it out of my head. It doesn't matter. He… well, he actually had some weird theories."

"Like what?"

Adrian shook his head. "Does it matter?"

"Maybe it does."

"He asked me if I knew anything about a place called Katalpa, which sounded… familiar, I guess, but only in the way that your friend, Marion, the way her name sounded familiar. I don't know if that makes sense. At first I thought he meant the creek, but no. He said he heard about Katalpa from some guy who'd been in and out of a few hospitals for several years because of a major depressive disorder. He said he didn't even really know what Katalpa was, just that it was a place that might be real or might be a symbol, like… I don't know, it was weird. I always thought Travis was just anti-social, not someone who'd be into esoteric shit or anything like that."

Charlie sighed. The smile she'd given Adrian earlier had been genuine, but even the relief at seeing him again was eclipsed by a bizarre sensation deep in her gut, a sensation that weighed her down, made her feel restless in her own skin.

"You can't do this again," he said. "You can't shut me out. It's like… maybe it's my fault for, I don't know, for having a certain perception of you when we first met. But it's like you were more honest back when we met. We witnessed some fucked up shit together, and then you vanished for a whole month and—and apparently you show up here in the middle of the night, you look like you haven't slept in days and are barely even here right now, and… god. I don't know."

"I know. I haven't been fair to you."

"Charlie, it's not like you owe me anything, all right, it's just… I'm trying to be your friend, the friend I thought I was, anyway, but you're making it hard."

She drew in breath, closed her eyes for a moment. There was a voice in her head that urged her to belittle Adrian's words. *Oh, it's hard for you? Tell me how hard it's been for you.* She could see the cold beach, the shadowed hills of The Aching Plane in her head, could still feel the distorting wave that pulsed outward from the great void.

He said, "I mean, I'm sure I can't imagine whatever it is you've been through the past month, from the look of it."

"You wouldn't understand."

"Try me. Please."

"If you think I'm being unfair to you, Adrian, I'm sorry, but it'd be more unfair if I explained everything. It would make you part of it."

"And it's fair for you to get to decide that? I've told you, Charlie, I've told you it's okay. I'm asking you. I'm fucking embarrassing myself asking, *begging*, practically—"

"You *wouldn't understand*. Okay? You wouldn't understand. I have all this unbelievable, indescribable *shit* in my head that'll probably haunt me until the day I die. It's right in front of me every time I close my eyes, and I happen to know that every person who's ever seen the stuff that I have, it... it never got better for them. *Okay?* Excuse me for struggling to find the words to explain it to you when I can barely even make sense of it in my own head, and I can barely even believe any of it was real even though it *fucking happened to me*."

Adrian pulled away from her, disbelief on his face.

She went on, and all the unsaid things felt like a bubble that had inflated in her chest, full now to bursting. "I couldn't contact you because I was lost in a place where there are cathedrals made of rotting flesh, and people mutate into giant deformed spiders with human faces and hundreds or maybe thousands of eyeballs in their skin, and the lost people in the dark hills lose their physical bodies, as in their skin *literally melts* and their bodies just become puddles, and all I remember feeling in that place is this horrible fear and something like... like aching, like I was in so much pain but I couldn't figure out where or, or why, and... I lost my friend. I couldn't find her, and I wasn't strong enough to stay, I was *so* scared I thought I might die just from how scared I was, so... I gave up. I left her there because I wasn't strong enough to turn back and keep looking."

"Charlie..."

"Katalpa isn't just a place. And it's not some stupid esoteric shit. It's embedded in our consciousness, and we can always feel it somewhere underneath everything. I can feel it *right now*, and you probably can too. As long as anything has ever been alive to *feel*, there was *the ache*, the heartbeat of Katalpa. That's what I know about it. That's all I want to know. I was right there in the middle of it, I had to *see all of* that, and it's in my head. And don't fucking look at me like that, Adrian."

"Charlie, no, hold on, I'm just—"

"You wanted to know, now you know. Believe me, it's the last time I'm talking about it. You can think whatever you want, and tell people whatever you want to tell them about me."

"What the fuck, no, if you'd calm down for a second—"

Charlie stood from the porch, limped several steps away, arms folded against her chest. Tears shimmered on her bottom eyelids and she wiped at them frustratedly. "Our own consciousness is an illusion, and everything about our existence is just an extension of that illusion. By its very nature meaningless, doomed. That's what we amount to, all of us."

Adrian stood from the porch. He began to reach a hand out for her.

"If you had seen it, you would understand. But no one should have to see it. Marion shouldn't have had to. *I* shouldn't have had to. I... I don't know how I'm supposed to—"

Despite himself, he did reach his hand out, placed it on her arm.

She pulled away as if his touch burned, hugging herself tighter. "I'm sorry, Adrian. You've been one of my favorite people ever since I met you."

"Would you come sit down? We can talk this out and take our time."

"No. I need to be alone."

"At least let me... I don't know, let me take you home."

But she didn't stop, and he didn't pursue. He stood on the sidewalk and watched as she walked down the street. He was still standing there, watching, when she rounded the corner and disappeared.

4

The backyard of whoever's house this was became a tilting vision through Charlie's eyes. Two propane fireplaces, dangling string lights, and the scattered circles of people with plastic red cups in their hands. The murmurs of nearby conversation were indecipherable from where she sat on the cinderblock wall at the edge of the yard, not far from a steaming hot tub of mellower college students who were passing a smoldering joint amongst themselves.

"*And I felt it, you know?*" someone was saying as they described a recent mushroom trip. "*It was like this peaceful vibration under every-thing, connecting the whole world.*"

She knew Adrian wasn't here, but her eyes searched the islands of gathered people anyway, hoping or dreading to recognize his figure, his face, his modest posture. It was easy to imagine the sound of his laughter, or the subtle baritone of his voice reaching her ear from the murmuring of a nearby circle.

These crowds were full of strangers. People with death far from their minds. People whose minds didn't present them with fresh memories of unimaginable horrors when they closed their eyes.

She nursed her drink, sipping the burning gin around chunks of ice. It was her fourth glass of the night. The buzz tingled through her body, but she registered it as a fact, neither positive nor negative. It felt strange, she thought, to *have* a body, to lift a hand in front of her face and feel control over every individual finger, to feel the crisp air on her skin. She felt these things—the air, the alcohol's buzz—as if from a great distance. It had been a long time since she'd felt anything like herself.

Then again, she thought she wouldn't recognize it if she *did* feel like herself. If there was a consistent sense of self beneath everything she'd felt, everything she'd seen, everything she was still wading her way blindly through, it was a fragile, crumbled illusion. She felt like a pair of floating eyes, no body, no face, just the act of observation perched at the edge of a yard, surrounded by other floating eyes that imagined themselves to have bodies and faces and minds.

More voices wafting from a nearby group: "*And I just thought, what a miracle to even just be alive, you know? The whole universe conspired to bring us here to this exact moment. How can you even look at the world and feel how it is to be alive and not just feel joyful, you know?*"

Charlie was staring at her drink, studying the melting ice, when footsteps approached her across the lawn's tufts of grass.

"Well look at that," said Travis, lifting his own glass in a cheers gesture. He wore dark clothing: a black jacket over a brown shirt buttoned all the way up "What's a girl as interesting as you doing at a party as dull as this?"

Charlie returned the cheers gesture halfheartedly as Travis leaned against the cinderblock wall beside her. One hand held his glass, the other was stuffed into his pants pocket.

"You know," he said, "ever since that night at the lake, you know the bonfire, I was hoping I'd run into you again."

She looked out across the yard. "Was an interesting night."

"I don't mean this in, like, a creepy way or anything, but I actually think a lot about some of the things you said to me. Even just from a philosophical standpoint, it kinda got to me, I must say."

"It got to you?"

"Yeah, you know, it made me think."

"I wasn't trying to upset you or anything. I was just—"

"You were just being honest, right?" Travis grinned. "That's what I thought. I could tell, actually, by the way you said it. Especially those things right before your boyfriend, um… right before Adrian, I mean, kinda dragged you off."

Charlie raised her eyebrows. "Right."

"Adrian here tonight?"

She shook her head. "What did I say that bothered you so much?"

"Oh it's not like it bothered me. I'm actually pretty familiar with a lot of nihilistic philosophers and whatnot. I've just never actually met someone who genuinely sees things the way you do. Most people… I mean, just look around." He gestured with his drinking hand to the circles of others at the party. "How many of these people, do you think, would not only believe, but would want to talk about how nothing in the world is important on its own, like you said? How many of them would want to hear more about how we'd probably lose our minds in the face of what Shirley Jackson would've called *absolute reality*?"

A memory flashed in Charlie's head of that night. Travis, wide-eyed, starting to follow her as Adrian led her to the truck.

She turned from the party and looked right at him.

"Katalpa," she said in a low voice. "You knew that word."

As they had that night at the lake, Travis's eyes widened. "Holy shit. I *knew* you knew about Katalpa."

"What do you know about it?"

"Not much. But I know it has to do with what you were talking about at the lake."

"How so?"

He raised his other hand. "Am I being interrogated here?" A careful laugh. "It's just something I heard about. I used to know this guy, actually… he had serious chronic depression on top of a whole bunch of issues, the main thing being that he couldn't even feel pleasure. I mean, maybe in small doses… but that was his life. Going around being chemically unable to feel almost any real positive emotions at all, I'm guessing. Just—"

"Void," said Charlie.

"Exactly. Sometimes though, this guy would have these little flashes of emotions. It was almost like his brain was constantly malfunctioning and would just… be normal, I guess, for a little bit. When this happened, he said he felt something aside from the usual numbness. I only remember because of the way he said it. Like he got scared all of a sudden. When I used to talk to him, he was pretty monotone. But he got scared this one time. He said when he felt his emotions come back, it wasn't for very long, but he said it was an *ache*. And when he felt it, he'd dream of Katalpa. That's it. I swear that's pretty much all he said about it."

"That's it?"

"Pretty much. He implied it was… I don't know, maybe a place, or like it was a representation of something. It just stuck in my head is all. And then I started having these weird dreams, and so did everyone else. You know, like… before the fucked up things with the church and all those people, I heard what you said that night at the lake, about, like, how there are things in this world that make our existence seem unbelievably fragile."

"Well," said Charlie. "If you're hoping to hear more about this Katalpa thing from me, you're gonna be disappointed."

Travis laughed. "Hey, makes no difference to me. I've heard enough crazy shit to last me a lifetime just from the last month and a half."

"I know what you mean." She looked at him, mining for answers from his facial expression. "It sounds like that friend of yours was right about at least one thing."

"What's that?"

"What it's like to exist, at the core of it all." She spoke between sips of her gin, which was running low near the bottom of the glass. "It isn't neutral, it isn't bliss, it isn't even pain, exactly. It's... *wrong*. Peel away all the layers and there's only one thing left: the mistake that anything exists at all. Once there was nothingness, and then there was something... and it aches. Nothing is supposed to be. This world is a mistake. *We* are a mistake. Your friend must've come to prefer the nullity. When he felt anything, it was pain. It was aching."

Travis looked upon her with dawning awe. She didn't know how much alcohol he'd consumed, but it must've been comparable, because he wore it all on his face: wide-eyed, desire-filled awe. "Well I... I don't know about my friend. I haven't seen him in years. Actually, I don't even know if he's still alive. But I do remember him saying, once, that he wouldn't know what to do if one day there was ever a cure for depression. I think he meant, like, it was so deeply a part of him, after all that time. Maybe you're right. I mean, *I* think you're right. I just don't hear truth like that spoken... ever. But doesn't it ever scare you?"

"What?"

"That you might be right about all that?"

Charlie sighed through her nose. "As a species, we have an inclination toward illusions. It's how we survive. Without the ability to convince ourself into illusion, we'd be able to feel it all the time—the wrongness, the aching, at the center of existing. Meditators would back away in horror at the emptiness they found underneath everything rather than singing its praises, because they'd at least start to understand that what some people call enlightenment is just a door... and no matter the key you use to open it, no matter the path you took to get there, it opens on the same darkness. One step beyond serenity and it's savage indifference, all-consuming chaos, and then *nothing*. Nothing at all. People would resign their investigations into the mystery of consciousness because they'd discover it doesn't really exist, it's the word we give to the illusion of having *selves*, and it might be the only thing shielding us from being torn apart by what's underneath it. We'd lose our identities because we'd see there are no individuals, no people, just brains chemically inclined to cope with the incomprehensible chaos and horrors beneath what we perceive as reality."

Travis set his glass aside, shaking his head. "I swear to god, I've spent time with a lot of people who'd probably call themselves nihilists, but I've never met anyone like you. The way you see things, and the way you can articulate it all. My god."

"You wanna know my first impression of you," said Charlie, "that night at the lake?"

"Please."

"I thought you were pathetic. Regurgitating pop nihilism to impress girls at social gatherings."

"Huh... yeah, uh, I guess I, uh..."

"But you're not a nihilist. You're just curious." She finished off her drink, set it down with a *clink* atop the cinderblocks. Her vision swayed. "I like that better."

"I'm not just a poser, if that's what you think. I'm pretty sure I see things how they really are."

Charlie smirked. "Must be quite the burden, gifted with such sight."

"Come on. You aren't the only one who's an actual realist about things." He gestured to the house and the many people gathered across the backyard. "Sometimes I can barely even engage with what most of these people consider important or meaningful. It all seems so shallow and, like, silly almost, doesn't it? I don't care what Carl or Genevieve thought about last night's episode of whatever shitty show everyone's been watching for twelve seasons too long, you know? Sometimes I feel like everyone's playing this really stupid game just to keep themselves occupied, but everyone also pretends it's not a game, it's real. And most of them are happy to, like, forget who they are under the masks they wear for the game. It drives me crazy, because it's like… you want to shake them sometimes, you know? Say, *Wake the fuck up, I know you're in on it, too*, but then you think more about it and kinda just wonder… does it even matter? May as well play along as well as you can. Drink, dance, watch stupid shows, talk about nothing, fuck. Party it up while we're here, basically." He shook his head. "Oh god, I sound like Camus."

"Don't flatter yourself."

He chuckled, most of his defensiveness gone. "But I'm glad I came tonight, actually. If I'd known I'd run into you, I wouldn't've even hesitated. I mean, it's practically metaphorical. We flounder around hoping for answers, but the only answers that come are those we come up with ourselves. In a sea of faces all regurgitating the same lines, I run into you."

When Travis placed a hand on her arm, she didn't pull away. There was no weight, she thought, behind his touch. No substance.

Let him think his musings were special, or impressive, or whatever he needed them to be. She felt nothing and was under no illusion that anything she did tonight would alleviate that. What did it matter? Maybe there'd be a moment—no more than a breath, a passing second—when she didn't see Marion in her mind, or her father's urgent look, or the Ocean of Hali, or the floating form of Terrence Forgaill, or the skin of a woman's face melting from her bones.

Charlie didn't pull away from Travis's hand. Nor did she decline when he asked if she wanted to leave with him.

*

In the middle of it, her mind went to Marion—of kissing Marion in her bedroom, with the window's blinds glowing dimly orange from the streetlight below. Of holding Marion's hand in the sunlight on Catalpa Creek in what felt, now, like a different life.

Travis's pace grew more intense and his breath deepened and caught, his thrusts stiffening into spasms, and Charlie thought of Adrian scooting closer to her in the dark, under the covers of Marion's bed. Adrian's hand caressing her back, tracing the contours of her spine. His eyes on her, gently, in the dark.

It didn't matter anymore, she thought, how she loved him. Whether it was as a friend or maybe something more—the hope, the imagining, of something more—it didn't matter. She was far away from him. A shape growing blurry. A pair of brake lights vanishing around a corner.

Adrian, she thought, would've been gentle, impassioned—and attentive, most of all. Now that it was too late, she could imagine it in a way she had never allowed herself to. It stirred a restless bundle of desire in her stomach, a spreading warmth where for

Travis and his motions there was only flatness. Once the physical sensation of pleasure was gone, it receded to nothing.

With Marion, a single kiss had set her alight for hours. With Adrian she could only imagine, but it was a vivid imagining.

While Travis was in the restroom, Charlie dressed herself in a hurry and left before he came out.

In the driveway of her house, she closed her eyes and sagged into the seat. Somewhere in the numbness she felt the need to cry —not for herself, but for how the empty spaces inside of her seemed to hurt—and for the house, how its emptiness was like her own. She missed her father. She missed her friends. She missed herself.

Charlie didn't cry. She sat in the driveway for a long time, letting time have its way with her.

She spoke aloud in a low voice, maybe to her father, maybe to Marion, maybe to Adrian, or maybe to herself, the version of herself that had once sat in this same spot for too long on too many nights, aching and longing for something other than what she had.

"I'm sorry. I didn't choose to be this way, and I don't want to choose it now." Finally she started to cry. The night sky and its stars reeled indifferently above. The coldness of the air made warmth seem a treasured, fleeting memory. "Is there an end to this feeling," she said, "or will it always be like this?"

5

One year to the day since she returned from The Aching Plane, Charlie went back to Catalpa Creek.

Her house was emptied out, the rooms cleared; the books, shelves, clothes, dishes, silverware, keepsakes packed up; her father's things either donated or thrown away; the carpets vacuumed, the floors swept, the lawns mowed. The *For Sale* sign had first been modified with *Sold*, and then removed altogether. The house wasn't hers anymore.

The moving van sat in the driveway of an apartment building in a different town, miles from here. Of her old life, only a few small things remained: the boxes packed into the backseats of her car; Charlie herself; and Catalpa Creek.

Charlie stepped out of her car in the dirt parking lot near the quarry, tackle box hanging from her fingers, fishing pole resting on her shoulder. She made as if to begin the trek into the woods, along the path that would take her to the creek.

She stopped where the path began. Followed it with her eyes as it led up through the trees. Her eyes glistened, betraying a stir of emotion on her otherwise expressionless face. She recalled something she'd said what seemed, now, a long time ago: promises made to a girl she loved. Something about an empty picture frame, poetry books, and a fishing pole.

Her hand trembled around the cork grip of the rod.

A year had passed. In that time, she had placed no empty picture frame on her desk. She had avoided Catalpa Creek both physically and in her mind, retreating from the thought of it like a shadow from light. She read no poetry, carried with her no chapbooks or collections. None of the things she had promised while inside the nightmare of that other world.

For a long time she stood at the entrance of the woods, far from the sound of what had once been her riverbank, a place that was as much home as her actual house had been. The afternoon sun beat down. Time bore on, uncaring. She wondered if her own life would ever feel real again.

She returned to her car, placed the tackle box and fishing rod behind the back seats without ceremony. She cast one more look at the woods before climbing into the front seat and driving away.

"Bye, Dad," she said.

If she cried, she wouldn't have admitted it, not even to herself. She took no detours, no final drive by the empty house that was no longer her own—the place she had grown up in with a father who had loved her—and no stops to say any last goodbyes to anyone along the way.

Later she told herself she felt nothing as her hometown shrunk in the rearview mirror. Lying to herself was something she'd become—if not good at, then consistent with.

She was, perhaps, not yet old enough to understand the difference between forgetting and eventually no longer remembering. But she hoped, in time, that all the things she felt now—pieces of shattered glass in her chest—she would someday forget, or at least no longer remember. Some things were better that way. Forgetting was one of life's few mercies.

The freeway's asphalt thrummed beneath the rubber tires. The open road seemed a reflection of her own emptiness, aching without hope to be filled.

EPILOGUE

River Bug (II)

1

The boy was twelve, his dirty blonde hair longer and wilder than his mother cared for, and his clothes were the same he'd been wearing yesterday. He knelt on the couch and stared out the window, waiting with his chin in both palms, fingers splayed along his cheeks. Every few minutes he sighed.

His father passed by on his way to the kitchen, suppressing an amused smile at the image of his horrifically bored son.

"No sign of them?"

"Nope. Lily probably took too long to get ready, or they'd be here by now."

The father rinsed some dishes, placed them in the washer. He looked out through the kitchen window, saw his wife out in the backyard. Atop her head, the wide sunhat he'd bought her last Christmas. She held her thumb over half the garden hose's nozzle, making the stream shoot out in a wide fan to cover more of the backyard plants.

They'd been together for fourteen years. When she turned slightly on the lawn to redirect the water across a different cropping of plants, the swell of her belly became visible. A few more months and their little girl would emerge into the world. Their son wasn't looking forward to having a second little sister—that was what he claimed, at least.

As if on cue, the little sister—nine years old and unquestionably more mature than her older brother, according to herself—came bouncing out of her bedroom. Like her mother, her blonde hair was almost white.

In a singsong voice, she called, "Thomas?" Went up to the couch and hopped up beside her brother, even mimicked his pose of staring out the picture window. "Hello? Earth to Tommy?"

"Jesus Christ. Dad!"

The father snapped out of the trance he'd been in. "You two can settle it on your own," he called to his kids. "And don't swear, please."

"You say it all the time!"

"Well… yeah, okay. Fair point." Trying not to laugh, he dried his hands, went out the sliding-glass door, shutting only the screen behind him in case the kids needed something… or in case they started fighting.

He hugged his wife from behind, rested his hands gently on either side of her rounded belly. She leaned back into him, smiling. He kissed her cheek. "Any news from the little one?"

"Figs."

"Huh?"

"Figs. She wants figs today."

"Honey, when's the last time you had figs?"

"Honest? Mmm, probably like twenty years ago. My grandma's house. She had a fig tree in her backyard."

"Ah. Well, I'll pick some up when I head into town."

"You're the best."

He rested his head on her shoulder. His eyes widened. "Hey, felt a little kick there."

"Mmhmm. Someone hears her daddy's voice."

"More like someone knows she's getting figs today." For a moment he touched his head to hers, and the scent of her ivory hair filled his senses. "You're beautiful."

"*You're* beautiful."

"No, I was just watching you through the window—"

"Stalking me."

"Yes, stalking you. And I just felt, you know… amazed, I guess. Happy." She leaned back far enough to kiss his lips. "I guess it's true what they say about pregnant women," he said, letting her go. "You look like you're glowing."

She blew him a kiss, returned her attention to watering the plants.

He was at the screen door when she called after him. "Adrian?"

"Hmm?"

"Did you call Lupita yesterday?"

"Oh… yes. She said no."

"She said no?"

"Well, what she actually said was we were crazy if we thought she'd let us cook for her. So, if you're up for it, looks like we're headed over there tonight. Again."

"Did you tell her I insist?"

"Well yeah, but, Honey, she insisted harder."

"I'll call her in a few minutes. She has us over every time. It's about time we hosted."

Adrian laughed as he opened the screen door. "Bet you ten bucks she'll be insulted if you try to change her mind."

His wife sighed with feigned drama, then laughed, too. Adrian shut the screen door, stuffed his hands into his pockets, and watched her. Her name was Jane. They'd met at a writing convention where he'd been networking with publishers and promoting authors, and she'd been attending lectures and pitching to panels of agents. Her third book, released less than a year ago, had been her first piece of nonfiction. Its subject: the horrible event that still felt like an open wound in the town of Matheson, and which she had lived through firsthand.

The book was called *The Church: Matheson, Oregon.* The subtitle, in True Crime fashion, did most of the work: *A Survivor's Investigation into the Unexplainable.*

Fifteen years had passed, and Jane still awoke sometimes from nightmares about that day. Writing the book had helped her a little, but the shape of its narrative resembled exactly the results of her investigation. It was a hole in the earth, a black void with no visible bottom and no explanation for its existence. Her research and the book that came from it was the equivalent of being lowered into that hole with a rope and a flashlight. She had descended, but eventually reached the extent of the rope, and the light petered out into only more darkness.

If there were concrete answers, if there was an explanation for what had happened in the church—why, and how, and if it could happen again—she still didn't know. No one did.

When she spoke about it, she cried. The things she'd seen—and what had happened to the people around her—were things she could never forget. But as time passed, the hungry madness of those memories softened, even if only a little.

Adrian never brought it up first. For Jane, it was about how her parents had died in that church, a horror he could only imagine and comfort her through. His own aunt had died there, but he had never known her well; the best he could do was listen when Jane opened up about her grief. And that was all he wanted to do: listen. His memories of those days were like images from a distant, fading dream, and talking about them—even just thinking about them— brought with it a familiar ache.

Sometimes he opened his wife's book, flipped it to a page near the end, and read. Her words gave articulation to a place in him that he mostly hid away, even from himself.

After that much time and all the things these people were able to tell me, I felt myself circling around conclusions I'd been afraid of. What if it was a mistake, after all, to pursue answers for what had happened? It's a deep-rooted human need, isn't it, to thirst for explanation. We need to explain ourselves... we need things explained to us...we need for there to be a reason something happened.

Only seven people, myself included, survived the incident at the Evangelical Free church in Matheson, Oregon. We were each altered in some way by the horror of what we experienced, but none of the other survivors share the depth of my curiosity. Almost unanimously, they would welcome answers if I unearthed anything more than what I'd learned and shared with them, but to my surprise and, I confess, my disappointment, they covered up this part of their lives. Every day they gave the event a wide berth, tried to move on, tried to live.

What if it was a mistake, then, to continue to pursue answers for what had happened? I felt I needed it to make sense, I felt owed an explanation, answers, and catharsis. But just because most things we experience in our lives do have tangible explanations and reasons, doesn't mean the world works that way.

It was as though the world opened up and an unfathomable darkness revealed itself behind everything, just for an instant. That instant was enough to destroy dozens of lives. Even as I write this, I can't say I feel ready to let it go. I can't say I believe the words I'm saying. I do know that this search could consume me for the rest of my life if I let it, and for all I know, I would come no closer to answers or explanation or catharsis, no matter how many years I give to it.

I survived. I would have to go on living in spite of the guilt. I have to imagine that if my parents could see me now, if they could see how hard I've searched for answers about what happened to them, maybe they'd be proud. Maybe it would break their hearts, too. I can imagine them telling me it's time to let it go. Something my father used to say was: There are no answers, there's only starting points. An instant is all it was when the darkness of the world left a permanent scar on the people of this town, myself included. But for those of us that survived, that instant cast a shadow over our lives ever since.

I like to think it's possible to begin stepping out of that shadow. I like to think that, one day, stepping out from it will seem more worth it than stepping deeper in.

"Dad? Earth to Dad?"

Adrian realized his son had been calling his name for several seconds now. He turned. "Huh?"

"My friends are here."

They were all pulling their bikes into the driveway, dismounting, tossing playful quips and insults back and forth. To Adrian's surprise, there were fishing poles in their hands, the rods gleaming in the sun.

"What's the plan for today?"

Thomas shrugged. "Dunno. I think Anthony and Lily wanted to go fishing."

"Catalpa Creek?"

"I think so."

"You guys know how to get there?"

"I think Lily's been a few times, so yeah, we know."

"The trail out past the old quarry?"

"I think so, yeah. Anyway."

"Ah, shoot. If I still had a fishing pole, I'd lend it to you."

"That's okay, Dad." He pulled on his sneakers. "Peyton's dad had some extras, so I have one to use."

The little sister jumped out the front door to greet Thomas's friends before he could. They high-fived her, asked her what she was up to, and she—ever the supreme confident one—high-fived them back and returned each one of their quips.

"Hey, bud," said Adrian, before his son could say goodbye and run out the door. "Would you mind bringing your sister along?"

"I guess. We don't have an extra fishing pole though."

"Maybe you can share. Or, you know, she might enjoy just—"

"Yeah, okay. Bye, Dad." He gave Adrian a quick hug, then hopped out the door. He said to his sister, "Get your shoes if you wanna come."

Adrian watched them pedal away. Theirs was a world he hadn't been part of in decades, but seeing it in front of him brought a smile to his face.

Fishing, he thought. A touch of melancholy found his eyes. After the kids disappeared down the sidewalk, headed into their golden summer day, Adrian returned to the backyard to hold his wife, to kiss her again. Deep down, though he wouldn't have been able to explain why, he wanted to cry. He felt something inside, as if a chasm had opened up beneath his feet. But Jane's glow lifted him up again. She told him to please not forget the figs when he went into town. He replied that he loved her.

The group walked upstream without any specific purpose or destination in mind except just to walk, to keep up their jumble of conversations, and maybe to find the perfect fishing spots. When they reached a place that opened up almost like a beach, they laid out blankets.

Everyone spread out along the banks of the river.

Thomas was stuck with his sister.

"Can I use yours?" she asked, sipping on a Capri-Sun.

"When I'm done with it, yeah."

"Are you gonna take forever and then say, *Oh*," she lowered her voice to do an unflattering impression, "*Oh, I forgot, maybe next time, sis. Or are you actually gonna—*"

"Jesus. I don't sound anything like that."

"Actually, you do. Sorry. Nothing I can do about it."

He punched her on the shoulder. She punched him back, giggling. "You're so weird."

"*You're* weird."

His sister elected to hop along the rocky parts of the creek.

Thomas told her not to wander off, and he made his way a bit farther downstream. He'd seen a spot that looked perfect while they'd been walking, but he hadn't said anything to the others. Let them find their own spots. This one was his. There'd been a few boulders to sit on, and a place where the water pooled within a half circle of rocks.

When he reached it, it was unmistakable—but nearby, a few strides downstream from the spot, a woman stood alone at the creek's edge. She was around his dad's age. Beneath a gray beanie she was blonde—not unlike his mom, except this woman's hair was darker. She was dressed in slim jeans with straps that crossed her back over a simple burgundy shirt. Her hands were stuffed into her pockets. She appeared lost in thought, staring into the water.

He considered turning back, looking for a different spot, but after a few seconds he went ahead. There was nothing threatening about the woman. The opposite, in fact. She looked like someone who was in no hurry to get anywhere. Someone who would concede this fishing spot to a kid, and she'd probably be friendly about it.

Thomas was only twelve, but he also couldn't deny how pretty he thought she was even for an adult, someone his dad's age. It occurred to him that she appeared sad, somehow, but he dismissed his impression. How could he know?

A boulder sat embedded just at the river's edge. He sat atop it, reaching for the end of his fishing pole.

The lure, it turned out, was not tied to the fishing line.

"Aw, crap." He ran a hand through his hair. Now he'd have to trudge all the way back upstream to find Lily or Anthony, either of whom would know how to tie the lure properly to the line. A few seconds' more consideration and he decided to try it on his own. After a few more mutterings of "Aww, crap," the woman's voice cut him off from his frustration.

"Having trouble there?"

He looked at her. She had stepped toward him, away from the riverbank, but stopped at a polite distance with her hands in her pockets. The corner of her lips had tightened into a smirk.

"I've seen my friends do this part before," he said. "But I've never done it myself."

"Which part? Tying the line?"

"Yeah."

"Need help?"

He sighed. "I don't know. Lily knows how to do it. I might just ask her."

"Is that her over there?"

"Nope. That's my sister."

"Oh."

"Is it just like a regular knot? Like when I tie my shoes?"

The woman took another step closer, but stopped herself, as if remembering she was a stranger and this was a child. "Close, but a little different. I can do it for you, if you'd like. Or I can walk you through it."

"Okay. What comes next?" He held it up so she could see, and she took this as permission to approach his boulder. He'd gotten only one step in the process: feeding the fishing line through the eyelet at the end of the lure.

"You're doing great so far. What's your name?"

"Thomas. Thomas Benedict."

For no longer than a second, the woman's eyes widened, her mouth slipped open. Did she recognize his name? His last name, maybe? She quickly reigned in the expression, refocused on the lure and fishing line he was holding out for her to see.

"Okay, Thomas Benedict. You're doing great so far. Pull a little more line... good. Next, you twist the line together four or five times."

"Like this?"

"Like that."

"Then what?"

"Loop the rest of the line back through again."

"The same way it went in?"

She grinned. "Yes. And then tighten it."

He couldn't contain his smile when the knot tightened. "Wow!"

"You're all set."

"Thanks. Holy shi—crap. Thanks."

She stepped back, smiling with only her lips, a simple friendliness glittering in her eyes. "You got it."

He stood up on the boulder and walked himself through the motions of casting. This was the only thing he remembered with any clarity about fishing, because the rest of it was mostly boring.

"Nice cast," said the woman. She hovered nearby, eyes aimed at the river. "If you can get it right in that pool there, just to the left of where yours landed—"

"Yeah, I know, that's where I was aiming."

"You're still in a good spot, though. You'll get there."

He looked over at her. Beneath that friendly smile, beneath her helpful demeanor, there was something weighing her down from inside. Maybe it was in her eyes. Maybe her posture. Thomas didn't think these things consciously, but a subconscious piece of him sensed it.

"So, uh… you seem to like fishing," he said. "Or, I dunno, you seem like you're good at it. Like you know stuff."

"When I was your age I used to come here almost every day. To this exact spot, actually."

"Really? When you were my age?"

"I spent as much time here as I did at home. Sometimes with my friends, but usually by myself. I loved fishing. It was a way to clear my head."

"You should've brought a fishing pole."

"Maybe I should have. I haven't been fishing in a long time. A very long time." She bowed her head, appeared—for just a moment —to close her eyes.

He thought to ask her why it'd been so long if she loved it, but that question seemed too personal. It was something his sister would've asked because she had no filter.

"The last time I went fishing," the woman continued, "was actually the last time I was here. Before I moved away."

Thomas didn't know what to say to that, either, but he didn't mind. This woman wasn't like a lot of adults he met. She spoke to him as if he were an adult, too. And it seemed important to her that she was here, remembering things. He tried to imagine what she must've looked like when she was his age, but it was impossible. To him, adults looked like they had always been adults.

"So you used to live here, in Matheson?"

"I did."

"You grew up here?"

"Yes. You too?"

"Yep. Me and my sister." He gestured upstream where his sister was splashing around in a shallow part of the creek, getting her pants all wet, probably ruining his chances at catching any fish. "She just turned nine. Dad says she's more mature than I am, but I think he's just messing with me. I mean, *look* at her."

They both laughed. It was nice to share a laugh with a kind stranger.

"I take it your sister doesn't like fishing?"

"I don't think she's ever done it. But I might let her borrow this one, when I'm done." He reeled in his lure, then cast again. This time, he landed closer to where he'd intended, where the woman had suggested.

The woman clapped for him, then appeared to consider something, her eyes flitting behind her, toward the woods. "You know… I might know where there's a fishing pole nearby, in case your sister didn't want to wait."

"What? No, it's fine. It's probably a long walk back to your car or, or wherever—"

"No. Just nearby. When I was your age, I had this hiding spot where I always kept a fishing pole. It's… it's probably still there."

Thomas laughed. "A hiding spot for a fishing pole? You must've *really* loved fishing."

"I did. It was like coming home."

He reeled in his lure. "I don't know if it's something I'd do more. I like casting, but it's kinda…"

"Kinda boring?" she said for him. "That's okay. It's not for everyone."

A comfortable silence fell between them, filled only by the sound of the water and of his sister's splashing upstream. He thought of a dozen different things he could bring up to keep the conversation going as the woman paced gently toward the river and then back, as if she were trying to decide whether to say good-bye.

"I guess it's kinda fun. I've caught just two fish before."

"Yeah? Out here?"

"No, it was out at the lake with my dad."

The woman nodded. "I used to go to the lake when people had bonfires."

"Umm…" He cleared his throat. "Maybe you know my parents? They grew up here, too."

"It's possible."

"My mom writes books, so maybe you've read one of them?"

"What are they called?"

He told her the names of her first two books and did his best to explain, in brief, what they were about. They were hard for him to remember, though, since they were, as he used to say, *boring books for grownups*. "Her new one won an award though. That one's called *The Church*. It's a true story about something bad that happened here a long time ago."

"I know," she answered. "I know a little about that."

"That's my mom. My dad works for the publisher in town."

The woman took a long breath. When she brushed a few strands of hair from her face, Thomas saw her hand trembling.

"Are you... okay?"

"What? Yeah." She smiled that friendly smile. "Of course. Your dad... his name's Adrian, isn't it?"

Thomas smiled. "Yeah!"

"I used to know him. A long time ago."

"You knew my dad? Like when he was my age?"

"Not quite that young. We were in our twenties. But yeah... I knew him."

"Trippy! I can tell him you said hi! Or, uh... or maybe you could come over. He's had old friends over from when he was in school and stuff. He'd probably be happy to see you."

"That's very kind of you to offer, Thomas Benedict. But I'm... I'm not staying for very long." She turned her eyes back toward the river. "I just came to... to..."

"To remember things?"

"Yeah. To remember."

"Well, thanks for helping me. It would've been really annoying to go all the way back that way to ask one of my friends to do it for me."

"My pleasure. You take care, Thomas. And... and do say hi to your dad for me. He was... well, he was beautiful. He's one of the best people I ever met."

"Wow. I bet he'll love to hear that."

She laughed, but it was a sad laugh. And then she began to walk away, not along the edges of the creek but toward the woods. She stopped, though, and nodded upstream. "Can I ask you something?"

"Yeah, sure."

"That's your sister?"

"Yeah. In a few months I'm gonna have another sister, too, so basically dad and I'll be outnumbered by girls."

That tight-lipped, suppressed-emotion smile appeared on the woman's face again. "Can I ask what their names are?"

"Sure. My baby sister's gonna be named Harper."

"Pretty name."

"I guess. And my sister over there, that's Charlotte. Charlie for short."

The woman's smile faded. She lifted the hand back up to her face, this time to wipe at her eyes. Thomas worried if maybe he had upset her, but when her smile returned, it was more real than before. "Her name's Charlie?"

"Yeah. I can call her over to say hi, if you want."

The woman shook her head, still wiping at her eyes. "No... no, let her play. It was very nice to meet you, Thomas."

"You too. Maybe I'll see you around? Like if you stopped to say hi to my dad?"

"Maybe."

"You should. If you want, I mean. We're going to Grandma Lupita's house for dinner tonight, though."

"Oh... Thank you, Thomas. Maybe I will." She waved. And then was gone. Stepping into the woods.

Thomas watched her go, wishing he could do something, or say something, to comfort her. It occurred to him, with no small amount of shame, that he'd forgotten his manners. He hadn't asked what her name was.

A few minutes later, his sister Charlie came and sat beside him on the boulder. He reeled in the lure, and then—playing up his reluctance—handed her the fishing rod. And taught her how to cast the line out, over many laughs and frustrated huffs.

3

Before coming to the creek, Charlie drove to the house she'd grown up in. The sight of it struck her like a bell and she remembered everything. Sitting in the glows of campfires and bonfires by the lake at night. The bustling coffee shops. Lupita and her house, her unyielding sternness and warmth. Adrian, who had once been a young man, begging Charlie to let him share those unthinkable agonies with him. And herself—the tormented young woman she'd once been, paralyzed by grief, longing, and fear.

The old house didn't look quite as she remembered it—the color was different, the trim new, the lawn redone. But she could see underneath the changes. She could see to its heart, where it was still the same. The windows of her bedroom she used to look out from. The front porch where her father had liked to stand for a few minutes every morning, still in his pajamas, a mug of tea in hand. The driveway where she'd spent too many nights asleep in her car during her early twenties.

It was a stranger's house now.

She slowed the car to a stop, sat for a long time just looking across the aching hours of the past. Her father had stepped out onto the front porch, holding a cup of tea, a surprised smile coming to his face. Somehow that was so vivid, it was almost as though she could see him—right there, at the entrance of their old home. She could see how he would look if he'd been able to grow old. Hunched a little, maybe dressed up like he was ready to head to church. Gray beginning to dominate his hair. And how filled his heart would've been, how deep his smile, to see her after so much time apart. The light that would've come to his eyes.

"*River Bug? Is that you?*"

*

Charlie navigated over rocks, upturned roots, and came upon a cluster of thick bushes beneath a circle of trees. The little girl, she thought. Adrian's daughter. Her name was Charlie.

She stood for awhile in the trees, wiping the warm trails of tears from her cheeks, and studied the bushes in front of her. To anyone else in the world, these were just bushes. To her, this was a landmark, a groove in her brain left by so many distant memories.

Charlie dropped to all fours in the dirt. She crawled until she was beneath one of the bushes, head and shoulders scratched by its sharp branches. Carefully, she reached her arm out. At first all she felt was dirt and pine needles. Her fingers slid back and forth—and then found the cork grip of a long-abandoned fishing rod. Something she had left here when she was young. Something she had almost forgotten.

Okay, she thought, and she could hear her father saying what she already knew.

*

Afternoon became early evening. In a few hours it would be dusk, but for now it was still light out, still warm. She journeyed far upstream.

At one point, she looked across the creek and saw someone out there, someone standing far out in the trees. They were *waving* at her. Charlie's breath froze in her lungs.

The person looked like—

No. Charlie looked away, breathed deep. She cast her gaze out there again and it was just the forest, the trees, the rocks, the beams of late sunlight filtering through.

When she found an adequate boulder, she sat. This spot was farther upstream than she'd ever been before, but it was exactly where she needed to be. And she knew what to do. This was something she could never forget, no matter how much time went by.

She brushed off dirt from the rod. The lure on the end of the line was cosmic blue, adorned with frills and gold sparkles. Her father had given it to her on her nineteenth birthday. It was called a River Bug.

"Hey, Dad." She kissed it and held it over her heart.

4

"Dad. Dad, I forgot to tell you—"

"Tell me in the car, Thomas. We're gonna be late."

"I know but—Dad, it was, it was really cool—"

"I caught a fish!" shouted Charlie. "I caught a fish and Thomas didn't!"

"Shut up. You *hooked* a fish, you didn't catch it."

"Guys, seriously, go grab the casserole for Mom and then we'll head out. Thomas, be nice to your sister."

"But Dad, that wasn't what I was gonna say, I was gonna say I met someone who said—"

"*In the car*, Thomas. I'm gonna get your mom and we gotta go."

In the Benedict household, this was a standard Sunday evening. Once a week they invited Lupita Del Rosario over for dinner, and once a week they ended up going to Lupita Del Rosario's house instead—on Lupita's unwavering insistence, of course. And every time, they were at least fifteen minutes late.

Adrian had learned to subdue his impatience amid the chaos of his excited kids, their mother who always stressed about being on time but also didn't know how to hurry—especially now she was pregnant—and his own disorganization. He would probably forget something, maybe his wallet, maybe his phone, or maybe the entire casserole he and Jane had put together.

"I got it!" Charlie said, the plexi container for the casserole cradled in her arms. She swung her hips to and fro as she stood by the front door. "*Let's go*, everybody! Dad's gonna bust a cap!"

Adrian burst out laughing as he sat to put on his shoes. "I'm gonna *what?*"

"She means blow a cap," corrected Thomas. "Jesus, Charlie. Bust a cap means shoot someone."

"What?"

"Dad's gonna *blow* a cap, not bust a cap. That means shooting someone."

"With a gun?"

"Yes."

"Let's *go*, everyone!" Charlie shouted again. "Dad's gonna shoot someone!"

"I think you both mean *blow a lid*," said Adrian, but his kids didn't hear him, and it didn't matter. He laughed as he finished with his second shoe.

*

Lupita was waiting for them in her swinging chair on the front porch. Little Charlie and Thomas ran to her, shouting her name, and she embraced them, laughing.

She told Adrian he looked well but could use to gain some weight, as always, and she put one gentle hand on Jane's belly. "Won't be too much longer before I'll have to get the baby seat out from the garage," said Lupita, her eyes twinkling.

Adrian gave her a quizzical look. "You have a baby seat, Lupita?"

"Oh, yes. Haven't used it in… oh, I don't even know how long anymore. Never thought it'd need to be used again, but never could bring myself to throw it away."

Adrian thought to ask why she had it—he had never known Lupita to have had a child—but the thought slipped away from his mind as they stepped into the house.

5

Something was different this time. Adrian felt it just under his skin, behind every word he said and every expression he made. They'd been coming here to have dinner with Lupita once a week for a few years now.

But something felt different this time. In the short-lived silences between the conversations, he found his mind wandered toward the past. Memories from long ago briefly surfacing, like a fish breaking water for a moment before vanishing.

Later, while Jane and Lupita were deep in conversation in the kitchen and the kids were watching something on the living room TV, Adrian removed himself. He walked down the hallway, past the bathroom, and to a bedroom he hadn't stepped foot inside in—Who could say how long, exactly? He could count the time in years, but it was more than that. He'd been a different person back then, living a different life. More than just years had passed.

He put his hand on the doorknob, twisted it, but didn't push. This motion alone brought everything swarming back.

Years ago: being in that room, in the dark, with Charlie Louise. Trying to get through to her, begging her to be honest with him. He had been so afraid. They both had. He could remember staying up as long as he could, running his hand along her back. That was as intimate as they had ever been—it was hard to say, even now, whether things could've progressed between them under better circumstances—but this memory remained sharply vivid, a splash of clear color in a gray, foggy mire of half-forgotten images.

His hand on her back. Her eyes in the dark. The shelter they had provided each other.

That was before she had disappeared. Before everything went wrong and she left—and he had tried to live, for the first time anyway, with the possibility that he might never see her again.

Adrian took his hand away from the doorknob, wiped at his eyes, left the hallway. Stepped out the front door for the cool air of dusk.

This street. He and his family had driven down this street so many times, and it was such a casual thing… but it was different tonight. Tonight he remembered what he had seen transpire on the asphalt of this street, in broad daylight. The sight and smell of blood. The sound of gunfire.

Trembling, he made it to the sidewalk and sat on the curb. Cried silently into his hands.

Time was, he thought. It wasn't nostalgia he felt for those times, it wasn't longing. It was an ache.

Maybe there was something he missed about it, as terrible as it had been. Some piece of himself long forgotten, maybe. And his friend. He missed his friend and everything they had meant to each other among all that chaos and all that darkness.

If I could speak to you now, Charlie, I'd want to say thank you. I didn't understand back then—I couldn't—and I know it hurt you. I know we hurt each other. So much of it still haunts me in some part of my mind, even though I don't think of it as often anymore.

But if I could speak to you again, if you could hear me now, that's what I'd want to tell you. I'd say thank you. You tried to protect me from something unexplainable even though I didn't want that… and look at me now. You gave this to me. You know that, right? I love you for that and I forgive you for everything. I wish I could tell you that.

Through his tears, he turned his eyes up at the sky. Only a few stars were visible, popping through the fading light. Darkness loomed.

When her voice spoke from his right, just a few feet down the sidewalk, he thought it wasn't real.

"Do you remember the night we met?"

He looked at her—*gasped* at her. She was barely more than a silhouette with the orange streetlamp glowing behind her. There was no way she was real.

"You looked like you were in pain when you stepped out from the house."

"And you were throwing up in the grass."

Adrian stood, moved closer. "You took care of me. And I knew right then that you were someone I wanted to know better." Realization dawned in his eyes, followed by tears.

"Adrian," she said, her voice soft.

"Charlie?" His eyes brightened. "How? I mean, I… I thought I'd never see you again, but— But you're here!"

"I needed to come back. One day I just… I knew I needed to find you again and ask if you remembered. And…" Her voice wavered. "I needed to apologize to you f-for… for *so many things.*"

"No. Don't even start." He pulled her into his arms. "Don't even start. Charlie there's… there's so much I have to tell you."

"I know." She wiped one of his tears away for him, started to laugh with the lightness in her body. "Me too."

They sat on the curb like kids after a long day, two people in the orange glow of a streetlamp, their voices and tearful laughter cutting through the street's silent darkness. It was a gift, Charlie thought as she looked at her friend. A gift after all, knowing everything and everyone would one day end. She had known that once. Had known it well.

Adrian was telling her about his family, about how he'd met Jane, and about their kids, when Charlie noticed movement in the darkness behind him, at the end of the road. When she focused, she distinguished the figure of a person out there. A girl.

Marion Del Rosario stood where the road's asphalt ended. She looked no older than the last time Charlie had seen her—a twenty-two year old girl, lost in fog, muttering incessant apologies to those she'd left behind.

In one hand, Marion held something. Charlie couldn't see it clearly from here, but she knew what it was.

With her other hand, Marion was waving. As if to say, *I'm still here, waiting for you.*

But she would always be there. Charlie knew that. She saw her sometimes in the darkness of her bedroom. Or on the sides of empty roads at night. Or across an uncrossable distance, waving her arm, trying to get her attention, trying to draw her back. Sometimes Marion's skin was gray. Sometimes it appeared loose, as if she were hollow. Sometimes her face began to melt.

Charlie returned her attention to Adrian. The sadness didn't vanish, but it retreated like daylight to the far edge of the horizon.

When she began to tell her side of things, Adrian reached out and took her hand. About leaving the way she had, she said: "At the time, I told myself it was what I needed. I told myself it was for the best. And maybe it was, for awhile. But it never really felt right."

Adrian was still holding her hand when they stood and he led her toward the house where his family and Lupita waited. The front door opened and Adrian's children came to see what was happening. Charlie looked back toward the road, just once.

Marion stood now on the sidewalk, shadowed by the orange streetlight. She was waving. Written on her face and in her sorrowful eyes was a piercing, human desperation. A call for help that never ended.

Behind Marion, emerging from the shadows, was Charlie's father. She knew he'd be there, she knew he would always be there, but knowing never made it easier.

He, too, was waving.

THE END

Acknowledgments

There are so many people I'm overwhelmed with gratitude for on a daily basis.

My parents, Kevin and Eileen Lakin. There are any number of reasons why the world, why life itself, can seem dark and bleak—and only more so all the time. It's thanks to my parents that I find myself still able to believe in a kinder world.

My brothers, Ronnie and Kevin. How lucky am I to have family about whom I can say, "Those are my people."

My Grandma Clara, always for the wonderful conversations, the subtle wisdom, the humor, the strong, strong heart—the source of so much of this family's strength and love.

My family, whether near or far, here or gone. I love them and miss them all the time, and I meant what I said earlier—it's a privilege to be one of them.

Anjali, my partner. There are too many things I could say, but if I may be specific for a moment: She was there through this book's entire process, including when its darkness became too literal. I've known for a long time how to weather depression when it comes —but I've never seen it so clearly through someone else's eyes, through the eyes of somebody who loved me, cared for me, was patient with me, enough to try and support me through it, and to be there waiting on the other side of it. There's a gratitude there that I do not have the words for.

Cain Brookman, who suffers greatly at the horror aspects of my writing, but who's also kind enough to mention that "I hated it" usually means "It's effective, damn you."

Nic Anderson, who offered valuable insight on this book's first few chapters.

To those friends who live in my heart. Lipika, Chris, Zyon, Coyah, Espen, Stine, Mike, Adam. I don't know what I'd do without you.

More and more I realize: It's the people I love, and who love me, that save me. Every day.

To anyone who's known the nullity and aching of such things as depression, grief, sorrow, longing.

There are a few people I'd like to name, many of them writers and authors. Some of them I know only by way of social media, yet who I'd nearly—or would like to, someday—consider friends. Others I know only through their work. It's their foundations that I've mapped my own from, and I continue to owe thanks for so many reasons: Stephen King; Peter Straub; John Langan; Shirley Jackson; Sally Rooney; Mary Oliver; Thomas Ligotti; Raymond Carver; Carl Phillips; Edgar Allan Poe; Robert Chambers; Arthur Machen; H. P. Lovecraft; Mariana Enriquez; Paul Tremblay; Dan Simmons; Brian Evenson; Shaun Hamill; Robert McCammon; Richard Matheson; Jac Jemc; Mike Davis; and Zdzisław Beksiński, whose artwork accompanied me on my path through The Aching Plane. It almost feels presumptuous to put such incredible names down here, but also it'd almost feel wrong to leave them out.

Finally: To you, the reader. Thank you for joining me here, in these dark places. I hope to see you again, in the next one—but for now, for the time you've given me here, I can't even begin to properly express my gratitude.

Photo by Kevin Lakin

Cody Lakin is a writer and bookseller living in Southern Oregon. He is the author of the novel *The Family Condition*. Connect with him and receive updates on future works on Facebook, Instagram, and codylakin.com